Th

Offe

Nemesis

Pete Haynes

First Edition
Published 2016
NEW HAVEN PUBLISHING LTD
www.newhavenpublishingltd.com
newhavenpublishing@gmail.com

Cover design © Pete Cunliffe
pcunliffe@blueyonder.co.uk

newhaven
publishing

'For people who have stood by, and the animals I have known.'

Thanks to
Terri George. Colin Gould. Brendan Loughlan, Garry Bushell

One

A man is running; he is running for his life. It is winter on a cold early evening, and because of the artificial illumination given from the streetlights, the man's breath is clearly visible as it escapes in great belching puffs from his mouth and nose. His eyes claw at a distant place where he is struggling and praying to reach, a place where he will be safe; he is terrified.

And behind him are people who are also running, but these people are chasing the man and they are brandishing pieces of wood and iron bars, which are to be used as weapons to beat the man with. Their faces are torn with violence, mouths open through lack of breath, yet charged with lust for inflicting pain and the prospect of a kill, and then, possibly, they will experience sensations of warmth and calmness that the feelings of satisfaction and pleasure brings. The men are shouting at the man they are chasing as their excitement grows, because they are gaining ground on him. The man turns in an alleyway, but as he runs down what he thought might be a route for him to get away from the mob he suddenly stops, realising it is a dead end. He turns around, but then driven by panic continues to turn in a circle as he searches for an exit. Looking at the entrance of the alleyway, he decides to retrace his steps with hopes of making his escape.

The man starts to run, but just as he reaches the entrance the mob is turning into the alleyway, and on seeing the man they raise their weapons in triumph before attacking him. The man is powerless to defend himself and the first few strikes knock him against the wall; the constant barrage of blows are the only thing stopping the man from falling to the ground, but eventually he does. He falls, cradling his head in his hands, and attempts to assume a fetal position but the men pull at his arms and drag him away from the wall so they have more room to beat him, but their actions are hindered as one of the men places his hands against the wall for support and jumps up and down on the prone, defenceless man. The other men club and dig at the man for a short while and they too start to jump and stamp on him. The attack is vicious and prolonged with one of the men holding onto another man's shoulder for balance as he stamps down on the man's face and head in measured strikes.

There had been no resistance from the man, his pleading was momentarily before crumpling under the ferocity of the attack, and now his body shudders and gives way to the heavy stamping and kicking as every part of the man's body is targeted with aggression, intensity and a precision as if to destroy the body's very existence. The man's face is

5

unrecognisable from only moments earlier, swollen to twice its size. It is completely mutilated, looking like a piece of bloated flesh that had been pulled from the sea.

The beating in the alleyway is being shown on a screen in a studio to rapturous applause and cheering from a crazed audience expressing an unquenchable desire for more violence. A camera pans around and picks out a young boy who appears to be in an apoplectic rage, it zooms in on the boy showing clearly the heated emotions of anger and hatred etched into his young face. The camera pulls back and we see the boy is stamping on a cardboard head, emulating what he has seen on the screen. The boy is impervious to everything around him as he stamps on the cardboard head in an uncontrolled fury.

Cut to the show's presenter, a man having a slick and slimy presentation who is surveying the audience with gloating pride; the man's name is Alan Manville. His manner is cool and detached from the mayhem going on around him. Knowing he has successfully delivered, he regards the audience with what could easily be understood as a patronising smile. He speaks in a condescending manner, just as a teacher might do when allowing a class of children to get overexcited. 'A good ole fashioned stomping – you can't argue with that – kiddie fiddler got kerunched – it's what you wanted and it's what you got – as always,' he gives a big smile and swipes his arm in front of himself, 'because this is The Offender's Nemesis, and you always get what you want.'

Cut to an attractive young women wearing glittering hot pants and pink boots, she is stamping on the floor in time to a song having a simple construction with the words, 'Stomp them down, stomp them down, stomp them down – into the ground.'

As the song ends to an explosive fanfare of music, noise and lights, the camera turns to the young boy stamping on the cardboard head, his face transfixed by the atmosphere as he continues to stamp down, and then he stops and looks upwards, staring at something only he can see he lets out a scream with all his might, discharging excitement, but also releasing anger from his small, young body.

The word Justice, which is drawn in childishly large primary colours, appears on the screen with Alan Manville's voice speaking over it in a clear and commanding tone, 'Remember – only The Offender's Nemesis can make you feel this good.'

The Offender's Nemesis is showing on a screen in a large bar. Beer sprays and faces contort in pleasure as men grapple and playfully grab at one another, but it is not only a male spectacle of excited behaviour, women are also celebrating, raising glasses and cheering. A chant breaks out, gaining momentum to a near deafening volume that fills the bar, 'One less weirdo – one less weirdo – one less weirdo.' Although there are a few people who are not celebrating and do not share the feelings of the vast majority in gaining pleasure and enjoyment from the brutal spectacle, or an ostensible need to participate in mass hysteria.

An old couple, a man and woman, sit by themselves against the wall watching the mayhem, mindful not to disclose their thoughts. They are not the only ones who aren't participating in the revelry who also keep their thoughts to themselves. A few lone men nod an acquiescing agreement when catching the eye of someone taking part in the shouting and euphoria, fearful of the consequences if not consenting to the common demand; ridicule, accusations and beatings is a common response from a fired up mob if they suspect someone of disagreeing with them. There is a man rushing towards the exit with a phone to his ear who is also not involved in the high spirits.

The man speaks into the phone when he gets outside the bar, although not so much speaking, but blurting in a wild panic. 'Chris, Chris, they've killed Steven, it's just been on now, it's just happened, I can't believe it, it was Steven, they called him by another name, but it was Steve, your brother – Jesus, I can't believe it was Steven.' He holds the phone away from his ear as he tries to compose himself, as taking deep breaths he continues to speak into the phone. 'Chris, Chris – I don't know what to say – I can't believe it, I can't believe it – oh, Jesus Christ.' He listens to what is being said to him before continuing. 'On the show, The Offender's Nemesis – Chris – oh Chris I can't believe it.'

Two

Ten months earlier.

Chris Kirby looked around where he was standing, taking in the general décor and items on the shelves, while thinking how dismal it all was. He was in a Rummage Room. Rummage Rooms might be their formal title, but they are usually called 'rubbish rooms' by the people that use them. They are everywhere in and around the poorer areas, selling miscellaneous items cheaper than in normal stores. The goods are mainly second-hand, damaged or 'nearly new,' and there is the old stock or end of line products that have ended up in them, which can be bought for a fraction of the price they are sold for in stores found in wealthier areas. Some of the things are considered as 'essentials', which includes candles, cheaper brands of sanitary towels and cough linctus for the very young and old. These can be bought with state coupons, known commonly as 'tickets,' the state coupons can be used, provided they meet the criteria of need while other things are bought with cash. The coupons are also accepted in the massive stores, when buying 'essentials,' where the bulk of shopping is done in the impoverished areas. Candles are commonly used because of the constant occurrence of power cuts in those areas, although the television remains on during a power cut because it is powered by radio waves, while other electrical household appliances and lighting will go off as they are powered in the traditional method through meters.

The country had changed, and the many changes have created a condition of austerity for the vast majority of people who live in a society ruled by an illiberal state, although this state of affairs is not only experienced in this country, but also in other countries that had the same system as ours. The previous situation where a comprehensive system of welfare existed is no longer in place, but the state does provide coupons for those with the responsibility of looking after children and the elderly. The coupons are for those existing in "subsistence-level" living standards and are exchanged for items deemed as absolute necessities.

These thoughts were drifting through Chris's mind as he looked around at the stock where he was standing. The Rummage Room was in a quiet road very close to a housing project, which was typical of most projects throughout the country, in that it housed poorer people. A state policy to stringently group people together from low socio-economic backgrounds in them has had a dramatic effect on the country. Housing in regular areas, once occupied by poorer people, were often forcibly acquisitioned by local authorities and sold off to those earning good incomes or with the wealth to buy properties having undergone renovation in areas where improvements have been made to community services, so areas that once suffered inadequate conditions and amenities symptomatic to places where poorer people live, now benefit from good local services and resources.

There are other projects that house people not seen as 'indigenous' – the 'non-indies' – to the country and segregation between them is clearly demarcated. The main projects house people who are now known as Ancestral Nationals, or A.N.s, they are people whose family have been in the country for generations and are seen as 'indigenous' to the country in race, as opposed to projects that house 'foreign nationals;' or, F.N.s. They are places completely set aside, physically in that they are often geographically in places away from towns, and poorly serviced in terms of infrastructure. The people living in them are treated with distrust and often hated by mainstream society; these projects house people who came to the country near to the time when the country changed, but there are also projects housing people who are not viewed with such suspicion and hostility that have come from other countries and are descendents of people who had come to live in the country. All of these people are a different skin colour from what is called the indigenous population. They also include people known as B.B.s, an abbreviation commonly used for Blended Blood.

The influx of people from different cultures having different belief systems placed a strain on integrating diversity in relation to religion, but nowadays that is not seen as a problem as there is not the accommodation or acceptance of other religions and belief systems. There are facilities, although meagre, for the practice of non-mainstream religions and social gatherings, but they are viewed with distrust and not funded by the authorities. They are often associated with bodies that conspire against the state and are connected to terrorists. Terrorists are seen as the enemy from within, who bomb indiscriminately, rob to fund criminal activities and at any opportunity undermine the morale of the country. Nearly all of the alleged terrorists, who are seen as a constant threat to the security of the country, live in the projects for 'foreign nationals', and in many cases it is claimed they do so illegally. The people who are referred to as "foreign" suffer poorer health, have inferior housing and less job opportunities. They are people who are not represented in any positive way and are alienated from what is generally going on in society, and it is seen as entertainment rather than a serious news item when raids on their homes and arrests take place are shown on television.

There are also the people who came to the country years ago and their descendents who were, and are, middle class and have mixed in the better off areas. After the change in society many people went back to where they had came from, or to other countries, but it was not a simple procedure and the state washed its hands of taking any responsibility for the welfare of people in vulnerable situations. It was a bloody episode fuelled by bitterness that left many dead and a lasting legacy of distrust.

The country had, as had most other countries in the world, gone through a change that had a seismic effect on the running of its society. It was brought upon by environmental factors that caused a collapse in the economy, which had a catastrophic impact on the material wealth and quality of life once experienced by many people in the country. To say simply that things have changed when describing the transformation in society would be a gross understatement. There was a near complete failure in the maintenance of the economy, brought about by the principles of craving immediate profits. The people running big business were blind or indifferent when seeing the damage being done to the environment through unsustainable practices, which ultimately upset the ecological balance by depleting natural resources.

The blaming of those responsible was not aimed at those in positions of influence and responsibility in financial institutions and corporations that caused the problem, but rather the practice of scapegoating came to the fore in order for the ruling elite to maintain their positions of ascendancy. The laying of blame on the changes that occurred went through a brief indeterminate period until a common target for blame was constructed. The focus is on people who are commonly called 'liberals.' Liberals were, and are, blamed for the level of crime that previously existed, which was seen as the main cause for what is often termed "the breakdown in society". It was, and still is, seen as entirely their fault, and as a result there has been a resentment and hatred of the 'liberals.'

The previous system of law and order has been dismantled, and in doing so defied hundreds of years of progress. The state's strategy to demonise the previous system and the people who worked in it is continually worked at.

It is true that, before the radical change, society had been beleaguered by street crime in the form of violence and robbery against the individual. There was also spontaneous rioting by the criminal and the bored that usually resulted in looting and vandalism, where many innocent people who were caught up in the disorder lost possessions, were injured and in some cases lost their lives, although there were also planned riots organised by religious and political groups who declared their intentions of bringing down the country. Fraud became so prevalent and in some circumstances the price of security had become greater than the worth of one's personal savings, so in some areas the insuring of one's car became a rarity rather than the norm. People lived in what had been termed 'Total Fear.' Fear became the central talking point, fear of going about one's life without the constant anxiety of being attacked by thugs, burgled, raped or murdered. The situation had got to a point where there were large no-go areas in every town, and the police viewed theft of one's possessions as no more than an irritant. In many urban areas, drug deals took place on nearly every street corner, and the country was dealing with internal threats to its security from anarchists and foreign terrorists. People felt powerless in not having the means to address what was ruining their lives, and felt let down because of not having the representation to advocate their views. Their lives were destroyed and for many, any attempt to improve their quality of life was impeded by criminal activities and behaviour.

The legal system had failed in its duty to protect people and the average person felt the law and other public services appeared to work in the interests of people who did wrong. The majority of people felt they had been forcibly detached from having any meaningful involvement in having their feelings aired and acted upon. Their anger was directed at what are called the 'liberal progressives,' who were seen to pursue their own interests above any other consideration and crime, for them, was a lucrative product while the taxpayer was just a cash cow. They were seen as a growing body of people with a quest to defend and protect a self-perpetuating culture of professions with society having become little more than a name to justify their actions while the average person suffered.

After the international economic disturbance, those people who can be called the higher or ruling elite made an evaluation of the country and a process took place that is commonly referred to as the 'big change.'

The state dismissed the legal, social and educational services and 'despatched,' which means killed, many individuals who it held to blame for the way conditions had sunk to, often publicly in the form of a grand execution to demonstrate the state's commitment in honouring the wishes of the masses to punish those they held responsible, and as a public declaration to show a real change in how things are now to be done. Making its position clear, the state virtually wiped the slate clean in preparation for a different age that had dawned, and with it a vastly different way of implementing order. Since that time, which is nearly two decades ago, not a single day passes without there being some reminder to perpetuate anti-liberal 'progressive theories' and to ridicule its politics and practices. The message is maintained through the use of politics, the media, education, literature and the secret police. There was, and is, an organised incitement for people to wreak revenge on those who are blamed for letting the social fabric of society be ruined. One reason blamed on the 'liberals' for destroying national identity was their policy of allowing a great amount of people from other parts of the world to settle in the country, another reason was how the liberals were seen as constantly attacking and rubbishing the country's history and traditional culture by undermining it by any means possible.

The tackling of crime was welcomed, but it had not brought an end to violence and fear, as people with less advantages and opportunities in the run-down areas became segregated from wealthier areas and became more and more economically impoverished. Violence and brutal behaviour was confined to the rapidly evolved housing projects, where vigilantism was encouraged, and became a constant presence. The ubiquitous sight of loafing yobs waiting to attack their prey with impunity that previously existed has now gone and so too has there been the virtual eradication of the housebreaker and street mugger. The term 'mugger,' along with a lot of the language previously applied to this kind of behaviour is no longer in use. The term 'mugger' was discarded because it implied the victim was a fool for being on the receiving end of a criminal act, and in a way seen as a 'loser while the perpetrator was the 'winner' by gaining at the victim's expense. Now there is a different assessment of the situation, where the perpetrator of a crime is severely punished without having any defence to justify his or her actions. Other words once associated with crime that might be used to lessen the magnitude of an offence, such as 'petty,' have also disappeared, all language related to crime is now assertive with there being no excuses. Also there are self-appointed groups, or gangs, that deal with anti-social behaviour in brutal ways, which is monitored by the police or security officers who are always present.

The wealthier areas are now practically free of crime, and one factor for that being so is the way social mobility has become limited, which also stops would-be criminals travelling into wealthier areas to commit a crime and then retreating back to the place they came from. A system of 'zones' was created where passing from one area, or zone, to another requires a relevant pass or permit. In practice, a system of segregation took place as one area became divided from another. There is no longer autonomous movement within the country and reasons for travel are needed. The freedom to travel to other countries is now tightly restricted and is basically limited for those occupying high positions in business and government work, the excuse given is the threat of terrorism, but the vast majority just don't have the money to do so. The concept of everyone having a passport does not exist, and therefore there are no conversations among the average people about different countries they have visited. The wealthier obviously enjoy a better quality of life than the masses and see the loss of the freedom to travel throughout all areas as a small price to pay, although they are given far greater access to travel within the country than poorer people, even though the more comfortably off have less material luxuries and choice than before the change in society.

The constant anxiety hanging over the middle class regarding crimes and anti-social behaviour has been replaced by the persistent fear of finding 'qualified' work. It has become their single most overriding concern, although it is something that has always been of importance. There are now extreme consequences if one does not secure the right form of employment, failing to do so would result in living in a poorer area, possibly and in many cases probably, living in a project and suffering the conditions existing there. Once displaced to a project, it is impossible to escape and move back to what one once had. This is because of the lack of opportunities to do so, and other limiting factors that exist for those in the housing projects such as decent education and the negative stigma that goes with living in such places.

A liberal democracy, or arguably what was the appearance of one, is now gone and society is controlled in a different manner in many ways. There is the stringent monitoring of citizens by means of a personal identification system where everyone has at all times to carry an ID card that, when checked, contains all possible information about a person the state has gathered, and when implemented was remarkably well accepted by a populace feeling threatened by crime and terrorism and therefore seen as a necessity to maintain safety and order. The theft or the production and dissemination of counterfeit ID cards carries such a severe penalty it dissuades anyone who might consider it. For example, thirty years hard labour is the standard, but nobody survives long enough to see out his or her sentence. Once the worth of the prisoners is extracted they become ill and die.

It was suggested to also have a barcode tattooed on poorer people containing information about place of birth, where one lives, employment, genetical code, insurance number and all details the state wants about a person. That idea was abandoned, although in recent years it has become popular for the foetus to be coded by keyhole surgery in particular areas and in families judged to be posing a risk to society. The practice of 'chipping' began just a few years back, just as it is done with pet animals to keep track of their whereabouts. At first the chips were inserted in the

13

bodies of those who had committed a crime, then quickly broadened to associates of those people and to a situation where 'chipping centres' sprung up in the car parks of shopping centres with financial incentives given for anyone to be 'chipped'. The scheme rapidly explored all social areas where it could be done in a person's leisure time, and in doing so could be seen as light- hearted, especially when performed in booths set up outside bars and the people putting themselves forward for the 'chipping' had been drinking. It is thought that 'chipping' will soon be made compulsory and the meagre welfare support that exists and medical services will be withdrawn if a person fails to comply with the ruling. Already there is a slogan broadcast by the state on television and on posters in doctor's surgeries, No Chip – No Treatment. Although, this practice will not be compulsory for everyone in the country, which includes people like Chris or his family and friends who therefore enjoy greater freedoms. Chris belongs to a group in society referred to as, 'professional,' or having 'qualified status,' who are legally required to carry an ID card and also a mobile phone that has all their data held on it. The phone allows the state to track exactly where the person is, and can only be used by the owner as it is triggered by a genetical print exuded by the person's skin on contact with the phone.

There is much made in the media of a country sharing a national unity, pride and identity, but in fact many people think what really exists is a system of one against all, lived to a backdrop of rage where the use of fear regulates social order. The committing of violent acts still exists and is an everyday occurrence in the poorer areas, yet there is the perception that it does not, or that it is acceptable because it is rationalised in understanding it, as empowered members of society use proactive means to deal with acts of deviance in their environment. The practice of violent and aggressive retribution is reflected and exploited by television shows concerned with addressing crime, or which have crime as their subject matter for what has become the most popular type of entertainment in the country. The Offender's Nemesis, or TON as the general populace commonly calls it, publicly names, shames and punishes 'criminal offenders', 'terrorists' and people seen to be subversive. It is a lavish, well-funded show that presents explicit and perversely imaginative methods of humiliation, punishment, torture and death.

The Offender's Nemesis is by far and away the most popular and influential show of this kind and is employed by the state as an important means to control the population. The public are treated to be a spectacle that ranges from the outrageously gruesome to the childishly crude as capital punishment is now exploited for entertainment. Its formula mixes notions of revenge and ethics, and presents itself as being concerned with 'honesty' and 'truth'. The spectacle of seeing a 'criminal' get his or her (but it is nearly always his) comeuppance satisfies the general public who are constantly reminded how they were once alienated from the process of dealing with those who commit crime and ruin their lives. The humiliation and punishment metered out on the show goes beyond anything that has preceded it in the era of what is often called modern civilisation. It is so perverse it would have been unimaginable to contemplate them being practiced on mainstream television and viewed so ravenously by members of the general public before the changes that occurred in society.

The methods of punishment used on the show, and the bizarre scenarios that are enacted for the public's enjoyment and entertainment, would cause any stable person to doubt the mind or reasoning that invented them for a public to derive great pleasure. They are punished in the most brutal fashion and new ways of inflicting humiliation and methods of killing an 'offender' are continually sought and used, in order to maintain popularity and gratify the consumer. The show employs various methods of punishment, with medieval practices of punishment being popular and revisited many times. It must be an arduous task having to keep thinking up new methods and scenarios to keep their audience interested, and although some of these are thought up by people working for the show, the majority of ideas for humiliation and punishments are taken from suggestions given to them by the viewing public. This helps the makers of the show and, most importantly, it gives the public a sense of participation in punishing criminals, which is part of the state's new ideology of dealing with crime.

You Have The Power, is a slogan that appears in newspapers, magazines of all kinds, billboards and the sides of buses, a message pertaining to the alleged involvement of everyone in an all embracing society, and, for the economically deprived, that means the power to deal with crime that affects them personally.

The show trawls back through time and takes to task those people judged as flouting their positions of authority. Public officials who worked in the legal, social, educational, health, or political fields are discredited. They are people who occupied 'qualified' positions in what were often called the 'professions', but that very term is now bracketed and viewed with critical examination. The show takes special delight in dealing with these people, who are often grouped together with artists and musicians and the like, who are seen to have shared what is called 'liberal progressive thinking.' They are paraded in front of a raucous studio audience and humiliated for their amusement in an act of retribution and entertainment. All of them are in their middle and old age as nearly two decades have passed since the massive change in the running of society took place.

The 'offenders' are presented on the show with their crimes explained, which is met with an excited response and cries for rough justice by a rowdy audience that is as encouraged as it is controlled by those that make the programme. There are staged scenes where the supposed perpetrators of crimes are entrapped and dealt with by acts of sudden retributive justice in the most violent ways.

Certain 'criminals' or 'terrorists' have found fame because of their notorious reputation. Their arrival on the show becomes a great talking point as it is marketed to exploit the event for maximum effect and to create hysteria in the public, who have an insatiable appetite for the show, especially, and essentially those in poor areas. People buy scratch cards in shops, although there are many other ways of getting tickets such as winning them in a competition, and they vote on their computers for the criminal of their choice to appear on the show. The scratch cards have the name and photograph of a criminal or terrorist on them, and if that criminal or terrorist appears on the show on the concealed date they win money and tickets for the show. As successful as The Offender's Nemesis is in offering entertainment and amusement, it also succeeds as an effective strategy to stir fear and ignite hatred while offering a diversion from the realities of life. Game shows have a formula of taking sides, and The Offender's Nemesis takes this procedure to extremes as divisions are established by clearly demarcating 'them and us,' the 'criminal' and the 'decent person.' It is a simple model consisting of the 'normals' and the 'deviants' where the 'dangerous outsider' is contrasted with the 'innocent citizen'.

The show is justified as a meaningful response to crime because it eradicates unwanted 'criminals' and is relentlessly compared to the previous system when the criminal disappeared into a complicated legal and social quagmire, which left the victims of crime feeling the dealing of an offence was unresolved. The act of retribution satisfies the general public. It is perceived as an immediate and honest response to crime because social ills are now dealt with in what is called a no-nonsense manner. Although there does exist a contradiction that is generally unspoken about, namely creating an overt show of feeling safe by the public, because of the way in which the state is dealing with crime, contrasted with a constant sense of foreboding at breaching the parameters of control, even when doing nothing wrong. The Offender's Nemesis encourages behaviour that is charged with a witch-hunt mentality and as a result creates a general mistrust of the other while accepting the violent acts used upon people seen as being 'criminal' or 'deviant'.

The Offender's Nemesis is childish in the extreme with its slapstick scenarios, but it is out of bounds for children in the homes of qualified people. They do not want their children to witness the sadistic violence and base crudity that peppers each show. The qualified people feel they have a greater stake in society, which often gives them a sense of occupying a higher status and are encouraged through cultural conditioning to view the tastes, activities, behaviour and values of those coming from housing projects as uneducated, brutish and crude. This refined sensitivity is very different within the culture of the poorer people as antics on the show are aped in all social settings. Animated characters have become celebrities, and their distinctive voices are heard in school playgrounds, pubs, clubs and work places. Crime is entertainment, and it is used to amuse people who are forced to live on the bare basics of everything from the material to the spiritual. It has made famous media personalities out of the most prosaic people who are really nothing more than third-rate sales people who have the ability to smile inanely while bowing to their leader, the glib Alan Manville, the modern media prince within celebrity culture.

Something that is widely known about The Offender's Nemesis, which is never discussed in the media or has any political platform to debate the matter, is that the 'offenders' and 'terrorists' appearing on the show are sometimes, and it is said often, innocent of the crimes they are charged with. The most credulous will believe whole heartedly what they are presented with, and with that being so, combined with apathy and fear, the system can continue to make the show and the accusations it does.

The show makes a big thing of having an interactive relationship with its audience and utilises various forms of communication that includes the use of people's personal computers, which almost everybody owns, but without the facilities people would have expected from a computer in the previous era. Their function is not the same, using one's computer for personal research is not a common activity as it used to be. There is the Internet, but it is not a resource available for mass accessibility as it once was. Things are now very different because all information is censored and filtered through line entry and all methods of connection are by means of a cable system. There are satellite aerials, but they are only seen on buildings the state has sanctioned for them to be on, such as government research departments and their affiliates. Otherwise it is illegal to install receiving technology and the punishment for contravening this law often includes the death penalty, as it is seen to be treasonous.

In essence, unless censored, computers have ceased to be a method of communication between people within their own country or internationally and to be used at will. A type of intranet system exists, which is usually installed in schools and colleges for communication which has carefully collated contents. Where once before there had been various forms of communication, television is now the main source of entertainment and outlet for the authorities when deploying initiatives employed for rousing anger and excitement for purposes to control.

The way things are now organised makes it easier for the state to disseminate what it wants the populace to see, hear and think. Even though, ostensibly, companies privately and independently own programmes and channels, it is fundamentally orchestrated by the state as the directors of those companies also occupy positions in the government.

Chris is fortunate that he can travel through many zones, including the one he was now in, because of his qualified background. He can also travel extensively throughout the country by getting the relevant permit at a main railway station without having to give a detailed explanation of his reason for wanting to travel, although there are areas used for 'Government Activities' where the public, whoever they are, cannot 'trespass'. All this being so, Chris would have to give a good reason for being in the zone he was in if stopped by the police or other security service. It is the normal practice to alert the authorities for people with qualified status if they travel to a poor area such as where he now was. Chris did not do so because of not wanting the state monitoring his whereabouts as he had arranged to meet people who are judged as subversive. This would be bad enough, but he had two thousand Euro dollars in his pocket and the security officers would view Chris with extreme suspicion. The money was to do with the person or people he planned to meet, and at that moment, what with his nerves, the envelope containing the money felt so bulky, in fact it felt about one metre wide. He would most definitely be taken to a police station or a nearby Police Holding Units that are known as PHUs. They are used to hold people before being taken to a police station or prison, and are useful places, as they can contain more than two or three people without the attendance of a police officer. Chris had heard stories of them being vandalised because people resented their presence, and even attacked in attempts, sometimes successful, to free friends or relatives, although this was never reported unless it was in the interest of the state to do so. There are in fact regular acts of rebellion against the system, and it is known that riots deep inside housing estates go unreported, albeit not on a large scale, and there is

18

access to crude weapons along with homemade explosives, but everything is monitored so meticulously things can't really gather ground, so it is just individuals or tiny groups that commit the acts of defiance and they are nearly always caught and dealt with swiftly with a death sentence handed down with no trial. These people do not appear on The Offender's Nemesis as the state wishes their actions to be unknown about by the masses.

Three

Chris noticed a small piece of a mirror that had been wedged behind a water pipe. He stepped up close to it, checking over at the woman behind the counter to see if she was watching him, which she was not, and looked at his reflection. What he saw shocked him because he was surprised how pale and fatigued he looked; deep, dark lines were beneath eyes that had a haunted look. He noted how the taut strain of anxiety had altered his normal expression. Chris fingered the envelope that contained the money, and as he did so was weighed down by a heavy weakness and the ragged upset that had become a constant feeling, and these emotions were exacerbated by his stark surroundings and his reflection in the grubby fragment of a mirror. He looked more closely at the face, and because of tiredness a thought flashed through his mind to question if the reflection was actually his own, and the longer he looked it only increased the tiredness that enveloped his body and mind.

The shop door opened suddenly, which made Chris jump and turn quickly to see who was entering. It was a man, but the way he was startled on hearing the door open told Chris how frayed his nerves were. The man spoke in a loud voice as he pasted a notice on the wall just inside the doorway. Chris took a last glance in the mirror and walked towards the man, who had finished with his pasting. The man wore an old raincoat and as he spoke to the woman behind the counter a cigarette remained, as if stuck, in the corner of his mouth. The cigarette had been loosely rolled, and Chris noticed by the smell the tobacco was the new synthetic type, real tobacco is shortly only going to be a privilege for the wealthy. It was a cheap substitute aimed at those in the poorer areas, and it has been said the substance is laced with a drug to subdue emotions. His face was red, very red, with deep purple patches spattered on his cheeks and neck, and as he spoke just two teeth showed in the black chasm that was his mouth. Chris looked at the notice the man had just pasted on the wall, it gave warning of dogs and rats in the area that have rabies and that an organized cull was to take place the following day. Chris looked from the man to the poster, noticing how clumsily it had been written and how the misspelled words were made up of crudely shaped letters.

The man put down the brush he was holding and showed with his hands the size of a rat that was in his granddaughter's cot. The man huffed and spat as he told how the cot was dragged outside and burned, and that it was lucky his granddaughter was in another room at the time. The woman he was talking to pulled faces of disgust and raised her knee slightly, lifting her foot from the floor, as if the rat was next to her feet.

The man continued in his loud voice, talking about diseases and the lack of hygiene in the flats.

The shop door opened with a sudden bang, causing Chris to jump, his nerves were extremely frayed. A young man entered, he was tall, in his late twenties with a face that had become set in a bad tempered scowl.

The man with the brush stopped talking and looked at the young man as he strode up to the counter and pointed to boxes of candles that were stacked on a shelf behind where the woman was standing. He articulated his request, saying he wanted four boxes of candles, in verbal communication that was no more than a grunt, and as the woman turned to get them he dropped a screwed up coupon on the counter.

Chris looked from the coupon to the young man's face. It was grimy, worn and furrowed, and Chris noticed how the skin appeared hard. The young man's eyes flashed a brooding resentment, barely concealing anger as he watched the woman place the boxes on the counter and check the coupon for authenticity. His large hands looked strong, dirt was packed under the nails and inscribed on the chafed skin on the back of his hands were different tattoos of symbols and signs indicating his allegiance to a particular gang.

His eyes then flitted over to Chris, who quickly looked away, as if his interest was taken with the first thing he looked at, which happened to be a small umbrella that was designed for a young girl. It was yellow and had been knocked about by its previous owner, or owners. Chris saw that the young man was still looking at him, so he turned his attention to the next nearest thing, which was a floor mop that was in a nearly new condition. Chris glanced towards the young man, checking to see if he was still looking at him, and he was, although not glaring. Chris knew it was obvious to the people in the shop he did not come from the area and it was probably for that reason he had caught the young man's attention. When Chris looked again in the direction of the counter he saw that the young man was leaving, and the door slammed shut behind him. The man with the brush nodded at the door before looking at the woman and rolling his eyes, but the woman's expression showed she did not want to make any remarks about the young man who had just left the shop.

'He was one of them the other night,' the man said, 'right in the thick of it he was.'

The woman nodded, she was uncomfortable at not publicly wanting to be seen taking sides over the young man's actions. She looked away from the man, and then over at Chris who was pretending not to listen to their conversation and that his interest was concerned with a jigsaw he was holding, which had a note on the box informing a prospective buyer one of the pieces was missing. The man also looked over at Chris and lowered his voice, but it was still loud enough to hear clearly what he was saying as he spoke about the different gangs that existed in the area, of the punishments they carry out and of how they were at loggerheads with each other. The gangs separated crime into different types and graded them for their contemptibility, which determined the punishment they were to deploy. For example, a thief who stole property from a person's house is treated differently from a gang who waylaid an unsuspecting person, beat him or her and robbed the person's possessions, and they are treated differently from a man who sexually abused a child, who is treated differently to a man who had raped a woman.

The man continued with his attempt at hushed tones, which failed because what he said could be heard by anyone passing outside the shop.

'Yeah, the other night – it was that weird looking fella, you know, the one who's always carrying that manky shopping bag with old newspapers in it – always alone and dressed the same – dirty looking and always wearing that scruffy old jacket – looking down at the ground as he's walking along.'

The woman raised her hand to the side of her face in a sign of distress, having no heart to hear of brutal behaviour and violence inflicted upon someone, but the man did not share her sensitivity as he went on, pausing only to moisten his lips with his tongue and to check over at Chris, who was holding the box containing the jigsaw to his ear and gently shaking it.

'Yeah, those small bungalows off by the side of the project, that's where he lives – or lived.'

The man's last two words caused the woman to physically cringe, although showing an appearance of composure so that the man did not notice her feelings.

'Yeah, by heck, they gave it to him,' he went on. 'You know the one I mean, don't you?'

The woman nodded and said something to verify that she did, but her voice was too quiet for Chris to hear. And then she braced herself for what the man was going to say.

'That's right – he lived with his mother, for years – well, the old girl died a couple of years back and he continued to live in the bungalow – he shouldn't have been allowed to, he should have been moved to a single person's flat, but he lived with his mother because he cared for her. Anyway, they said he started to drink more after his mother died, but he had always drunk a lot beforehand. They reckon he, his family, were professionals, lived in a nice house in a posh area, and he had a good job – something to do with technical stuff, bit of a scientist, that kind of thing

– worked for a big company and then the government – he was married at one time – that's what they say – don't know if he had any kids, but he lost his job – because of the drinking, and apparently he touched up a couple of young girls at his work – that's when it all started to really go down hill – he lost his job and was put on a register for sexual deviants, so his work record and character was ruined – brought shame upon his family – it had a knock-on effect. They say there was a lot of illness with his parents – his father died and they lost the family home – came here, and she, his mother, got one of the bungalows and he came with her – he worked over the municipal dump, as a gatekeeper – apparently blokes who work there used to urinate in his tea – and he took a few smacks, for being a perv.'

The man paused and looked at the woman as if waiting for some kind of response, but she remained silent and waited for him to tell her the grisly details.

He went on, checking the door of the shop and glancing over at Chris, who continued to study the jigsaw puzzle.

'He'd been warned a few times, and given a few digs for making comments to girls, and women – some of them were married, but he really let himself slip with a young girl who works in the social club bar – must have been drinking more than normal. He put his hands on the girl and said he'd pay her – give her some money for her knickers – and when she told him to sling his hook he made a grab for her, and pleaded with her not to say anything about it.

'She – the girl, reckons he held on to her – holding her close like, to his body, and she said he stunk horrible – and then he started crying, asking her not to say anything, but his hands were all over her body. So, she pushed him off, and told her brothers, and her father, and they got a gang together – went round his place the other night and got hold of him. Some of them wanted to kidnap him, keep him locked up in a garage or somewhere, and then they could go round and torture him at different times – really make him suffer, but that didn't happen. They gave him a right beating in his place, by all accounts, then took him out onto the green and finished him off there – bricked him to death, but before he was actually dead they set fire to him – you could hear the cheers around the whole project.'

The woman's face gave a slight flinch as her eyes dulled and cast a downward glance at a place where the depths of human conduct had sunk.

'They then tied the body to the back of a car,' the man went on, 'and towed it around the green and some of the back streets – people were cheering, and then they hung his body, or what was left of it, over a street light – it was like something from that television show, TON, only they were doing it themselves – that's what a lot of them were saying – yeah – and that fella, that young fella who was just in here, he was in the middle of it...'

The man continued to speak, but Chris could not hear what he was saying. Everything in the shop, the man's voice, the lights, the miscellaneous items, all that was around him fused into a sheet of fear that seared through his body, leaving him deaf and completely cut off from his present surroundings. It was at that instant when the man mentioned the name of the television show that Chris fell into a state of panic. An all-encompassing bright light blinded Chris and unsettled him to such an extent he had forgotten the reason why he was actually in the shop, and it was as if all the planning and conjecture had been completely obliterated. Chris found himself walking towards the door, although he imagined he was stumbling in its direction. In actual fact he was not, to the man and woman he just seemed like a person who had whiled away some time in the Rummage Room and was now leaving, but it did not feel like that to Chris. He saw himself as a great lumbering form fumbling his way through the doorway, and he was conscious that he did not say anything to the woman, something like, 'thanks' or 'bye', considering it was a thing he would ordinarily do as he had spent quite a while in there looking around.

Once out of the shop, Chris stood on the pavement looking around the street where he was standing like a man who had suddenly found himself in a place that was foreign, frightening and with no knowledge of how he got there. Why had he responded with such anxiousness when hearing the word TON? The sound of a heavy chugging engine from an aircraft pulled Chris from his thoughts. He looked up and saw a large helicopter, a troop carrier, not one of the 'spy choppers' that are a common sight flying over the poor areas. Chris looked at the helicopter, thinking how it looked like a mechanical insect, ugly and ominous, set against a dull sky that was low and ready to break, and in doing so discharge a shower of polluted water on whatever lay beneath. It passed directly over his head, the sluggish rhythm of its engines and the deep sounding whirring of the blades so loud it was all-consuming, and Chris could quite clearly see the pilot, although his face was hidden because his head was encased in a helmet that had all the other accompanying gadgets attached to it.

Chris took his phone from his pocket and saw there were not any messages, although checking his phone was not related to the reason why he had come to the Rummage Room. The planned meeting that was meant to take place on that day was made with a man called Simon who works in the in the area of mental health, a trained psychiatric nurse with a job title of Community Engagement Officer who worked closely with Chris's brother Steven. It was very secretive, with Simon telling Chris all communication has to be conducted face to face and any written instructions have to destroyed immediately after reading them The reason Chris was in the Rummage Room, with the money on him, seemed implausible to him and usually he would not have gone along with what he was doing, but Chris was desperate to help his brother, and after a long period of time of trying to do so, events had led him down a path to the situation and place where he now found himself. Chris thought back to when he was a child and of how Steven had always been a constant concern and worry for him. There were signs that showed themselves in Steven's behaviour, when he was not more than a baby, of him being different, which later on caused difficulties on a social level as other children did not want to play with him. Teaching staff, parents and other children felt uncomfortable with Steven because he was different, and this continued as Steven exhibited behaviour which made it impossible for him to attend mainstream schools. His journey into adulthood grew increasingly hard and hurtful as he suffered alienation and experienced daily the draining blow of rejection from the looks, actions and words of others. Finding a job was extremely difficult to at times impossible.

Steven was very intelligent, but his condition, which was once associated with what was called autism, caused him to be different from the norm and essentially made it problematic for him to fit into a workplace and develop relationships with people. He could pick up and understand the most complicated mathematical equations almost instantly and from a young age his ability to solve complex formulae confounded some educationalists while others refused to accept his capability. Preferring to ignore his positive talents, they condemned him to a segregated school for children with learning disabilities, and such schools have neither the facilities, skilled teaching, or interest to support their pupils in attaining their potential. It damaged the family and it placed what Chris felt to be a persistent cloud hanging over him that dampened his heart because he felt anxious for his brother and anger at the system.

It is said that people can be cruel, and this adage was learned by Chris at an early age as he saw how many people can indeed be cruel, and very often in preference to offering compassion and understanding. As a child he thought about why many people act this way, and from what his parents told him, especially his mother, and from what he deduced, the young Chris came to believe it was because of fear. His experience of being Steven's brother opened up insights in the world around him that, probably, most other children of his age who did not have his experience would never encounter.

Chris came to accept that people, in general, are afraid of someone or something that is different. This realisation, and sensitivity was developed because of his situation and it made him conscious of the injustice suffered by many, and he became vocal in speaking out against iniquity when he came across it. The propensity for him to be like this caused extra worry for his parents, again especially for his mother, whom he was closer to. She would carefully explain to Chris that it was the decent and honest thing to be opposed to cruelty, whatever form it might take, but it was also equally important not for it to ruin his life, because that is what he had to get on with, living his life to the full in realisation that he was fortunate to do so. His mother was a pleasant woman, kind and generous, wanting the best for people, but it seems her down-to-earth honesty, thoughtfulness and selflessness was not rewarded. As Chris grew older he became aware of the mechanisms employed by the state to control society, particularly the use of fear, and to be precise, fear of the other. Chris saw from first hand experience how disability rouses fear just as that which is exotic can cause suspicion and fear because of it not being felt of as natural because it is foreign and different. The thing that is perceived as different is pushed farther away, for safety, and in doing so severing any kind of likeness and connection to it, to a point of hating it, which causes feelings of anger. Chris saw how a parallel can be drawn with attitudes towards people with disabilities and those people who are seen as standing in opposition to the desires of the state - people referred to as 'terrorists' and 'dissidents,' because both can be seen as deviating from what is commonly called 'normality.'

Steven was the only member of his family Chris had contact with, his parents split up when he was seventeen and his mother died two years later. She had cancer, but Chris believes she committed suicide in order to save her children the upset of seeing her deteriorate and suffer a long painful illness until her death. She was always an anxious person and the adaptations that had to be made as society changed unsettled her deeply. She then discovered that Chris's father was involved in a relationship with a woman he met though the course of his work and was devastated. Chris's father left his mother and moved in with the woman, and Chris had not any meaningful contact his father since that time.

Chris's father was an engineer and had been in partnership with another man. As Chris understood it, they owned a small company that employed no more than two or three people. A lot of their orders were from foreign clients, but as international trade for many smaller companies dried up when the change happened, customers had to be sought from within this country, and that brought about the collapse of the company. Chris's father found work with a corporation, which was essentially government owned, that processed waste materials. It was not ideal, but at that time his father had turned fifty years of age. Chris has a sister who is older than him, thirteen years older, but they were never close and haven't been in contact with one another for years. Steven was just a year younger than Chris and how much his condition had affected the family is difficult to say, but without doubt it put an enormous burden on it. Chris often thinks back to how his father would lose patience with Steven, and then what with his mother defending her son it put a strain on their relationship. Chris was always worrying about his mother, Steven's condition caused Chris to feel responsible for him, and it also made the bond between him and his mother closer, and her leaving him at such an early age compounded in Chris a sense of unfairness in the world.

While Chris was standing outside the Rummage Room thinking back about his family, his nerves were getting the better of him, and although he wanted to get away from the area he was in he also wanted to see through what he had set out to do, but while he was thinking this he was unaware of being watched by a man who was standing further down the street. Chris was also not to know that four weeks earlier, the man watching him was present at a meeting in an office used by the secret police. A decision was put into action in that office, deep in a building where the affairs of the state's security take place, and the man watching Chris was given orders to monitor the activities of a person who had come to their attention, that person being Chris. The man given those orders is called Garman, a seasoned state security officer who has dealt with many cases over the years. He is a heavy set man with strong dark features, his eyes almost black, piercing and unyielding, and those eyes were the last thing some unfortunate people had seen before being 'despatched' in whatever way it was after he had interrogated or tortured them. Earlier on that day, in his office, Garman picked up what looked like an official ID that had been dropped into a tray on the desk he was sitting behind, his thick fingers toyed with the ID and the muscles in his strong hand flexed slightly while his eyes narrowed as he looked at the photograph on the ID. Written across the photograph were the words, CASE TO BE RESOLVED. The face on the ID was Chris Kirby's.

Four

As there was still some time to kill before his planned meeting, Chris decided to go for a walk, and hanging about outside the Rummage Room would only cause people to be suspicious of him. He began to walk with slow doleful strides, looking at the buildings in the street, all of them houses except for three shops. There was the shop where he had arranged to meet his contact, which was a general hardware store on the corner, the Rummage Room and what looked like an antique shop, but it seemed that it had not been open for years. Chris looked at the upstairs windows of the house that looked like an antique shop, the heavily stained curtains had dulled from white to grey and they were drawn shut, and for some reason Chris felt someone had died there and nothing had happened since. He looked at the roof of the building, and then at the roofs of the other buildings in the street, they would have been built during the late Victorian period.

Chris looked up at the little gargoyles on the roofs of the buildings, each one different from the other. Their grotesque and misshapen faces had lost the sharp contours of their features through age, neglect and the corroding processes of pollution. Chris thought about the men who had built the houses and shaped the gargoyles that did not serve any function other than being decorative. The builder had left his mark on uniformed houses built to a specified standard, but the character of the little gargoyles stood in defiance to systematic order and measurement as each figure had its own personality. Chris thought about modern buildings and the people that build them. They would not have been that different from the people who had built the houses in the street he was standing in, but it seemed to Chris that a craftsman back then wanted to inscribe and shape a piece of work that was personal to him, and in doing so showed his character for future generations to look at.

A feeling of loss momentarily took hold of Chris, as it often did when thinking of individual thought and action. Shaking himself out of it, he walked towards the hardware shop with more purpose in his step.

Chris stood outside the shop looking through the window, but seeing inside was difficult because it was dark and stacked against the window was a heap of materials and tools that looked old and was discontinued stock. There were two men inside the shop and Chris supposed that one of them worked there and probably owned it, while the other man was a customer or someone just passing the time of day. The weather was dull and overcast, and a cold wind was a reminder that winter had not gone and snow or sleet was threatening. Chris looked across at a piece of the green in the housing project that was visible from where he was standing, and was aware that his loitering around so close to a housing project would attract the attention of the security services if they were around so he decided to start walking.

A car went by, making its way towards the project, and there was something menacing about the car that caused Chris to feel anxious. He had glanced at the inhabitants of the passing car and it did not go unnoticed by the three men inside it who all looked at Chris as one. The car was beaten up and tattered, and the young men inside it were the car's human equivalent in that they looked scruffy and rough. Chris saw that one of them had a black eye that was so severe it was noticeable from just taking a quick look.

Chris checked the time, feeling a tremor of apprehension run down his body he pleaded internally to something or someone for the person he had planned to meet to make an appearance, but it had not reached the pre-arranged time. His nerves were spiralling to a point that he felt he was going to explode. He was walking in the same direction the car had gone, and stood on the side of the road leading into the housing project. Chris looked over at a rectangular concrete block that housed four shops, and without thinking began walking towards them, looking about himself like a person who had disembarked in a town that was foreign, unknown and dangerous. The project was a stark and brutal construction, a complex made up mainly of flats built with security in mind so that it could be 'locked down' easily with only the one road leading into and out of it, and once inside cameras were everywhere, so the security services could control what went on there with ease.

Two children were clambering over a mechanical horse that was outside one of the shops. They kept shaking the horse in an effort to make it move, but the horse was resolute. The benign smile on its face was unmoved by the demands of the infants who began to curse it for its obstinacy. One of them slapped the side of its face, and then slapped it again, only harder, and the other one kicked the flanks of the horse as they swore in voices with a deep gravel tone that Chris found surprising for children of their age. One of the boys looked directly into Chris's face and asked him if he had twenty five cents to give him, for that was the required coin needed for the horse to come to life.

Chris thought about giving him the money, but did not for a couple of reasons. One of the reasons was that he did not like the boys' attitude or the way they were behaving. He disliked them even though they were very young. Chris did not like the way the boy had looked at him before asking for the money. It had made him feel uncomfortable. It was as if the boy had made a judgement about him and the type of person he was. Maybe a crazy thing to think, considering how young the boy was, but all the same that is how Chris felt about it. And that led to the other reason that stopped him from giving money to the boy. Chris knew it was common practice in the housing projects for young children to accuse men of being perverts and paedophiles, or a 'paedo' as they were commonly called. There were always stories in the papers, and on the television, of an accused man who had been hounded down and killed by a mob. Although the media did not sanction the behaviour, there was usually a comment to the effect that if people persisted to behave in that way there will be people who get very angry about it.

Fear of the 'other' is rife as circumspection is the normal state of affairs, even though the state continually proclaims that its salient principle is of having a society where a person who has done nothing wrong should not become a victim of theft or physical attack.

'Anger is fear'. Chris had read that in a book written by a monk, or a philosopher, coming from an Eastern religion or philosophy, and it came to his mind as he surveyed the dismal looking housing project. The resonance of chickens clucking and squawking is a constant background sound. It is the norm to keep one's own poultry, as is evident by the rows of chicken runs lining the front and back of the flats and a bitter smell that twists in the wind, which at times is so acrid it burns one's eyes and inflames one's nose and throat. The meat and eggs are a cheap source of protein in a time when there is a shortage of many goods that would have been taken for granted in other periods of history, but for many there is not the money to purchase food and other commodities if they were available.

Theft of another person's chickens, or vandalism of coups and runs, is pretty much non-existent, because the consequences if caught or found to be doing such a thing is so harsh it deters even the most inherent light-fingered person or vandal. It is prevalent within the culture to show one's abhorrence to crime committed against the individual and to always confirm one's belief in law and order by being seen to participate in, and support, any initiatives and measures implemented by the state or local authorities directed at addressing crime. There are days set aside in schools that concentrate on a particular offence. It could be shoplifting, drink-driving, stealing another person's property in the street or from their homes, or inflicting violence upon another person. Although the youngest children do not have days that dealt specifically with rape, murder, paedophile behaviour or acts of terrorism. The activities that take place range from a project in the classroom to the whole school

30

presenting a theme in a gala-like affair. There are multi-school events, which are very popular and are often covered by the media, which is either local or national. Many children and youths belong to an organisation called the Anti Crime Crusaders, which is known as the ACC, which is massively popular and promoted by schools and the state.

Nearly all names of organisations, television shows and phrases in society are abbreviated to a snappy, easy to remember epithet.

Chris looked into the face of the boy who had asked him for some money and guessed he would have been a VM, a Vigilant Minor, the junior part of the ACC, the senior's being the OY, Observant Youth. To a large degree the organisation had replaced the scouting movement, having taken from it many of its ideas to do with a ranking system based on achievements and chiefly for it to be self-governing as it is a principal ethos for rules and discipline to evolve and be administered from within the organisation. The ACC is a powerful organisation in that it has a high profile and is listened to by the authorities, but it exists primarily in the poorer areas.

Chris looked at the amount of discarded lottery stubs that littered the ground outside the shop, and he watched as the wind collected a wave of the tickets and splashed them against the mechanical horse. The boy was still looking at Chris, and he thought of what the man with the loud voice had said earlier in the Rummage Room, about the man who was beaten by a mob and dragged behind a car. Chris looked up at the streetlights, just to see if there was any evidence of where the man had been strung up. It might have been in another part of the project, but the green that the man was talking about, where the mob had gathered, was next to where he was standing. Chris checked the way he was standing, because his body language might have been projecting what could be judged to be a shortcoming, and that may well be detected. Some small facet of speech, expression or posture could be noted and identified as different and wrong. The thought of the boy shouting out he was a pervert or paedophile – 'kiddie-fiddler' is the common term – and running into the shop screaming and accusing the man outside of some action caused a sudden wave of sickness and fright to pass though his body and re-ignite the panic he felt earlier in the Rummage Room.

A woman came out of the shop just as Chris thought the boy was going to ask him why he was hanging around. He felt a massive sense of relief on seeing she was with the two boys. The boy who had been looking at Chris gave one final kick at the mechanical horse as he turned to leave.

31

'Stop piss balling about you little cunt,' the woman shouted at him. The boy sneered with a look of contempt and hatred at the world around him with such conviction and intensity that it shocked Chris, because he thought the boy too young to feel such emotions so deeply. Chris looked down at his watch as the woman stared at him and pulled the other boy by his arm, and he shrugged her off with the same disdain that the other boy held for the woman. The three of them walked off with the two boys running around the woman like young dogs let off a lead. Chris pretended to be occupied with searching for imaginary information on his phone.

The facility on one's phone for noting specific details and information in a most functional way is the normal way of writing down one's plans and not writing in a book or diary. The facility on the phones for doing this are never called a personal organiser or log, because the word 'personal' is not used as it was in previous years. The notion of 'privacy' has become, in the main, a fairly foreign concept and private journals can be seen as leading to subversive behaviour. Nowadays, writing down one's innermost thoughts has diminished to a point of keeping a book and giving it value as something personal to log down one's reminiscences has all but disappeared, because the concept of owning a book to record one's reflections, describe one's feelings and note subjective observations is unusual. The majority of people would just not see the purpose of doing it. Personal emotions and responses to external matters presented in society is not a shared experience, and neither is it encouraged for it might trespass on the condemnable act of being critical.

Chris had bought a diary in the past, and he is not alone in doing so, but he did not maintain the interest in keeping a regular update of his experiences and thoughts. Chris had once read that the keeping of a diary was an important factor in the common person gaining a consciousness of one's life. It was primarily young woman working as maids in service in the employment of the wealthy. The 'lady' of the house would often bond with her maid and teach her to read and write, and to emulate her by owning a diary. It was by reading these accounts of the young women working in service that many significant insights were gained of the subjective understanding of the working class and of their experience and the conditions in which they lived. The diaries gave an account of their hopes and aspirations, and what it was like in the households of the wealthy by reading the thoughts of those young women coming from the poorer classes who worked for them and lived under their roof.

Chris looked up and watched the three figures as they made their way over the green, the deep voices of the children echoing around a space boxed in by concrete and brick blocks that housed the inhabitants of the project.

He looked at the toy horse. The once colourful designs that adorned it had faded and it was peppered with chips and divots. The smile on its face was perversely incongruous to its surroundings, and on taking a closer look Chris read what was printed next to the coin slot: Giddy up – Galloping Giggles.

Two of the four shops had closed down, one completely shuttered up, the other just having the windows whitewashed so people could not see inside. One of the shops not closed down was a miniature Rummage Room that looked open for business, but it was not. Wooden boards had been placed against the window making it difficult to view the contents from outside. There were only two Juice Saver light bulbs in the shop that did not give off much illumination. It is common in poorer areas to have minimum lighting in shops and public places because of electrical energy not being an abundant commodity, and it is too expensive to use freely even if it is.

Chris thought about the young man earlier who bought candles in the Rummage Room and wondered why he did not get them in this one, but then it occurred to him that he had exchanged a coupon for the candles and he would not have been able to do that because the smaller shops do not have the license to accept coupons as a form of payment. The shop in the project would most likely be owned by an individual dealing only in cash, and probably operating a kind of pawning system for deferred payment.

People open small versions of the Rummage Rooms as there is a market for such a service because cash is thin on the ground and credit is not available. The culture of paying at a later date for products and services is no longer an orthodox practice in society and credit cards are no longer issued and controlled by private banks.

Nearly all of the small retail outlets have closed down in the poorer areas, which has left just a skeleton service of shabby shops in defunct precincts. The mass of shopping is done in a GS, a Gigantic Store, which are everywhere. They sell almost everything anyone needs and also accommodate doctor's surgeries, opticians, dentists, undertakers and other essential services. They also house local authority departments such as housing offices, employment sections and administer benefits to those who qualify, which is meagre and often only amounts to the coupons. The stores are austere places, some looking nothing more than sealed mammoth steel and plastic boxes, and from the outside one cannot see inside the vast constructions that are constantly patrolled by heavily armed guards monitoring people in and around the store. The security guards give the impression they are not to be approached as they patrol in small groups looking through smoked visors that are fixed onto their helmets.

The immense stores are a focal point of the surrounding community. As well as housing the necessary facilities, there are also rooms and spaces for multifarious functions, such as public information lectures where films are often shown. The most popular films are those giving warnings to guard against diseases and information to be vigilant against terrorists, who are always illegal immigrants or the sons and daughters of people who entered the country illegally years ago.

The Gigantic Store's presence as a visual landmark is monolithic and their function is of essential importance. The influence of the state is ever present by showing films on screens in the stores where people are shopping. The films often show market places in other countries where there are long queues for any food that is available, which results in rioting because of the shortage of food and the conditions people have to live under. It is the films of the rioting that are most popular with the majority of people who are visiting the Gigantic Stores. The images are contrasted with what is presented as efficient farm production in the idyllic countryside in this country. The shoppers are told how fortunate they are to live where they do, and are reminded that it needs constant protection, because there are those that come from other lands where life is harsh, culturally backward and violent who want to destroy the way of life we have in this country.

The usual method of payment in the stores is through the use of the ID cards that among others things contain one's banking details. The security guards often ask for them to be produced as it sends a clear message that the state is vigilant in its professed quest to challenge and eradicate what is relentlessly reported as the 'scourge' of illegal immigrants who are among us and involved in terrorist activities, people who think nothing of killing innocent members of the public to highlight their cause, which varies from religious to political grounds. This message is constantly propagated and believed to be true by the masses.

Methods of obtaining goods exist aside from formal practices. The 'alternative economy', even though illegal, is in full existence and plays a significant part of how the poorer people trade rather than participating in the orthodox economy. At times it is little more than a barter system where items, services and goods are exchanged because cash is so hard to come by.

Chris looked across the green at the woman and two boys as they were disappearing into the flats. The booming voices of the boys faded with them, leaving a dull stillness hovering over the worn and uncared-for piece of grass residing beneath low clouds that were full of dirty water. Chris looked at the doorway of the other shop that was open, which could be described as a general store, and taking a deep breath he entered by pushing the door that sounded a bell.

The inside of the shop was as neglected as its exterior. Chris looked at the tinned food, shelves of cheap bread and the contents of a small freezer. The shop sold the basics that people run low on, and so they go in the shop to buy what is needed to get by before doing their main shopping at the local Gigantic Store. There was a stack of tinned beer of a type found in the poorer areas. The beer comes in bland packaging and always has the details of some kind of competition printed on the side of the can, usually to win more of the beer, but sometimes to win tickets for a sporting event or some other form of entertainment. The beer itself is weak and made with different 'flavours' or 'tastes'. Some of it tastes no different from children's fizzy drinks, and there are rumours that the use of hops is not part of the ingredients at all because it is not so much brewed but concocted in a laboratory. The beer is said to contain a chemical that has calmative effects, as is the case with the type of tobacco Chris had noticed earlier.

In one corner of the shop was a display of children's toys, some costing no more than a few cents. There were masks of famous wrestlers, toy imitation badges and ID cards representing anti-crime organisations, plastic guns, daggers, truncheons, itching powder, plastic excrement and chewing gum that tastes of onions.

A man and a woman were watching Chris. They were sitting behind the counter looking as if they were refugees waiting for some kind of transport to take them from the trouble they live in. Their faces were lined and their bodies were depleted of physical strength and the energy to challenge or question anything that might confront them. They looked beaten. Their drab clothing was basic, well worn and of poor quality. Chris offered a smile, but there was no response in their weak eyes. Chris walked up to the counter and neither the man nor the woman made an attempt at standing, but merely looked up him, and Chris felt he could have pointed a gun at them and their expression would not have changed.

Chris looked at a large display of different scratch cards that were on the side of the counter, and took an involuntary sharp intake of breath when seeing the faces of men on the cards that were purported to be 'criminals' or 'terrorists'. He looked closer at the faces, trying to see if he recognised any of the men. Some scratch cards are of a lottery type to win money, but there are others just as popular that give the winner a chance to participate in deciding the fate of a 'criminal' who was to appear on a forthcoming television show, which would probably be The Offender's Nemesis. The show has mass appeal and is marketed so generally it is impossible to escape it. Some of the cards have points and when a person has collected the required amount he or she can apply to be in the audience of one of the transmissions, but there are also 'prizes' giving the winner an opportunity to vote on the methods of punishment or humiliation that will be used on the 'terrorist' or 'criminal', which is usually done by casting votes on a computer. The punishments, torture and humiliation are base and hideous. They are created to be a spectacle of horror and range from the outrageously gruesome to the childishly crude. Capital punishment is now exploited for entertainment.

Chris looked at the cards with the distorted faces of condemned men staring out. Printed beneath the face is a name, supposedly their real names and nearly always foreign if they are 'terrorists'. Those people labelled as having had a liberal understanding are not on the cards and although they do appear on The Offender's Nemesis they are never killed. These people are used on the show for light entertainment in between the punishments of those accused of being criminals and terrorists. The 'liberal professionals' are humiliated and discredited, which is an important part in maintaining a hatred for the previous system's ideas and practices.

Chris looked at the selection of cigarettes on the wall behind the counter and decided to buy some, even though he had a full packet in his pocket. He saw the type that the man was smoking in the shop earlier, the cigarettes with a synthetic smell. They were considerably cheaper than normal tobacco, and without consciously doing so Chris felt the words leaving his mouth as he asked for a packet.

The woman stood up and turned to get the cigarettes as Chris counted the money in the palm of his hand. He had never smoked the cigarettes before and decided to try one when outside the shop and throw the rest away. He paid the woman and thanked her, and she looked up at him as if surprised and said, 'Thank you,' in a tone of voice and manner that made Chris take a second look at her.

The man also looked at Chris, and the dullness in his eyes dissipated as he saw Chris more clearly. They looked like they wanted to speak, maybe just some pleasantries, but were too afraid even to do that, and not wanting to draw attention to himself Chris gave a quick smile and said, 'Thanks, bye,' as he turned to leave.

The woman raised her hand in a feeble gesture and the man raised his chin slightly. The old couple watched Chris leave their shop as if he came from a world they once knew, and that he just might be able to offer some chance for them to escape to freedom, but he was now departing with their hope.

Chris stood outside the shop and unwrapped the packet of cigarettes, all the while thinking about the old couple. He knew they were not from the social background they now lived and worked in. Chris was more than ninety nine per cent sure of that as he thought about how they probably ended up where they were. They were a couple from the professional class and for some reason a job or jobs were lost so they could not keep their house, which relegated them to living in a project where they suffer the stigma that goes with it from people they previously knew, and here in the project they have difficulty connecting with people in the situation they now find themselves. It was common for it to end with people taking their lives because the transition was too much to take. There are stories of people committing suicide and also taking the lives of their children because they cannot bear the thought of them having to live the life they were fated to.

Chris put one of the cigarettes in his mouth and was conscious of how the acidic smell from the chickens tingled on his tongue. He drew on the cigarette before lighting it and could taste it was different from an ordinary brand, and when lighting it his taste buds were filled almost instantly with a scented flowery flavour that left a pungent taste in his mouth. He smelled the smoke as it drifted from the tip of the cigarette and thought about it being drugged for a short while, before turning to take a last look through the window of the shop, but the clutter in the window restricted a clear view inside and he could not see the old couple. Chris turned away and, taking another drag on the cigarette he wondered about it being drugged and if he felt anything, or if the effect would be immediate.

He re-traced his route through the project, noticing the cigarette did not seem to have any effect and of how the weather was changing. It had become dark and the wind whipped up its pace with a damp chill. There was nobody about, and this made the place feel ominous. Chris looked around at the flats and over to an area he had been in only a few weeks before when visiting a person who lived in one of the flats. He had seen a man called Bill Copley, who he was told was part of an underground movement that held meetings and encouraged like-minded people who wanted to contribute to a critical analysis of the system and take part in the covert process of printing and disseminating pamphlets and journals. Bill came from a qualified background and had been involved in campaign groups since his mid-teens, having fallen foul of the authorities, because of his activities and views, he had been ostracised from opportunities at work and of living in a better area. Chris had been put in contact with Bill during the course of his search for groups and people who might be able to assist him in helping his brother Steven. Chris felt a lot of the people he had met were well intentioned but naïve.

As Chris looked about his surrounding he wondered how somewhere like the project that houses so many people can be so devoid of colour and is so often very quiet. He came to the opinion that the place was an unmitigated construction of monotony.

Chris stopped walking because his attention was drawn to a colourful card lying by the side of the path. It was the size of a playing card and probably popular with school children who swapped them. He picked it up, but froze when turning it over and seeing what was on the other side. It was a picture of Alan Manville pulling a face and striking a pose that was his trademark. Chris looked closely at Manville's face, at his tanned skin, his teeth, bleached white and shaped by extensive dentistry skills, and his smile, set deep, giving the appearance of a mask, but it was his eyes that Chris really noticed. They were colourless, dark, piercing, staring out and they could have been saying, ' I love you,' or 'I hate you.'

He is a person who commands a lot of power in the massive market of trite media entertainment. Chris believed that just because of his association with what is often judged as crass, sensationalist popular culture, people should not underestimate the influence Manville has within the media or of his importance as a public figure, and that Manville had risen to a powerful position with connections to those ruling the state because of his success in manipulating the public.

It is certainly true that celebrity culture and its values have saturated the imagination of the majority to a point where the opinions of a pop singer, however unproven, fickle or facile are held by many as a benchmark to measure values by. There are many people who believe 'celebrities' have a pivotal role to play for the state in the functioning of the system, seeing it as a distractive policy that amuses, entertains and educates, or maybe conditions rather than educates while rendering the targets of its effect as malleable subjects for state intentions. Politicians no longer parade themselves in front of the public with efforts to persuade people to vote for them. The affectations once used by politicians of attempting to pass themselves off as concerned elected representatives of people they share the same experiences with does not exist anymore. They are now ensconced in the background performing bureaucratic duties for those who actually rule things in entirety. Although there are those coming from a qualified background who write Manville

38

off as inconsequential in the greater scheme of things and do not agree he has a powerful influence in the running of society, Manville is seen as commercially popular and nothing more than that in a society where the 'celebrity' and 'popular' culture dominates the lives of poorer people making up the mass of society.

But, for Chris, Alan Manville, and the show he fronts, The Offender's Nemesis, has become an obsession. He hates the show for utilising low-minded reasoning to initiate a barbaric response to issues of crime. He sees it as pernicious and part of what has been created to limit people's imagination and to instil a sense of constant fear while living their lives in a state of bondage. The personal aspirations of poorer people are rarely realised, and yet they expect them to be fulfilled immediately, and because of this a perpetual sense of self-failure is felt, causing a void in their lives that is easily filled by respecting the status of celebrities such as pop singers, soap stars and models who are held in greater esteem than engineers or scientists, who are seen as figures having little or no relevance in their lives. The teaching of a broadly informed education has shrunk to a point where now all that is taught is a narrow spectrum that meets the needs of the state. However, the qualified class consider themselves to be more informed on important matters. They have a broader and higher education and take an interest in classical arts and politics. Public figures of virtue, such as military people, are deemed as significant. This class of people feel they have a place within the deeper fabric of the country and that is the reason for them being better rewarded by the state.

Chris looked at Manville's face on the card. The feelings that rose in him were not caused by revulsion, but dread. Chris had woken many times during the night lately, in a panic because of dreams, or nightmares, where Manville, the show and the ominous fear of the state's measures to control had closed in on him and triggered feelings of inextricable suffocation that left a lingering sense of dark foreboding throughout the following day. It was a recurring nightmare where Chris was trapped by state security officers and watched over by a gloating Alan Manville who decided his fate. The malignant pleasure shown in Manville's face said there would be no mercy, and humiliation and torture will be staged for the amusement of his audience until the inevitable act of killing Chris, which would be in the most macabre manner.

On many occasions Chris had woke up shouting, dreaming he was on the show, but the faces of those in the studio audience stayed with him, and the images of hysterical excitement at wanting to see him tortured and killed, and no matter how hard he tried Chris could not shake them from his mind. The effects left by the nightmares were haunting and at times all-pervading as Chris thought about the practices the state applies, and might direct upon him in the future. The reason he thought that might happen was because of him wanting to protect and support his brother Steven who he believed would become known to the authorities as a person that does not fit in the system and is at times vocal in his criticisms of it.

Chris looked around to see if anyone was watching as he placed the card in his jacket pocket before continuing to walk back towards the shop that sold building materials.

Five

Chris looked through the window of the shop and watched the two men who were still talking to each other, but his attention was snatched away by the sound of a door slamming. He turned around quickly and saw the loud man who was in the Rummage Room earlier, walking in his direction carrying the posters, a bucket and a brush. The man crossed to the same side of the street Chris was on, and even from a distance of about forty metres Chris could see the man's beady eyes were set on him. His ungainly walk carried him in uneven steps from one side of the pavement to the other, and as Chris watched him he cursed himself for not being more precise in keeping to the time he had arranged to meet the person, or people he had planned to meet. He looked through the window of the shop, feeling the eyes of the loud man burning into him, and then the sound of chesty wheezing signalled he was standing next to him. Chris looked at the man, his laboured breath and reddened face fighting against the effects of the cigarette that was stuck in the corner of his mouth.

'How do?' The man said, as his eyes searched Chris for information.

Chris did not want to get into a conversation, because he knew from listening to him earlier that the man liked to talk a lot, but he felt obliged to answer him.

'I'm okay thanks – yourself?' He said, knowing he should not have added the last part, and sure enough the man settled himself, pushing his face forward in an effort to read as much as he could about Chris.

The man nodded at the shop window. 'He's not got much in there – never got what you want and it costs way over the odds.'

'Small business, struggling to survive I suppose,' Chris said, aware his tone of voice and manner would rouse the man's curiosity.

'That's what he would say,' the man said, referring to the owner of the shop. Chris felt the man's eyes peeling layers from his face as he searched with greater concentration.

Chris offered an amiable smile and decided to stop any interaction by stepping over to the door and placing his hand on the handle, 'Ah well,' he said, and just as he was going to push the door open the man said,

'Not from round here, are you?'

It was as if Chris had walked into a wall, so impenetrable was the feeling that shut down upon him as his mind zigzagged in a frantic search to give a credible answer. Again he cursed himself, this time for not having prepared a reason for being in the area.

'No,' was all he said. He looked squarely at the man and shook his head as he proceeded to enter the shop. As Chris closed the door he saw the man looking at him and was relieved his face wore an expression of being rebuffed rather than harbouring any acutely suspicious thoughts. Chris turned and saw the two men in the shop were looking at him. The man behind the counter stood with his arms folded, his large angular jaw jutted out, which caused his glasses to shift on the bridge of his nose. Chris noticed one of the arms on his glasses was taped at the hinge on the frame. Both men regarded Chris with surprise at him entering, but they retained their reserved manner. The other man had stopped talking when Chris entered.

Chris walked over to the furthest corner of the shop from where the men were at the counter, and as he browsed the men continued with their conversation in quiet tones. Some of the items for sale were little more than rubbish. Chris ran his finger along the edge of a damaged sheet of plasterboard and noticed some of the stock was so old the advertising and colouring had paled or nearly disappeared on the packaging. As he was looking at a cardboard tray of small locks, which were of very poor quality, the man behind the counter raised his voice for Chris to hear as he asked him if the there was anything he was specifically looking for.

'Not really,' Chris said, and immediately regretted opening his mouth without thinking. 'Just having a look,' he added and smiled at the man who looked at him with no change of expression. This meeting with an unknown person, and people and going into the project had really unnerved Chris and he kept telling himself to calm down.

The two men continued with their conversation, which was about a model boating club they both seemed to be members of. The man on the customer side of the counter demonstrated with his hands the process of constructing a difficult joint on a model boat he was working on. He spoke of the intricate details involved and showed the other man what he meant by crossing one finger over the other and then wetted his finger before drawing a diagram in the dust on the counter. The other man watched him with what looked like a mixture of boredom and patience.

Chris felt the man behind the counter found the other man's conversation, with all his demonstrating and explaining, either monotonous or irritating. But then he joined in, pointing his finger at the diagram in the dust. Chris imagined them working on their boats, and he noticed how their hands looked seasoned and roughened from working with building materials and tools.

Chris checked through the window to see if the loud man had gone, and was pleased to find he had. He began to relax, liking the quiet atmosphere of the shop because it was a departure from the confrontation and rush that existed in most of society. It was an out of the way place and he liked listening to the two men talk of their interests which were away from the mainstream. Chris felt a deep comfort at seeing the little shop as a haven for those wanting to escape from the aggressive demands and mercurial values broadcasted by the media. He touched the envelope in his pocket, two thousand Euro dollars is a lot of money to have on one's person in a society where people carry hardly any amount of cash. The man Chris had arranged to meet in the shop was referred to as X, and he was going to be with another man.

Chris looked at his reflection in the window of the shop, again feeling the shock of how exhausted he looked. He looked away from the window to the different items around him and suddenly felt an acute awareness of how drab and threadbare everything was, and running through the poverty stricken baseness of it all was a nasty edge of hostility. His mouth dried as the feeling of exhaustion escalated and became like a heavy weight bearing down upon him and his mind reeled back, like cards in the hand of a dealer, going back over time and recounting how things in society had changed. The 'big change' happened when Chris was thirteen, and it remained crystal clear in his mind how his school was shut down for a couple of months as 'reorganisation' took place before it was re-opened. The process of changing the system was called 'rationalisation'.

Chris remembered how the word was used in all contexts and how his mother would use the term to describe what was happening, which confused Chris, as he had not heard her use the expression before. There was the practice of 'rationalisation' in the workplace, education, the health industry, immigration, social services, the running of the media and access of information, travel within the country and going abroad, and above all the foremost focus of 'rationalisation' was directed at 'law and order'.

There had been serious disquiet for years concerning law and order before the change, and although there was also general dissatisfaction about education, immigration, housing, employment and other societal matters, it was the problem of crime and anti-social behaviour that was the country's primary concern. Criminals were seen to act with liberty and the level of violence inflicted upon innocent people grew as its nature became more vicious and random. Many joked it was the perpetrators that felt they had been wronged if someone informed the police and wanted to press charges. The formation of policies and rights created a situation where the authorities were seemingly unable to do anything meaningful to resolve the matter.

It was commonly believed that the proposed solutions merely added to a growing industry that was made up of people seeking a status that secured steady wages and a good pension. Apathy took root as most people felt they had no one to represent them in advocating their interests. Dissatisfaction with the mainstream political parties grew as voting in many areas waned and the parties that previously had been thought of as marginal or cranky came to the fore. A growing number of people coming from different walks of life were beginning to join ranks and ask questions about the people and groups that had the controlling power over the running of government and the dominant institutions in society.

It took some time for the state to take the threat to the principal parties seriously. The message was clear - the general public wanted something done about the levels of crime affecting their lives, and they were becoming vocal in demanding an end to a system and its institutions that seemed little more than a self-propagating industry for those speaking in what was widely described as, 'liberal democratic' tones. The people who worked in those industries were seen as parasites, accepting good wages and conditions yet not taking responsibility for their actions. The involvement of the professions were seen to be intruding upon every aspect of life and were blamed for creating a situation where a large amount of the populace had become reliant on care and provision in dealing with personal matters in their lives, thus creating a situation where the individual took no responsibility for his or her behaviour. The excuses and defence given by the authorities for the breakdown of the fabric of society was viewed by the majority of the public as nothing more than convoluted language that proved itself to be meaningless. There was a call for change, although the situation did not only exist in this country and was comparable in all other technically advanced countries.

And then there was a global economic collapse of an unprecedented proportion which had an immediate impact on what had become accepted as the normal running of society. The owners of massive trans-national companies, the magnates and the landed, essentially those people holding the dominant power behind the state, intervened and brushed aside the existing democratic process. They banished the emerging fringe political parties that comprised of segregationists, religious reactionaries, racists, the greens, fascists and communists, and in doing so created a new face for the state that laid the entire blame on a liberal ideology that, in practice, had failed the citizens of the world. The whole liberal democratic process was overthrown, and forever since has been denigrated while the position of the ruling elite has been preserved.

Chris pondered over his investigations and of the people he had come into contact with in his effort to help his brother. He had become involved in action that was critical of the state; and he was scared.

Six

Time passed in the shop, and Chris kept looking at the two men were still engaged in their conversation, in low tones, the man behind the counter periodically looking over at Chris, for he had spent an inordinate amount of time in a shop having a limited amount of things to browse among.

'Are you okay there, sir?' The man said, 'You've been looking around so long I thought you were doing a stock-take.'

What he said might have been light-hearted, but his eyes said something very different, because the man had become impatient with Chris looking at items he obviously had no interest in buying, and constantly checking the time by looking up at a clock over the counter; which was a quirky clock that read the time backwards and could have been put up on the wall by the owner as a harmless statement of rebellion against the way of things.

Chris made a bit of a hash in his apologies for spending so long looking around the shop and stumbled on about how he thought he had arranged to meet someone down the road but must have got the time wrong, and he thought the shop interesting.

'You thought you were meeting someone?' The man behind the counter interjected, which caused Chris to stammer as the stony, humourless faces of the two men looking at Chris made him feel even uneasier. Chris told the man behind the counter he would ring his friend and check to see if he had made a mistake, and then he did something he could not believe he was doing, he pressed numbers on his phone and spoke to an imaginary person. It was farcical, and as Chris was talking he thought why he did not tell the two men his friend had his phone switched off, but then it all seemed so absurd, and all the while the two men watched Chris as he walked towards the door to make his exit, and as he did so, Chris waved nervously to the two men and apologised when closing the door behind him.

The relief Chris felt as he stood outside the shop lasted only for a few seconds as a thought flashed through his mind of the man in the shop phoning the police - although he had not stolen anything his behaviour could be construed as suspicious, and what with having the money on him, Chris felt the burn of anxiety return. He began to walk, cursing the man or people he was supposed to meet, he felt let-down and frustrated, and there was Rosie, his wife, she had told him it was 'madness' and 'dangerous' to be doing such a thing and now he had to tell her that the whole thing failed. She would not gloat, but she would tell him to learn from it and stop mixing with such people who tread a path away from the normal thoroughfare in society. He started to walk towards the train station with anti-climactic feelings of tiredness as the anxiety he felt had been replaced by the heavy weight of frustration.

Chris took his phone from his pocket and phoned Brendan, his friend of fifteen years who had always been very supportive to Chris and his worry over Steven. Chris met Brendan when he started college and they hit of off immediately - although they were studying different subjects, they shared similar views and had become very close friends over the years. Chris respected Brendan's intelligent reasoning, exceptional in his area of electronics - he had a good humour, sense of fair play and an astute understanding of the way society is run. Brendan had always got on with Steven, the two of them discussing technological intelligence and its uses, as well as politics. Brendan had planned to marry a woman he met when young, but it did not work out and he had lived alone for the last four years. Their relationship felt stronger as they had both lost their parents while young and this was something they could both relate to. Chris and Brendan spoke with honesty and trust with each other and had remained just as close since Chris got married. Brendan came round for meals or just visited to chat and became Godfather to Nina, Chris's twelve year old daughter, a responsibility Brendan took seriously.

There was no answer so Chris left a message telling Brendan he would speak to him later and explain what happened, and just as he was putting the phone in his pocket it began to ring. It was Steven. He was in a state of anxiety as he asked Chris what he was up to, but Chris placated him and told Steven they would meet up straight away. Chris arranged to meet Steven in a café area in one of the Gigantic Stores that was a few miles away and close to where Steven lived. Chris went to the station, going over the worry of how Steven had known what he was doing.

As Chris entered the café area he saw Steven seated at a table, and in his normal manner he was staring intensely from the quick of one of his nails to points in his surroundings, his eyes hardly ever settling in a relaxed repose. Chris noticed this as he stopped for a second to look at his brother before going up to the table. Steven was a little taller than Chris, with a rangier build and had long thin fingers that were nearly always fidgeting with something, which was one of his mannerisms making him appear physically awkward. His eyes were lighter in colour than Chris's and always fiery, and when observing a thing or person securing a fixed concentration that made people wary of him. He rarely spoke when in a group, appearing withdrawn or even sullen, but then he might unleash an outburst in an obsessive manner as he endeavoured to press home a point he wanted to make. His high intellect and lateral thought patterns caused

46

him to present an argument or reasoning in such a manner it was difficult for most people to understand, which often resulted in him being misunderstood or ridiculed for talking what was often perceived as nonsense. Steven spent most of his time alone, a voracious reader who scoured where he could to find books on mathematics and developed profound theories on artificial intelligence, but his knowledge and talent in the sciences was only part of his intellectual scope.

Steven had always taken a fervent interest in the political system, and would explain to Chris how it can be viewed as a multifunctional machine, like a computer, and his interest was in those people, or organisations that programmed it. He felt the way of things had been created so that the vast majority of people within it are ignorant and poor, a perfect situation for the creation of anger and resentment at that which is most immediate in one's experience, and not conscious of how their condition came about or for what reasons. Steven would say how the system allowed the ruling-elite to remain in control and so have power and wealth. Chris saw his brother as a man who was ostracised by others and felt alienated and yet was preoccupied with the plight of the average person not having opportunities to fulfil his or her potential as fully balanced human beings as long as they live in a system like the one that exists. Chris felt the reasons for the ridicule and antagonism people direct against people like Steven was a consequence of fear, and they are fearful for themselves because of the way in which society dictates its messages of appropriateness and conformity.

He lived alone in a single person's flat and was barely able to pay the rent with what he earned as a tutor in a college. The job at the college was found for him by Chris, who worked there at set times arranged by his employer and the college, it being normal practice for people who had gained qualifications to work a specific amount of time, although not that many days, in an institution for higher learning. It is seen as paying back the state for one's education and the opportunities that afforded, and as Chris trained and works as a draughtsman, the state demands he arranges a set amount of time to work on a course relevant to his subject. While working at the college he saw an opening for Steven, who at that time was unemployed, which was not unusual for Steven as it was difficult for him to secure a full time job of any worth, and certainly not one where he used his abilities. Chris made enquires and after some cajoling, Steven went for an interview and got the job.

Steven worked part-time, tutoring on one of the basic numeracy skills courses running at the college which provided a rudimentary education for those who had left school without gaining, or taking, any qualifications. These students are classified as 'educationally subnormal', a term revived from the past and used without criticism of it being insensitive. The college has a reputation as a place of no great distinction whatsoever and accommodated young people who travelled in from poorer areas. It ran a few courses for higher learning, as in the case of Chris, tutoring on part of an architecture course, but primarily its function was for the provision of courses aimed at low achievers. The course Steven taught made up part of what is called Nationality Studies. It is not academically challenging and does not lead to higher educational qualifications, but is part of the curriculum which, when completed, gave the learners a certificate showing they had achieved a standard level of understanding in what is regarded as relevant knowledge of the running of modern society. The student who successfully completes the course is proclaimed as an Informed Person. Steven gains little or no satisfaction in teaching his students as he found none of them to be conscious of their situation in any political way and most of them do not want to learn, but just go along with the content matter of the course, which, besides basic numeracy and literacy skills, is little more than reciting the changes of statutes that has led to strengthening the country's military and trading position in the world.

Chris approached the table, and he could tell by the look on his brother's face that he was not pleased with things, which was often the way it was with Steven. Before Chris could say hello and sit down Steven snapped at him, 'What have you been up to? Eh?'

'What do you mean?' Chris said, conscious of how weak his words sounded.

Steven told Chris of how he knew what he was doing and of the meeting that was meant to take place that afternoon, and as Steven spoke, Chris mulled over how he would have known and thought about the different people Chris had spoken to. Chris told him everything, of how he was walking around with two thousand Euro dollars in his pocket with intentions of meeting a man only known to him as X, because he was told there was an option of getting Steven out of the country. At first it sounded far-fetched to Chris, but the more it was explained to him, and the more anxious he became about the safety of Steven, the more the idea gained credence. He had been told of a passage that exists to get people out of the country by means of a fishing boat that docks in Holland, and once there, a network of related sympathisers and people who were dissidents in this country offer support in giving the 'refugees' a place of safety. Apparently, the Dutch authorities know what is happening, but turn a blind eye to it as the 'refugees' do not pose any problem or threat therefore they are accommodated and live in the country as essentially 'non-people' in a self-sufficient community.

Steven became increasingly agitated. 'Oh don't worry, just go out there and make me look a fool – that's what they'll say, he doesn't know what he's doing, that's why his brother sorts things out for him, because he's not capable, see? Not to be taken seriously, just a deluded idiot with too much time on his hands – don't worry though, his brother will see to it…'

'I care about you,' Chris said to Steven as he looked directly at him, 'and what's wrong with that?'

'You're always there, worrying, going on about things, getting in the way - I am a bloody adult you know, it's a bit, embarrassingly stupid having an older brother trying to sort things out for me - and now, getting involved with this, and making a mess of it - to begin with, I don't want to go to Holland, have you ever thought of that?'

He stared at Chris. 'God you're bloody thick and stupid at times.'

Steven looked down at the table with signs of deep worry etching itself into his features. He refused to tell Chris when he asked him who had told him about the meeting.

'I know you've been nosing around,' Steven said, and then he snapped, 'So, stop it, because it's none of your business.'

Steven looked at Chris and an expression of hurt came over his face as he said, 'Just go home to your nice little wife, and nice little daughter and family - because you're not like me, never have been and never will be, so just leave it and let me get on with my life.'

They looked at each other with nothing being said. A silence established itself as the two brothers sat at the table in the café area feeling too awkward even to look at one another, so they looked down at the table or at things or people around them. After a while Chris asked Steven quietly if the 'colony,' as the place of refuge in Holland was called, really existed, and that he had heard there were such places in other countries as well and not only in Holland.

Steven answered him, now less heated, but speaking with irritation and impatience. 'Of course it exists, as many things exist that aren't encouraged or allowed to be talked about freely.'

Chris shook his head as he said, 'I've made right idiot of myself – walked straight, and naively, into a trap,' and he began to think about the implications of him doing so, of who was involved, of what consequences there would be and what he had opened up; Chris was worried.

Steven looked at him. 'You were probably followed, well, almost certainly, for a few reasons, one of them being to see if you went through with it - and now they know you are prone to participate in, subversive action, as they would put it.'

Steven asked Chris whom he had been talking to and arranged it with. Chris told him it was Simon, his health worker, and he had put him in touch with a guy called Bill Copley who lives in a project close to where he was supposed to meet X, and on saying 'X' Chris flinched with the humiliation of it all. He told Steven how the meeting had been planned to be face-to-face and was given instructions on a note that was to be destroyed immediately after reading it.

Steven sighed heavily as he looked around the café area, his eyes not taking anything in, because his mind was absorbed in thinking about his brother's actions. He began to speak about Simon and of how community mental health workers are no more than agents of the state whose findings and opinions contribute towards the condemnation of perfectly harmless, well-meaning people who lose their liberty, become imprisoned, are abused with a chemical attack on their minds through the application of drugs, and even worse like being used as laboratory guinea pigs for a whole host of investigations, and then often murdered. Steven told Chris how things in that respect had not really changed at all, as it was the same as before the 'big change' in that the medical profession has always been instrumental in the state's endeavour to implement methods of social control.

Chris had heard these condemnations of the mental health industry from Steven on many occasions, and so his confiding with Simon the mental health worker made him and his actions appear stupidly credulous when the situation was so potentially dangerous.

Steven told Chris a contact he has in the 'underground' had told him about the supposed meeting, and 'in the manner that it had been put together it seems the operation was organised from a proactive arm of the state's security which tells us not only that I am I under investigation, but also you are.'

He gave Chris a long searching look. 'You've been tricked - and why didn't you tell me what you were doing?'

Chris found it difficult to look Steven in the eye as he said, 'Simon told me it would be wise if I didn't say anything to you, because you might mention it to people and they might talk and the authorities could then hear about it, and not only would the plan be thwarted, but it puts yours, mine, Simon's and the other people's lives who are organising the trip into jeopardy.'

Steven stared down at the floor, disgust showing in his face and all the while his thin fingers fiddled with a piece of paper, which had been torn off one of the leaflets that were on the table promoting a certain product being sold at 'cut-price'.

Chris spoke, his tone a quiet enquiry, 'Why didn't you contact me before, to let me know?'

Steven did not look up as he answered, telling Chris he was only told a few minutes before ringing him. And again silence enveloped the two of them as they sat at the table, as if isolated and separate from all around them. Nothing more was said as a nagging trepidation built in Chris's stomach, a feeling he knew would not diminish with time and that trouble would be coming their way. Chris asked Steven if he wanted to walk to the train station or bus stop with him, but he declined with the slightest shake of his head as he stared down at the floor, and Chris felt his brother was mulling over an ambiguous conundrum embroiled in a certain danger that threatened his life. As Chris stood up to leave he took a breath before venturing to tell Steven to be careful at the college as it had been mentioned that he has strong opinions, which translates to having too much to say about matters regarding the state and politics in a public place. As Chris predicted, what he said was met with a scowl as Steven glanced up at him briefly before looking down at the floor.

'Oh, has it?' Steven said, with indifference and sarcasm.

'You have to be careful Steve,' Chris said, saying Steve instead of Steven, which was what he always did when he wanted to impress something very important upon his brother, and maybe it was said more strongly with emotion. Steven continued to look down at the floor as if he was the only person at the table and Chris did not exist.

'Remember what Brendan is always saying,' Chris said, "if you've got something to say, say nothing."'

Steven took no notice of what Chris had said and did not look up when Chris said goodbye and left the café area. Chris took a final look at his brother before leaving and going home to his wife and daughter, his mind troubled about how far Steven had become involved with people in the underground movement, and of how he was now also implicated and had been brought to the attention of the state security for wanting to meet up with dissidents and those who are rebelling against the workings of the state. He thought about how dangerous it is, and then he reflected over what Steven had said about him being duped, and that what he had believed was a fabric of rubbish. Chris felt so stupid as he went over what was said to him about constructing detailed and secret planning to get dissidents, or those whose lives are under threat from the state police, out of the country to a 'colony,' and of how he had gone along with it.

Chris left the store without looking up, or not noticing a large screen over the exit door. A trailer for The Offender's Nemesis advertising a forthcoming show was being shown, and as well as details about the imminent show there were updates and competitions, but there was no sound, just the images flashing on the screen. People walked past and beneath the screen taking little or no notice of it, and in a way it was as if the thrust of the show had become impotent because of there being no sound. Not one person stopped to look up at the screen, everybody just walked by, and judging by their response one might well assume they did not care about it.

Just inside one of the aisles leading towards the café was a man standing alone, it was Garman; he was watching Steven, who was looking down at the floor with intense deliberation.

Seven

When Chris arrived home Rosie was already there, having got out of work a little early, but Nina was at her friend's house. He had not called Rosie to let her know what had happened, she knew all about what he was doing and of his making contacts with people in the 'underground movement' as Chris kept nothing from his wife, in many ways he was an open book and shared all his concerns with her. Their relationship was strong and there was a meaningful commitment on behalf of both of them towards each other, their feelings were discussed and they cared very much for each other's welfare. That being said, Rosie was not enthusiastic at all about Chris getting himself involved with people in the margin of society in his pursuit to help his brother. Rosie kept telling him it would only lead to trouble and after that day's experience she was proved to be right. She told Chris how he had let things slip, that talking to people he did not even know is a risky thing to do and taking days off work to do it is not the smartest thing in the world.

Rosie watched Chris as he told her what had happened, not only about Steven and the meeting that did not take place, but also about the man in the shop with the bucket and posters, what he was saying and in the project with the young boys on the horse and the old couple in the shop, and then finding the card with Manville's face on it. Rosie placed her hand on his shoulder as he sat looking down at he floor, her eyes moistening as she felt his anguish, but she was concerned for what harm his actions could bring upon their family. She leant close to him and, whispering in his ear, she smoothed his hair, 'It's too much baby, let some of it go - this Manville, creature, he's got too big in your mind, keep to what is practical, we'll both try and help Steven, but you will have to start withdrawing from meeting with these people you've been in touch with - you're getting too involved in the wrong way darling, from now on we'll go through the conventional channels.'

Chris dropped his head further onto his chest, knowing the normal established route of enquiry would not bear any positive results, and now it was too late, he was involved, he was fraternising with dissidents who were undoubtedly known to the authorities and it was also known he was willing to take part in a plan to smuggle people out of the country. He knew deep in his heart it was too late and he knew he had put his wife and daughter in danger. They spoke about it for a while, and at times Chris was overcome with the trouble he had brought to them all and his fear of what might happen to Rosie and Nina. Rosie tried to steer Chris away from becoming hysterical, telling him if he stopped what he was doing then maybe the authorities would let it pass as it being understandable for a man to be concerned for his brother. They hugged and held each other close for a long time, it not unusual for them to do so, but the length of time they stood holding one another showed clearly the apprehension they both felt.

A couple of hours later Chris's phone rang; it was Brendan. Chris told him everything that had happened that day, and when Brendan told Chris to be careful of what he was saying, implying that the authorities listen to conversations on phones, Chris took no notice and carried on, telling Brendan the authorities knew everything he had done anyway. Brendan told Chris to keep his chin up and if it was convenient they would meet up the following evening for a chat and a beer; they arranged a place and time before ringing off.

Nina came into the room, Chris was alone, Rosie was elsewhere in the house and the television was switched off. It was quiet, and if his mind had not been so worried it would be a peaceful scene as he watched Nina look for a book she needed for school. Chris watched her search under cushions and listened to her as she spoke impatiently under her breath. He thought about her age, twelve years old and getting older with every day. From being a little girl she had a pleasant character, kind, friendly and considerate, always seeing the feelings of the underdog, but strong enough to say something about it in their defence. She laughed easily and was pleased by the simple things, although Chris often thought maybe too honest for own good, but then again that might change as life brought its lessons, some of which are cruel and unfair. His thoughts stopped with a sudden realisation of the situation he had made for himself and his family. A dismal worry clouded his mind and a heavy weight formed in his stomach as he looked at Nina; all he felt was fear.

The next day was Saturday. Chris had a couple of chores to do, he would meet Brendan for an hour or so, and then he was staying in for the night with Rosie, and probably Nina, unless she went to a friend's house. Chris knew he should not contact the health worker, Simon, but it was nagging in his mind, he wanted to tell him that he intended to give up on his plans of smuggling his brother out of the country and he was not going to get involved any longer in talking to members of underground groups as he realised its stupidity; at any rate, that was his plan.

Chris rang Simon the following morning, but there was no answer, and so after ringing a few more times he left a message with details of his new intentions of not getting involved with the underground movements. The rest of the day was taken up with minor chores, but a foreboding feeling stayed with Chris the whole time as he went about his domestic activities, and a regret that Simon had not answered his phone so he could get off his chest what he had planned to say. He was looking forward to meeting Brendan in the evening in a bar the two of them occasionally went to - they had planned to meet early in the evening and stay for a couple hours, although Brendan, being a single man, might well move on to another place to spend his Saturday night.

As Chris walked through the doorway in the bar he spotted Brendan sitting at a table, and Brendan, who had seen Chris enter, pointed with a disappointed look on his face at a large screen set on the wall of the bar. This stopped Chris in mid-stride as he looked at the screen, and the two friends shrugged at each other in a gesture that said they were both unaware of it being there. The presence of the screen shocked and dismayed Chris, because the main reason the two of them met in that particular bar was because it did not have a television screen dominating the place, and it was one of the few establishments in the area where one could go for a chat without there being loud music or a television blasting out frenzied and unintelligible hysteria. Chris ordered two beers at the bar and took them over to Brendan.

'It was put in during the week,' Brendan said as he pointed at the screen, and they both agreed it was not too loud, but all the same they would be looking for another bar to meet up in the future. Chris took only a fleeting look up at the screen as he sat down, noticing that what was being shown seemed a bit odd; it was a man showing another man how to do breathing exercises.

Brendan and Chris discussed Simon, the other people he had met who were connected to the underground groups and the meeting with X that did not take place. When Chris looked back up at the screen he saw a cartoon was being shown, and every time one of the animated characters spoke it caused two men, who were standing up at the bar, to laugh. The animated character was a large animal of no discernable species, a made up type of animal with a tiny voice that was completely at odds with what one would expect because of its large body. Chris noticed the character had a speech impediment that made pronouncing words difficult, and it seemed to be this aspect to the character's speech that caused the two men to laugh. Brendan also looked at what was on the screen, and they spoke of the urgent need to find another place to meet up, and maybe even that night, but before they did so Brendan said he would buy another beer.

As Chris waited for Brendan to return, he turned in his seat and took a quick look at the men who were laughing at the cartoon. They looked like ordinary people and judging by the football programmes they had rolled up in their back pockets they had been to see a match earlier in the day, and by their behaviour had been having a few drinks. Their swaggering manner was bordering on becoming potentially aggressive, and it was as if they were out to ridicule anyone who did not fit in with mainstream fashion. Chris felt they were bullies, noticing how one them made a comment about Brendan as he turned from the bar holding the drinks, and that it was possible they were looking to make trouble with people who did not want it.

As Brendan set down the glasses Chris told him that maybe it would be best if they moved on after finishing their drinks. Brendan shrugged, his gesture implying he did not mind if they stayed where they were or went somewhere else. Chris and Brendan continued to talk about Steven, Chris's concerns for him and the way he had now involved himself and his family in the whole depressing affair, and the more engrossed they became with their discussion, the more Chris forgot about moving on to another bar or one of the few public houses that had survived the alterations that happened during the last years before the 'big change'.

They decided to stay where they were, because by the time they found somewhere quiet, it being Saturday night, it would be time for Chris to go home; he told Rosie he would only be a couple of hours. Chris went up to the bar to get their drinks and found it was considerably busier than when he came in earlier, but the two men were still standing in the same place, their demeanour showing the increased amount of alcohol they had consumed. Chris returned with their drinks and the two friends continued with their conversation. For as long as they had known each other they found it easy to talk about anything from politics to personal matters, and both shared similar views and humour. They were good friends and they thought a lot of each other, it was a solid friendship and one bound by loyalty and respect, although their conversation that evening was not as jovial as it often was because of the recent events with Chris and the meeting with X that did not took place.

Their conversation was interrupted as the volume of the television suddenly rose to a point that made normal conversation impossible. The theme tune of The Offender's Nemesis cut across the air of the bar that was filled with the noise of customers talking and congested with cigarette smoke. There had been many changes in society since the 'big change', and one of them was the reintroduction of smoking in public places such as bars. Brendan and Chris swapped discouraging looks just as the two men at the bar cheered and did a dance in a circle with each other, a dance that was emulated throughout the country as it had been demonstrated on television so many times when the theme tune of The Offender's Nemesis was played.

'Good evening good citizens, I hope you've had a pleasant day – whatever you've been doing, and let's hope it wasn't something bad - but I'm more than sure it hasn't been,' the voice of Alan Manville seemed to penetrate every corner of the bar. Chris looked up at the screen and saw Alan Manville standing in his trademark pose, pointing into the camera with a smirk on his face that looked ready to break into either a smile or a sneer, but his eyes remained constant, dark, hard, probing and judgmental, separate from any expression he put on his face. A sick feeling formed in the pit of Chris's stomach, which was followed by a feeling of depression with a heavy sense of doom, as it always did when he saw the show, and especially so on seeing Alan Manville.

Eight

The show's distinctive theme tune continued to play as the camera swept across an audience of cheering people, many holding up placards and posters with either the face of a 'criminal' or a 'terrorist' on them. The camera stopped and the screen changed into an explosion of lights, which then settled and a cartoon figure showed on the screen of a furtive man looking about himself with a sneering smile that implied he had got away with something, and then from the side of the screen a coach load of smiling people who were waving to the television audience reversed into the picture and over the stealthy offender. The word SQUELCH filled the screen for a second before dissolving. The people on the coach continued to smile and wave as the bus drove off, leaving an imprint of the offender on the ground.

The cartoon faded and the camera zoomed in on a member of the audience, a balding, middle-aged man with straggling hair and a greasy complexion. A bubble appeared from his mouth containing the words 'That's my favourite.' The bubble disappeared, but the camera stayed on him as he continued to cheer and shake his fists in the air, and turning in his seat the man looked into the camera and gave the thumbs up sign.

A man's voice introduced the show with a cheery, overly exuberant,

'Good evening viewers, the PPC is honoured to be allowed into your living rooms this evening - so sit back because all of us at the People's Pleasure Corporation are proud in knowing that we have a show that is presented for your enjoyment while raising the standards of justice that we know you want maintained - welcome' and the man's voice continued with the lengthy introduction to the show.

As well as being watched in the living rooms of people's houses The Offender's Nemesis is screened in many public places. It is also common to watch the show in clubs where the atmosphere can be drunken and boisterous and it is a popular event bringing together people whose excitement grows the closer to the day that the show is on. Betting takes place as people wager on what particular punishment is going to be meted out to an 'offender'. Scratch cards are brought along and swapped, and bets are placed on what 'offender' on the cards will be appearing on the show that evening. Chris looked down at his lap, he felt drained and looking at Brendan he thought about asking him if they should leave the bar as the theme music for the most popular media show in the country was finishing and one of the state's leading mechanisms to maintain social control was underway.

The theme music, all the effects and the clapping and cheering disappeared as an image of a van parked in a quiet street appeared on the screen. It was during the day and had the feel of an overcast afternoon. The back doors of the van were yanked open with such a force it made a hard clanking sound that reverberated around a bleak square in the middle of municipal housing blocks. Four burly men dressed in paramilitary style clothing, their faces covered as they wore balaclavas, dragged a young man into the back of the van. A pretty young woman holding a microphone and a young man carrying a camera ran up to the men and she was shouting so excitedly into the microphone that her voice was breaking into shrill hoarseness. The young woman threw her head from side to side, causing her long hair to fly into her face. This action of shaking her head is a distinctive trait of hers that has established her as a known celebrity. Comics mimic her, caricatures of her appear throughout the media and she has also recorded songs for a leading music company.

Four other men dressed in stone grey uniforms holding snub-nosed machine guns appeared and stood next to the van, their faces hidden behind visors attached to their helmets. The young man being dragged into the van started to shout, proclaiming his innocence of a crime or deed that had led him to be in his present predicament, as the high-pitched shrieking of the young woman echoed around the drab environment.

The young woman's face filled the screen. 'And to think,' she panted eagerly, 'not just two - no, one minute ago, this slime-life thought he was getting his grubby, nasty little hands on the hard earned, and thoughtfully saved, dollars belonging to an honest and decent citizen in this housing project'

The young man's head struck the side of the van as he was bundled into it and the young woman looked at the camera pulling a feigned look of pain as she said, 'Ouch - now where did I put those pain killers?' A dull roaring of laughter from the studio audience responded to her humorous line as she said, 'I've got something that will keep him company on his trip to the station,' and she threw a small vial into the back of the van, which she had taken from a pouch hanging around her neck. The word STINKBOMB appeared on the screen in primary colours and was met by a roaring of applause and laughter from the studio audience. The young woman held her nose as she said to the young man, 'Now you know what it's like for everybody else who has to stand next to you,' which brought more applause and laughter from the studio audience as the camera closed in on the young man shouting and gagging. Holding back the desire to laugh, which is a common mannerism among the presenters on the show, the young woman pointed into the camera in a characteristic pose that is shared by all the presenters on The Offender's Nemesis.

The picture spiralled into a multicoloured design and opened out to show Alan Manville in the studio pointing at the audience. The sound of cheering grew louder as Manville stared at the audience with an unwavering expression that was serious and determined. His face dissolved and was replaced by another man pointing at the camera with exactly the same pose, and then Colette, a young woman who is a popular presenter on the show appeared and the cheering and applause became even louder. Two other presenters joined the three of them, and all five presenters were standing side by side and pointing at the audience. This was 'the team,' as they sometimes called themselves.

The camera swung around the audience as the noise became wild with excitement, many of them waved placards and posters, or held up small cards with the face of an 'offender' on them. The faces of 'offenders' ran along at the bottom of the screen in a continual line, and when one of them corresponded with a placard being waved by a young boy in the audience the camera picked this out and cut from one to the other to show that the face of the 'offender' was the same. The 'offender's' face grew so large it took up the whole screen and the word GUILTY appeared across his face as if stamped by an old-fashioned ink block, and the cheering and clamour heightened to what sounded like uncontrolled chaos.

The 'offender's' face dissolved and was replaced with a shot of a male presenter wearing an expensive suit standing on the stage in the studio. He stood with his arms folded, looking at the audience with a swaggering manner as he nodded triumphantly at what he surveyed. The man looked as if he took a lot of care in being physically fit and the manicured and tanned features of his face crinkled as his large smile took shape to show evenly shaped bleached teeth. The shot changed to the audience waving their banners and placards, some of the children waved papier mache heads they had probably made at school, with faces painted on them representing a particular 'offender'.

The presenter pointed at the camera in the show's trademark pose and said, 'Let's get on the road and see the good folk from different parts of the country who are watching what's going on this evening,' and he pointed to a dot on the floor that enlarged to show an outdoor scene with thousands of people looking at a huge screen.

'Welcome Manchester,' the man said and the cheering from the crowd in Manchester increased.

'Let me hear you,' the man said and the crowd responded by cheering louder, and other places in the country were visited in the same manner.

The man looked at the camera and said, 'Okay – I'm ready – are you ready? And the studio audience chanted, 'Are you ready' with him, as it was one of the many catchphrases that are repeated by the audience, and the man shouted, 'Well let's go!'

A photograph of a man's face spun onto the screen. It was the 'offender's' face that the boy in the audience was waving earlier. Almost immediately the mood changed and the audience booed and hissed as the presenter said who the man, supposedly, was and what crimes he had committed, which was being a paedophile, but the audience did not need to be told because the man's background and the things he had been accused of had been read out over the preceding few weeks and had featured in the popular newspapers and magazines.

The 'offender' was middle-aged, gaunt with hollow eyes and was almost bald except for strands of greying hair combed forward across his head.

'Charming looking specimen, isn't he ladies? I bet you would give your right arm to have a dinner date with him, wouldn't you?'

The presenter smiled at what he had said, 'But don't worry,' he went on, 'he isn't available for dates, because he's going for a drive.'

The audience erupted into cheering and the man could just about hold back laughing as he said, 'Let's go outside and meet Marcus who is going to present this man with his free ticket for travel - but it's just one way.'

The audience cheered and shouted louder for a few seconds before the sound lowered as an outdoor scene showed a bus in a car park with Marcus, the presenter, standing next to it, who also had the tanned and manicured look.

Marcus struck the show's trademark pose and said, 'Hi ya, all - if he's a no, no - he's gotta go, go,' and the audience chanted the final part of the slogan with him.

Marcus went on, 'But before we pack our bags, let's meet some of the good people who have been lucky enough to win tickets that allow them to be on the bus this evening.'

He walked over to a queue of people waiting to board the bus, whose ages ranged from the young to the old. Some of them held up banners with the 'offender's' face on them and others were holding horns and sirens. They all waved at the camera and began to cheer and make a noise with their horns and sirens.

Marcus said, 'Okay, okay - these are the lucky people who have had their names picked out of the hat to hitch a ride on the school bus.'

He spoke to a man and woman aged in their sixties, asking them if they had sent their names in for the draw by post, by means of a scratch card or the intranet system. Marcus then went through other options people have in order to win the chance of appearing on the show and participate in one of the punishments; although this was a 'special' one as it would culminate in death. Some times the people participating in the punishments are victims of a crime the 'offender' had committed, or they may be relatives of an 'offender's' victim. The couple could barely answer Marcus's questions as they stammered and giggled embarrassedly until he turned to the camera in his slick manner and said, 'I see this lucky couple are excited about going on a bus ride – and who could blame them?'

Marcus walked to the front of the bus and pointed at a steel frame that had been attached to it. 'Now, it's like a school bus - only different,' he laughed and said, 'and here's the PC.' He wagged his finger at the camera, 'No, no, no, not that kind of PC.' Marcus shivered at the thought, 'But this is politically correct. That,' he said patting the steel frame, 'is a paedophile clip - PC, a paedophile clip.'

A rousing cheer and clapping sounded from the studio audience.

Marcus said, 'If he liked hanging around schools so much, maybe he'd like a ride on a school bus - but sorry, Mr Poison Slime - in fact - I'm not sorry at all,' and the audience chanted the words in time with him because it had become his personal catchphrase.

He continued, 'There isn't a seat in the bus available for a piece of repulsive rubbish like you, so - we have kindly provided you with your own special place - that's right, strapped onto the PC on the front of the bus - specially made for repulsive, vomitous creatures such as yourself.'

He pointed off camera as he said, 'And here it is ladies and gentlemen, and boys and girls, excuse my language, but here is the puke inducing piece of matter, who is no matter at all now, because he is no longer a problem in our streets and lives.'

The studio audience cheered their approval at what he was saying, 'So please gentlemen - strap up the scum,' and the studio audience repeated the words 'strap up the scum.'

Four men dragged the man towards the bus, their faces hidden beneath balaclavas and the man's head was hidden in a hood. The people getting on the bus blew horns and sounded their sirens and the studio audience began chanting and shouting. The presenter looked into the camera and said, 'Back soon, by which time we will have strapped the scum in his own special seat, all safe and sound - be back soon now,' and he pointed into the camera.

The shot pulled back to show the man struggling as he was strapped to the frame, and as the people on the bus waved through the windows the show's logo appeared on the screen, and The Offender's Nemesis broke for a commercial break.

Chris looked around at some people in the bar who voiced their agreement about the man getting his 'comeuppance' for the crimes he had committed, and the two men who had been to football earlier started to clap and chant as they got in the spirit of the show and wanted the man to die in some horrific manner. The raised voice of a woman standing along the bar caused Chris to look over at her. She shouted over the rim of her glass she was holding to her lips, 'They should cut off his private bits before putting him on the bus, put them in a soup and make his family drink it - they would have known about him, disgusting lot, bad as each other they are…'

Chris looked at the woman, shopping she had done earlier was lying in bags at her feet, and he noticed some frozen items that would have thawed out a while ago. She was standing next to two men, but she did not seem to be with them, and the two men did not seem to be together. Chris took an internal bet that all three of them had randomly struck up a relationship imbued by the shared desire to drink enough alcohol to aid them in their quest to nullify all thought that reminds them of their reality and so escape from the drudgery filling their waking lives.

The first advertisement was about The Offender's Nemesis and most of the others were promotions for entertainment packages contracted to companies owned by Quality Entertainment, the company that owns People's Pleasure Corporation, which makes The Offender's Nemesis. Chris looked from Brendan, who was staring absently at the screen, to down at the floor with thoughts of what had recently happened, the people in the bar, their behaviour and that it was a shame the bar had put in a screen. When Chris looked up he saw an advert boasting about an 'exclusive offer', which meant if you purchased four of the scratch cards for The Offender's Nemesis you got one free. Chris could not stop looking at the screen and just like many other people he knew who professed disgust at its purpose and contents, he was attracted to the activities on the show, and it was a macabre and morbid feeling that made him feel trapped by it. He was repulsed by what he was looking at, yet he was also fascinated by its power.

The theme tune for The Offender's Nemesis sounded and a cartoon appeared on the screen of a man behind a desk who changed shape into a reptilian creature, but not in a scary way, it was childishly humorous. Phrases, terms and words flowed from the character's mouth and floated around the room he was in. The words and phrases were academic jargon used before the 'big change' associated with social work, the welfare and education professions and the legal system. The animated film lampooned people who worked in those professions and made fun of the elaborate rhetorical verbiage they used. There is a regular section on The Offender's Nemesis allocated for the ridicule and punishment of those people who once held qualified positions in work that is now totally discredited and the people themselves are reviled. The cartoon character has a name, Christopher Correct, and he has become hugely popular with the general public as a figure of mockery. There are various Christopher Correct collectables for children, such as toys, stickers, posters, towels and inflatable replicas of him that are used as lilos or chairs, which also come in sizes for adults. The character is also seen on hoardings promoting political messages by the state and has also been used by different companies to advertise their products. There is a female equivalent called Dolly Do-Gooder, although she has not caught the public's imagination as much as her male counterpart.

The cartoon evaporated from the screen and was replaced by a slick presenter pointing into the camera, all the while holding a fixed grin as he said, 'Welcome back, you good folks of this great land. As you see,' he was referring to the cartoon, 'we have a toad to taunt later in the show...'

He had to stop talking because of the increased noise from the audience, and then putting his smile in place he said, 'Wow, what have they been putting in your tea today?'

The presenter explained the show's format to the audience before returning to Marcus and the outside broadcast. The opening shot showed that the space where the bus had been parked was now empty, and the camera searched around for the missing bus to an accompaniment of what was meant to be funny music. It cut back to the studio with the presenter resting his chin on his hand and scratching his head as if confused.

'Where did it go?' He appealed to the viewers, and then to the studio audience he said, 'Who stole our bus?' Children laughed and some people booed and shook their fists at the thought of the bus being stolen.

'Only joking,' the presenter said, pointing into the camera and striking the show's trademark pose, 'Once we get them - they don't get away,' and the studio audience chanted 'they don't get away' in unison with him. The picture cut to a shot of the man strapped onto the front of the bus, his face now shown as the hood had been taken off. The studio audience burst into cheering and applause as they watched the bus as it was driven down a busy street by the side of a housing project. A long camera shot showed people on the side of the road shouting and making gestures at the man secured to the front of the bus, which incited louder cheering from the studio audience, and also cheers from a number of people in the bar, including the two men standing at the counter behind Brendan and Chris. The location where a scene of public humiliation is set up is always a cause for popular conjecture. Newspapers and magazines have articles about where the show has planned the public spectacle to take place. The actual location is a great talking point in pubs, clubs, places of work and in schools, and gambling is widespread as people bet on their choice of place.

A camera shot inside the bus showed Marcus sitting behind the driver, acting as if he was excited and caught up with the fevered atmosphere on the bus. He could hardly make himself heard as he tried to shout over the noise of the bugles, sirens, horns and chanting as he started to walk down the aisle and spoke to people about how they came to be so 'lucky' by having a seat on the bus. A young boy told him he was there because he won a raffle they held at his school, and a woman said her husband won a ticket to have a place on the bus and had kept it for her as a birthday surprise. Marcus turned to the camera and said that the people on the bus had made up a song and that earlier on they had been singing it, but his voice disappeared as the passengers on the bus chanted their ditty, 'Pulp the paedo - pulp the paedo - pulp the paedo now!' They repeated the line with Marcus cheering them on, before turning to the camera and holding his hands over his ears with an exaggerated expression of pain.

The picture cut to the presenter in the studio who was pointing into the camera as he said, 'It just gets better, and you gotta know it - 'cos I know it.' The audience chanted, ''cos I know it,' with him and he began to speak rapidly, 'This show motors faster than a racing car with no brakes and is packed with more action and fun than a house full of good-time girls serving free bar - that's why our competitors don't stand a chance - they don't compare - they wouldn't dare, and that's why we're the greatest.'

The audience broke into cheering and shouting and the presenter made a show of trying to quieten them because he wanted to say something. When the noise settled he introduced a regular piece on the show, which is very popular with the viewers, called a 'dish wish.' It ignited loud shouting from people in the bar, causing Chris to look around and become concerned that the bar was filling with people and the atmosphere was not as it normally was; The Offender's Nemesis had instilled an aggressive feel.

The 'dish' is always an attractive young woman who is a celebrity, a media personality known for being a model, pop singer or an actress, and is often all of them. She always appears holding her 'magic wand' and makes a wish of what she wants to happen to an 'offender'. She does not say what her 'wish' is, but waves her large sparkling gold wand and the picture dissolves into colourful stars as yet another musical jingle with an easy to remember verse or line plays and the shot cuts to the scene where the offender is to be punished, tortured or killed. On this evening the 'dish' waved her wand and the scene that came onto the screen showed a male presenter holding the show's trademark pose, standing in front of what at first looked like a warehouse or factory of some kind. His tanned face creased as he fixed a grin to show dazzling and evenly shaped white teeth, which is an aspect shared by all presenters on the show.

He dropped the pose and began to speak. 'Remember old rotten teeth, with his grimy skin and dirty neck?' A photograph of the 'offender' spun onto the screen and the audience reacted immediately by hissing and booing.

'That's right, he embezzled old people out of their savings and eventually ended up actually killing an old lady who wouldn't give him the security number of her account - well, the dish's wish is that nothing should save his bacon, and that he needs a damn good wash - in fact he should go in the hot tub - after all, that's what you do isn't it? If you have a piece of dirt and scum you have to scrub it away.'

This stirred the audience to cheer and chant and the presenter began to walk inside the building as he was speaking.

'He thinks he's going to spend a day boiling the skin off pigs.'

The camera drew back to show a grim looking building, and then it zoomed onto a sign showing it is a slaughterhouse, which roused the audience.

The presenter continued, 'Because that is what they do in this building, when old oinker has oinked his last oink he's put in this container.'

He stepped up to a steel case and spoke over a film showing dead pigs being released from the case, their bodies steaming, stripped of hair and surface skin.

'And given the hottest steam bath you can imagine, and then out the pinkie comes - really pink, red raw pink, and the skin is peeled off him.'

Colette appeared on the screen, pulling a face she said, 'You would need more than a skin factor ten to deal with that.'

The audience laughed and Colette continued, 'I've never seen a pig do an impersonation of a shrimp before,' and she pressed her fingers against her lips to show her manicured nails. The audience laughed some more as Colette's face dissolved and was replaced by the face of the 'offender'.

The audience's laughter suddenly turned to jeering and the presenter in the slaughterhouse appeared on the screen with his finger over his lips. He spoke in a hushed voice as he explained that the 'offender' had just arrived to start what he thought would be his first shift in the slaughterhouse. It cut to the 'offender' walking with another man into the slaughterhouse, both dressed in overalls and the 'offender' was putting on large gloves. The noise of pigs broke out loudly when the shot cut to inside the slaughterhouse, but because of a hidden microphone on the man with the 'offender' the audience could hear what they were saying to each other. The man talked about the process of slaughter and the 'offender' remarked how loud the squealing was. The man told him how the pigs can sense fear because they are sensitive creatures, and he told the 'offender' he would also be squealing if he knew he was going to be killed in a couple of minutes.

The picture cut to the presenter who was now crouching down and still with his finger over his lips as he spoke 'That's right - he would be squealing - and old rotten teeth doesn't know, but he's just about to find out, that he's going to join the oinkers, and the man he's talking to isn't an operative at the slaughterhouse - he works for a security agency, and some of his colleagues are going to direct old rotten teeth's snout where it belongs.'

Cheering and shouting erupted from the audience as the presenter stood up from his crouched position and dropped the pretence of whispering. He pointed into the camera and said, 'Come on folks, i-t's,' and the audience joined in with him as he said, 'countdown time.'

This is another slogan where the audience count down the ten seconds that appear on the television screen. The 'countdown' happens just before offenders are told what is going to happen to them or moments before they are caught doing something, and sometimes before a death penalty is carried out. The unsuspecting expression on the face of the 'offender' is clearly shown during the countdown, which adds to the pleasure and amusement for the audience.

It returned to the slaughterhouse. Four men suddenly appeared from behind a machine and grabbed the 'offender', and, although he struggled to free himself and shouted out his defence to the crime he had been convicted of, his efforts were useless. The presenter faked yawning by flapping his hand over his mouth at the 'offender's' pleas to be listened to and a cartoon of a pig appeared on the screen with the words, 'Don't ham it up - you've had your bacon!'

The shot cut a number of times from the studio audience to the 'offender' as he was beaten and thrown against a machine before being shoved into it. The shot cut to outside broadcasts around the country, showing the crowds breaking into paroxysmal states of emotional outbursts. Some people were aggressive, others were nearly breaking down with laughter or hugging one another, and there were those who stood or sat alone, chanting outwardly or inwardly. Armed guards, who are always present at outside broadcasts, as they are in the studio, stood by vigilantly monitoring over-exuberance.

Chris looked away from the screen, conscious of his heart beating hard and a constricting pain filling his head. He took deep breaths and although not wanting to look at the screen he found it difficult not to take quick glances, and each time he looked, the 'offender' was nearer to meeting his inescapable doom. Chris had often thought how the intensity of feeling shown and felt by people in the studio audience, or wherever they were watching the spectacle, was increased because the man, the 'offender' who was being humiliated, beaten and tortured was powerless in his situation. Chris felt that he shared the fear the offender was experiencing, and that was one of the primary intentions of the whole thing, to demand complicity and submissiveness to the regime, because this is what happens if you are not - you are brutally beaten, demonised, alienated and even killed. To publicly show one's anger and support in baiting a victim of punishment is to demonstrate one's support for the governing system. One has to suppress feelings of fear and of powerlessness and Chris wondered how widespread the feeling was among of empathising with the 'offender's' suffering and feeling his or her fear. Chris felt it could not just be him and a minority in society that felt a constant anxiety when having thoughts that challenge a system that is perpetrated by those who are commonly regarded as normal, right and just.

Chris heard the television audience chanting, which was accompanied by people in the bar, and when he looked up at the screen he saw scenes of adults and children who had been stimulated to a crazed state. They laughed, shouted, screamed, shook fists, waved banners and pictures, and then it cut to the slaughterhouse just as a steaming, lifeless body was extracted from the machine. The sight of the man evoked laughter from the two men standing behind Chris and Brendan, and they laughed even more as a cartoon of a man's face with steam blowing from his ears appeared on the screen for a few seconds before returning to the presenter who was looking into the camera. He said that the body was to be pulverised in another machine and a cartoon appeared showing a large weight landing on a man with the word CRUSH written across the screen.

It cut to the audience in the studio where there were scenes of distraction and a thunderous sound as the audience pounded the floor with their feet.

The shot zoomed in on a young boy, his face screwed up in anger as he jumped and stamped on a papier mache face, which was that of the 'offender's' in the slaughterhouse. Most vocal were the children as the crowd chanted, 'crush, crush, crush, crush, crush.'

The shot cut to the slaughterhouse as the man's body was dropped into a machine and a heavy steel door closed down upon it. The picture changed to the young woman who has made the 'dish wish,' showing her laughing as she waved her 'magic wand' as if to start the machine. It cut to a shot in the slaughterhouse of a green light flashing on the side of the machine, indicating it was operating.

Scenes of erupting pandemonium were shown in the studio audience and among crowds in the outside broadcasts, which were replicated among some people in the bar, and then the show's logo appeared on the screen before going into the advertisements.

Nine

Chris watched the adverts without really taking them in, he and Brendan both sat as is if in a near state of comatose, wearily witnessing something terrible they had been caught up in. The Offender's Nemesis's theme tune sounded louder than it did before as it introduced the show, and a female presenter ran through the show's 'rules and guidelines' while maintaining a stretched smile. Every week the viewers are reminded of how they can be a member of the audience or participate in administering a punishment, and the various ways of getting tickets are explained at least twice in every show. The presenter went on about winning a ticket for a friend, known as TAF, Treat A Friend tickets, and of how tickets can be won by entering a competition in one of the many magazines, which included solving a simple quiz and sending the answer in, or by purchasing scratch cards, entering intranet competitions as well as the variety of competitions that take place at work and school.

The presenter explained how different punishments are worth different points and members of the public can win a punishment and when a sufficient amount of points are accrued it allows them to be in the studio audience when a major punishment is to take place, even a death.

A fast cutting montage of the various forms of punishment and torture flashed on the screen, some real, some in animation. Different presenters talked over the images, explaining how 'winners' can swap punishments among themselves. One presenter said, 'A cropping,' and a cartoon showed bolt croppers snapping a man's shin, another presenter said, 'A group kicking,' and a real image of a man lying on the ground being kicked by a group of people was shown, which was followed by several other types of punishments, and then the pace of the background music slowed down as the capital punishments were shown, which included being 'tossed' in the back of a garbage truck, and a cartoon of a body disappearing in the crusher at the back of a truck showed on the screen, or 'tossed' out of an airship, and a long shot of what looked like a human body falling from the undercarriage of an airship appeared.

The picture cut to a male presenter pointing into the camera. He smiled before saying, 'Use your imagination - remember, it's your choice because they're your offenders to do what you want with.'

The images were repeated and began to spin before exploding, the fragments forming themselves into the show's logo, which after a few seconds dissolved and Alan Manville appeared holding the trademark pose of pointing into the camera. He said, 'There is never too much excitement, and there has never been a show like ours before - is this what you want?' A pre-recorded shot showed on the screen of young children who had been filmed in a school shouted back excitedly in reply to his question, 'Yes it is.'

Manville stared into camera, as if struggling to hold back a smile that wanted to break across his face, 'They say we pack too much into our show - they say there is too much for the audience to take in - they don't know what our audience want, and that's why they will never understand or be as successful as us - our show is packed with fun and it's packed with retribution - it's what our audience wants, and it's what our country needs - so let's keep it going.'

The sound of an engine revving up over fast music played as rapid intercutting of different presenters appeared on the screen with each one of them saying a single word, 'thief,' 'crook,' 'sneak' 'thug,' 'bully.'

It cut to Alan Manville standing with his hands on his hips. 'Joyriders,' he said, 'older people will remember that name? They used to be called that by people in authority who allowed the perverse meaning of joy and driving to be confused, a term that became accepted because there was a feeling that there was nothing we could do about it - a term created by people who were idiots. 'Let's face it, people who steal another person's car and drive it around our streets in a reckless manner are just pests - they are more than a nuisance, they're cretins - and they're murderers - and we see them as nothing more than a germ in our system - and you know what to do with germs in your system? That's right, flush them out,' and a prerecording of a crowd chanting 'flush them out' played. It was a new slogan they were introducing to the audience, knowing they would be repeating the catchphrase after it had been played a few times.

'Watch what happens when we have the joy of riding - over a thief,'

Manville said as a recording was shown of a group of men who were all dressed in the same uniform dragging a young man out of a car. Manville told of the alleged crimes the young man had committed and of how he was driving a car he had stolen and how it was involved in a hit and run incident, which resulted in the death of a young mother and her child was left with brain damage. Manville explained how the young man sped off from the scene and was later seen laughing and bragging with his friends, some of whom were in the car when he ran into the woman and her child. A series of fast cutting images showed an enactment of the night when the hit and run happened, with young people laughing and drinking inside a car to a backdrop of the music with the sound of a revving engine.

'Glamorous, isn't it?' Alan Manville said over the pictures as the music lowered in volume, 'But it really gets exciting when this happens.'

71

The picture changed to a deserted area of wasteland and a different piece of fast racing music played as the young man was shown being dragged along the ground by four men in uniform. The uniformed men tied a hood over the young man's head, cuffed his hands and bound his feet and then the camera pulled back to show three cars with bull bars attached to the front of them. Standing next to each car was a person dressed in a uniform, and although their faces were covered and they were wearing crash helmets it was obvious one of them was a woman.

The music died down and Alan Manville's face appeared on the screen. He raised his hand in the style a pastor might do when addressing his congregation before speaking.

'Okay, you great folks of this great land, we'll take a slice of breathing space from this week's show which is bursting with sensational acts of real justice.

'The amount of people who contact us with requests and ideas of punishments is growing by the week - and by the way, what a pitiless lot you are.'

The audience laughed and Manville nodded before continuing.

'And the people wanting to participate in our spectacular spectacles just grows day by day. Some have suggested we film members of the public dealing with offenders, such as chasing an offender and then giving him a good old fashioned beating. You want to do all kinds of things to an offender, but let me say this again, members of the public aren't allowed, I'm sorry to say, to touch the offenders.

'A huge amount of you have written in this last week, and we value your contribution - the response we have had for your suggestions of punishments has been massive, but as I say, you can't carry them out. You can participate in the punishments we organise, and you're very welcome, and I know there are many of you who can't wait to participate - but I'm sorry - it would be illegal for you to enact them yourselves.'

The audience began to boo and Manville held up his hand as he spoke.

'It has to be carried out by security agencies who are lawfully allowed to do so - they work very closely with us in making the show what it is - so keep your suggestions coming in - just like Maggie from the Midlands region has - she says, if her offender liked doing nothing all day and hanging around, and getting money by burgling people's homes by climbing though the window, she thinks he should hang around if he wants - hang from the ledge of one of the windows he has climbed through to steal people's belongings - Maggie says nail him to the window ledge and leave him hanging there for everyone to see - oh yes, thank you Maggie, and there have been some great suggestions - some are old favourites like dragging an offender behind a car, or throwing an offender out of a building, and of course let's not forget a stampede of shoppers trampling a pickpocket - and the good people from the Blue Coat Boy in the western region have sent in a photo of themselves, they say their combined weight is one and a half tons, and they do look a cheery bunch - they have been nominated by Cheryl, the manager, to crush an offender.'

Manville looked down at a piece of paper and read out loud, "Get the waste of space down, put a beer barrel on his head and let me and my friends sit on it - it will give him a headache, and it will be one less headache for the rest of us."

Manville looked into the camera, 'There you are, decent people everywhere - and by the way Cheryl, if you and your friends sit on the barrel, doesn't it make the beer flat?'

The audience laughed and Manville waited before continuing, 'But as I've said, we have to organise everything - you just can't go out there and perform these imaginative, well intentioned acts yourselves...'

And again the audience started to boo, which caused Manville to stop. He raised his hand as he said, 'I know, I know, but it isn't up to us at People's Pleasure Corporation, it's sanctioned by above - way above our heads, they're the ones you have to get on to.'

He laughed as he stepped backwards, pointing into the camera as he said, 'You choose - because it's your show - and there is plenty of scum to choose from.'

It cut to a male presenter pointing into the camera as he said, 'Stand on a turd!'

There was the sound effect of a raspberry noise and squelching. The audience went crazy because it was a popular piece in the show. Different punishments come and go out of fashion and the producers encourage viewers to send in their ideas as they are always on the lookout for new ones to amuse and keep their ratings up. The presenter adopted a painful expression as he said, 'Ever trodden on a piece of - well, let's say it - shit - there, I said it - when walking down the street? Well we have a vicious killer here tonight who needs to be put in his place.'

A series of different presenters read out criminal offences over photographs of victims and the aftermath of crimes that included: burning down a hospital, stamping on the face of an eighty-eight year old woman, stealing charity money which had been raised for a children's hospice, and among others, conspiring to plant a bomb in a busy shopping centre. The audience responded to each crime with booing and jeering. The list of crimes was interrupted by a fanfare that is played to introduce that week's 'lucky winner,' the person who had been chosen to enact a punishment. A woman called Marie was shown bouncing up and down excitedly backstage. She had won the chance to participate in her 'suggestion,' and the 'offender' she had chosen was a 'terrorist'. His face appeared on the screen and was met by jeering. The 'terrorist' was speaking, pleading his innocence in a broken accent and his poor command of English incited the audience further.

A male presenter spoke over his image, 'Not only does this ingrate not want to integrate with the good people of our land and be thankful for what this country has given him - this contemptible person has taken it upon himself to plan and conspire with others of his ilk - some from abroad, but also with others who live in this country and enjoy the opportunities and advantages they are given - they want to murder and maim innocent people who are trying to get on with their lives.'

The narration continued over a film of a bomb that had just exploded in a public area showing scenes of destruction, distress and mutilation as the dead and injured were shown in graphic detail, which was met with booing and jeering from the studio audience that was echoed by people in the bar, some pointing at the screen and shouting for the people who planted the bombs to be killed and, 'torn to pieces.'

It returned to the 'terrorist' and the voice of the presenter. 'Odious specimen, don't you agree ladies and gentlemen, and boys and girls? He worked as a school teacher, grew up in a housing project, and this is how he repays this great country and its equally great people. He was given the opportunity to train through one of the extremely generous community education initiatives called, MOM, the Model of Meritocracy. His studies were grant funded...' The audience showed their dissatisfaction at public money being spent on such things by booing and hissing.

The presenter continued as the noise of the audience quietened. 'And he won The Exemplary Achievements by Diligent Citizenry Award - and didn't this piece of gutter slime just show what was on his mind? As honest people worked hard and paid their taxes for him to benefit at our expense by attending one of our educational institutions to gain qualifications, and get employment in a position that carries a great deal of responsibility - but that is what this viper and his type do, take from the country while harbouring desires and plans to destroy it, and by the way, find pleasure in causing trauma and murdering and maiming innocent people - it's just luck for us all that the real diligence was shown by the pupils, boys and girls of eleven years of age, who became suspicious of the monster that taught in their classrooms - but the children are Vigilant Minors in the ACC, and are alert to the ways of these people...'

The audience cheered and applauded and the presenter talked about the good work that the ACC does and how proud the country is of the young people in that organisation. He returned to Marie, that week's 'lucky winner,' and told the audience and viewers she had decided upon his punishment. The presenter placed his hand on Marie's shoulder and smiled at her as he said, 'Tell me Marie, you most gorgeous of creatures,' and his flirting brought whistles and cheers from the audience, 'did you think up the punishment yourself? Was it your pretty little idea, or did someone else inspire you to think of such a thing?'

Marie looked around with a timid smile before speaking quietly, obviously finding it difficult to go along with the rehearsed script. 'Mistress T,' she said, and the presenter stepped back in mock surprise as the studio audience cheered loudly and began to chant, 'Mistress T, Mistress T,' over and over again.

An effect of fire erupting slowly rolled across the screen to an accompaniment of heavy orchestral music and thunder crashing. The screen cleared to show a woman in a dungeon sitting on a throne glowering into the camera. She is Mistress T, a character introduced to the programme over a year earlier who had proved to be extremely popular. She is a dominatrix, her character is anyway, and she is always visited in her 'dungeon' where she presides over what punishment would be suitable, but it is always one that is sadistic and often related to the crime the 'offender' had committed. Her appearance is that of a classic dominant mistress wearing black clothing with heavy Cleopatra style eye make up. Over the time Mistress T has been on the show she has had different assistants to aid her, and although it is tongue in cheek and intended to be humorously entertaining the use of her character has obvious sexual connotations. There is always some banter between Mistress T and Alan Manville, who really hams it up when showing her respect and appears to enjoy himself when she appears, to a point where he finds it difficult to hide his feelings of finding her attractive, so much so some say there is something going on between them or maybe it is just play-acting to make good viewing.

Mistress T has a large fan club and is liked by adults as well as children, and although having an overwhelming male interest she has good-looking muscular young male assistants, known as attendees, that are brought in to encourage an appeal for women who enjoy the spectacle of handsome young men acting as her slaves. She is a huge hit and as children swap cards at school with Mistress T being a current favourite, men also collect photographs of her and any information that is available about Mistress T, many applying to be her slave, sometimes as a joke to be on the show, but also privately. Mistress T has proven to be a powerful aid in selling products so she is used extensively in advertising, but she is also an influential figure in promoting state policy, appearing in public information films and making mock threats to people who do not obey the law.

After the presenter told Mistress T what the young man had been found guilty of she leant back on her throne before giving judgement. She spoke about the supposed car thief, the paedophile, the terrorist and the killer of an old lady, her face pulling expressions of hatred and disgust as she said, 'It is to be the ultimate penalty for all these human weasels this evening, one of them has already been disposed of,' and she paused to lick her lips before glowering, 'for the other three - press the flesh,' and she raised her eyebrows exultantly.

The crowd cheered loudly and enthusiastically and it cut to the studio with the presenter shielding his face with his arm, 'Oh no,' he said, 'she's in a bad mood this evening,' and it cut back to Mistress T who widened her eyes as she said slowly and deliberately, 'Squash them, I want to hear the pips crack,' and her face faded from the screen as she licked her lips to the sound of thunder cracking and loud music. The studio audience chanted her name as the presenter tried to make himself heard, which he could not, but, smiling at the bedlam in the studio, he just nodded and pointed at a monitor showing outside broadcasts where similar scenes of excitement were taking place in different locations around the country.

Brendan and Chris looked from each other to around the bar, noticing how the appearance of the Mistress T character had excited people. Brendan leant close to Chris as he began to speak about Mistress T, 'She's an interesting addition to the show, power and dominance with a clear sexual association...'

Brendan stopped speaking as the two men behind them became suddenly loud as one pushed the other one in fun accusing him of having secret fantasies about Mistress T, 'You fancy her, don't you?' he said, and the more he pushed the other man, the more he denied having any desires for her. Brendan looked at Chris, their look showing a shared understanding, but then one of the men began to shout in an aggressive manner with a tone of violence edged to it. He was shouting at a man sitting alone at a table apart from everyone else, as if trying to find a place away from the mood and noise associated with what was going on, but his sanctuary had now been trespassed upon by the two men who had singled out their prey. The drink had lessened their inhibitions to control themselves and they were becoming increasingly hostile as they shouted insults and damning accusations at the man, and he responded as most

76

helpless victims do - by self-consciously looking away and down at the floor, probably praying for the baiting to stop and not escalate to anything worse, or even violence.

'Look at him,' one of the men shouted, fucking perv, aint he? Loves her, don't he?' and the other man shouted, 'See him looking at her, fucking eyes were coming out his head, silly looking cunt - wants a spanking off her don't he?' and his associate walked towards the man, sneering as he said, 'What you doing, wanking under the table? You'd like her to give a right beating - probably want to her to cut your dick off and stuff it up your arse, you dirty old cunt - then have her sit on your face with her big arse and rub her fanny all over your stupid face, you fucking pervy old cunt.'

Chris went to stand up, he had heard and seen enough, but Brendan stopped him by gripping his arm with a look of warning not to get involved. The man shouting the abuse looked at his associate, they both laughed and after insulting the man at the table some more he returned to the bar where both men went though various ways of killing the man sitting at the table and getting rid of his body. The man looked up at the screen, relief already showing in his haggard face as he realised this episode of taunting and bullying was over.

Brendan leant close to Chris as he said, 'They're blaming him for all the things lacking in their own lives - placing the hatred and contempt they feel about their own predicament and their sense of being powerless to change anything for the better - and power is the key element here with this Mistress T character, her appearance has probably incited their anger.'

'But even so,' Chris began to say as he looked at the men, although he did not continue what he was going to say and looked around the bar, agreeing with Brendan that the appearance of the Mistress T character had changed the mood and behaviour in the bar. Chris looked from the two men at the bar to back up at the screen and saw the location had returned to the studio, but to a different set from the one the audience were in. A male presenter smiled and winked before introducing Marie. The camera pulled back to show the 'terrorist' was standing next to them.

'No touching,' the presenter said as Marie stepped towards the 'terrorist' and attempted to push him, 'Remember, we keep saying this - you aren't allowed to touch your offender - or call them by their name - they're just the offender - a non-person, just as they saw their victims to be - so remember Marie,' he pointed playfully at her in a jokey, reprimanding way, 'Don't call him by his name,' and placing his hand over his mouth he turned sideways to the camera and said, although you might want to call him a 'c…'

His mime left no doubt what word he meant and the audience broke into laughter. The presenter also laughed as he pointed into the camera and said, 'Let's get this on, or should I say, lets get the people on.' The audience cheered as the camera followed the presenter as he walked away from where he was standing, 'Okay - we've found just the place for him - Marie listened to Mistress T and has decided to use the press - but not the press made up of news reporters, no - the press made up of the weight of people used against vermin like this poisonous weasel who wanted to murder our children as they go out to play with their friends or to buy a present for a grandparent.'

The noise of the crowd became so loud it drowned out what the presenter was saying. A large appliance with a platform was shown and the presenter had to shout to make himself heard over the shouting and chanting from the studio audience, 'And guess what? We've allowed Marie to bring her friends along, and we've invited more members of the public to add their weight to squash evil.'

A group of people began moving around in the shadows behind the presenter as he explained to the audience and viewers that a floor was to be lowered onto blocks that had been placed on the 'terrorist's' chest and head. The lighting in the studio dimmed and a drum roll sounded. There was silence, except for the sound of people laughing and talking to each other as they climbed onto the platform. The lights went up and the shot pulled back, showing a large group of people standing on the platform of the appliance. They were cheering as the audience chanted 'Squeeze - squeeze - squeeze.' Marie was shown standing on the platform clenching her fists and mouthing the word, 'Yes! Yes!'

This scene continued for a few minutes to a fanfare of noise and the two men behind Brendan and Chris chanted 'squeeze' and hurled insults at the 'offender.' A women in the bar stepped towards the screen, pointing at it she laughed drunkenly while cursing the offender to his fate before laughing and waving and shouting, 'goodbye.' Messages were shown on the screen and shots of the crowds from outdoor broadcasts were intercut with presenters making gestures. A close up shot of the platform part of the appliance was shown, although there was not any sign of the terrorist as he had been secured beneath it and was completely covered.

As the group of people began to climb off the platform they shook each other's hands and hugged one another. The shot cut to the presenter who pointed into the camera and said, 'We'll be back after this break - and remember, this is the only show that offers you terrorists in a flat-pack form.'

The picture dissolved and altered into the show's logo before disappearing and then the advertisements came on.

Ten

The noise in the bar began to settle down. Chris saw some money passing hands between two men sitting at a table, people gamble on a multitude of variants that might happen involving a punishment or 'kill,' as it is often called, and these men had most probably wagered a bet on some outcome or detail. That particular week was a 'bumper show,' a 'special,' there was usually one capital punishment per show, but on that evening there were four. Changing from the grim intensity of violence to a lighter feel of introducing something humorous was something that always happened and is remarked upon by many people, although not in the media, as it being a ploy to confuse emotions. The show returned, and there was Alan Manville, who changed his expression from a big grin to one of seriousness as he said with a heavy hint of sarcasm the word, 'professionals,' and as he did so the cartoon character Christopher Correct appeared on the screen in an assortment of situations that depicted him expressing his heartfelt commitment to the aims of his work, which was to improve the lives of impoverished and put-upon people, but it contrasted what he was saying with scenes of him basking on a beach, sitting by the side of a pool and residing in a large house with fine furnishing as evidence that he did not really care at all.

In this part of the show, ex-lawyers, social workers, educationalists, health professionals and the like are brought in to be humiliated in various ways, all done in a fun and light hearted way, yet the aspect of revenge is central as is the maintenance of hatred for any person using progressive language. The exercise is performed through the well-used tactic of combining anger and laughter. One scenario is of having a 'debate' in the studio with members of the audience posing questions to the 'professionals' about their actions and the policies they created while in their former jobs. The 'professionals,' or 'liberals' also answered telephones as members of the public phoned in with questions and the 'professionals' defended themselves by justifying their former positions and made excuses for their way of thinking. There are the familiar questions such as why they avoided all responsibility yet earned a huge wage while sanctioning polices and implementing practices that were socially divisive and supported the perpetrators of crime rather than help the victims. This sentiment is perpetuated by the media and written into the history books for all school children to read.

Manville pointed into the camera and then at the audience as he said, 'Well ladies and gentlemen - boys and girls, we have a treat for you, and we here at People's Pleasure Corporation know that you're going to enjoy

80

this - because we believe you deserve to question these invertebrates - and do something to them...' A slow rousing of cheers, laughter and clapping from the audience caused him to stop speaking and Manville nodded as he looked around the audience and raised his voice.

'That's right, that's right - it's time to spit in their faces, shout at them and let them know what you think - and remember, don't listen to their answers and excuses because we know it's all lies - so slippery and deceitful are these purposeless rag worms, but now the industry has been taken away from them they are worse than useless - something we - you, knew all along.'

The audience chanted 'Squash, squash, squash.' Alan Manville held up his hand and shook his head, 'No, no - not that - not for these people - God knows they deserve it,' and he quickly placed his hand over his mouth as if guilty of saying something he should not have. 'Oops, I'm not allowed to say that - no, no, no - we will - you, will have a bit of fun with these cowards,' and Manville stopped and looked at the audience shaking his head, 'Jeez, Mistress T has really got into you this evening, whatever it is that high priestess has, it's certainly something - she says, "squash them," and we say, "yes please mistress" - and who are we to disagree with her,' he smiled and the audience cheered and laughed.

Manville stared at the audience before speaking. 'Ever heard of "Restorative Justice"? Mm? Well, let me inform you where people's hard earned money went in those days when these self-appointed mini-gods put their scheming minds together with objectives of creating an industry for them all to pursue their self-seeking personal interests at the expense of the decent people that live in this country. He made quotation marks with his fingers as he described the 'liberals', and the audience jeered as he spoke.

'Those people in qualified positions - as we know, the psychologists, therapists, housing officers, social workers, psychoanalysts, probation officers, councillors - and it goes on and on, a plethora of 'qualified' so called professionals invented and concocted a host of different jobs, theories, organisations and courses - and so it went on, mainly to mystify the honest, hard working person and defend a very good thing they were making for themselves.'

He looked into the camera for a long while with a look of serious contemplation before saying in a concise manner. 'Liberals,' and the audience erupted into booing and hissing.

'We've got a lot to thank - I think not - Christopher Correct and Dolly Do-Gooder for.'

The audience started to clap, and, finding a steady rhythm, they clapped in unison. This had become the thing to do before a 'liberal' was brought onto the show.

Manville clapped his hands and said, 'Well, let's get one of these all caring, well meaning professionals on here to explain herself - so, without making all you good people wait any longer - greet a sheet - or should that be shit.'

The line generated laughter from the audience, which quickly turned to heckling as a middle-aged woman was brought onto the stage. She looked around nervously as Alan Manville waited for the noise to subside before giving a knowing smile at the audience and into the camera, as if he, the audience and the viewers were together and in on something and the woman was ignorant of what was planned for her.

Manville turned and inspected the woman distastefully before speaking, 'Your name, is Patricia O' Keef - is that correct?

The woman fumbled with the collar on her blouse and was hesitant in giving her answer, 'Er - well, not now, er - it's just Keef, Patricia Keef - I dropped the o.'

She looked up at Manville, squirming as she waited for his response. Manville looked at her like a person examining the waste collected in a drain before turning to the audience. He said, 'She can't even answer the easiest of questions - just asking this person to clarify her name is too much for her, because it's too direct, and straight - and to be straight is not the way for these people.'

This caused some of the audience to laugh while others jeered. Manville sneered at the woman as he said, 'Could you please tell us your name, if it's not too difficult for you, and I do hope you don't find such a question like asking what your name is as, too intimidating - or, that you feel victimised.'

The audience laughed and clapped, and the camera picked out a poster someone in the audience was holding with the words, LOSE A LIBERAL written on it.

After chiding the woman for a couple of minutes Manville looked into the camera and said the time had come for her to explain what she actually did.

She spoke in a quiet and nervous quiver. 'I managed a team of Youth Offender Officers who delivered a range of interventions and activities, and I supervised the provision of community reparation projects...'

Manville interjected, mocking her, 'I like it, I like it - I love the language, give us more.'

Her eyes flitted around nervously as she licked her dry lips as if thinking of saying something that would please Manville and therefore, hopefully, be spared the worse of the treatments. She continued in her weak tone. 'I - my team, investigated causal factors that put young people at risk of offending, and implemented session plans that included the development of self-empowerment, coping strategies and activities to formulate a more positive self-identity...'

Manville interrupted her, making a show of holding back laughter, 'I'm sure you did, I'm sure you did - and all for the best possible reasons, Patricia Keef, or whatever you want to call yourself.' He then raised his hand, 'Enough, enough of that for the moment - one of the things that Ms Keef wasted her time with, was putting into practice restorative justice - mm, it sounds so lovey-dovey I think I might need a tiny tissue to dry my eye - let's find out about this restorative justice ladies and gentlemen.'

Manville turned to Patricia Keef and said, 'Could you explain what it is - without going on for two days, please,' and as she spoke, Manville nodded as though deeply interested in what she had to say and he gave a contrived smile of sympathy as she tried to control her breathing because she was so nervous.

'Restorative justice is a problem solving approach to crime that involves the parties themselves, and the community generally, in an active relationship with statutory agencies - it involves making room for personal development for those primarily concerned, particularly the offender and victim, but also their families and communities...'

Manville held up his hand to stop her from continuing, 'Please, please - I was going to say spare us the details, but I'm not because that's why you are here this evening, to demonstrate what a lot of dangerous bullshit you were paid handsomely to peddle - bullshit that had the most damaging consequences for society.'

The audience clapped and cheered their approval at what he had said. Manville continued, 'We will show some film of you later, which gives evidence to your past as well as having another of your type on the show who worked - if that is the correct word - in a system of complete madness which was allowed to take root and flourish, with results that were to the detriment of all right-thinking people, but first,' Manville pointed into the camera, 'we at People's Pleasure Corporation have put together a little piece of fun for your amusement.'

It cut to a recorded montage of Patricia filmed years back when she was in her job. The piece was intercut with presenters dressed in infantile clothes performing a pastiche of presenting restorative justice. A clumsy and childish diagram of a triangle with the components of

RESTORATIVE JUSTICE written on it appeared on the screen. The presenters shouted out words that were associated with the industry they were deriding. 'Reconciliation - mediation - resolution - reparation - significant other,' and there was film of Patricia Keef standing in front of a screen delivering a computer presentation to an audience. As she spoke cries of 'shame' and jeering came from the studio audience.

In the film they were showing, Patricia Keef looked young, on top of her game, the very model of a confident woman making positive strides in her career. Manville gestured for the studio audience to quieten in order to hear what she was saying. The shot zoomed in on her face as she spoke. 'We have to see crime issues in their social context - it is progressive and forward-looking to be preventative, to be flexible in one's practice and be creative by taking a problem solving orientation - a common definition of restorative justice is a process whereby parties with a stake in a specific offence resolve collectively how to deal with the aftermath of the offence and its implications for the future - let me guide you through the restorative justice pyramid...'

The film continued with other footage of Patricia Keef at work, until eventually it was brought to a close and Alan Manville began to ask her questions. The audience loved this part, watching the former 'professionals' squirming and laughing at the language they used.

Patricia Keef was trembling as she spoke to Manville. 'Well, essentially my role purpose was to develop constructive relationships within the role dimension itself - I was responsible for signposting and referring young offenders to other agencies as appropriate - to take a holistic view of their needs - my response was appropriate to the level of my post and within the remit of my role, and I would use my expertise to formulate an informed judgement - confidentiality is paramount...'

Manville cut her off, looking into the camera he said, 'And remember folks, she always demonstrated a commitment to her clients, above their victims - us, that is - well she would, wouldn't she? After all, they were the product that she made a very comfortable living out of, and provided her with a career giving her a cushy number and a big fat pension - that we all paid for.'

Manville smiled bitterly as he said, 'Just look at this.'

Another film recorded years ago was shown, it was of a man talking about his work before the 'big change.' The man said, 'Of course one has to retain a strong commitment to equal opportunities - one has to have the ability to translate complex assessments and initiate creative intervention programmes to prevent youths offending, and protect young people from negative effects within their social situation...'

84

'Stop!' Alan Manville shouted - we've heard enough - and now let's meet the excuse for a man itself who said those words - its name is Ken Mathews.'

Booing and jeering met Ken Mathews as he walked onto the stage. He was hardly recognisable from the man in the film and Manville smirked as he looked from the man to the audience.

'Listen, Ken,' he said, 'tell us about your skills and abilities.'

The audience laughed as Manville shook his head in dramatic dismay and looked from Ken Mathews to a piece of paper he was holding. He began reading from it, 'You worked in a multi-agency team that had a, "multitude of staff and qualified practitioners, each having responsibility for one's own input to a holistic package that contributes towards the most positive outcome for"...'

He stopped reading and held the piece of paper in front of Ken Mathew's face for him to continue reading what was on it. Ken Mathews was an utterly broken man, and the audience loved it. He stuttered as he began to read, 'Positive outcomes for victim recipients and those responding to what can be seen as a negative stigma within the dimensions of his or her situational world structure...'

Manville pulled the piece of paper away and said, 'Victim recipients! And those responding to negative stigma! You mean people who had been physically attacked and traumatised, and criminal scum.'

The audience burst into cheers and Manville rounded on Ken Mathews, sneering as he pushed another piece of paper at him. 'And read out more of this perverse academic verbiage - with your 'dynamics,' 'cross-fertilisation of theories, 'methodologies,' and your 'expertise' - go on, go on you excuse for living crap...'

The audience broke into wild cheering and laughter that was so loud Manville waited for them to settle before continuing, his eyes fixed on Ken Mathews. 'Come on creep, read what you said about yourself in your job "self-appraisal,"' and he shoved the paper in the man's hand, folded his arms and watched his agony. Manville snapped at Ken Mathews, telling him to speak up as he read what was written on the paper, but he could barely form the words as he stuttered his way through. 'I have overseen the creation of a self-empowered team which has shown success in campaign deliver...,' but he got no further as Manville snatched the paper from his hand and said. 'Don't bother - just don't bother - I had to read this nonsense for purposes of research, but please don't inflict it upon our audience, because they just don't deserve it.'

The taunting and teasing continued as Manville turned to Patricia Keef and said, 'Let's see - this is what you wrote while being paid to do what was outrageously called a job. He read from a sheet of paper, 'I couldn't possibly negotiate the concluding effects of offender outcome as it falls within the parameters of a negative agenda - I couldn't possibly negotiate that discourse unless there was a veritable paradigmatic shift in the focus of my role dimension...'

Manville stopped reading and rounded on her. 'Shameful - absolutely disgraceful - how could you bring yourself to speak in that way? Just for the money, and the self-appointed crowns that you all wore, denoting a status you all craved?'

The rowdiness in the studio grew to a darker mood, and Alan Manville was confident he could conduct the audience with ease. He stepped back and adopted a lofty pose as he spoke to Patricia Keef. 'As you liked "muggers" so much, the viewers have voted for a "mugger" to give you a personal gift - another "mug" who profited handsomely out of his activities. You and your type went along with using this corrupt language, engaging with your clients, when really they were nothing more than filthy pieces of scrotum scum that couldn't let the possibility go by of attacking, hurting, terrifying and robbing people - in the knowledge they could get away with it because their victims had no one in an official capacity to defend them, because all efforts were focused on defending the scum themselves - so they targeted people who were weaker by virtue of the fact they were old, infirm, alone and scared - and it was this state of affairs that you personally fed upon - and so we, at People's Pleasure Corporation, have decided to fulfil the wishes of our audience, which is for you to continue dining off the existence of a piece of scum - we have prepared a little delicacy for you - just because you can no longer feast off the actions of a piece of scum in your work, we have a criminal who was arrested for attacking and brutalising his victim before robbing her, and for old times sake we want you to still be able to feast off him - from his actual body, or what's left of it.'

The audience bristled with anticipation as they waited to see what was going to happen. Manville led Patricia Keef to a table that had been laid for a meal complete with candles and flowers. A young woman dressed as a waitress came onto the stage carrying a silver platter, placed it on the table, gave a little curtsey and giggled at Alan Manville before leaving. As Patricia Keef sat down Manville picked up a napkin from the table and said as he gave it to her, 'Yes, you dined off of the actions of the offender - now you can dine off the body - a dish freshly prepared by a world renowned chef - may we entice you, for your delectation - spotted dick - that favourite dish from yesteryear, brought bang up to date, we have prepared for you the broiled penis of a serial rapist and thieving piece of scum...'

The audience broke into hysterics, and it took a while for them to settle before Manville could continue. What was on the dish certainly looked like a penis, whether it actually was, and Chris thought it probably was, it caused Patricia Keef to break down and fall to the floor clutching her face. Manville bent over her holding the platter and asked if he could tempt her.

After a couple of minutes Manville turned to the camera and said, 'Watch this - we offered Patricia - whatever she calls herself, a choice of drink when she arrived here earlier. She chose tea. Just watch her drinking her favoured choice, in a refined manner.'

Manville spoke over a film showing Patricia Keef drinking from a fine bone china cup, 'Little did she know that her delicate cup contained, water, milk, tea, and - the urine of a young offender who broke into old people's homes.'

The audience responded noisily and Manville exploited the joke to the limit by miming her drinking the tea as he walked from one side of the stage to the other.

After the audience calmed down they were invited to fire questions at Ken Mathews under the supervision of Alan Manville. They wanted him to justify his old job and the theories and practices he pursued.

A member of the audience held up a placard with the words, Fart In Their Face written on it, which related to a part of the show called, Phut On A Professional.

In past shows the 'professionals' have been made to sit in a chair known as the Fart Chair and a member of the audience wins the opportunity to push his or her bum into the 'professional's' face and break wind. There have been stories of people who have been picked 'going into training,' as they eat a diet of foods known to create flatulence and a bad smell in order to achieve the much-wanted potent Ass Aroma as it is called.

During the humiliations, members of the audience come onto the stage to shout abuse and scream into the face of the 'professional,' and at times even spitting in their faces. The 'professional' goes through all this to escape jail. They have lost their jobs and pensions and the state is now calling them in to answer for their philosophies and actions. Some think they should serve hard labour, some even worse, such as the death penalty. They escape further punishment by allowing the public to take revenge in this way and publicly admitting their 'stupidity' and that they were wrong. In past shows the ridicule has included 'professionals' having a vat of bull's blood poured over them and then for it to be hosed away with cow's urine; apparently that was a punishment sent in by a viewer.

The show moved away from the 'professionals' as different presenters spoke over a trailer of past punishments. One was of a man pushed out of an aircraft, another of an 'offender' inside a wooden crate that was run over by a steamroller and one of a coach load of people who were members of a club for people wanting to lose weight driving over an 'offender'. A female presenter looked into the camera and pulled a face as she said, 'I've heard of shiatsu, but that's what I call a back massage,' as it showed an alleged thief being trampled by a group of people. Future punishments were promised by a smiling presenter who said, 'Don't worry, there are plenty more goodies on the way,' and as The Offender's Nemesis was breaking for another commercial break it showed a water cannon hosing an 'offender' down a street and over a car.

The atmosphere that had been generated in the bar was nothing like Chris had felt before. Where it had once been a place for people to go for a relaxed drink where it was relatively quiet, it had been turned into what the majority of the large bars had become - impersonal spaces with a large screen dictating the focus of attention. Chris and Brendan had hardly spoken, they sat looking around at different people in the bar like aliens visiting a strange planet, but both their heads turned towards the screen as the theme tune of The Offender's Nemesis introduced the final part of the show; Chris and Brendan looked tired and tense.

Eleven

The last part of The Offender's Nemesis opened with the young man in the beginning of the show who was thrown into the back of the van. He was now stripped to his underpants and being led down a busy street. People hurled abuse and laughed as he stumbled along with his feet manacled. Making a reference to his nearly naked and puny body the presenter said, 'Let's show everyone what he really looks like.'

The offender was paraded around a while longer before guided to a set-up of two men digging up the road. One of the men was operating a heavy mechanical device that hammered and flattened mud and broken concrete.

The presenter told the men they were to be joined by another man who might not be very good at the heavy work because he was so 'light fingered.'

It ended with the 'offender' having to pat down the mud with his hand, and the man operating the hammer machine, as if by accident, brought it down on the 'offender's' hand a few times. It showed the 'offender' clutching his pulverised hand, barely able to stand because of the pain while people shouted and laughed at him. The female presenter who was with the young man when he was thrown in the van appeared by the side of the road, buckled over with laughter. 'You've got to hand it to him,' she said, and the sound of laughter from the studio audience sounded loudly. She continued, 'It's a serious disease called flat finger that thieves can get,' and pointing into the camera she said, 'He'll find it difficult to put his hand in his own pocket now, let alone anyone else's.'

The show finished with the 'offender' who had been strapped to the front of the bus as he was driven around a built up area and then to an open space where the bus was driven slowly into a wall. Just as he was crushed a cartoon appeared on the screen of a man being squashed into a wall with the words, PAEDO PULP across it. The next day a photograph of the man who was driven into the wall would appear in all the popular newspapers, owned by the same corporation that makes The Offender's Nemesis.

The show had ended and maybe a minute or so had passed, but Chris and Brendan were not speaking to one another, they just sat looking around the bar. The atmosphere had quietened and the two men standing behind them were now making their way to the exit, with one of them looking at his watch telling the other man his wife will go on at him because he was meant to have taken his youngest son to the wrestling over an hour before.

Chris and Brendan were beginning to return to their senses, or that is how it felt for them, but what they had just experienced left a bad taste in their mouths and, checking their glasses were empty, Brendan rubbed his hands together and playfully slapped Chris on his shoulder to lighten their mood. He asked Chris if he wanted another drink, which he did, but was stopped from standing up by sounds coming from the television. A cartoon was showing - although aimed at adults having state messages and information. It is conveyed through childish rhymes and songs. Corporations also use these cartoons to propagate their values and sell their commodities, and it is said that this time on a Saturday is a good slot as many people are off work and many of them have been drinking for most part of the day. Chris thought about the use of language, the abbreviations and acronyms and how the content, whether it be frivolous or important, can cause one to view almost everything in the same way and not consider the meaning because they are often so much alike they can all be understood as trivial, easy to remember and to associate with, but difficult to have an alternative interpretation and meaning.

They decided to leave the bar and head off somewhere else for one more drink before going home. It had not been a relaxing time and they had not discussed the situation of Chris getting involved with people who had seemingly deceived him.

While walking down the road the two men spoke about how Chris had implicated himself and his family in trying to help Simon, and they talked about The Offender's Nemesis, the people in the bar they had just left, the way in which the country was going and how the authorities have carte blanche to change laws and bring in any policy they wish to. They talked about how, over the years, human rights had eroded, and in relation to being arrested for a crime, to a point where in many cases suspicion alone substantiates guilt. When an alleged criminal is held in custody and appears in court there is no longer, as there once was, a fund to pay for advice, defence or any legal proceedings. The jury system operates in cases where the accused has the means to defend him or herself, but generally money spent on discussing exhaustive details and circumstances in a case is seen as money wasted. Brendan spoke about the 'offenders' on The Offender's Nemesis and how the faces on scratch cards for the show are nearly always foreign when the offender, or supposed offender, is a terrorist. The primary group in society who are always treated with suspicion are those labelled as foreigners, the poor ones, even though many of them were born in this country. They spoke about the faces on the ubiquitous scratch cards and that names given underneath them are not their names at all. Chris spoke about the people he had met in the 'underground movement' who had told him they have evidence that innocent people are tried and sentenced as guilty on the show.

While concentrating on talking, neither Chris nor Brendan had noticed they had walked in a different direction than the one they intended to. Although they were not lost, it was an area they were unfamiliar with, and one that could possibly be unsafe as it was very close to the edge of a housing project. They started to walk towards the high street from where they could catch a bus, but while doing so they passed a bar, and after a discussion of whether they should or should not go in there for a drink, they decided it looked decent enough and entered the bar.

It was not a large place, and at first sight not unfriendly, but like all bars occupying similar positions close to the projects, it had an ingrained repressed feel where there is suspicion of the other. A television, although quite small, hung on the wall, but nobody was taking any notice of it and what little sound there was coming from the television could not compete with the noise of the patrons' chatter.

As Chris entered the bar he was conscious of a feeling residing inside him of wanting to find answers about the society he lived in, and that he was tired of standing on the side, so to speak, and keeping quiet.

Brendan bought the drinks, draught beer, the type they nearly always drank, and they found a place to stand, as there was no available seating. They spoke about the meeting Chris was supposed to have, and the person X that he was meant to meet, the conspiracies, the people in the 'underground movement' and of how it must be closely monitored by agents working for the state, and they spoke about Steven, the way he is and what danger he could be in. Time elapsed, and with their glasses empty, Chris suggested they should have one more before going home, and as he was already late he phoned Rosie, letting her know he'll be later than expected. Chris bought another drink and they remained in the place they had found, deep in conversation and remarking how the bar had filled with people.

A sports programme broke for the news and scenes from a battle in another land was being shown on the television. Many of the soldiers shown who are on 'our' side had a foreign appearance, and as always, the scenes on the film were disjointed and clumsily edited in such a way it gave an unreal feel to the spectacle. Subtitles ran across the bottom of the screen saying how the 'Special Army' had been deployed to break down a particularly stubborn and vicious resistance. The 'Special Army' exists separately from the regular armed services and is involved in a continual activity taking place in different countries all over the world. It is made up of people who did not volunteer to join, but were forced to do so. Among

91

them are those serving prison sentences in this country who sign up because they had been promised to have their sentences dropped if they join, which is an empty promise, and there are the people who are forced into it from other countries. These people make up the vast bulk of the army, people who have never been to this country and are fighting for its name and interests, a situation that has arisen through corrupt governments in the pockets of those heading the large corporations.

There has in essence been a reintroduction of the press-gang system. Agents of the state infiltrate gangs or groups of unemployed poor in this country and feed back information on the ones they consider being troublesome or potentially prone to criminality. They are approached and made offers of earning good money, far above what the regular army personnel receive, with the opportunity to work abroad on behalf of the state as part of the 'Special Army.' Most people, or nearly all of them, decline the offer, but the state does not give up on its intentions and coercive methods are employed, such as arresting and charging them on trumped up charges that incur lengthy prison sentences, which is not just incarceration but involves forms of hard labour. An alternative choice is offered, and that is to sign up and serve the country overseas. What they actually do is take part in brutalising people in parts of the world who are resisting the demands and interests of big business, because they know their way of life and environment is going to be ruined.

It does not come in for any scrutiny by any form of media as all meaningful information is muted where the interests of the state and companies are concerned. When a regiment in the 'special army' finish operations in a particular country they are not repatriated to the place where they come from. Their 'disappearance' or deaths are reported as losing their lives in action or in one of the many 'accidental incidents' that occur during transit. Nobody, in their right mind, would make any enquiry into what actually happened because of the consequences that criticisms or persistent questions would bring, for it is widely known what happens to those who do. They are arrested for crimes they have not committed, are involved in accidents whilst driving, lose their jobs because of some trumped up reason and even have a family member killed on the road or die from a 'mystery illness.' People know what is going on because they have been told by those serving in the forces and had been in areas where the 'special army' were deployed and saw things they are not willing to report because they fear what will happen to them.

The people pushed into the 'special army' are often troublesome in a street criminality way, not those harbouring subversive ideas against the state or having any political interests. These people, often the educated

92

'dissident' type, are also dealt with, but in a different way. One popular method is to falsely accuse them of some crime, usually something important that carries a severe sentence. It is common to make accusations of serious fraud at work where plans of embezzling huge amounts of money are concerned, or stealing important information and using it for personal gain, and, if working for the state, accusations of contravening secrecy acts is the norm. The penalty is extremely harsh whether one works for a company or the state as both are seen as stealing from the people, and thus the interests of country. The charge is loaded in language where the 'offender' is found guilty of committing a treasonous act in that it is a serious betrayal of trust and loyalty, and that incurs a long prison sentence and the loss of one's home.

A group of men standing near to Chris and Brendan looked up at the television and one of them raised his fist and shouted, 'That's right boys, give them hell - the foreign bastards.' Some of the men in his company nodded in agreement while others took no notice, and the man who had shouted turned, looked at Brendan and nodded in a way for Brendan to respond. Brendan's response was not what the man wanted because a weak smile and conciliatory nod did not satisfy him.

'What do you think then? Eh?' The man punched out the question to Brendan, his eyes filling with hostility and hot temper, 'You two look a couple of brain boxes, what do you think we should do? Bomb them back into the Stone Age? The dirty foreign cunts.'

Chris and Brendan looked uncomfortably from the man to the people he was with.

'Well, come on then, you must have an opinion,' the man said as he took a step towards Brendan, 'Don't you think we're doing the right thing out there? Eh?'

Brendan nodded, tight lipped before saying in an effort to pacify him, 'That's right it's got to be done, you're right.'

This stopped the man from stepping any closer, but his look said he did not find Brendan's answer convincing and his eyes searched Brendan for any discrepancy he could seize upon. The man took a step backwards and diverted his attention to Chris, 'Your friend there is keeping quiet,' he said and then at back to Brendan, 'Just like yourself, about what you think.'

'Not at all,' Brendan said in an even tone as the man joined his group. Some of the man's group were looking from Chris and Brendan to the man.

'Old Christopher Correct over there, keeping quiet about what he thinks,' the man said, and one of his group shouted out, 'And his mate,

Dolly Do-Gooder,' which caused them all to laugh, and thankfully, for Chris and Brendan broke the tension by taking the man's attention away from the two of them.

Brendan looked at Chris and said, 'We shouldn't have come here.' Chris nodded in agreement and said they would finish their drinks and leave, and have another one elsewhere before going home, but Brendan told him he had had enough for the night. So the two of them drank their beer and walked towards the exit, but just as they were nearly there, a man, who had been propelled backwards by a shove he had received, stumbled into their path followed by an angry looking man who was pointing into his face as he snarled, 'Don't tell me to, "behave," saying "behave yourself" to me, you cunt – I'm not a child – and listen cunt,' he said, pushing his face close into the other man's face, 'even if you like to be treated like one, I don't, get it?'

They then grabbed at each other's shirts, grappled and traded insults though mouths clenched tight in anger for a few seconds before a few other men who appeared to be their friends pulled them apart.

Chris and Brendan continued on their way to the door to exit the bar and into the street outside, and as they did so Chris thought about the scene they had just witnessed and what the man said, saying he was not a child and that he did not want to be treated like one. Once outside the bar they looked at each other with relief and then walked towards a main road. Chris told Brendan he wanted another drink, and maybe they could find somewhere pleasant to have the final beer of the evening, but Brendan was adamant in his desire to get home. When they reached the main road where buses could be caught to take one in most directions Brendan tried to persuade Chris to go home, but to no avail, Chris felt unsettled and he wanted to stay out a little longer. Brendan boarded a bus with an expression of misgiving on his face as he left Chris on the pavement. The two friends waved at one another as the bus passed Chris who was walking in a direction away from the main road towards a housing project. He was feeling very unsettled. It was the tension and apprehension brought about by the meeting that went wrong the day before. The constant concern he felt about his brother and what was to become of him had been a lifelong worry, and now it had proven to be that Steven's life could be under threat, and that was the reality of the situation. The authorities had Steven in their sights and it was going to end up in something he had always feared. Chris had never been a big drinker in any sense, but he felt he needed another drink in an effort to banish the feelings of worry.

Twelve

As Chris walked along a road running next to a housing project he looked down a side street and saw lights coming from some shops; they drew him towards them like a moth to a lamp. He began walking in the direction of the lights, not really thinking, but hoping there would be some company or contact, for he felt a hollow emptiness deep inside. Chris was not lonely, and he had the support of Rosie his wife, but there was something he was in search of that might give him hope.

Within twenty seconds of walking down the street the physical environment changed to dereliction and the feel altered to severe intensity. The street was leading onto the project itself and Chris reminded himself it was a place that was unsafe to enter, although nowhere near as dangerous as the ones with foreign nationals, but all the same there was the real potential for trouble. Chris stopped outside a shop that was lighting the pavement. It was a Rummage Room, although not a massive one - it was the size of three old shops. Chris looked through the window before entering, and as he did so the smell of dampness hit him immediately. Heaps of drab items were piled on trestle tables. There were coats, hats, pullovers, shirts and all types of clothing in sizes for adults and children jumbled together. Chris watched the few people in the shop picking around what was on offer. One table was stacked with candles. 'New but smoke damaged,' a sign read next to a table lamp, which was on a table that had items on it labelled, 'From houses of distinction.'

An old motorbike engine was next to fishing reels which were being scrutinised by a tall, earnest looking man. The man's demeanour, and the way he attempted to maintain tidiness despite his threadbare clothing, led Chris to assume he had maybe once occupied a qualified position at work. The man's eyes grasped at the objects he handled, and then he stopped, as if calculating the cost with the money he had in his pocket.

Chris picked up a tent mallet. It was old and had been well used, probably for jobs other than hammering tent pegs, and Chris wondered who on earth would possibly want to buy such a sad looking thing. Music was playing from an old music system that had a price tag stuck to its side. The music was quiet and unobtrusive, as if selected to fit in with the doleful plight of the people and their surroundings.

Chris left the musty, depressing place, but had only walked a few steps before stopping in the middle of the street. He turned around and looked at the Rummage Room. An insight into the running of the whole economic system flashed upon his mind, but then his attention was broken by a man coming out of a doorway. The man had just left a bar, although it was difficult to tell it was a bar because the windows were boarded up with black sheets of wood, which made it impossible to see inside, and light only escaped when the door was opened. Chris walked towards it, checking the money in his pocket as he did so. He wanted to go in and experience the life within it, even though he was nearly shaking with trepidation at the prospect of doing so. Chris imagined a voice of reason telling him not be so stupid, but it was smothered by a burning need to open that door and enter the bar, in maybe the same way an astronaut wants to explore the unknown in space, or a mountaineer has to continue to a summit and a racing driver has to press for greater speed. But why? Why did he have this compulsion? This is what Chris asked himself.

The door opened suddenly and a young man came out at a pace that made it impossible to avoid bumping into Chris. They both blurted apologies, and as Chris watched the young man briskly make his way down the street he realised that he was holding the door open. Chris looked into the bar, and from where he was standing he could see only one person sitting on a stall up at the counter, although he could hear the raised voices of others and the sound of a television

He entered. It was quite small and had a compact feeling. There was just one person serving, a young woman in her early twenties, and as she walked towards Chris her eyes remained trained on a football match being shown on a television that was fixed high on the wall in the corner, and all the while her jaw moved lazily to accommodate the gum she was chewing. Chris ordered a large draught beer, and, still looking at the television, she asked him what type of beer he wanted, but Chris had difficulty in hearing what she was saying because she mumbled her words while pushing her tongue through the gum in her mouth, and the volume of the television was just too loud for normal speech to be understood. He eventually communicated successfully, and as she poured the beer Chris looked around his surroundings. The place was not worn and dingy, as Chris had thought it might be, and it had a style in keeping with the standard theme of the chain of bars it was part of. The smell of synthetic tobacco wafted over from a group of men who were standing under the television, some of them looking up at the television as they shouted at each other; he noticed that nearly all of them were drinking the same beer as he was.

Chris lit a cigarette, sat on a stall up at the bar counter and while looking at the television he also watched the group of men, but took care to be discreet, because he did not want to be caught looking at them. Their conversation drifted from football to their work, which by what they were saying was to do with either building work, refuse clearance or driving. The tone of their voices was abrasive and the main content of what they were saying was to put someone down and undermine them. The person being criticised and derided was sometimes one of the group, or it was said about someone who was not present. The conversation was in essence materialistic, with an evident covetousness and aggressive one-upmanship. As Chris was considering this, and noting their basic observations and the principles of immediacy that took precedence, he became aware of the man sitting on the stool at the counter. The man was looking at Chris, watching him, and so Chris nodded and the man gave the slightest of nods while his eyes searched Chris as if he was trying to place him.

The man's stare unsettled Chris. He picked up his glass and was not sure whether to finish his drink and leave or stay for another. One of the men from the group came up to the counter and shouted his order. The young woman nodded and set about pouring the drinks with her inert eyes staring up at the screen as she chewed on the gum. The man engaged in a bit of banter with her about the football match. It seemed that neither he, nor any of the people he was with, supported either of the teams, but she did. The entrance door of the bar opened with a heavy thud and a group of men ambled in who were loud, excited and had been drinking. They knew the men by the television and the two groups shouted friendly insults at one another. Items of clothing came in for barbed humorous comments, as did hairstyles, lack of hair, size of stomachs and mental capacities. Chris sensed that most of the people being verbally abused accepted the comments as intended to be just a joke within the ambit of bar room revelry, but their eyes hardened a little as they considered there was a line that when crossed the supposed joking became blatant personal insults.

The rough caustic wit was replaced by questions about work or home-life, and sly innuendos were made concerning women who were being seen on the side. The arrival of the men had made Chris forget about the man on the stool, but when Chris turned he saw that he was still looking at him. Chris took a more detailed observation of the man. He was in his early forties and his bulky overcoat concealed a thin and bony body beneath it. The man had coal black eyes that burned into Chris. His large hands were put to use in heavy manual work that was dirty, which was obvious by the ingrained grime showing clearly on his thumb and forefinger, which were gripping a hand rolled cigarette. All the while, the man made no effort to look away, but just steadily watched Chris as if adding confirmation to what he was thinking. Chris thought he might engage the man in some small talk, but he had already nodded to him and that was practically ignored, so it was unlikely he wanted to strike up a conversation.

Chris ordered another drink, and while doing so caught the attention of a man who had just left the group of men and was walking up to the counter. On reaching the counter he asked Chris how he was, and Chris replied that he was fine and enquired after the man's welfare. The man gave a stock response, saying that things were going well. His delivery of speech was fast and hard as words were thrown out as if despatched with apathy and disgust. He stood back, raising himself to his full height and cleared his nose, sniffing forcefully before he spoke. Chris guessed they were about the same age, and he noticed his dull eyes showed an edge of suspicion as they fixed on Chris and assessed him. He had a red face that was soft, although hardened by weather, work and alcohol. The scars showing above and to the sides of his eyes were a clear indication he had been involved in violent battles. His sturdy frame was resolutely anchored to the floor and his thick hands hung loosely to his sides, as if waiting to be employed in a physical effort. The man picked up his glass of beer, and looking down at Chris asked him where he was from. Chris was immediately nervous, and, hoping it did not show, he answered the man, telling him where he lived while adopting what he intended to be a passive and affable manner, but he now deeply regretted wandering down the side street and being so inquisitive to enter the bar.

The bar was a long way from the grimmest part of project culture and the people in there would consider themselves to be socially above most people within the place they lived in, because they were not the poorest. They are the type of people that are proficient in using their ingenuity to make ready cash, and because of that it elevated them to a higher status than the majority in their social environment, which can often cause them to gloat with arrogance at those less fortunate themselves. Their particular way of life is hard and physical, and, although in absolute terms having more than many around them, they would find it tremendously difficult to transcend project life because of education and other social opportunities. For many of them it is satisfying enough to just compare themselves with the poorest in the situation they live in, who they will scoff at and treat with contempt, even though they would undoubtedly have members of their families that are very poor, and because of the scantiness of support if things went wrong they live with the continual worry that they can also drop to that level.

Violence is the common currency within the culture of the people in the bar. It is what streams people into their place within their system, and it is this factor that Chris was concerned with as he told the man where he

98

lived, and he started to ramble as he went on about needing a drink because he had been through a rough few days.

The man's eyes did not show any change of expression as he asked Chris what he did for a living, which instilled an increased intense wariness in Chris, and so he told him that he did a bit of tutoring and bits of other work when he can find it. The man looked at Chris's hands, noting by their cleanliness and smoothness he did not do manual work. Not that impressed, but seemingly satisfied with what he had learned about Chris, the man chinked his glass against Chris's and said, 'Well good luck – doesn't sound like you're making many dollars.'

Chris felt a great relief at having passed a test of acceptance, and he raised his glass towards the man as he turned way from the counter. The man was right in that the wage of a tutor employed on a casual basis is low compared to what the men in the bar could earn when things are going well, and Chris was happy for the man to think that, because he might have felt different and been resentful if he knew Chris had a full time professional job. The man sitting on the stool was still looking at Chris, but the suspicion in his stare had weakened because Chris had successfully survived the other man's examination and had been granted an approval.

The man who had asked Chris the questions stood amongst his friends as a fresh bout of raucous banter erupted between the two groups. After a few minutes the groups intermingled and catchphrases, probably coming from popular television shows, were shouted out. Chris observed that the repeating of phrases and mimicking well known media characters and their actions took the onus off the individual, and possibly a relief is felt because one did not have to cast his opinion and create a personal response as attention is diverted to group participation, of aping one another and shouting out slogans as a tag to tie one to the crowd, and it is all fused with loud harsh laughter.

Chris ordered another beer, no longer caring about the man sitting along the counter as the noise in the bar grew louder, and at times the young woman behind the counter struggled to cope with the demand for beer. She was short tempered with some of the men who she saw as taking their remarks too far, and her annoyance was increased by the ribbing she took because her football team had lost. The atmosphere could have been described as good-natured, but it was obvious there was a thin brittle lid holding physical violence in place, and Chris felt that was part of the reason why there was a presentation of two contrasting emotions. On the one hand there was aggressive humour that was antagonistic, and on the other a wary friendliness and circumspection.

It was tribal etiquette, and Chris was very aware of how difficult it is to successfully interact and participate within the group because of the complexities that make up the acceptable behaviour and customs. The conduct became more drunken as choruses of songs were sung and popular sayings and catchwords were shouted out and repeated in unison. Pack boundaries were clearly defined as safety and security was felt by acquiescing to the rules.

A few of the men began to chant a phrase that immediately caused Chris to feel uneasy. It was from the television show The Offender's Nemesis, and one of the men mimicked the actions of a presenter who is associated with a simple phrase that had made him a household name.

'Ooh, I'm glad I'm not you,' the man repeated the phrase, and right on cue the door to the bar opened and a solitary looking man entered who was physically disabled, facially disfigured and on first sight looked to be mentally impaired. The group fell about laughing as their pack member pointed at the man who had just entered and repeated the phrase. Some of the men could not contain themselves, holding their sides, they spun in circles as they fought to catch their breath, while a couple of them made baboon-like grunting sounds. The man who had just entered walked up to the counter, his face reflecting a disposition that was resigned to insults and rejection. Chris admired the man's forbearance and the way he continued see through what he had come in to do, but then thought it was a daily experience for him, and unless he completely gave up he had no other choice but to carry on.

The man ordered a drink, and the young woman serving him tried to hold back laughter because of comments the men were making about the man's physical deformities. The man took a preliminary sip of his drink and judged its taste as if it was an exclusive variety rather than the standardised, mass-produced beer he was holding. He looked around his surroundings, his eyes not lingering for a fraction of a second on the men, two of which continued to repeat the phrase, 'Ooh, I'm glad I'm not you,' with their arms around each other's shoulders and wiping tears from their eyes.

Their bullying behaviour caused Chris's stomach to tighten and his mouth dried, a reactive sensation causing him to ponder how the emotions triggered by anger and fear are one and the same thing.

One of the group came over to the man and asked him what he was doing in the bar, and as the man looked down at the floor and mumbled something the group member shouted out, 'Have you come in here looking for women?' and then he broke into laughter as he looked at the others by the television. A few of the men broke into hysterics as their

100

group member drew attention to the man's shoes, pointing at them he laughed and shouted out about where the man had got them. Chris looked at the man's shoes. He conceded that they would be considered as inappropriate for a man of his age. They were a sports design, the kind of style a young schoolboy would wear, and Chris thought they had probably been bought in a Rummage Room, or maybe the man had found them somewhere, possibly in a rubbish bin.

One of the group became nasty towards the solitary man. He was a stocky man and fairly short in height, 'Get the scabby fucking thing out of here,' he growled through gritted teeth, and his eyes lit with rage as his face flushed in anger. One of his companions told him not to bother himself, but he continued to glare at the solitary man and said something about throwing him out of the bar and setting fire to him. 'He's not right,' the man said, and he went on about how the solitary man should not be allowed in places where 'families or working men go'. Chris would dearly have liked to intervene and defend the solitary man, but was fully aware of the danger if he did so.

Chris ordered another drink knowing it was not a wise thing to do, he should have gone home earlier and the atmosphere in the bar had become taut with aggression. His anxiety when entering had lessened, which was mainly because of the alcohol, but he was still an outsider and it was clearly evident how outsiders are treated. The more he thought about it the more he regretted ordering the drink and he decided to leave it on the bar and make a hasty exit. Chris looked around the bar and saw that the man who had been sitting on the stool looking at him was now standing in the doorway talking to a rough looking character in a surreptitious kind of way. Chris felt there was something unpleasant about him, and thought that maybe it could have been because he was anxious, but he saw the man as someone who would make trouble for a person who had not done him any harm. The man looked like he might be giving information to the rough looking character and conspiring for an attack on someone, and Chris could not help feeling that it might be him. Just why he thought that, Chris was not sure, he had not done anything wrong, but then neither had many people who had been attacked, murdered and accused of things they had not done. Chris looked at the solitary man and asked himself what had he done wrong and was afraid the verbal abuse might lead to a physical attack on the man; it had descended into a nightmare and Chris wanted to get out of there.

Chris looked around and gained some consolation from seeing that nobody was looking at him, the men in the bar were in the main just shouting at one another, some only a few centimetres from the face of the person they were shouting at. Having made his mind up to leave, he walked past the solitary man, who was looking up at the television, but suddenly changed his direction and went to the toilet. The reason why Chris altered his course was because of the man talking in the doorway, he could not get it out of his mind that the man was collaborating against him; Chris was now very nervous.

There was nobody in the toilet and he hoped it stayed that way while he was in there. His bold attitude had gone, and he felt as if he had not drunk any alcohol at all, but his head ached and his mouth was dry. Chris rinsed his hands in the sink, and, noticing how they were shaking he immediately felt faint and remembered he had not eaten for a long time.

Taking a last look at his pale face in the mirror Chris turned from the sink and left the toilet.

On re-entering the bar, he heard a man shouting above all the other noise. It was the stocky man's voice, and it was loud and hard. He had hold of the solitary man by his collar and was shouting at him, although two of his friends were asking him to leave the solitary man alone. They were trying to calm the situation, but the stocky man began to shout at them. His face was bright red, his eyes were bulging and his lips were pulled back showing his gritted teeth. He swore and shouted, but Chris did not stand and watch, his principal intention was to get out as quickly as possible. Chris approached the doorway to leave the bar, focusing on the door itself and not at the man who had been looking at him.

He had made it. Chris pushed on the door, and as it opened he took a quick look at the man who had been looking at him, and there he was, staring at Chris with a long searching look, 'Be careful out there,' the man said, but Chris did not answer him, he looked away, panic scorching though him as he hoped there had not been an attack planned to take place outside. As he left the bar Chris heard the men shouting behind him and the grunting baboon-like noises.

Thirteen

There was no group of men brandishing bats outside the bar, as Chris feared there might be, waiting to beat him into a coma, it was just as it was earlier when he had walked in there. Although Chris did not relax, looking around for signs of danger he walked as fast as he could to exit the intense atmosphere residing in the project environment, and when reaching the end of the street Chris nearly collapsed with relief. Talking out loud, he asked himself why he had put himself through the ordeal he had just experienced, and he felt the effect of the alcohol, which made his nerves more jagged than they already were. Chris realised he was quite drunk, although tiredness, lack of food and worry contributed to how he felt. He stumbled as he walked, once or twice bumping into a shop front, but he then suddenly straightened and maintained an even walk, and with his head erect, he employed a brisk and businesslike approach to his bearing. The reason for this change was that a police car was driving slowly down the street, and the two policemen inside it were looking at Chris. His breathing became short, and on seeing one of the police holding units across the street he rapidly sobered up. There was no light on inside the small building, signifying it was empty.

Chris stopped walking, realising he had turned the wrong way and had been walking down a street that skirted the housing project. Nobody was around, except for the policemen who had stopped their car and were watching Chris, which made him even more nervous. He began to walk, although not knowing where he was going and for a second thought about going over to the police car and asking them which way he needed to go in order to get home, but changed his mind when considering the questions they might ask, and how one thing can lead to another, which caused him to think of the stories he had heard of people who had been going about their way in an innocuous fashion when they had a chance meeting with the police or security services, and it led to them becoming embroiled in a situation that grew so nasty it ruined their lives. And then Chris stopped thinking as one of the policemen opened the car door and looked directly at him.

'This is it,' Chris thought, 'now I'm going to be pulled in for questioning, and God knows where it will lead to.'

'Everything okay?' The police officer called across to Chris.

Chris just nodded and said that it was, but his voice would have hardly been audible to the police officer.

'Stay where you are, I want to ask you a few questions,' the police officer said as he climbed out of the car in an awkward fashion, as if his knee and hip joints had temporarily seized up. He was a big man, and, adjusting the holster that held his gun to the side of his waist he walked across the quiet street, his eyes watching Chris carefully. Chris looked from him to the other officer who remained in the car, sitting behind the steering wheel impassively watching the proceedings.

'Right,' the police officer said when he reached Chris, 'you've had a drink, and I want to know where you've been and where you're going, and as you're telling me, take your ID out of your pocket, very slowly.'

Chris had been asked to produce his ID many times. It was an everyday matter of modern life, but this felt completely different because he had not been asked for his ID while being in the type of area he was now in, and the police would be suspicious of his reasons for being there. His nervousness was inflamed as his mind raced over the people he had recently made contact with who are involved in the 'underground movement' and the plans he was making for Steven. Chris nervously handed his ID to the police officer, who took it without taking his eyes from him, and before Chris answered his first question he asked another one. 'Where do you live?'

Chris told him and then the police officer wanted to know what he was doing in the area as he continued to inspect the ID. Chris told him where he had been that evening, but as he was speaking the police officer interrupted him and asked Chris why he had not gone home with Brendan, and as Chris was trying to explain that he wanted to stay out a little longer the police office looked up from the ID and shouted, 'But what are you doing now?' He spat out the question and stared at Chris in a manner that was becoming hostile. Chris rambled as he told him that he had made a mistake in the direction he was walking, and that he was in a world of his own.

'Come with me,' the police officer snapped as he turned and walked towards the patrol car. Chris was nervous, and he knew it showed as the police officer asked for his phone, which he placed in a holster on the car dashboard that read the relevant details. Chris was told to place his hand on a rubber plate that took his fingerprints, and almost immediately his details showed up on it. The police officer in the driving seat watched Chris with an expression that was a mixture of boredom and amusement.

The police officer read out the name of the college where Chris worked and his occupation with the address of his place of work, nodding as he did so. He looked at Chris and said, 'You're in a fine state to be going home to your family, and is this a way for a man in professional work to behave?'

Chris told him it was not a habit of his to drink much in any way, and with a wry smile said that his wife is understanding, but his attempt at informality was not appreciated by the police officer talking to him, and the other one looked at Chris as if noticing him for the first time.

The first police officer asked Chris if the students in the college knew he got drunk and staggered around not knowing where he is going in areas where he should not be.

Chris told him this was the first time and that he took his work very seriously.

'Is that so?' The police officer said, letting his question hang in the night air, which for Chris at that moment felt noxious and cold.

'You set a good example for your students,' the police officer behind the steering wheel said, with an expression that made it clear he did not like Chris, or his behaviour at any rate, and both of them queried his suitability to have a job that carries responsibility. Chris parried their questions with apologetic explanations, feeling increasingly worried they might make trouble for him at work.

'Come over here,' the first police officer said as he walked across the street towards the little construction known as a police holding unit. Chris followed him, finding it difficult to breathe, and he was aware that he was speaking, telling the police officer he was really sorry and that he was going to sort himself out and he just wanted to go home. What he was saying reminded Chris of people he had seen in the street who were being beaten by security officers and of how they pleaded with them, or even the offenders on The Offender's Nemesis. The police officer opened the door and gestured for Chris to enter.

'This is it,' Chris thought to himself, 'now I'm going to find out what a PHU is really like.' The door closed behind Chris and he looked around, surprised how small it was inside. It was an empty, global shaped space without any sharp corners or edges and completely covered in white tiles, which made the floor, walls and ceiling appear to merge into one another with no distinction between them, and it was dimly lit by lights hidden beneath some of the tiles. The feeling of austerity was driven further home by the police officer's manner and the way he told Chris how it was cleaned. He stared at Chris as he explained that the whole inside of the building was simply hosed down and the dirty water and bleach drained through a filtering system in the floor.

'Bit like life really,' the police officer said, and a spiteful grin creased his mouth as he said, 'All the dirt and filth that builds up gets cleaned away - scouring the unwanted scum down the drain, where it belongs.'

And he looked at Chris, defying him to meet his eye, which Chris found difficult to do. Chris could hear his own breathing, irregular and sharp, and for a fleeting second he thought the police officer was going to lunge forward and strike him. So he flinched and jumped backwards.

'Bit nervous aren't you?' The police officer said, and Chris nodded to confirm he was, and said that he was tired.

'You've got a clean record - keep it that way. You don't want to be holed up in one of these,' the police officer said and he ushered Chris out of the little building with its damp atmosphere that smelled of urine, vomit and bleach. Once outside, the police officer gave Chris directions to the main streets where he would be able to get a bus home, and all the while the other police officer watched him with a contemptuous look.

Chris could feel a massive discharge of tension leaving his body as he walked away from the police car, and for a few seconds the relief he felt was so great he thought he was going to faint, but just as that feeling began to subside a powerful sensation rushed through him, and all he wanted to do was laugh out loud. Without turning to look back at the patrol car he walked to the end of the street and followed the directions he was given. Having strayed a fair distance out of his way it was a long walk back, and at times he became scared when some of the cars that passed him slowed down and the people inside stared at him.

Fourteen

Rosie was already in bed when Chris got home, although not asleep. Having rung her on his way back she knew where he was, and was worried rather than annoyed he had stayed out and was a little worse for wear with beer. The grating sound of the evening, which was of harsh aggression, rung in his ears, and Chris spoke to Rosie about the evening, telling her everything in a hushed tone as if not wanting the poison he experienced that night to sully his young daughter who was in her bedroom only two metres away. Rosie listened, carefully taking note of what Chris told her with concern showing on her face. She told him to rest and they would speak in the morning when emotions and anxieties would be less magnified. Chris lay staring up at the ceiling, his mind a cauldron of heated thoughts and Rosie lay next to him, her eyes closed, but unable to sleep because of her worry for Chris and for them as a family, now that he was involved in something he should not be.

After a while Chris did close his eyes, but at first had to keep opening them as images of the television show The Offender's Nemesis flashed into his mind, and there were the men in the bar who had been to football, their voices and attitude, the people in the bar baying for another human being to be beaten and killed with no thought to the truth of the accusation that has led the doomed people to be in the position they were, and then the next bar, with the sight of armies killing people and then Brendan being threatened by the man who wanted resolution to the anger he felt, so he hit out at a person he knew could do so in safety, as was the case in the next bar, when he was alone, full of fear, being stared at by the man, and the other man, asking questions about who he was, where he came from and what he did for a living, a miniature inquisition, taking place in every interaction in a society obsessed with suspicion, and there they were attacking the solitary man, disfigured, alone and helpless, and Chris thought maybe this is how they all feel inside, but then the police officer, his face full of antipathy as he questioned Chris as one might imagine one would be interrogated in a concentration camp, but he had not done anything wrong, he was just walking down the street for Christ's sake, and the other one sitting in the car, all heavy with power and indifference to a person's innocence, Chris was just the quarry for that moment, as an innocent animal is in the sights of a gun held by a man who wants to kill him or her, and the police holding unit, the PHU, it's cold interior, with its very own horrific smell, and the roads near the projects, deserted, broken only by the passing of cars that brought possible danger.

Chris fell to sleep, but it was not a peaceful escape from his worries as he journeyed down a tunnel of unpleasant intangible images played to a chorus of malevolent voices.

Alan Manville's face was broken into a smile that was so exaggerated it threatened to tear it apart. The make-up was so crudely applied it looked grotesque and clown-like. In fact he was a clown, and he was performing in a small tent, a tiny circus that was incredibly hot and full of gaudy colours with an overpowering smell of sawdust, sugar and sweat.

Manville spoke to the audience, which consisted mainly of children who were crammed into the tent. They were laughing hysterically at Manville as he clowned around; but then the whole scene changed and the feeling was completely different. Manville was now his normal self and he was talking to a studio audience on the set of The Offender's Nemesis.

Manville began to speak, 'Here's a particularly odious character - a man who hates his country so much he is involved in smuggling illegals into this land of ours with the purpose of blowing women and children apart as they go about their daily lives.'

The audience's anger shifts from jeering to stamping their feet and shouting. 'Well, it's lucky we got him in time,' Manville said as he nodded at a female presenter who was dressed more glamorously than usual. She was walking towards Chris, her big smile in place as she swayed her hips in an exaggerated manner. Chris looked around where he was standing, and jumped back in fright on realising he was on the stage. Alan Manville was grimacing at him and Chris looked at the audience who were going wild, noticing that some people were holding up posters with his face on them. Manville shouted over the noise at the audience, 'And you decide how we deal with him.'

The audience cheered and a chant of 'crush, crush, crush' thundered, so loud and deep Chris became deaf and his insides felt strangled, and then Chris woke up.

His heart was beating hard and his mouth was dry. It was another nightmare with scenes of horrific violence and cruelty. The dream of being an offender on the show The Offender's Nemesis was so real, yet obviously surreal. Chris found it difficult to breathe, and as he gradually relaxed, a massive weight came upon him that was filled with fear and despair. Trying to calm his breathing, Chris lay in the bed, next to his wife, the woman he loved and cared for so much, but his mind was being taken over by worry and obsession about his brother and the ways of system in which he lived in.

The next morning was taken up with driving his daughter to a club she belonged to which met on Sunday mornings - partly arranged and organised by the local schools, it was to do with artistic activities such as painting, drawing and putting on plays, but there was also a component that got young people involved in helping those in their communities who find it difficult to help themselves. Nina, being the way she was, wanted to be involved in developing a rescue centre for animals that have been abused and are homeless, this being the 'social' aspect to her club activities, but there was also her drawing, in which Chris believed she had a real talent. There are numerous clubs having different activities running in the evenings and weekends offering activities across the spectrum, although the fee to join them, even though not a great deal, excludes the poorer young people from being able to participate, and there is also a cultural ethos that sends out a message that the groups are aimed at the professional class and not those from poorer backgrounds. Chris had often thought how the children coming from middle class families, if one could still classify social strata in that way, are involved in more meaningful interests in that they can access activities having a personal stimulus with educational insights that further detaches them from the children coming from poorer backgrounds. The clubs and groups also perform the function of presenting a positive reflection on a young person's personal history, showing their interests, skills and experience when looking for a job in later life. Conversely, the poorer youngsters belong to clubs or organisations that are primarily to do with sport, although a limited range of sporting activities are on offer such as football, boxing and other combat sports. There are also the militaristic organisations, having ranks to aspire to not rising above sergeant, and other organisations such as the Anti-Crime Crusaders.

When Chris returned home after dropping Nina off at her club he spoke to Rosie about his dream, and again went over the events of the night before. They sat on the sofa, Rosie watching Chris carefully and patiently as he spoke, her eyes moistening and just as they were going to spill with tears she stopped Chris with the flat of her hand. 'Okay Chris, okay - stop it now,' she said.

Chris looked around the room, shaking his head, and looking at Rosie he said, 'And that show, that, sickening excuse of a show, TON, as they call it, giving a license to the bullies, the inadequate and the cowards out there to target people seen as weak, and different, because they're oh so scared of being singled out themselves...' but Rosie stopped him from continuing, placing her hand on the side of his face as she leant forward and gently kissed him. Chris looked from Rosie to around the room, his eyes settling on a photograph of the three of them, his family, Rosie, Nina and him, smiling at the camera; and Chris closed his eyes.

Fifteen

A couple of months later, as Chris was walking down a high street, he suddenly stopped on seeing a man sitting at a table next to the window in a café; the man's name was Paul. Chris had met him a few years earlier at a meditation class he had found out about one day when his attention was drawn to a piece of paper pinned to a tree. Details of the classes were written on it explaining how the meditation techniques used in the classes were influenced by an Eastern religion and philosophy. The classes were held in the house of an elderly lady called Kendra. In the days before the 'big change' she had travelled to the East many times, pursuing her interest in religion and philosophy. Chris saw her as a good woman who would have been considered cranky and eccentric by most people, and although he did not see her as sinister in any way, she did appear to have a cult-like status among some of the people who attended the meetings. They were her followers, and among them were some that believed Kendra had powers to heal, and Paul was one of those people.

He was a talented artist having his own ideas, but over the years had become increasingly out of step with all that was around him. Paul once told Chris he had never been involved with any campaigning organisation that had politically subversive inclinations or objectives, although his work was often critical of the authorities and what he saw as the inflexible will of the state. This was reflected in his paintings, which examined freedom and the possibilities of developing our potential capacities to pursue positive creativity. Paul was expelled from Art College for straying away from the official structure of the college's curriculum, as he found the set format constrained his inspired ideas and he confronted the college for what he saw as placing limitations on his art. It was a period of friction in Paul's life, and never accepting the situation it had left a lasting bitterness towards institutionalised thinking. Something that Paul was concerned with, and at times was quite vocal about, were the practices of the medical profession, which he saw as the major means used by the state to control its citizens. He said the medical profession, 'nullified through sedation,' and labelled and sectioned people whose behaviour or attitude challenged the system. Paul echoed the views of Kendra who believed the authorities have a vested interest in the drug companies and sanction the creation of drugs that are nothing more than a chemical cosh, which leaves patients profoundly stupefied and so too passive to respond to their situation. She maintained there is collusion between the companies and the establishment, and there are financial considerations before objectives to heal. When people want to cure themselves with alternative medicine and practices it is made unlawful and policies are passed to ban medicine even if it is harmless. She saw it as a condition of mass poisoning and social control. Kendra was not reticent in venting her views, which she did publicly.

Chris entered the café and joined Paul for a cup of coffee. Paul was pleased to see him and greeted Chris like a long lost friend. He told Chris how he would sit by the window watching life pass by, often with a piece of paper and a pencil, but never a pen, making small sketches of anything that came to his mind as he gazed through the window. The sketches were usually abstract and often surreal, sometimes depicting a slice of a person's time with a pencilled shadow of an expression as a passing person was immersed in matters weighing upon her or his mind. Paul would record it as evidence to the hidden emotions of our time. Yet, the drawings were not seen as important to Paul, they were merely doodles that were possibly peripheral to an evolving idea forming in his mind, which would manifest itself in a piece of art he was working on.

Paul told Chris that Kendra had died a couple of years ago, and Chris remembered she had been ill for a long time and her health was failing when he first met her. Paul believed Kendra was killed and was convinced she was murdered by agents working for the state because of her critical investigations into the major drug companies. Paul had once told Chris he saw himself as a disciple of Kendra's, and that his own experiences had strengthened his belief and support in what she stood for. Chris watched Paul as he spoke, the intensity of his feelings showing as the veins in his neck stood out, and his fingers toyed with a spoon in such an agitated manner that it eventually spun across the table. Paul sat back exhaling deeply, and Chris was reminded of his brother and of how he fidgeted nervously with things. Chris thought Paul seemed more restless since the last time he saw him and wondered if it was because he was becoming increasingly estranged and frustrated because of his marginal position in society, or maybe there had been things happening that had caused him to be so troubled, and then maybe it could be both.

Paul had been a patient in what is called a clinic for the treatment of psychiatric disorders and illnesses. There are many small clinics as well as large long-stay sanatoriums for chronic psychiatric illnesses, known as Healing Centres.

Not long after meeting Paul, he invited Chris to view an exhibition of his work. It was in a small room in the basement of a building that was once used by a large and well-known mechanical engineering company which had closed down and the local authority annexed the building. The offices are used by various council departments and rooms are hired out to societies that range from model railway enthusiasts to flower arranging. There are no government grants to subsidise the activities, so the person or the group organising it meets the cost of hiring the room. Paul had hired a room in a quiet corner, he did not advertise his exhibition, but relied on word of mouth to let people know it was on. Paul trusted Chris and told him of his experiences and of how the state is killing 'outsiders' with prescribed medication.

'They medicate until you are in no fit state to look after yourself, and then they section you - and then you've lost all your rights, because they cease to apply if a person is labelled as DF - dysfunctional - and then they increase the medication until you're dead.'

Paul's artwork reflected and symbolised what he had told Chris in unusual glimpses of an individual up against an all-pervading and absolute force. He had made his opinions known to those he came into contact with who work for the authorities, such as doctors and other people working in the medical profession.

Chris watched Paul as he spoke, and every now and then he looked around the small café they were sitting in, all the while wanting to tell Paul about Steven, and about his involvement in trying to help him, but it was difficult because the conversation was one-way traffic. It was barely a conversation at all, but just Paul venting, and then he told Chris how 'they' had taken his dog, a constant companion of Paul's. He asked Chris if he remembered her, which Chris thought as an odd thing to ask him because he had met the dog on numerous occasions. Paul called her Dee Dee, although her real name was Diana. She was a friendly dog and was made quite distinctive because she wore decorative collars Paul had made for her to wear. He told Paul that he remembered her and liked her very much. Paul watched Chris carefully as he told him and then said Dee Dee liked Chris because she knew he has, 'A kind soul - something humans are having drummed out of them.'

Talking about Dee Dee had quietened Paul as he told Chris that he was convinced the state had stolen her, and he became silent as he stared wistfully down at the table. Chris began to speak about Steven, telling him everything, the history of Steven, of his own feelings and concerns he had felt over the years and of how he got involved in trying to help Steven, the people he had met like Simon the health worker and the plan for Steven to flee the country and the meeting that did not take place. Paul listened intently, only interrupting Chris once to ask if he had ever met Steven. Chris told him he had not, but he had talked to him about him in the past.

'Don't ask too many questions, not when speaking to anyone working for or connected to the authorities,' Paul said, and he stared at Chris, his eyes burning as if sifting through pages telling of a history beset in fear and danger. He warned Chris about those involved with the underground movements and told him everything he did from now on has to be done after planning and with caution to the possibilities of an attack from the state. He told Chris that every act the state considers to be a misdemeanour is observed, graded to the level of threat it might pose and then ultimately dealt with, in the inimitable way the state does such things. Paul said, 'They are underhand, hypocritical and cruel - it's what empires have always been made of - and when will this promised time come when the lamb is to lie down with the lion? Not under any ruler, King or otherwise has it been true, and if we keep thinking in this way it never will - it's a conception of the leaders and the led that disempowers us and keeps us enslaved, mentally and often physically.'

Chris told Paul about his nightmares and of the obsession he was developing about Alan Manville and the show The Offender's Nemesis. He spoke to Paul of the power it has within society and of how depressing it is to see young people so fired up and delirious in wanting to see people tortured and killed in the most gruesome manner. Paul spoke about the show, of how it is an important tool for the state to maintain social control and the way in which it works at different levels.

'The language they use, for God's sake.' Paul said as he leant forward and looked directly into Chris's eyes. 'Crushing, smashing, battering, and it has connotations of being anarchic with words like destroy, eliminate, get rid of and eradicate, but it is directed inwardly, to repress, to flatten and squash - aggressive language of hate and fear, and as the offender is dehumanised, so too is the audience as their minds are desensitised to the violence and callousness by cartoons with comic strip language like, splatter, squish, kerump and kerunch. It has proven effective in exciting the audience and public, and especially children, it is real but not real, the bad man being beaten, it is only right that he should be, so why not make it fun - as long as we don't think what we're doing, we'll just continue with our free fall into the dark abyss.'

Chris left Paul sitting in the café, concerned for his welfare as he was for his own and his brother's; and the knot in his stomach was tightening its grip.

Sixteen

Nearly four weeks had passed since Chris had spoken to Paul in the café, and what Paul had said persuaded Chris to withdraw from his involvement with meeting dissidents and planning to get Steven out of the country. Chris thought how Rosie was right about it all, like she seemed to be about most things. He was powerless to do anything and he was likely to bring trouble upon his family, so he decided to get on with life and hope the authorities got on with targeting someone else who was actively raising his or her head above the parapet. It was just before Chris was going to take a lunch break that he received a phone call from Simon, Steven's health worker. He said that he knew it was about the time when Chris took his break and was wondering if he had some time to spare for a talk. Chris was unnerved by his call and told himself to remain resolute in not getting involved any further with anything to do with Simon, but he did ask him why he had not been in touch when X did not turn up at the shop. Simon told him in a cool manner that it was a matter out of his control and what they were doing is dangerous and X reported that he saw a person he knew was part of the state's security. He apologised to Chris and told him it is one of risks when operating in this way and these things do happen so do not expect things to run smoothly.

Chris told Simon he wanted to stay out of any business he had previously been pursuing, but Simon persisted in wanting to meet up with him, telling Chris he should not be afraid, as he had not done anything wrong, and they should meet up for a farewell chat and that will be the end of the matter. Chris yielded to Simon's wishes, his resolve was simply not strong enough to resist, and so he agreed to meet him in a café near to where he worked.

When Chris arrived at the café, Simon was already there, sitting at a table talking into his phone. Chris stopped for a moment and watched him, noticing his very businesslike manner, which was not what he felt a health worker should be like. Simon brought the conversation he was having on the phone to an abrupt end when seeing Chris approach his table and he stood up, the features in his face softening as he greeted Chris warmly, as if he was an old friend he had not seen for a while. As Chris was sitting down he repeated what he had told himself to say when meeting Simon, which was that he had only a few minutes to spare because he was very busy at work. Simon told him he understood and how he appreciated that Chris had made the effort to fit him in with his busy schedule.

After preliminary questions, which Simon asked in a polite and unobtrusive manner, about how Chris was, he quickly got on the subject of Steven and if he had seen him recently. Chris did not parry Simon's questions skilfully and found himself stumbling over his words as he hesitantly told him that he had seen Steven just the once, and he had made a decision not be involved in Steven's affairs. Chris knew he was showing signs of anxiety as he went on to tell Simon he was going to keep his distance, and after all he had his family to consider and he did not want to bring trouble to his home. All the while Simon nodded slowly in agreement to what Chris was saying, and just as Chris stopped speaking he said, 'Why do you think you are going to bring trouble to your family? Have you been speaking to anyone? Have you spoken to Steven about this? What did he tell you? Chris, we decided it was best not to talk to him about what we are doing.'

Chris did not say anything and Simon smiled as he said, 'Keep your nerve, and remember, the common language is Chinese whispers, so please don't believe everything you are told about other people, because it is simply not true.'

Simon was persistent, telling Chris it was normal to feel the way he did and he had only one attempt at meeting up with a contact who can organise an important piece of work. 'Some people spend years,' Simon went on, 'you can't give up after only having tried the once - that's ridiculous, and remember, you are doing this for Steven - we all are, that's my priority, and I have to take this route because my hands are tied if I try and give him the help he really needs in the orthodox manner through the course of my work, but I've built up connections with people over the years that can give that help - and they do, Chris, believe me they do,' and he looked into Chris's eyes as they averted to different points around him, as if searching for a convincing resolution to his predicament. Simon put his hand on Chris's arm and patted it lightly before giving his arm a supportive grip to reassure him, and as he did so a smile broke on his face, a smile that could have said I'm with you all the way, even though our journey is against the odds.

Simon told Chris about a man called Kim Blakely, and how one of his contacts has met Blakely on a personal level. Chris knew of Kim Blakely, he is a principal figure in the underground movement. Blakely is the central instigator and motivator for political campaigning, and has been credited with raising awareness to issues affecting the lives of people in society. His identity is a secret, it has to be and what Kim Blakely looked like, who he was and where he lives remain unknown. Simon also told Chris about a person he should meet up with called Roger Edgebury, a musician who lives away from town in the country who could be of great help to him, and that he should really go and see Bill Copley again, the man he has already met who lives on the housing project.

'These people will help us, Chris,' Simon said, 'and they can help Steven, so stick in there and don't back off now.'

Chris sat at the table not knowing what to think, becoming aware that he was nodding at what Simon was saying and that he had already stayed talking to him longer than he intended. He thought about what Steven had told him, and the manner in which he said it when they sat in that café area on the day Chris was supposed to meet X. It was going though his mind, and then he thought about why Simon had asked him if Steven had said anything about the meeting or anything else. He looked up and saw the look of 'trust me' was still on Simon's face. Chris started to speak, but not clearly or fluently, as he told Simon that Steven had asked for him to give his word to stop his involvement in what he is doing, and all the while as Chris spoke Simon gently nodded his head sympathetically. Simon waited patiently for Chris to finish speaking and then explained in a soft tone that Steven was a very intelligent man, but had found it difficult to socially interact and build a close relationship with another person, and over the years this has led him to be overly suspicious of others, even those who are trying to do him a good turn and help him.

'But don't worry,' Simon said, 'I don't take it personally, it is my job, at the end of the day, but I do get close to people, the people I like, I wouldn't be human if I didn't, right?'

Chris was slow to take the prompt and answer him, so Simon said it again and nodded to press a confirmative response from Chris, 'Right?' Chris found himself nodding without really considering what he was agreeing to, but that was enough for Simon to press further. 'That's right, that's right, I knew you would understand if it was explained to you - you're in a difficult position, what with the emotional attachment in this matter, your brother has always been a concern for, because you love him - right?'

Chris nodded again, this time aware of what he was agreeing to, although not want to be drawn in, he was struggling to fight it.

'You're a good man Chris,' Simon said, 'with honest intentions, and because of your honest heart you are open to manipulation and then self-doubt sets in, as it has now, but here's the thing Chris, you haven't been manipulated, it's just that you have no experience of what you're dealing with - and that's why you're confused, your openness can lend you to become exposed, and that can make you vulnerable, which you feel, so you then batten down the hatches, so to speak, in an effort to ward off scary and uncomfortable feelings with the hope of keeping away from danger.'

Chris nodded and looked around the café.

'How does Rosie get on with Steven, Chris?'

What Simon had said caused Chris to turn quickly and look at him.

Simon went on. Does Rosie get on with him? Do they, you know, as a brother and sister-in-law spend any time together? Have a coffee and a chat, that kind of thing.'

The question confused Chris, but he told him Rosie got on with Steven and they liked each other, although at times Steven was difficult to reach.

Simon watched Chris as he looked down at the table, noting his dilemma as if he were watching a film on a television screen, a film he had seen many times before, and for the first time since they had been speaking the concern in his eyes dropped as he looked down Chris's body, as if taking in his whole essence, everything Chris was as a person, and the look of concern in his eyes was replaced by one of coldness and contempt.

Seventeen

Chris began to walk across the green in the housing project as he had done over three months earlier when had come to meet X. Two weeks had passed since Chris met up with Simon in the café, and on this afternoon he received a phone call from him prompting Chris to meet up with Bill Copley that same day. Chris had not told Rosie he had met Simon in the café, and neither did he tell her where he was going when he left the house about an hour earlier.

It was early evening, and Chris thought back to the last time he had been there. The weather had changed, it was bright and a hint of sun was breaking through light clouds, so very different from the dark heaviness of a few months back, although that being said, even the sunniest sky could not lighten the spirit of a housing project. Chris remembered the two young boys playing on the mechanical horse and the fear he felt of one of the boys accusing him of being a paedophile, and he remembered their deep, gruff voices and the anger that showed in their faces. He looked over at the bleak concrete area that housed the three shops, and there was the horse, as if a symbol of hope in a world blighted by misery and despair. Chris thought about the old couple that worked in the shop and wondered if they were still there. A thought flashed through his mind to go over and check to see if they were, but he decided against it and continued walking across the green, thinking of the old couple, their faces and what their history might have been.

A sharp, powerful smell cut through all of Chris's senses and stopped him thinking of the old couple. It was thick, acrid tasting and Chris felt it was burning his eyes, but as soon as he heard chickens he knew what it was. Walking alone into a large housing project scared Chris, and even though Bill Copley told him he would be safe, it was not something someone like him should be doing.

He reached the end of the green, entered a block of nearby flats and started climbing the steps in a concrete stairwell that was open at the sides to the elements. By now he was finding it difficult to breathe without retching because of the bitter stench of chicken waste. The sweet smell of synthetic tobacco was evident, making the biting smell of urine all the more sickening and from various flats loud music of the type that is popular with youngsters blasted through closed and open windows. Chris stopped walking and looked at the door numbers in a panic as he realised he was in the wrong block. A youth of about fourteen came out of one of the flats and glared at him, his look and manner guarded and aggressive. Chris nodded and told him he was visiting a friend but had come to the wrong block of flats. The youth shrugged in a way that said it had nothing to do with him. Although not wanting to draw attention to himself, and it would be obvious to the youth he did not live in the project, Chris decided to ask him where the block he wanted was, and told him the name of it. The youth shrugged again, and having determined that Chris posed no danger he grunted something inaudible and nodded in the direction of the block next to them.

Chris walked down the steps, all the while uneasy and waiting for something to happen; but it did not. And so he climbed identical steps in an identical stairwell and thought that because there were no discernable features that differentiated the flats many people must go into the wrong block as he had done, even though he had been there before and it was not that long ago. On reaching the floor he wanted, Chris walked along a balcony that was crammed with chicken hutches at one end and at the other bicycles and what looked like children's toys dumped in a heap. The balcony was cramped and lottery tickets were strewn everywhere, causing Chris to think they looked like fallen leaves on the ground in a forest. Chris looked at the scene people saw when they look over their balcony and across the grassed area to the shops, and with it were the smells and having to go through the daily grind of existing in a confined space blighted with poverty and apprehension, and he contrasted it all with pleasurable sights that exist in an environment where wealthy people live, and the more he thought about it the more he felt it was all so wrong. A word, quite perversely, came to his mind; it was *joy*. Why on earth, he thought to himself, could he think of a word like that while standing where he was? 'The hopelessness felt by these people is to the delight of the state,' he said to himself, the words popping into his mind from seemingly nowhere. Chris thought about this as he stood on the balcony looking across a landscape that could only have been constructed by human beings.

A woman, who was probably in her thirties, came out of a flat and scuttled along the balcony. Chris noticed her eyes were like everybody's eyes that live in places like the one he was standing. They appeared dead of any emotion, yet hostility and suspicion resided beneath their aggressiveness, declaring the knowledge they were beaten, and Chris contemplated how the system could very easily be compared to a game show, with its rules of winners and losers, with these people being the losers while the winners are not seen, and although being part of the game they are the ones that make up the rules.

Chris knocked on the door of Bill Copley's flat and waited, and in those moments he knew what he was doing would probably get back to Steven.

Bill Copley answered the door. He was in his late thirties, his well-spoken accent having been dropped in order to fit in where he now lived. Bill paid little regard to household tidiness and his clothes were scruffy and worn, although Chris noted his clothing was part of a style many people in the underground movement wore, which was a mode of dress Chris did not wear; his clothing would be considered very bland and everyday.

Bill was friendly as he greeted Chris and took him into the living room where two men and a woman were sitting. Cups, glasses and bottles were scattered on a low table and over the carpet. There was a strong smell of cigarette smoke, but it was not the synthetic type. Chris was introduced to the people in the room, as he had never met them before, and offered a glass of wine, which he took and settled himself on the settee next to the woman.

When people such as the ones Chris was with in Bill's flat got together they would discuss politics, read articles, some of which they might have written themselves, which have been published in pamphlets and 'underground' journals, watch films and plan strategies for evangelising their ideas to bring about change in the system. Chris reminded himself that when he was in their company he was there to find help for his brother.

'We exist in a degenerated society', the woman said, 'where those in power, rather than guide and put in place policies to give examples for self-betterment, have conversely sought policies that limit opportunities for people to explore their initiative and imaginative development. The use of brutal, primitive customs and the values of immediacy is a tactic employed to distract from self and experience, and it is an old method that has been used throughout history.'

She went on to talk about how, just as the liberal management before the 'big change' had allowed crime to escalate, so too has the new regime, by sanctioning widespread violence. She believed social control is maintained by the use of fear and when people are scared they do not think rationally and that people have given up rights once fought for, such as freedom and choice, for the promise of safety and in doing so hand over power to the state to have control over their lives.

'The state deliberately prohibits a person to develop mindfulness,' she said, 'because a still mind is thoughtful, reflective and clear when looking at one's situation. The state has created a situation where the individual lives in confused disarray with no insight into what is causing her or his discontent, because when attempting to explore and understand that which is bringing about the discomfort in her or his life it seems distant and beyond their control - one becomes alienated from one's very self.'

A précis of the conversation that began to take place went like this. Any resistance to the state is eradicated by means of various approaches and methods deployed by the state, such as psychological approaches, which incorporate initiating covert operations that manipulate fake dissident groups that discredit well-intentioned people working to improve people's lives and fairness. The pseudo-groups that are constructed by the state will carry out bombings of innocent people in public places and indiscriminate assassinations to terrorise the population, and blame it on terrorists and illegal immigrants, which has the effect of causing public opinion to be set against people rebelling against state practice or showing resistance by not going along with the way of things.

Chris began to speak, talking about the show The Offender's Nemesis and how it plays an important part in the practice of social control, and that it is wrong to, as many do, just dismiss it as slapstick nonsense that feeds what the masses want. Chris spoke about the format of the show and how they have to keep it fresh and simple to grasp, while being something that can be watched with others and identified with. There are all the slogans, the inane songs and different characters that come along which are popular with men and women in the workplace and children in the school playground.

One of the men in the room spoke about how the use of crime and criminals has been used historically to maintain social control. 'Deviance can be seen as necessary because it performs a positive function in drawing the so-called ordinary members of society together and to judge themselves as normal in contrast to the deviant. Deviancy is used as a tool to control the populace, but when it gets out of control, such as the rate of crime rising too high, deviant behaviour becomes dysfunctional. It creates an imbalance, destroying stability in society as shared values, moral beliefs and collective sentiments are brought into question.'

They talked about how the public punishment of criminals and terrorists on shows like The Offender's Nemesis gives support to, and justifies, the new approach that replaced the courts, the prison, the rehabilitation programmes, the psychodynamic approaches and the community-led strategies. Crime is kept at the top of popular concerns, as it has been for years, because when controlled successfully it is a positive device for creating divisions within society, and maintenance of power for those making up the ruling elite.

Bill Copley led the conversation saying what The Offender's Nemesis is doing is not new at all. 'The state has regressed to former practices by employing medieval methods of punishments. The criminal is publicly castigated, humiliated and even killed, and people are encouraged to witness the act of revenge and retribution. It also performs the function of bringing the masses together, as it did in the village square, and in doing so accentuates community values and shared moral norms, as opposed to understanding and accepting the ethics and behaviour of the criminal and terrorist who are clearly seen as the enemy.'

They all discussed this, agreeing that such is the power and influence of The Offender's Nemesis that it has become the modern equivalent of the medieval village green or town square, in that it is a place where community ills are aired for public viewing, a setting where there is a public declaration of guilt, trial and punishment, and justice is seen to be done.

Bill Copley said, 'It is a return to a basic set up of personalising punishment, which means retribution that can be seen and is practiced in public, and just as it was in those medieval times it is today as fallacies are spread and innocent people are tried and punished to hide truths in order to protect and defend the interests of those that administer rule - they are providing this national village green, or town square.'

Bill went on to explain the different but interconnecting parts of the corporations and the company that makes The Offender's Nemesis and how it is controlled by the state. He went on to say how the directors of the corporations also occupy positions within the government and higher echelons of the state and that the show is made to make a profit for the company's owners. They discussed Alan Manville, his popularity and how he is a valued overseer of what have become the obtuse obsessions in society for poorer people. The people in the flat spoke of how the poor admire and trust Alan Manville because he is seen as ordinary and in touch with them. He carries the air of authority that many people have come to expect from a leader. Manville is fun, his persona is vibrant and it's good to be on his team because he is so obviously a winner, and not to be on his team is to be a loser. In tune with the ordinary people he will stand with the crowd and cheer and jeer, sharing their feelings and sentiments. He is seen as capable of being light-hearted, but also a heavyweight in that he will support the desires of the masses by performing acts like handing a petition on their behalf to political leaders. They spoke of how Manville is the voice of the people, it is a fact and it has been a successful ploy by the state to deceive the mass population with the use of a personality such as him. He is the quintessential man, and without any doubt whatsoever, has more trust and admiration than any political figure, but as one of the people in the room said, although he performs a machine-like function for the state, the state own him and when he becomes defective they will replace him with another model to perform the same function.

Chris became upset as they spoke about how the general public are apathetic to truth, regarding whether innocent people are being killed on The Offender's Nemesis.

'It's sick, and disgusting,' Chris said, 'and it's humiliating, and cruel - any positive, progressive and creative potential is reversed and abolished.'

Chris looked around at the people in the room and said, 'Killing innocent people - people like my poor brother - and they don't care, because they're so - they're so...'

'Scared,' Bill said, cutting in. 'They're scared Chris - they're all as scared as you are - they too are scared of having one of their brothers accused of something he had not done - but that hasn't happened Chris, so don't torture yourself.'

Chris looked down at the floor and the room fell silent as wine was poured and cigarettes were lit. One of the men spoke about how the 'offenders' on the show are little more than props and mere accessories, expendable resources in the process of putting the show together.

Chris shook his head despairingly as he said, 'And that one they have on the show, she's been on a while now - the fake dominatrix, people are just crazy about her.

One of the men in the room said, 'She is part of the control mechanism, it's an age-old strategy to use charismatic figures - take Manville for example, and this Mistress T, politicians don't have to bother trying to create some kind of character the public will connect with, it's easier and more successful to have constructed media personalities because the general public relate better towards them, for many reasons.'

He carried on, saying how many people will find the dominatrix character exciting and desire her sexually and enjoy seeing power demonstrated in a context where a sexual association is involved, however jokingly it might be presented, and that it is the state's objective to use sexual sublimation for purposes to control the mind.

'She is a dominant mistress who displays and wields power, having people at her disposal, at a mere whim her desires are enacted upon - creating a feeling of deference that isn't so much to do with respect, but fear, afraid of being told off for doing something wrong - it's simple and basic, it's childish, but it works, the little children are obedient - to some in different times she is a regal figure, to be worshipped and never questioned, but of course there is resentment, and it can show itself in different ways, to someone committing an act of cruelty on a person, or animal, unable to defend his or herself, vandalism, joining in with other to bait an 'offender' without caring if that person is guilty of what they have been accused of is immaterial, both the state and public get what they want, blind compliance and a sense of hurting that which is ruining their lives - but of course, it is all displaced.

'Subliminal feelings of wanting to be sexually dominated are toyed with and twisted, a state of sexually stimulated emotions becomes confused - where passivity and submissiveness are sublimated with political notions of strictness and order, to repress, suppress and subdue, and the language of the dominatrix is to crush, to squash, repel, stamp on - clients are told they are insignificant and worthless, an insect to be stepped on - the connection can me made to naughty little boys who must be punished in the "nanny knows best" culture existing in the public school echelons of society, and these yearnings have been disseminated more broadly across society - it's violent, there are roles to play, it is a sadomasochistic chaos, but it has proved to be very influential in conditioning and controlling the mass populace - they are tapping into sensory feelings, hidden emotions, to fuse enjoyment, comfort and personal pleasure within an individual and connect those things with cold, objective politics.'

They spoke again about The Offender's Nemesis being a successful strategy in the plan used to distract thoughts from one's reality of existence, and in this instance the sexual connotations that are being employed.

The man continued, 'This mistress caricature, and the others out there that tempt and tease and yet are unobtainable - innate urges, sex, aggression, these are repressed, yet the feelings of instinctual expression are felt, that is real, they are felt through the sublimation of these desires, therefore there is a real feeling of experiencing satisfaction, although the desires themselves have not actually been addressed, but only transferred by being satisfied through an expression that is appropriate and socially acceptable - but this leaves, in the unconscious, feelings of inadequacy and frustration.'

Chris said he had noticed that many people use language associated with chastising a naughty child and mentioned the incident he saw in the bar when the man said 'behave yourself,' and how the man it was said to reacted very aggressively saying, 'I'm not a child.'

The man who was speaking earler said, 'That man, Chris, as many others, resents feelings of repression, of being told what to do - "I'm not a child," it's evident what the meaning is, he resents being told to, "behave," being told he's naughty on a daily basis, by all the conflicting messages he receives through the media, of being spanked by nanny for any misbehaviour, little boys who are badly behaved get punished, and it's only right they do, because they deserve it, for being naughty, and this is what they are told on a daily basis, through the different arms of the media. This resentment resides just beneath the surface, it's always there, just under whatever façade a person presents in public, whatever character they are trying to pass themselves off as - grudgingly having to openly show consent to the demands and expectations made of them. People feel the pressure of having to conform, and all the while the feeling of dissatisfaction, frustration and anger rises to one's consciousness and is constantly hidden, but throughout it all a reoccurring impulse cannot lie dormant, and that is the atavistic desire for freedom, and it's confusing, and in order to achieve this sensation of freedom there exists an ever present feeling that there is something like a cocked gun residing deep inside one's self, and one's finger is itching to pull the trigger to blow away, and so obliterate, all that is self-confining, all that which keeps one from having one's liberty.'

The woman sitting next to Chris spoke about the 'psychology of social control,' and how The Offender's Nemesis has proved to be very successful in instilling fear by the use of punishment.

Chris said the public are obsessed by torture, punishment, inflicting pain and humiliation, and the women looked at him as she said, 'These practices satisfy and stimulate - truth has nothing to do with it. To control millions of people is no easy task, and no successful authority has retained its power by the club or bullet alone so other more persuasive methods are drawn upon, whether it be creating and implanting ideology that many people take up and feel part of, as in the case of religion or specific models of political thinking where segments of the population feel it relates to them and that they have a significant vested interest in the system, even though the whole model is a ruse created by the authorities to take them in, make them feel important and valued, and, crucially for the state, to create a division between different factions in the population, as is, or was the case with class interests.'

One of the men spoke about the use of language in the process of social control. 'Embedded in language is the meaning to our thoughts, thoughts we use in creating a notion of self - and although, especially in our present epoch, the state ridicules and undermines academic study of what is seen as the intangible and therefore irrelevant to the real needs in society, and strongly criticises those academic enquiries that went on before the 'big change', it utilises all scientific research into the mind for itself in order to maintain power, and use the of semantics plays a central role in achieving that.'

The discussion was moved on by one of the men who talked about the practice of what he called 'mentacide' and how it is worked upon on a daily process through a changing pattern of meaning, disseminated by means of the media, education and all other outlets of information that instil knowledge, values and language, primarily through the use of suggestion.

The same man went on, 'The will of the state to control the mind has always been a feature of power wanting to maintain its position of influence, some methods of attempting the art of mind persuasion have come and gone, some laughable, as in the case of certain devices and strategies, especially in the Victorian age with James Tilly and the Air Loom, but as easy as these might be to deride for their paranoia, it is a reality that the state employs various means to control the mind, and because of this, does that make the state schizophrenic? Are we run by psychotics? Indeed, is it the way for humans to be led by the mad sectors among them, those who despise good will and throughout history have to be forced to act in way that is fair and just - is it the sick, the greedy and the brutish who are the dominant apes that head the different colonies of the worlds we call nation states, and have developed politics as a so-called civilised response to base intentions and violent behaviour? Who knows?'

The man smiled at Chris, in a way as if he knew the answer even if Chris did not. He continued. 'The use of language to control the masses by persuading the mind to act upon a suggestion - it was well documented how techniques were used by those running cults and institutions and organisations presiding over a cult, but what about those strategies used by a government, employed by the state to serve its interests - we all live in a thing called a society that is nothing more than a cult, and embedded in the language used by the leader or leaders of a cult are the mind persuading messages and triggers that are employed to create the desired response for successful influence. Language lies at the core of controlling the masses, used in conjunction with physical coercion, working to prevent thought or resistance to the demands, wishes and dictates of the state or other powerful entities, and it is marbled through all fabric in society, from the obvious political acts of legislation to popular culture, because they are one and the same, both working to create the desired culture that produces passive and manipulative robots to obey the dominant wishes bestowed upon them.'

Chris felt the talking was seemingly endless, and had to admit he was relieved when Bill Copley asked him if he would like a cup of tea or coffee as he had hardly touched the wine he had been given. Chris watched Bill Copley leave the room and sat back on the settee listening to the voices in the room, to their tone, undulating with either force or complicity, but as to what they were actually saying, Chris had stopped paying attention.

Eighteen

Chris checked his watch - nearly three hours had passed since he had entered Bill Copley's flat. He should have driven, but decided to take public transport as he thought he would be drinking alcohol, which did not happen. Everyone in the room was as keen and fresh to talk about the state and society as when he entered. Chris knew Bill had contact with Simon and wanted to ask the others if they knew him and what they thought of him if they did, but then Chris decided not to bring it up.

Bill Copley read an article he had written, which had been published in one of the 'underground' pamphlets. Its subject was crime and how criminals and terrorists are a benefit to the people that run society. His article explored methods of maintaining the status quo and how there is a constructed facade called the government that is understood by the masses to be ruling the country, but is little more than an instrument serving the interests of people who have put them in place and hold the real power. Bill's view was that crime, or law and order, has been used to control society throughout history, although it differs in the ways it is done. From medieval times to liberal scientific thinking to what exists now, crime has had and continues to play an important function, in that it is used by the power elite for purposes of social control. One of the methods devised to control the populace has been the use of what is called 'moral panics,' a term that is not now in use.

Bill Copley read what he had written. 'In its modern context the various means of communication are saturated with the intent of the powers that be. A moral panic is created and demands a call for action against the specific social matter that is held responsible for destroying societal cohesiveness. A panic is whipped up as people feel their values, family, traditions and standards are under attack, and so will support measures to address the problem. Moral panics can be seen as a construction that is essentially created in order to gain the support of the populace for incoming regulations and polices that might lead to limiting personal freedom, but the restrictions are sold to the public as necessary for the general good of society. The process is presented as a model of good versus bad, yet its purpose is to do with social control.

'The sensationalist reporting of the threat to the moral fibre of society is a tactic that has always been employed by the power elite to retain control. Before the 'big change', high profile cases reported as the principal public enemies such as muggers, terrorists, paedophiles, drunken youths and racists, were splashed over the media and moral barricades were erected to defend the law-abiding public. The resultant outcome was that the majority, the innocent regular people, became the victims because of the implementation of increasingly stringent laws by the establishment to address the new menace intruding upon their lives. The laws were restrictive and the penalties for breaking them became so punitive, a social climate of fear developed among the law-abiding general public who shared the same moral and ethical beliefs. They felt isolated and personally threatened in their daily lives as they saw standards and their quality of life deteriorating, and they felt let down by the professionals, the government and other dominant agencies in society and saw the penalties inflicted upon them as so severe they were outrageously unreasonable.'

Bill Copley continued to read his article which questioned if things are any different in today's society with a system that is harsher, but believed to be more honest because people can see that direct action is used against a public menace. He said, 'There is less material wealth for the many in today's society, but it is seen as a sacrifice worth paying. When the present system was brought in it was described as a new democracy where the normal person has a say and can actually participate in dealing with criminals and those that destroy society. The general public believe they now have a voice and it is heard in a way it has never before. They revel in this sense of self-empowerment, feeling they are involved by the state in controlling crime, which is seen as the most important aspect that ruins their lives, and that their opinions are listened to by the state. The state agreed with their criticism of the professionals involved in education, the medical industry, social work and the legal system. The 'meddling', liberal bleeding hearts were seen as having been given too much power and they ruined society and the lives of people who lived in it by letting crime get out of control with their strategies, such as the psychodynamic approach that analysed the interrelationship of the offender, victim and society, but did not forget to carve themselves a nice salary and pension out of it all.'

Bill finished reading his article, which in essence said how it served the purposes of the higher elite to do away with the 'liberal progressives' and the justice system, for in reality it was just acting as a smokescreen to blind people from what actually exists. By successfully doing so it allowed those same individuals and their families, which make up the higher elite, to remain in power. A whole complex administrative order was, incredibly, wiped away and it then it was business as usual. In conclusion, Bill wrote that moral panics were, and are still, used as a mechanism of social control because they are a proven means to bring together the general populace through the use of fear to supposedly preserve cultural values from being destroyed by deviant groups.

A conversation began about how fear is used to maintain social control and to rouse people to fight and hate, and goad those people who would not readily support going to war and have deep convictions that lead them to seek an alternative if possible rather than engaging in killing and bloody revenge. They spoke of how people are threatened with imprisonment, branded a coward and as being selfish and unpatriotic while enjoying a way of life that has been provided for them and their children, yet they do not want to protect the country or their family from an enemy intent on destroying the country and killing their family or even enslaving them.

And once again, as it had done throughout the evening, the room became quiet as the group contemplated what had been said.

Finally, the woman said, 'But, the absurdity of the 'terrorist,' this mythological demon that threatens the substance of our society is so childish, it would be laughable if it did not evoke the blind response of faith to state measures of using violence that it does.'

One of the men spoke over the rim of his glass, the alcohol evidently showing in his mannerism. 'Well, the creation of myths is one thing, but having success in getting the masses to follow and believe the myths is another - religion is very successful at this - it demands blind faith in something that can be easily pulled into question for its inconsistencies, although not everyone believes in what they say they do, as is the case with people showing support to demands made by the state - there just isn't the complete compliance as the great body of media will want people to believe.'

The man stopped talking, realising the alcohol was making it difficult for him to articulate his thoughts. They then discussed the character Mistress T again, and her creation as another means within the methods to control and 'bludgeon' the minds of people with diverse messages and suggestions.

'She is a symbol having a status of superiority with the power to reward or punish,' the other man said, 'Yet, although people are constantly told they are free to act in any way they feel, if one acts in accordance with hierarchical dictates one is rewarded, act in a way, however small the deviation might be away from those dictates, and one is punished - and not only is it all perpetuated by the media and the other means the state has at its disposal, it is also, and crucially, enforced by the people themselves in their daily interpersonal relationships - they self-police themselves, through fear. It is an ongoing situation where there is the suspicion of others, of nations, terrorists and neighbours - things, threats, they are exaggerated in order to induce perpetual fear - indeed, the maintenance of fear, with the contradiction felt for the state and all it represents, which is, to love what you fear.'

Chris told the gathering in the room how the strategy of using the terrorist to bring what could be called the indigenous population together is felt predominately in the poorer areas, and is fuelled by the media and other strategies to keep the subject fresh in their minds.

Bill Copley said, 'It is a very successful method to create cohesion against an enemy and a sense of 'them and us. The only thing is - the terrorist does not exist, although they are very real in the minds of the people that the propaganda is aimed at. And to implement further the fear and hatred of the 'terrorist' there are bombings, which cause death and mutilation in the areas where ordinary people live. And that is real, except it is the state that has planted them. This thought could, and usually is, discarded as merely a conspiracy theory and a belief held by liars or the mentally ill.'

As the evening was winding, up Chris spoke about Kim Blakely and one of the men stopped putting on his jacket to explain in reverent tones how Kim Blakely's understating and insights are profound and that he works assiduously to enlighten people to their situation and hopefully, one day, bring about change. Chris then asked if anyone had actually met him, and one of them nodded with a respectful air towards Bill Copley, and Bill Copley told Chris in a rushed manner how he had spoken to him on a few occasions when he had attended meetings, which, by what Chris could make out were open only to the chosen few in the inner sanctum of the underground movement.

Chris left Bill Copley's flat with the three other people and shared a taxi caught near by, and although it was not mentioned it felt pretty obvious to Chris that they left together and caught a taxi for safety.

Chris was dropped off at a railway station and as he made his way home, he went over the events of the evening in his mind. There was a huge amount that was said, but there was also the mannerism of the people in the flat, and he stopped himself from going down a line of thinking how they were a bit phoney and just playing at it all. He thought about the colony for dissidents, which had been discussed and how one of the men had said it has a positive function for the state in having like-minded detesters in one place, and it also removes them from society. The man told Chris of how there are objectives within the colony to overthrow the state, although it will be a war of attrition, and 'great thinkers,' especially Kim Blakely, have laid intricate plans to bring this about.

Chris thought about 'the colony' and tried to imagine it, conjuring up images of what it was like, and for a second his imagination threw up dramatic images of scenes he had seen in a film when a ship had gone down and people were rescued and taken to a place where there were people welcoming them with outstretched arms and helping to dry land and safety. He thought of Steven, of him going to this place, a place where he would be safe in a land where there are progressive minded people who would not hound him for being who he is, but then maybe it would be nothing of the kind. It might turn out to be just a bland town and its ordinariness could be hugely disappointing as it shows in the faces of people going about their lives. Signs in shop windows are a little different, as is the language on advertisements, but the sounds of traffic and the effect of adversities of everyday living and routine are present, but it would be different, because there would not be the repression, the fear, and things like Alan Manville.

Chris stopped thinking about the colony and thought about the evening he had spent in Bill Copley's flat with the endless talking. He had to admit it was boring, the debating went round in circles and there was something about the people in that flat, something Chris did not like. They seemed to have an elitist opinion of themselves, and quite often when talking of the 'ordinary person' and of their behaviour and tastes it could easily be construed how they disliked them with as much disparaging regard as the state did.

He reminded himself that there are those people who are well intentioned, but are involved in a pastime that is worthless if hoping to make any political or social change, and also, which was worrying, there are those among them who are government spies; Chris did not want to go over it anymore, and his mind began to swim when thinking about it all.

Nineteen

It was early Saturday evening, Chris had finished some work he wanted to catch up on, and, as Rosie and Nina were out of the house, it was an opportune time to do it. Rosie had taken Nina to a musical with one of Nina's friends and her mother, and Chris's friend Brendan was away visiting a relative. Chris had received a veiled message from Simon, Steven's health worker, about arranging to see Roger Edgebury, the musician he had told him about earlier, and it was this that Chris was thinking about as he decided to leave his work and watch the television.

It had become a tradition for Saturday evenings on the television to be dominated by shows that are referred to as family entertainment, and Chris knew Manville's face would be appearing in more than one of the popular shows. Chris sat on the sofa, pressed the remote control and watched the television screen break into light and shapes, and sure enough there was Alan Manville interviewing a female model, who was also a singer and an actress in one of the popular soap shows. They were talking about crime and the young woman recited her script without intonation, reiterating the common theme, which was how all upright people have to be vigilant if they want to live in a country where they can walk the streets without fear and live their lives in peace. This is the sustained battle cry, as the young woman said, 'A place for decent people to live their lives freely and go about their business.'

Manville spoke to her as if she was a patient and he was the doctor. His voice and manner assumed the approach of a professional practitioner, fingering his chin as he concentrated on what she was saying, his face feigning expressions of sensitivity and interest as he considered the profundity of her insight. The young woman is contracted to one of Manville's companies after she won one of the long running contests on the talent show WOW! Which is organised by another of his companies.

Manville spoke in a quiet sober tone as he told the audience that it had been a 'real pleasure and inspiration' speaking to Bonita Doff, who is usually known as Doffy. He said, 'I would like to say that this is obviously a serious matter, and there are people who are mistaken, and I would say they are even snobs, who would be surprised to hear Doffy's cogent and intelligent understanding of crime, terrorism and how it effects us all. They would be surprised to learn that she also has the intellect and courage to stand up against crime by pledging her time and talent to travel on road shows and attend school galas – and indeed she will be appearing after the break on this week's edition of The Offender's Nemesis.'

The interview ended with Manville asking Bonita Doff when her new song was going to be released, and he congratulated her, saying how she deserved her success because she had worked so hard. The show ended with the titles draining down the screen and Doffy crumpled up in her chair with laughter at something Manville had said to her. Chris flicked through the few channels there were on offer, and without consciously doing so had returned to the first channel he was watching. The opening credits of The Offender's Nemesis appeared on the screen, which suddenly caused Chris to feel nauseous and anxious.

'You creatures of habit,' Manville said, his face staring out of the screen. It was a well known saying of his, and he followed it with another popular phrase he often said, 'You insatiable individuals,' and as he began to introduce the show Chris pressed the mute button on the remote control, silencing the chaotic noise from the room, and sitting there he suddenly felt very much alone as he stared down at the floor and contemplated 'life.' He then specifically thought about his own life, and a realisation came upon him that he was not lonely, but just helpless.

Having inadvertently pressed the mute button, the theme music of The Offender's Nemesis pulled Chris from his thoughts, and as the music faded a young woman's face filled the screen. With a beaming smile she spoke in a childish tone and simple metre as she told the viewers that evening's show was a 'special' in that it was concentrating on the history of different forms of punishment. It cut to Alan Manville pointing into the camera as he began to speak. 'Yes, yes indeed you good law abiding people of this great land - they knew how to put the heat on criminals all those years ago back in ancient Greece - a device of torture called the Brazen Bull, which was invented by a discerning man by the name of Perillos who came from Athens - it was a popular method of punishment - and one that resulted in death, ladies and gentlemen - the bull was made of brass, a hollow bull having a door on one side - the condemned offenders were put inside and a fire was lit underneath it, thereby heating the brass bull until it was so hot it literally roasted the criminals inside it to death, and the head of the bull was designed with a set of tubes inside it so as the offenders screamed in pain it sounded like the roars of an enraged bull,' and as he spoke, a cartoon depicting the brazen bull steaming with heat was shown on the screen, as usual in a childish style with words and the screams of the condemned coming from the bull's mouth appearing in bubbles.

A burst of music, lights and different cartoons followed as various presenters told the viewers what was on the show that night. It returned to Alan Manville who spoke about how punishment has always been popular with law abiding people as a deterrent, and then, adopting what was supposed to be a coy expression, he turned side on and looked into the camera as he said, 'But we just have a little more fun with them I guess.'

After telling the audience they were not going to be 'let down' or 'disappointed' with what was on offer that evening he clapped his hands and said it was time to get on with the show. Alan Manville adopted a posture and expression that said what he was going to say was important and meaningful; it was something he often did.

'Peine forte et dure, ladies and gentlemen - boys and girls - a method of torture where an offender who refused to comply would be subjected to having heavy stones placed upon his chest, and the weight increased until he confessed or otherwise - but if not, the weight got heavier and the offender was pressed to death,' and he nodded as he looked around the audience before continuing.

'Well I've been informed that Mistress T favours this type of punishment for one of the offenders we have on the show tonight - a form of torture used to extract confessions, or to the ultimate - which will certainly be the case tonight...'

The studio audience broke into cheering and chanting, but by waving his arms Manville quietened them to a level so he could just be heard as he shouted, 'Put them in the stocks? Not on this show - we give them more than that - because we want to give them more than that - we want to be amused,' and making a weak fist that was loosely clenched he began to shake it, 'but we also want revenge...'

The reaction of the studio audience made it impossible for him to continue as the building shook in an explosion of noise. The audience chanted and stamped their feet, and there was a competition between sections of the audience as some held up banners and shouted out for a specific torture, while others held up the faces of 'offenders' and chanted for a different punishment.

A male presenter's face appeared on the screen, his voice fighting to be heard above the noise in the studio, 'We are the original, we are the best - we are the longest running show of this kind - we deliver to you what you want, rather than telling you what is good or bad - because we know - we remember the time when folks like you were told what is good or bad for you - we ask no questions of you - why should we? Why should anyone? Because you haven't done anything wrong - look at yourselves in the studio monitors - go on, have a good look at how you are enjoying yourselves - give yourselves a big, rip-the-roof-off, cheer.'

The audience cheered wildly as the presenter was joined by a female presenter and they both smiled as they watched the audience shouting, laughing, shrieking and clapping, every now and then, when catching a person's eye, they nodded encouragement and pointed at a monitor for that person to look at him or herself.

When the audience began to settle, the male presenter mentioned an offender's name and a chant started up that grew in volume, 'Burn - burn,' they chanted as the presenter told them about the offender who was to be electrocuted on a future show by a celebrity who had been chosen by the public. He then told the audience that it was time to deal with, 'some liberals.' A mock religious setting had been constructed on the stage and the 'liberals' were cross-examined by different presenters and the audience gave their verdict while goading them to 'confess to their sins.' The presenters used words to describe them such as molluscs, ragworms, and lugworms. 'Squelch a slug,' a presenter shouted and the crowd went mad.

The 'trial' ended and the audience were told a 'suitable' punishment had been chosen for the 'liberals' which would happen shortly, but they were then incited to levels of greater excitement as the fate of an 'offender,' which had been previously decided by the 'viewer's choice,' was shown. A shot of an outside broadcast suddenly flashed on the screen, and then of another outside broadcast in a different location, where again the crowds were going wild, and then other parts of the country were shown and the word 'Nationwide' filled the screen.

The studio audience and the crowds at the outside broadcasts cheered and chanted in unison the 'offender's' name, 'Rudo - Rudo,' and held up placards with a man's face on them. He was accused of being a terrorist and a ghastly way of killing him had been thought up and approved by the viewers.

'You wanted it - you got it,' the presenter said as he pointed at the audience, 'Let's go to the fish shredder unit,' the presenter then made a show of laughing uncontrollably as he leant forward resting his hands on his knees, which evoked shrieks of excitement from the audience. As the shot switched from the studio to a grim looking factory, Chris changed channels, pressed the mute button and stared at the screen. He thought about the foreign sounding names the terrorists always have, and who Rudo really was, and of how the professionals never get beaten to death or sentenced to die in some hideous way. They are humiliated and forced to apologise, but a person who had once held a position in authority is never killed or savagely beaten. Chris thought it had possibly something to do with status, and although liberal professionals were held to account

136

and blamed for ruining the whole moral fabric of society, rank and the structure of power had to be maintained.

Chris returned to The Offender's Nemesis at a point where the 'ex-professionals' and 'liberals' were being humiliated. A women, an 'offender,' was reading from a piece of paper, 'Young violent criminals need a meaningful package of robust parenting skills because they need help…' but she did not get any further as two men dressed in protective clothing with their faces covered ran around the woman spraying her with hoses connected to what looked like an industrial spraying apparatus on their backs. Manville jumped out of the way and said, 'You were taking the pi…. lady – so you can have some of it back.'

The crowd responded predictably, screeching and stamping their feet as the woman fell to the floor and the men continued to spray her. Her humiliation was brought to an end as three men dressed as clowns appeared on the stage holding incredibly large multi-coloured broom handles with massive mop heads on the end of them. The men proceeded to 'mop' the woman along the floor and off the stage to a screeching accompaniment from the audience. The Offender's Nemesis broke for the commercials with a presenter telling the viewers if they miss the rest of the show they would regret it for the rest of their lives.

Chris looked down at his lap, at some paperwork he had been going through to do with his job, and he thought about what he actually did as a job, and then a sense feeling so powerful and out of his control began to fill his mind of how meaningless everything is, but he snapped himself out of that train of thought and shifted on the sofa in an effort to dispel the feelings his wandering thoughts had brought upon him.

He pressed the mute button and so released a jumble of sounds that immediately shattered the stillness of the room. The Offender's Nemesis returned and as the fanfare of music, noise, lights and spinning images faded, Alan Manville appeared on the screen with a look of serious concern before he began to speak. 'Oh, I have some bad news, I am very sorry to report to you dear audience, and of course our wonderfully loyal viewers - and it is loyalty, or disloyalty - the lack of loyalty, that is at the heart of what I have to tell you. 'Breaking the confidence of a friend is a bad enough thing, I'm sure you will agree, good people of this great land - but when that confidence is violating the rule of confidentiality, as set down by the Honourable - esteemed, she who is to be obeyed, Mistress T…'

The audience were so excited by knowing Mistress T was coming on they made such a noise Manville could not continue, and so he waited for them to settle down until attempting to speak. Smiling and shaking his head he said, 'Mistress T demands loyalty, a respect that goes beyond what one ordinarily understands - I am talking about a devotion one will pay for with one's life to serve her,' and again the noise from the audience interrupted him, and again he waited patiently before speaking, smiling as he looked around the audience.

'Loyalty is a precondition demanded from Mistress T's attendees, but one of them has spoken to the press and tried to sell a story about a matter of privacy in Mistress T's private and personal life - but, luckily the newspaper that the ungrateful thickhead tried to sell it to had the moral conviction to make this known - it was The Triumph, actually...'

The Triumph is a mainstream paper read by the masses, which is owned by the company that makes The Offender's Nemesis, and over the last couple of years Manville has increased his influence and position within the paper. Manville looked around different faces in the audience as if addressing them personally while speaking.

'And so 'we,' have told Mistress T - and guess what? She said she is going to deal with this disloyal attendee only the way she can - and we thought, but how is she going to do it, good people of this glorious land?'

The crowd began cheering and chanting different punishments and humiliations as Manville shouted above the noise, 'And just as we were wondering what his punishment was going to be we discovered something that changed the situation completely - good people, good people of this great land - yes we did - and listen to this.'

The audience quietened to hear what Manville was going to say as he struck a pose he thought was correct to deliver a serious piece of information. 'We have found, after a process of a thorough investigation using the most professional methods known in the world, that he had committed sex crimes against a young boy and threatened the boy to remain silent...'

Manville stopped as the audience began to stir, but before they became fully excited he hushed them with his hand, his expression becoming graver as he continued.

'The young boy, full of guilt and remorse - for what happened to him, and remember, he wasn't consenting to any of it, but was coerced by a grown man, who has the physical strength to overpower most grown men, let alone a helpless and scared young boy - and the boy, who shall remain anonymous to save his family even more pain than they have already suffered, took it upon his poor self to take his own life...'

Manville could not continue as the audience burst into a loud rage of shouting and chanting. As the noise in the studio began to dissipate, Manville raised his voice.

'So, alone in an alley, this young boy cut his wrists in an act to destroy the body which he felt was now rotten with evil...' and again the noise in the studio stopped him from continuing, and again as the noise began to lessen he shouted over it, 'This muscle-bound abomination of a real man might be able to bully and overpower a young boy, but let's see how he gets on with Mistress T - because I know this homo pervert will be no match, and will be screaming for mercy - but will he get it?' And the audience chanted back a resounding, 'No,' as the shot changed and there was Mistress T in her 'dungeon' staring and pouting into the camera.

Manville spoke, as he always does to the Mistress T character in a mock deferential tone. 'Mistress T, thank you for allowing us into your dungeon,' but there was no response from Mistress T as she stared acidly into the camera.

Manville continued, 'May I ask a question to how you feel about the news of this attendee of yours Mistress T?'

Mistress T paused before answering. 'You may, I permit that allowance.'

'You must be very disappointed, my gracious superior?' Manville enquired in a fawning act.

She glowered into the camera before answering, 'I'm not disappointed, because I do not invest that much interest or trust in lowly men who are at my call of duty.'

The audience laughed as she paused before continuing. ' I expect nothing else - they are, just as he proved himself to be, utterly unworthy, and in this case sexually depraved. It is only strict discipline that makes them behave,' and she narrowed her eyes, 'but it was more than just discipline for this human maggot - the penalty has been exacted and the miscreant was fortunate to have his worthless life squeezed out of him by an uncompromising mistress, who, of course because her divine beauty, attracts the lustful gazes of craven men - lowly men like you Alan!'

Manville jumped back in shock at what she said, and the audience loved it, chanting her name over and over again as they were always on the side of Mistress T when she and Alan Manville talked to each other.

She went on. 'Although they desire her allurement, she, and all women like her, remain totally unattainable to them and will be for ever beyond their grasping hands - as all women should be if they decide that is to be the case.'

The audience responded with laughter, although there was some dissension to what she had said, which caused Manville to turn towards the audience in a great theatrical gesture and say, 'What? You dare doubt the word of Mistress T?'

This brought more laughter from the audience and Manville asked Mistress T what she thought of those in the audience who objected to what she had said. She arched one eyebrow before saying, 'They are only males who protest, and the female race know how to deal with protesting little men,' and pointed her finger downwards. The camera slowly followed the direction of where she was pointing, taking in her body as it did so, and finally settled on a close up of her high heel. She twisted her heel into the carpet, 'Grind the maggots into the ground,' she said, and there was a close up shot on her face wearing a satisfied expression that broke into a cruel smile.

It returned to the studio where Manville was marching across the stage 'Oh dear –she, who must be obeyed, has acted swiftly on this one - too swiftly I'm afraid, dear audience and viewers, for us to witness the push up perv get his just deserts, because it seems she has already dealt with him.'

He stopped walking and turned to the audience in a brisk manner.

'Okay , let us get this show moving here and ask our favourite mistress what happened to the despicable sex fiend,' and he looked up at a screen, 'Please, Mistress T, what do you mean his worthless life was squeezed out of him? And who is the uncompromising mistress you talk of?

Mistress T appeared on the screen, and the camera pulled back to show her standing over a dead body covered by a drape. Looking contemptuously down at the body she said, 'There's plenty more men around - and let's hope the next one doesn't try to deceive me, because they all get found out,' and closing her eyes she said slowly, 'and dealt with.'

'Wow,' Manville said excitedly, 'tell me more, please explain Mistress.'

Mistress T looked into the camera a few seconds before speaking, 'The mistress who administered the penalty was Thunder Thighs.'

The camera pulled back revealing a very muscular woman in a skimpy bikini standing over the body, a sign appeared on the screen above the body with the words Dead Perv.

'Well done Thunder Thighs,' Mistress T said, 'I'm proud to have you as my playmate, well done for demonstrating what real power is,' and Thunder thighs went through a routine of flexing her muscles.

'But, how did she do it, Mistress?' Manville asked, struggling to get his words out, and Mistress T raised her eyes and nodded at the muscular woman. There was a close up of her thighs and the muscles showing clearly as she tensed them and squeezed her legs together.

Mistress T said, 'His neck broke like a stick of candy in a vice – and he squealed like a puppy dog.' She showed her perfect teeth as she nearly laughed.

'Oh wow oh wow oh wow', Manville said as he shrank backwards in awe, 'Thunder Thighs has been doing some serious squeezing,' and the audience broke into a repeated chant of 'squeeze, squeeze.'

'Cripes,' Manville said, biting his fingers in mock fear, 'if that's how they deal with someone they know in Mistress T's dungeon, what chance has anyone else got? He then dropped his act and broke into laughter as looked around the audience, randomly pointing at people and nodding in a gesture to incite their excitement.

'What a way to go,' flashed on and off the screen as it showed Thunder Thighs tensing her muscles and Manville shouted over the noise of the audience, 'We will paying another visit to Mistress T later in the show - wow oh wow oh wow - just how lucky are you good people out there? With the People's Pleasure Corporation at your beck and call it's just one big round of treats - pleasures for you to indulge in for your amusement - remember you lucky people, you've never had it this good – and, after the break, you will be seeing more of what makes you feel good from the dedicated team here on The Offender's Nemesis - catch you in two,' and as Manville was speaking the different faces of the show's presenters revolved around the screen. The studio audience chanted with Manville, 'catch you in two,' as it has become another popular catchphrase of his.

The Offender's Nemesis disappeared from the room in a trail of highly charged noise, and again Chris looked down at the notes on his lap, and then up at the clock checking the time to see when Rosie and Nina will be home, but there was something else on his mind, he felt there was a feeling deep inside him, it was like a timer, and it was ticking off time until some awful event was going to take place.

Twenty

The Offender's Nemesis returned with all its frenetic noise and fast cutting images. Chris muted the sound, his mind was elsewhere as he thought about Paul the artist and some of the things Paul had said to him, not only when he met him in the café, but from before when he first met him. The way he spoke about the 'system' with it's sinister conspiracies reminded him very much of his brother Steven. He used the same language, especially when talking about mental health and how it is used by the state to maintain social control by 'eliminating' anyone who is seen as a possible threat by stigmatising them as mentally ill and in need of 'treatment.'

Chris pulled away from his thoughts and looked at the clock, again, thinking of when Rosie and Nina will be returning, and he became conscious of how the stillness of the room was broken by the flashing lights and shadows spraying from the television screen. He pressed the button on the remote control and by doing so released the hard aggressive sounds into what was a peaceful and private space. Alan Manville was speaking, addressing the studio audience and viewers with a smile that stretched the corners of his mouth, 'Let's see how our killer burglar is getting on - as we know, he fancies himself as a bit of a hard man - he beat up a women in her house, which he was burgling, and he beat her so badly she died of her injuries - and we've been told he boasted how he how could have gone to the top in boxing - so, we gave the champ some boxing gloves and asked him to show us just how good he is at using them.'

The audience were too slow to respond as they gradually stirred to what might actually happen and a chant broke out that quickly gained momentum, 'beat him, beat him, beat him, beat him,' but Manville stopped their chanting by raising his hand and shaking his head, 'No, no - no - good and orderly people - no.' He waited for the audience to quieten before speaking. 'Lets watch this champ of chumps as he shows us his skills with the boxing gloves - is he going to entertain us with his hard punching?' Raising his voice Manville shouted, 'Or is he going to turn out to be a bloater floater.'

A curtain opened behind Alan Manville revealing a large clear tank half full of water, and standing on a cherry picker above the tank was a young man dressed in boxing shorts, boots and gloves being held between two masked men. The audience began to clap and the camera showed a small group of children holding up cards with the face of the 'offender' on them. Alan Manville explained to the audience and viewers how the water in the tank would start to rise when the young man was put into it, and continue to rise until it was full.

'The big problem for our champ,' Manville went on, 'is that a lid is going to be put onto the top of the tank and locked - and as mister woman killer thinks himself such a big shot by breaking into people's homes, let's see if he can unlock the bolt keeping the lid tight on the tank and break out of that.'

Manville had to shout to finish what he was saying, 'Because we have been considerate enough to place the key of the lock on a hook hanging from inside the lid for him to do so - only problem for woman killer, is those darn boxing gloves - will he fumble and float ladies and gentlemen? Let's get right on with it and find out.'

The audience went into hysterics, with the usual scenes and images picked out by the camera, and their shouting became louder as the young man struggled with the two men as he was pushed into the tank. Almost immediately a lid was lowered onto the tank and the young man stood up, showing the water was up to his chest. Another presenter explained how the lock on the lid is locked from the outside, but can be opened from the inside. The same presenter then introduced a man and woman who had won the opportunity to lock the lid onto the tank. 'Let's meet the lucky couple,' he said as a man and women in their thirties walked onto the set.

'You didn't know what you would be doing to your offender, but are you pleased with what you've got to do?'

The couple nodded greedily, the man more enthusiastically than the woman, and he told the presenter how they could not believe their luck and that it was definitely something they would be telling their grandchildren. The woman added how the 'offender' deserved, 'everything he was getting - and more,' which brought loud cheering from the audience. Alan Manville appeared at the side of the stage with a young woman holding a cushion that had a key on the top of it. She is a known celebrity and very popular with many people in the audience who chanted her name and she responded by smiling and waving her free hand at them.

Alan Manville said, 'If I might intrude here and ask the lucky couple to take the key from our gorgeous guest,' and the young woman walked towards the couple holding the cushion out in front of her.

'It's an absolute privilege,' the man said as he took the key from the cushion and the young woman gave a little curtsy and showed her brilliant white teeth. Alan Manville said of the young woman, 'There she is ladies and gentlemen - she hasn't only got great looks and talent, she's got poise and good manners - but we have something to do here, although it's hard to stop looking at our beautiful guest, we have to lock down the lid and see if the light fingered killer is all thumbs and gloves when trying to open the lock.'

The man and woman stepped onto the platform of the cherry picker and waved at the audience as it as raised to a height where they could lock the lid onto the tank, and as this was happening the young man in the tank became aware that the water was beginning to rise and he began to frantically climb a little ladder inside the tank in an effort to get out of it. The man and woman both held the key and turned it in the lock together, and the audience went into a high state of delirium at the sight of the young man struggling to get out. It was at this point Chris pressed the first button his finger came into contact with on the remote control to steer him away from what he was watching.

Chris was aware of his heart pounding and that his mouth was dry, and a terrible thought flashed through his mind; was his physical response because of fear or excitement? He did not dwell on the thought and took a deep breath, but had to shake his head to remove an image of the young man struggling in the water as he tried desperately, and inevitably in vain, to turn the key in the lock while wearing the boxing gloves. He thought about how it was beyond reason or justification, but then was it? As sick, depraved and cruel as it obviously was, the spectacle of suffering satisfied and controlled a scared populace. Chris thought about the measures used by the state, and those in authority throughout history to maintain an order that benefited their aims and remembered what was said when he was in Bill Copley's flat. His breathing had returned to normal, and he would never be able to explain to anyone else or himself why he pressed the button on the remote control to take him back to The Offender's Nemesis, but instantaneously he pressed another button as the sight of the young man's lifeless body floating in the tank was showing on the screen. Chris stared at the wall in front of him, and feeling an irrepressible tension fill his chest, neck and throat, he was beset with an awareness of utter helplessness and that all efforts were feeble in opposing the system and way of things.

And yet again Chris pressed the button on the remote control, and in doing so realised he was consciously inviting what he saw as the punishment, which is The Offender's Nemesis, into his living room. The scene showing on the screen was chaotic and noisy. The lid had been taken off the tank and Chris looked away as the camera shot closed in on the body of the young man floating on the water. Cartoons relating to the method in which the young man was killed rushed across the screen, one of which prompted the audience to chant, 'bloater floater, bloater floater.'

The wild scenes of excitement and emotion in the studio looked perilously close to breaking out into a riot and getting out of control as the armed guards moved towards some sections of the audience. The camera suddenly zoomed in on a man in the audience who had lost control and was lashing out with his feet and arms as he rolled about on the floor. One of the guards threw a net over him and with the assistance of two other guards they started to drag him away, but as they did so some people shouted at the man while there were others kicking and hitting him with their placards, but the man was saved by guards who ran to the scene brandishing clubs and pushed them away.

The presenter pointed over to where the disturbance was happening and said, 'Now, now - come on good people - we're all friends here - just because he got over excited there's no need for that.'

Alan Manville appeared on the stage in what seemed to be an unplanned entrance to placate the audience. Standing with his hands on his hips he appealed to them with a broad smile on his face. 'Okay, okay, now - wondrous people of this beautiful land where freedom is our greatest privilege - let's show the loving families watching the show in their cosy homes how decent happy people behave when they're having a good time - eh? Now come on now, everybody give the person next to them a big hug, and join together to give a big hate towards a sex pest you have seen before and given your feelings about.'

The camera swung around parts of the audience, showing people hugging one another and laughing. Manville was pleased with how the audience were responding and he pointed at them in a mock reprimanding manner as he said, 'And be careful, well intentioned people, because I know just the person who will correct any misdemeanours,' and there was laughter as Manville pointed up at a big screen showing Mistress T glaring out at them.

'That's right - my champion chums, it is she, the most powerful of priestesses - and if I may remind you what I just said, when you were all too caught up in loving each other with your hugs and all that kind of malarkey - what I did say, good and honest people, is let us join together and turn some of that friendliness into good old fashioned hate for the sex pest we have already met, and see what our imperial, all conquering, she who must be obeyed, the mightiest and most magnificent, Mistress T has got to say before giving her orders on what to do with the waste of human chemicals who has lived his life slyly waiting for an opportunity to sexually molest young girls.'

The audience cheered and clapped in time as they chanted 'Mistress T.'

Alan Manville watched them, nodding his head with a smug smile, and as they began to settle he pointed up at the screen and said, 'If we may please, oh so benevolent Mistress, can we inquire if you have decided upon a fitting punishment for this dangerous pest?'

Mistress T took a while before answering while continuing to glare out of the screen before finally arching one eyebrow, which is a characteristic of hers, before speaking.

'Oh, hello Alan, why aren't you on your knees when you address me?'

'Sorry Mistress T, sorry - please forgive me,' Manville said as he dropped down to his knees with an over-ingratiating movement, and the audience loved it, responding to the sight of Manville acting in such a way they cheered and chanted her name.

'Good' Mistress T said, - 'then I shall begin - I intended to try out various appliances of torture until the pervert is finally released from this life - one being the toe wedge, and then the head crusher, and then left to rot in the hanging cage.'

The camera zoomed in on her face as she spoke and the audience cheered at every pause and facial gesture she made. 'But it has been brought to my attention that this mutant has been guilty of committing another sneaky act.'

Manville nodded, and keeping up the act of servility he remained on his knees as he spoke. 'He has indeed Mistress T, oh pre-eminent one who is to be obeyed - the offender stole food from an old person's home where he worked as a kitchen worker, but not just a little bit of food - oh no, he had set up a racket where he had built up a large stock of stolen food which he sold on, and in the process had made himself a lot of money, while the old folks went without...'

The audience interrupted Manville with booing and jeering for a while before he could continue. 'And, this isn't the first time the offender has stolen from people, as a youth he was a repeat offender and spent a few spells in a correction facility for criminal sociopaths...'

Manville was interrupted again, but this time by Mistress T. 'Silence! I have heard enough,' she said.

The audience broke into excited noise and chanted her name, but only briefly as they hushed themselves so they could hear what she was going to say. Mistress T went on to explain how she had chosen a punishment that would be suitable for the 'offender.'

It is common for Mistress T to select a torture or punishment that is related to the supposed crimes the 'offenders' have committed, for example, if guilty of stealing a car the punishment will involve cars in some way.

146

'Show me this cretinous excuse for a man,' she said, and Alan Manville obliged by obsequiously pointing at a screen, saying, 'This, Mistress, is the inexcusable human sewer rat.'

An incredibly thin man was standing in what looked like a cell staring up at the camera with a fevered look in his eyes showing how frightened he was. His only clothes were a pair of grubby shorts, which emphasised his emaciated body and so accentuated his weak and powerless state.

The shot changed to Mistress T in her 'dungeon' standing in front of her 'throne.' She sneered, 'He obviously didn't eat much of the food he had stolen - what a pathetic, skinny runt of a man - he is just too vile to look at and too disgusting for a supreme mistress as myself to cast my superior gaze at - but if he likes food so much, then let him eat - until he can eat no more...'

The audience stirred, chanting and cheering as they anticipated what punishment had been thought up, but quickly became quiet as Mistress T wanted to speak.

'Just as he stuffed food away to sell, let us aid him in stuffing food into his mouth - his punishment is forced feeding - as in the process of producing foie gras, where tubes and pipes are rammed into the mouths and down the throats of ducks or geese and grain and fat is pumped and forced into the stomachs of the unfortunate animals, swelling their liver to ten times its normal size - the animals will tear out their own feathers and kill one another in a desperate effort to escape the hell they live in - and as the animals are innocent, this offender is guilty, making the penalty he will receive just and correct...'

The studio audience began to cheer and chant and there was a quick flash around the outside broadcasts throughout the country showing scenes of wild excitement before returning to Mistress T's 'dungeon.'

'Strap him down,' she said contemptuously – 'force fat and grain through a pipe down his throat until his stomach is so bloated and swollen it is ready to burst, and then apply weight onto the swelling stomach to increase the pain - the weight of a person,' and she plonked down heavily on her cushion covered throne. 'Sit on the loser,' she said as a torn smile appeared on her face.

Manville staggered backwards as he spoke, 'Wow oh wow oh wow - sweet and dearest mistress - you never fail us, such is your greatness, and what you are saying is similar to the water torture Mistress T, if you don't mind me saying - the water torture is where the offender is bound with wire and rags are stuffed in his mouth, a tube is inserted in the nose through which water is poured until the stomach is fully bloated, and then someone beats the stomach until the lining bursts - and death will surely follow - divine Mistress, and wonderful people of this great land,' but he stopped speaking on seeing Mistress T beckoning him with her finger.

'You were not listening attentively to what I was saying,' she said, 'but then, you are only a man - I said, sit, on the loser - and as for you, and other male pests who don't pay heed to my demands - I crush them under my heel,' she hissed, and, widening her eyes, licked her lips lasciviously.

Chris pressed a button on the remote control, having had enough of watching the show, but then quickly pressed another button to escape the barrage of noise that hit the room because the channel he had chosen was some kind of game show with hysterical shouting and blasting sounds. He flipped from a documentary about pigeons to news programmes dominated with wars and social disruption happening in lands abroad, and then, deciding enough was enough, he turned the television off and watched the company logo wave goodbye as it disappeared into the middle of the darkening screen.

Chris sat in the silence, but his mind could not adjust to his quiet surroundings and relax. He was deeply troubled as he went over the problems he faced and the anxieties he felt for his family. The ringtone of one of his mobile phones only caused him to feel gloomier. It was the phone he used only for contact with Simon, Steven's health worker. Simon told Chris to change the chip in it every two weeks as a precaution against it being monitored, although Chris was unsure how effective it would be. Chris listened carefully as Simon told him about Roger Edgebury, the musician who lives in the country, the man he had spoken about over a month earlier. Simon gave Chris a number for him to ring to arrange with Roger a time to meet up.

Chris found himself nodding and going along with what Simon was saying, and all the while his brother's face was clear in his mind, shaking his head in despair at what Chris was doing.

Twenty-One

As Chris walked through the main gate of the college where he worked, he saw bunting that reminded him there was to be an exhibition in the afternoon organised by local school kids who are part of the ACC. A large banner had been unfolded in the car park with the letters CTC on it, which is an abbreviation for Crush The Criminals. Chris read a leaflet that was handed to him by a boy of about eleven years of age, which explained how the exhibition was part of an anti-crime week initiative. Chris looked into the boy's face and thought his expression and manner could easily have been that of a man in his mid-fifties.

Chris looked from the boy to some members of the staff, and noticed how they were acting and speaking in an excited manner with the children about the exhibition, and he felt it was surreal, except it was real. A sudden panic filled him and he tried to relax, but the anxiety he was feeling was inflamed by an upsetting dream he had during the night that seemed so very real, and he knew the dull feeling left by dreams that were disturbing would stay with him during the whole day. He had been having the dreams more frequently and stopped telling Rosie about them because he knew it worried her. Some of the more daunting dreams were of Chris on the show The Offender's Nemesis with the presenters ridiculing him, but it was always Alan Manville who had a central role in the scenarios. In some of the dreams it was vague, and it was like he was a bystander to what was happening, but then it all suddenly changes and he is an offender.

During the previous night Chris had woken in a panic with his heart racing as Alan Manville was mocking him and provoking the audience to a heightened state of excitement. The female presenter, Colette, had also appeared, just as she does in the show, flirting girlishly with the camera, yet a hard personality resided, cold and unmoving, beneath the smiley-girl persona she presented. Chris averted his thoughts, thinking he had arranged to meet Simon after work that day, but it was a thought that did not bring him much relief.

At lunchtime, a man in his fifties who was a tutor in the Science and Technology department came up to Chris in the refectory, and the anxiety he had been feeling all morning was exacerbated by what the man told him. Although Steven was careful to be guarded about his beliefs and activities while at the college, it did not come as a shock to Chris when learning he did drift from the syllabus to expound his own theories to the students. The man was only too pleased to tell Chris about it, and although attacking what he wanted to say with relish, he maintained an air of regarding Chris with suspicion as he spoke.

The man's opening line was, 'I hear your brother gave a lecture to a class of students yesterday about the history of crime and society? I don't think it was what they had in their syllabus.'

The man said that the students were confused by the way Steven had spoken about the 'state' and 'control.' Chris did not want to talk to him about it and tried to change the subject, but the man did not let it rest and went on to say how two of the students had given him written details of what Steven had said.

'And, as poorly as it was written,' the man said, 'it was a clear account of what your brother thinks and how he is not afraid to push his warped views onto young people who are not here to listen to them, but rather to gain the necessary qualifications that will enable them to secure a good future for themselves.'

Chris thought about what the man said and the way he said it, thinking how ridiculous it was, as the qualifications the students got from attending the course Steven taught on were worthless if a young person thought they could use them to gain employment above basic unskilled work. Chris did not say what he thinking, and he had to hide the fear he was feeling from hearing what had happened. The man leant forward in his chair as he spoke, his eagerness to tell Chris showing in his eyes and he was baring his small teeth, the lower ones were dark brown and filled with the food he had recently eaten.

'He told the class how the present "state," in its aim to deal with the immense amount of crime, had redeployed a version of the Poor Laws that were brought in over four hundred years ago because the use of incarceration, severe punishments and the death penalty for minor misdemeanours failed to control rising crime. He lectured them on how The Poor Laws regulated travel and limited a person's freedom as it stipulated that poor people had to stay within their parishes - and how some of the poor were deemed deserving, while those who broke the law were brutally punished and branded with a mark that would identify the person if he or she wandered from their parish.'

The man stared at Chris, as if waiting for him to respond to what he had just said, but Chris did not say anything, he just looked at the man, conscious he was nodding very slightly.

The man continued with increasing fervour. 'Oh yes, his views, as twisted as they might be, are scathing about our society as he preached about crime and punishment and relating what happened hundreds of years ago to today - going on about how the public are drawn together as

150

one to view the punishment of criminals on television, just like they did in the village green,' and the man stopped talking as he adjusted his seating position before continuing, 'Yes, he has very strong opinions - with ideas about the "state" and how they have "created the terrorist," as a means to control the masses while ingraining a false sense in their minds that justice has been done and it is all for the good and protection of law-abiding people in society.'

The man carried on speaking, but Chris was not listening, he was thinking about what he had just said, about the village green and witnessing punishments, it was exactly what he had heard round Bill Copley's flat, and he wondered if Steven knew any of those people personally.

The man began to talk about how things are much better nowadays, primarily because people can act with confidence against louts without fear of the government prosecuting them, and also in the knowledge the authorities will protect them if the louts take any reprisals against them. He pressed this point, saying how the behaviour of louts was the main concern for the average person, especially for those who live in certain areas, and pushing his face close to Chris's he said. 'You see, the tables have now turned - where before the young savages were aware they had power in numbers - a gang of say, fifteen twelve and thirteen year olds knew by making a mass combined attack using knives and bats they could easily overpower any adult male, and beat him to death - and then jump all over the remains - there were no consequences.

'Although years before that, there was respect in society, and people knew they had to hold back and not step over a line that takes us into the abyss. When an adult said something to a young person, it was listened to, but all that changed - the thugs had nothing to fear because the authorities did nothing and the savages learned from a culture steeped in cowardice. But now that's changed.'

He stared at Chris in a way that made him feel the man was holding him responsible for the decline of society and all the violent acts that were committed. Chris resisted the temptation to talk and nodded at the man in the hope he would say his piece and go away; but he had not finished. The man eyed Chris closely and said, 'Have you ever had a person very close to you, like a brother or sister, or your mother - or maybe your spouse or a girlfriend, who was beaten and robbed - or even worse, sexually abused and killed?'

Chris shook his head slowly.

'Well, what do you think that is like, then? The man asked Chris.

Chris looked down sombrely at the table they were sitting at.

'Eh?' The man went on, nodding his head at Chris trying to elicit an answer.

'No, I haven't. I'm very lucky,' Chris said.

This satisfied the man, and he leant back in his seat releasing pent up breath. He looked at Chris for a few seconds before continuing. 'The ridiculous nonsense spoken in the past by those working for the authorities was created for their own interests and not for the normal person. As I said, they - *we*, did not have any protection and were criminalised if we wanted to stand up against the louts.'

The man looked at Chris. 'It was terrible,' he said, with strong emotion, and went on to say the louts maimed, stole and killed while the system handed out petty sentences that were laughed at.

'But, that has now all changed,' he said, and his stare grew in intensity, 'Because *now*, people - like women who might be working in a shop, who normally would not interfere or harm anyone, *now* realise if they attack as a group they can overpower any strong man, or even two or three youths - the mindset of a mass attack held by the young louts has *now* been adopted by law-abiding people. Men and women who once stood back and looked the other way when they saw a person being beaten and robbed, or some other wrongdoing, *now* chant "together" - and maybe up to twenty people will attack the criminal with any weapon that comes to hand - because the fear of doing so that once existed has *now* gone.'

It was a predictable diatribe Chris would have expected and he thought of how it was a popular discourse that is added to and then contradicted and added to daily in the media so that it keeps fresh in the minds of those it is aimed at.

Chris sensed the man derived enjoyment and even a sadistic pleasure when he spoke of beating and chasing down young thugs. Chris felt the man exemplified the feeling of the masses in wanting revenge against *that* which they believe is the cause of their personal feelings of wretchedness and alienation. The sadism depicted on the television show The Offender's Nemesis induced desires of witnessing, as a voyeur, the suffering of others, which has created a state of wholesale sadism that is legitimised and has become the norm, and any attempt to turn against this tide of thought and behaviour would be fiercely challenged by the general population who demanded brutal punishment against dissenters.

'I would give your brother some advice, which is to stick to the syllabus,' the man said as he stood up, gathered his crockery together and put it on a tray.

Chris watched the man as he strode in large ungainly steps up to the wall where there was a rack to put one's tray. He looked at the man's clothing, at his shapeless trousers and his crumpled jacket. His worn shoes were cheap and of a kind that are meant to last for years, and his dumpy frame was made to look clumsy by the length of his strides that were too long for his short legs. Chris thought about the man, seeing him as a walking apology, a being where there was no spirit to push forward with hopes of realising one's dreams. A man who had been reduced to being nothing more than a husk, dried to his bones by a system he probably hated, but was too scared to think about for longer than two seconds, so he resides forever in a feeling of loss and resentment where he can only take at times what he imagines is pleasure by acting in a spiteful way to those that he can, in an effort to take revenge and 'get his own back.' And there are those times when he is invited to be part of the system and join with others to witness someone who deserves to be 'got back at,' punished or even killed on The Offender's Nemesis.

Twenty-Two

Chris went to meet Simon in a café at the back of a Gigantic Store straight after working at the college. It was out of the way for Chris, in that it was not on his way home at all, but Simon wanted to meet there, saying he was pushed for time and it was convenient. He was already there when Chris arrived, sitting at a table with a cup of coffee in front of him, reading through some papers and looking very officious. As Chris approached the table Simon looked up and put whatever he was reading in a slim case, and Chris detected there was something about him that had changed, he seemed different, and this was confirmed when they greeted each other and shook hands. His manner was brisk and direct, with none of the considerate and empathetic way about him he usually presented. Chris started to tell him about what had happened at the college with the man in the refectory and Steven veering away from the set syllabus, but he could tell Simon was not interested. He was business-like as he rushed through the exchange of pleasantries and buying a cup of coffee; the formal etiquette was in place, but forced, because attending to the pressing needs of his agenda was apparent.

Simon asked Chris if he had spoken to Roger Edgebury, and when he told him had not, he told Chris he thought is was a good idea for him to do so. Simon told Chris that Roger Edgebury wrote music, some of which has been very popular, and although considering most of his own creations to be bland rubbish, the money earned from the sales of it gave him the time and opportunity to explore music he was really interested in and found meaningful. His commercial music had been used by some well-known pop stars and as theme music for films and television programmes.

'The proceeds have rewarded him well,' Simon said, 'allowing him to have a lifestyle that is the envy of many people. He is married, has children and lives out of town in an area known for its wealthy residents where he and his family live in an old converted farmhouse in the country that has a sizable bit of land. Roger likes to participate in country activities, dividing his time between working on the smallholding he has built up, writing songs and managing the business side of his music.'

Simon explained how Roger could be of help to Chris because he is a person with connections in many areas and knows people having influence in significant activities that support people who have crossed the state. He went on to say how Roger had been to the colony in Holland himself, and the network of associates he has who are involved in securing a person's safe passage would be vital for helping Steven.

Although Simon became vague when Chris asked him why Roger would be involved with such people when having a successful career in mainstream society by writing music for large corporations, Simon evaded giving an answer and almost dismissed the questions Chris was asking, but did say that, 'Roger Edgebury is a very committed man to the cause, and that is all we need to know.'

The meeting was over. It was not announced as being so, but it did not have to be - Simon's actions spelt it out clearly as he stood up, checked his slim case and said, 'You look after yourself, don't worry, just keep going as you are and I'm sure we'll get through this,' and he turned from the table and walked off. The suddenness of Simon ending their meeting took Chris by surprise. He wanted to know more about Roger Edgebury and he had intended to tell Simon more about the incident with the man in the college refectory.

Chris watched Simon as he walked in a brisk purposeful manner, and he thought about how different it was from the lumbering trudge the lecturer in the refectory had who told him about Steven; he was like a broken man compared to the decisive upright bearing of the health worker.

The meeting had lasted just twenty minutes. Chris thought about this, and also the way Simon had answered him not long after he arrived when Chris had asked him if he was driving. Simon hardly looked up as he told him that he was, but was in a hurry to be somewhere else and could not give Chris a lift.

As Chris thought about these things he was unaware of being watched by someone standing in one of the aisles; it was Garman. He was standing there during the whole time Chris had been with Simon, and he continued to watch Chris as he sat at the table looking around like a man lost in foreign surroundings.

Twenty-Three

Chris decided to phone Roger Edgebury on his way home from meeting Simon, and was surprised how much Roger knew about him and the way he spoke in a friendly manner as if they had known each other for years. They arranged a date to meet up in a month's time, which would be the middle of August. Chris had decided not to drive as he wanted to travel there by train, so Roger offered to pick him up at the station, but as he wanted to make his own way to his house. Roger gave him directions and told Chris to ring the bus company to find out the times of the buses that stopped quite near to where he lived.

After speaking to Roger Edgebury, a heavy feeling came over Chris that left him drained and dark thoughts swirled in his mind; he knew what he was doing was wrong and he was being drawn further into a web of mystery. The feeling got too much for Chris and he suddenly stood up from the bus seat he was sitting on and got off the bus, even though it was nowhere near his stop.

Where Chris had got off was a long way to the railway station he was heading for, but wanting time to think he decided to walk there. He walked down what was an old fashioned high street that led into a small shopping centre, and as he was walking through the main square of the shopping centre he heard a voice shouting above the sound of everything else. Chris looked over to where the raised voice was coming from and saw a man lurching around and pointing his finger at something only he could see. He then pointed at people, objects, fronts of shops, the ground, himself and the sky, and he screamed with fear; it was a sound possessed by such hysteria it upset a woman who dropped her head and sobbed as she hurried away.

The man had set up a board on the ground with different photographs pinned onto it. One of the photographs was of a pleasant looking house with a neat garden and a car in the drive, and another of a woman with her head thrown back as she laughed in a carefree way; a scene probably taken at home during a family celebration in happier times. There were two other photographs of young children, a boy and a girl, smiling at the camera showing missing milk teeth and large round eyes full of innocent content; this was the man's home and family and having lost his job, he was condemned to live in a poor area.

He shouted at people passing by about how his wife had started to lose her mind because of the worry of it all, but nobody stopped to listen. They kept on walking, careful not to let the man see them looking into his face as they scurried by. Children were pulled away and hurried along, but

Chris did stop, taking shelter in a shop doorway to be out of sight, and from his position he watched the man and the effect his plight had on people as they passed him. They were not so much embarrassed or feeling pity, but reminded of how precarious their own situation was and of their vulnerability, because what had happened to the man could easily happen to them. The look on all the people's faces said the same thing. It said the man was doomed, they were helpless to do anything about it and that they were scared.

Chris left the shopping centre, but rather than heading towards the railway station he walked down a side road taking him to a main street, he just wanted to go for a walk in an area he had not been before. He stopped briefly to look in a shop window to read part of a display that was to do with government health information on keeping one's baby safe from illness and disease. After walking a short while he turned off the main street into a quieter road running adjacent to it, and as he looked around he thought how the area was at one time a good neighbourhood and probably an expensive place to live, but it had become rundown, and as he looked at the shabby shops his attention was taken by raised voices coming from a side road he was walking past.

A group of people were shouting and a builder's van was parked up on the pavement in a haphazard way that added to the chaotic scene. Chris walked down the road, knowing he should not, but his curiosity had got the better of him. The fracas was taking place in a primary school and two security staff were looking on, their presence was worthless as they stood like bystanders with their arms folded and expressions on their faces that said it was nothing to do with them. A man standing on the pavement shouted through the fence, 'What are they, paedos or something?'

Another man shouted back, saying they were seen trying to break into the school, and said, 'They were desperate to get something to sell on, but they've been seen round here before selling drugs.'

The man on the pavement shouted, 'No drugs - no way, not round here.'

Chris looked to see who they were talking about, and saw two young men being held in the middle of a crowd. They looked petrified and had already been beaten, judging by the bruising and blood on their faces and their torn clothes. Chris noticed how quickly they were breathing and it reminded him of a cornered animal who is frantic with fear, knowing the end is coming. One of the young men shouted over to the security staff, his voice barely able to form words because he was so scared. 'Help us - help - we haven't done anything wrong - it's a mistake,' his voice broke, but the security men were also fearful. They just tightened their arms close to their bodies, and one of them gave a short nod at the inevitability of the young man's fate.

The crowd pushed forward, trapping the young men against the fence and a woman shouted, 'We're parents and we don't need this.'

A big fat man wearing a tee shirt that had risen up his back, and jogging pants that had slipped down so the tops of his buttocks were showing, grabbed one of the young men in a headlock and repeatedly punched his face with his large fist. He was encouraged by the crowd to continue beating him. Chris watched a woman as she clenched her fists and said in such a quiet voice she was not heard above anyone else,

'That's it, and again, make it really hurt.'

Another man, who was also big and fat, belly-barged the fence from the pavement side, knocking the other young man to the ground. This produced a loud cheer from the crowd and the same man pulled a rope from the back of the builder's van. He said he was going to tie the young men to the back of the van and drag them around the streets. The crowd cheered again and started to pull the young men towards the school gate, but the man who had the young man in a headlock shouted for them to stop, telling them they would be in trouble with the law for doing that. He told the crowd to just give them a good beating.

Chris then did something quite involuntary, he shouted out very loudly, 'Stop. What the hell are you doing? Let the police deal with it.'

And just as he realised he was walking towards the school gate he felt hands grabbing him and pulling him away with such force it shook him from his state of mind. One of the women said to him, 'Do your kids go to the school? Do they? Do they?'

Chris muttered the word 'no' in what he thought sounded like a weak, detached voice.

'Well, mind your own business and fuck off if you don't like it,' the woman said.

Chris felt the woman's severity and violence, and then she called him a 'liberal,' which was met by nods from others in the crowd. The word *liberal* worried Chris more than anything else that was said to him, because such a slur could lead to him being attacked by the crowd. As one of the young men was dragged through the school gate a woman, who was very small and neatly dressed, jostled next to Chris and shouted, 'Get him on the ground so we can really smash him.'

She looked up at Chris and told him she was punched in a public place while having an evening out after work in the 'old days.' She said, 'And I was mugged, as they used to say, on more than one occasion and nobody did anything.'

The young man was tossed onto the ground, just as a butcher discards the superfluous waste of a body part from his chopping block, and the crowd swarmed around and upon him. The small woman shouted through gritted teeth, 'That's it - that's it,' as she tried to stamp her foot down on any available part of the young man's body, and amongst all that was going on Chris noticed what she was wearing on her feet. They were ornate shoes, which were more like oriental slippers with sequins embroidered upon them and designed to be feminine and fragile with soft uppers and delicate soles. The small woman struggled to gain a place within the mob as she tried again and again to find a part of the body, which was now as limp as a rubber dummy, that she could stamp on, and when she did connect with just the side of the man's wrist she expelled a grunt of satisfaction and relief.

Chris turned, holding his head in his hands and stumbled away from the scene crying out, 'Christ, no - no, this is wrong.'

The sound of the shouting and chanting faded as Chris turned the corner of the road. He tried to compose himself because people were looking at him and he was suddenly conscious how he had become one of the random, misfortunate people one sees in urban areas acting in a strange way as he waved his arms and shook his head.

Chris took deep breaths and concentrated on walking in an easy fashion, wanting to mingle in with all the other people walking down the street, and as he walked he thought about the people at the school when the youths were beaten, their faces flushed, just like the man's face in the bar who threatened the solitary man. A thought crossed his mind that maybe it was not anger, but pleasure as their faces were glowing with excitement at seeing a person beaten, and they become even more excited when participating in the beating themselves, and maybe it is just one of the emotional highs a lot of people can feel in their lives that are swamped in lows, and it is an emotional expression encouraged by the state.

Twenty-Four

When Chris got home he told Rosie about what he witnessed at the school, of the look on the faces of the people in the crowd and the small woman with her anger and lust for revenge. He told her about the man who had lost his mind in the shopping centre and about the man in the college refectory talking about Steven, and also about going to see Simon, but he did not mention Roger Edgebury and the plans he had made to see him in August. Rosie tried to placate Chris, telling him he was doing all he could and always had done for Steven, but not to let the problems of the world get to him.

Rosie went out that evening to a woman's group she was a member of. It is a group working towards good causes such as supporting mothers having difficult times with their families and young people struggling with the problems that arise because of lacking literacy skills. Nina was in her room doing homework, in between sending messages to her friends. Chris sat back on the sofa and looked around the living room. All was quiet and peaceful, yet Chris felt that all was not well. His life with Rosie and Nina was great, and Chris counted himself to be very lucky, but it had been ruined by the worry of Steven and now worsened by him getting involved with something he should not be, and he hoped it would not draw in his wife and daughter where harm might come to them. The thought of that happening caused Chris to sit forward and hold his face in his hands. After a while Chris picked up the remote control, pressed a button and looked at the screen of the television as it twitched into life. The news was predictable, and as there was nothing else that interested him Chris went into the kitchen, warmed up the meal Rosie had made for him and returned with it on a tray to look at the television, knowing he should be getting on with some work he had to do.

A programme began that was to do with state security and which has become extremely popular, with some of the officers who are featured regularly on it becoming national celebrities. Chris thought about this, and about the time he was once held up in traffic because of a procession of slow moving vehicles celebrating national sporting heroes, which had attracted vast crowds of people. As he sat in his car Chris watched the people in the crowd rather than the procession, noting how especially the young children and their mothers were more interested in the security officers than anything else, and the way in which they pointed out members of the security and remarked how they looked like officers on the programme that was just starting on the television. A group of girls were taking photographs of certain officers and squealing in hysterical delight as they waved at them and shouted excitedly.

Chris remembered two young men of about nineteen years of age and how they were also more interested in the security officers than the sporting 'heroes', especially the ones on motorbikes. The two young men clapped and cheered, as did many others in the crowd, as the security officers passed on the motorbikes with their lights flashing. The young men were bursting with excitement, and one of them pretended to be scared as he gripped the other one's arm and shouted, 'They might look friendly, but boy oh boy don't get on the wrong side of these guys - they'll take you down faster than a silver bullet.'

What he said had confused Chris, but it made him smile because it seemed so ridiculous, and he saw the look on the face of one of the athletes who was standing on the back of a truck, he knew the main adulation from the crowd was for the security officers rather than for him and the other sportsmen and women.

Chris stopped thinking of the procession and concentrated on the programme as different images of stern looking men in uniforms carrying high powered weapons flashed on the screen, some having their identities completely hidden under their protective clothing, making them look like some futuristic figure drawn in a science fiction magazine many years before. The show is called Serious Security, and of course when spoken about is referred to in its abbreviated form, SS. A voice heavy with warning and deep in tone said over the images, 'They are your friends - please, please don't be their foe, because you will live, if you are lucky, to regret it,' and then different types of security in different situations flashed onto the screen with titles explaining what they are, such as; Border Watch, Riot Busters and Terrorist Hunters. The public get to vote for an officer who has been featured, and the officers who have accrued the greatest number of votes appear in what is called the Extra Special Enforcers table, known as the ESE league, which is popular with people who vote for what officer they think will be climbing or falling down the table.

The face of a security officer filled the screen for a few seconds before the camera pulled back showing the man in uniform grinning as he held up his baton. The camera zoomed onto the baton showing transfers of skulls. 'Meet Skull Cracker,' the voice of the presenter said, 'he's only too pleased to show the notches on his "play stick," as he calls it, his trusted truncheon that he takes into work every day so that the rest of us can sleep unhindered by criminals in our bed at night - yes, and I think that deserves a great big hand of gratitude,' and the studio audience dutifully applauded.

The presenter went on, 'Skull Cracker has received the most votes this week and he wanted us to tell you how thankful he is to you all, and to show just how much, he promises to crack a few extra skulls the next time they raid a terrorist hideout.'

This brought whistles and cheering from the audience and as Skull Cracker waved into the camera the presenter shouted over the noise of the audience, 'And remember, Skull Cracker and all the other guys are there for your safety, because the state cares about your well being.'

It showed the presenter walking over to a panel made up of two men and two women, all of them celebrities with one being a pop singer, one a model, an actress and a television presenter. After asking them what they are doing in terms of work and what plans they had, which resulted in plugs for shows that are owned by the same group of companies that make Serious Security, which also makes The Offender's Nemesis, with Alan Manville being one of the producers of Serious Security. The conversation with the celebrities was heavy with hysterical laughter at seemingly nothing in particular and two of the guests kept pulling funny faces, and then one of the men stood up from his seat and walked around in a manner that must have meant something to the audience because they fell about laughing, which encouraged the man to continue doing his funny walk. The presenter asked them if they were enjoying the show and one of the young woman said how she was so grateful because she was asked be a guest, and that she would 'just love' go on a date with Skull Cracker, which caused more laughter and pulling of funny faces.

The presenter looked into the camera, still shaking his head at the antics of the 'celebrity guests' and said, 'Officer MacLean is still top of the ESE league and now we are going to closely examine him in action on just one of the many calls of duty this brave...' and he winked as he looked around the audience, 'amazingly good looking and handsome man makes,' and the audience cheered and whistled as the camera spun round to show one of the female guests on the panel nodding her head eagerly as she held up a card with the words, 'Officer MacLean, please take me out' written on it.

The presenter said, 'We have asked for an expert in the analysis of rioting, terrorism and violent criminal disorder, who works as a consultant for esteemed security services, to talk us through the techniques and intricacies of what exactly Officer MacLean is doing, and makes him so special as he goes about his work as only he can.'

The title, Riot Busters unfolded across the screen to a blast of music and a succession of different situations was shown of rioting before the music dissipated and it settled down to one scene showing a crowd disturbance with a heavy presence of security officers. Talking over the scenes the presenter said, 'Our specialist advisor, Clarence Buckingham, will guide us through what is happening here, so, please tell us, Clarence, the background to this mayhem and unpatriotic behaviour before explaining in detail the superior combative skills of Officer MacLean.'

The 'consultant' said the riot was instigated by a 'mob' having extreme political views and allegiances with other groups following an ideology 'hell-bent' on 'destroying the fabric of society.' He went on to explain how the intelligence arm of state security is forever hard at work in stopping any major disturbances by infiltrating workers' organisations in the workplace, where many of these groups spring up. The camera zoomed in on a violent skirmish and went into slow motion as Clarence Buckingham said, 'Here we are now, a perfect demonstration of leadership skills, bravery and a diligence to serve the interests of one's country.'

Three young men were shown having a confrontation with a security officer in full uniform, therefore identifying him was impossible, and an arrow appeared on the screen pointing at him with the words 'Officer MacLean' next to it. Clarence Buckingham continued, guiding the viewers through what was happening and the film was stopped at certain points, giving him time to go into more detail as Officer MacLean attacked the three young men, who were unarmed and by the look of things were trying to get away from him. 'Look at this,' Clarence Buckingham said, 'he hits rioter number one in the face with the butt of his gun, he stamps on the leg of rioter number two who is lying on the ground, and shoots rioter number three in his chest.'

At this point the voice of the presenter cut in. 'I guess he got unlucky, the other two got patched up while he got bagged up.'

His remark brought laughter from the audience and the camera shot cut to the 'celebrity panel' in the studio who were laughing and clapping each other's hands, one of the female celebrities was so overcome with hysterical laughing she was helped by two of the others, who feigned cooling her down by waving a towel at her. She stopped laughing and pointed in the air as if just having thought of something, 'Oh, that's right, that's what they used to call them, those trouble makers wasn't it? Commies? Well my hero Officer Maclean knows how to clean boring commies off our streets,' and she started to laugh again as she said, 'Did you see the expression on the face of that one on the ground.'

The presenter looked into the camera, and pulling a face he said, 'Isn't she great?'

Chris turned the television off and looked at the blank screen for a long time, listening to sounds coming from the world outside his home, his own little bit of space that was once his sanctuary, but was increasingly feeling as if it was no longer that way.

He stood up, and without being conscious of why he did it, Chris walked down the hallway and tapped on Nina's bedroom door. Hearing no response he tapped again, and guessing she was probably wearing headphones he opened the door, but just enough to poke his head round it. It was as he thought, there she was, sitting at her desk with her headphones on. Nina looked up quickly and gave Chris the thumbs up sign as he mouthed if she was okay. Chris smiled, closed the door and went into the living room with plans of getting on with some work.

Chris could not concentrate on his work, his mind flitted from one thought to another, each one to do with Steven and the people he had met, the things he had seen that day, Simon the health worker and how he had changed. He thought about the programme he had just been watching and of security officers being popular celebrities was so depressing. There were adverts for toys to do with actual members of the security, some to do with what he had been looking at a few minutes earlier, and he thought about the people in the crowd watching what was meant to be a procession to celebrate sporting figures, but were fascinated with the men in uniform displaying power and representing control.

Chris reflected over the different forms of security that existed in the country and how it has permeated almost every facet of a person's life, to a point where, it could be argued, individual thought and consciousness of self, with matters like personal creativity or original thinking are being curtailed at their formative stage by a psychological barrage that is unleashed perpetually by the state to sway a person away from such personal development. Chris thought about the way heavily armed militia are present at social events, and how he had seen photographs of sporting fixtures and other places where there had been entertainment such as large concerts from before the 'big change' and there was nowhere near the amount of an aggressive presence of security. Chris had noticed that troops, and not the police, are now always present in places of travel, and there are the different types of prisons designed to cater for people that have committed different forms of crime. 'Foreign criminals', are now incarcerated in separate prisons with 'prisoners' from wars the country is involved with in other lands, and he has heard how there are massive prisons built in areas where the public are not permitted to be so nobody really knows for sure what is going on. Chris has heard how laws are changed overnight and justified as being in the interest of national security. He thought about what he had heard regarding the use of, 'Stooge Bombers' by the state, which is when the mentally ill are used to carry out bombings and so innocent people are killed and people who do not know what they are doing are accused of being enemies of the state, and it is all fired up by news media companies that create a constant state of delusion.

Chris jumped to his feet, and taking a deep breath he went into the kitchen to make a hot drink and break from his disturbing thoughts; but his mind kept returning to matters of state security and circumspection. He thought about the meeting he had been to, and the character Kim Blakely, a figure of iconic proportions who is regarded in the most reverent tones by those involved in the 'underground' groups. Chris wondered who this Kim Blakely really was. He is a man that produces material for his followers in the 'underground' groups to buy or acquire, with films and pamphlets having titles such as, 'Unlock Your Mind' and 'Free Consciousness'. Chris had been told the purchase price is to pay for administration and materials, as Kim Blakely does not make any financial profit from his work.

Chris took his drink into the living room, and although picking up some of his work he could not focus on it. He sat on the sofa with his mood becoming increasingly low the more he thought about officer MacLean, the 'celebrity,' and grim faced men in uniforms, and the academic dissidents, and their leader, Kim Blakely; it was only the sound of Rosie coming in that shifted him from what he was thinking.

When Rosie entered the room she adopted a breezy manner in an effort to lift his mood. She asked Chris why he looked so 'glum', and was it because he saw his bank statement, but it did not have the desired effect she hoped for. Chris began to speak in a rush, telling Rosie about the programme he had been watching and it reminded him of when he was caught up in traffic because of the sporting procession, and how the security, guns and control are aspects in society that are glorified and admired. She tried to make light of it, saying she always wanted to marry a man in uniform, but settled for him because of his money. Chris did not reciprocate with her joking, and if anything her manner increased his despondence.

Rosie told him he was upset because of the man in the college refectory and meeting Steven's health worker had worried him, and he needed some respite from it all, and watching television programmes like he has been will only make him feel worse, but Chris was not listening to her. He looked at Rosie and said, 'It's like people aren't thinking, and it's as if they've lost the ability to think because of the constant indoctrination.'

Rosie watched him for a few seconds before speaking in a calm voice. 'They are thinking Chris and they can, but it's safer not to.'

'Safer?' Chris said, becoming agitated, 'Safer - what kind of life are we living? Steven wants to challenge a culture that restricts a person's imagination to such a degree they hate themselves and everybody else they feel is obstructing them from being what they have lost sight of - and that is their true selves. He told me once that people are blindly walking in a mindless haze, and living in a perpetual flux of fear. Steven is right, don't give up on people, the human spirit still exists, it's just trying to survive under the present conditions - things change, they have in the past and they will again, so, don't give up hope, there are many examples throughout history where there has been change for the better and fought for against the odds - the evil people are always there and will dominate if they can.'

Chris continued, becoming heated as he spoke of how so called criminals, the *offenders*, are brought over as entertainment and to maintain social control, and he talked about how he had heard the state gets them from other lands and they are either paid for or bartered as part of an agreement. He pointed out the irony of a system that declares its most important anathema as being crime, yet it is criminals they desire and need for its maintenance.

Rosie gave Chris a long cautionary look before saying, 'I, and people like me, Chris, understand that - of course we do, what's got into you love? It's getting you into a state where you are shouting out the obvious to people who know, but...'

'It's important,' Chris was nearly shouting, 'if innocent people are being murdered on the most disgusting television show imaginable - the mentally ill, the sensitive who can't keep up with things, artists who explore and ask questions - those who want reform so that society is more fair - and just look at the show, at what it's all about and the people behind it - our freedom, given away and people are just accepting it because the system hands them token trinkets, and for that small reward they suffer a life dogged by fear and suspicion in aggressive conditions.'

Rosie dropped her head and shook it desperately, and raising her voice in an effort to plead with him she said, 'Chris - this *is* life, this is where we live - we cannot create utopia, a place resembling heaven where everyone will be *free* and *happy*, and *conscious* of themselves and all that is around them - most people know, but have to get on with it...'

166

Rosie stopped speaking as Nina opened the door and stood in the doorway looking at her parents. Nina was upset at hearing them quarrel, it was something she rarely saw and was not used to them raising their voices. She asked what the matter was and why they were arguing.

Chris walked over to Nina, placing his hand on her shoulder, he spoke in a soft voice, saying it was nothing to do with her or her mother. He said, 'Listen love, it isn't to do with us as a family, believe me, it's just that I'm worried about uncle Steven, and I'm sorry, I shouldn't keep troubling you and your mum, it's upsetting but I will do what I can to help him...'

'Has anything happened to him? What's happened?' Nina said. Chris spoke quietly, and calmed Nina by telling her nothing had actually happed, but it was an ongoing worry for him, and then he changed the mood by telling her his friend Brendan will be able to get her tickets from a contact he knows for a symposium taking place in the school holidays made up of different clubs from around the country that are affiliated to the one Nina belongs to. Although Nina nodded and smiled, she was unsure as she waved at Rosie and Chris and said she was going back to her room.

Chris and Rosie watched her leave and continued to look at the empty doorway until Rosie turned to Chris and said in a quiet, but strong tone, 'Be careful Chris of these people you are meeting and what you are saying.'

Twenty-Five

During the following week Chris paid another visit to Bill Copley's flat; there were five people who had visited that night, two of them being a couple called Karena and Roy who were members of more than one campaigning group. Karena edited and organised the printing and publishing of a journal called PA, an abbreviation of Politically Aware. At first Chris found them difficult to speak to, in that they were reserved and they would talk to each other quietly, acknowledging one another's knowing looks and nods, but as the evening went on they became friendly towards Chris as he told them about Steven. Karena told Chris that she and Roy had lived together for a number of years but never married and did not have children.

Karena explained to Chris that Roy did a technical kind of job, while she worked as a secretary in a large stationery company, She was very open and had a dry sense of humour as she told Chris about the people she worked with, commenting on their lack of consciousness, and of how she keeps her conversations with them on the most rudimentary level. Chris told them about his friend Paul, the artist, and his experiences and of how he has been treated. They were interested to know about Paul and they were understanding and supportive about Steven, and as they spoke Chris became aware there was something about Karena he found attractive. She did not flirt with him, and she did not appear to be the type of woman that flirted at all, but there was something about her, a sensual quality that Chris found appealing. She was quite tall and slim, and wore clothes that did not accentuate her physical features, such as hips or breasts. Chris noticed her clear complexion and her skin was free from lines, which he thought was maybe because she had not given birth and raised children. When Chris first shook her hand he noticed her long slim fingers, how cool her hand was and what a remarkably strong grip the willowy and engaging woman had.

By what Karena and Roy told Chris they had a network of friends that could be described as unconventional, in that they were involved with the arts, especially music and writing, and although they professed a Bohemian lifestyle they all seemed to have good jobs and lived in wealthy areas. When Chris mentioned Roger Edgebury and that he was going to visit him, they both laughed and told him they had known Roger Edgebury for years. They had first met him when they were students and used to go to the bars and clubs where students like them gathered. As they spoke Chris thought about how he had avoided, or just was not interested in that type of student scene. He saw it as a culture that is supposed to be individualistic and challenging, yet it resided firmly in the confines of conventionality, being safe and only making superficial alterations to fit with fashion while the powers that motivate the system remain the same.

The articles read out in meetings by the people that had written them were nearly identical to articles written by others or by the 'underground' journal itself, which were to do with universal uprisings against mammoth corporations and the governments who appear to create legislation that serves the interests of the corporations. There were petitions against inequality and injustice of all kinds, such as inhibitive laws that restrict rights and freedom, and chemicals in foodstuffs that have the effect of inducing soporific passivity.

A young woman read from her article, which had been published in one of the journals, which she referred to as her 'essay.' It was concerned with a process known as 'linguistic sense' that has been introduced in schools and is used in nearly everything shown on television. She told how the state has a department studying 'semasiology' and that her interest is in the codes embedded in the semantics viewed in everyday settings.

Bill Copley led the discussion to the subject of fear, language and methods of social control, and how they have been used throughout history. The group discussed how there must have been stories told in caves to frighten people from straying too far at night. They talked about myths in feudal times and of how in a capitalist society tales of the economy are used as a stick to beat people into line. They spoke about the present society and the myth of the average person who is now supposedly empowered in addressing social order, when they do not have any power or involvement in the running of societal affairs, as all sense of freedom is designed by the state.

Bill showed a film made by members of an 'underground' movement that had the use of fear as its main subject matter. The film was really a documentary showing three people sitting around a table with coffee mugs on it. The people discussed how fear is a powerful weapon and is used to maintain control. They explored how it is used in war to vilify the *other* and to divide society into conflicting fragments on lines of race and class. They discussed how religion uses fear to control and of how it was at the core of major enquiries during the rise of the age of scientific reason. One of the people in the film spoke of the 'elite' and of how they manage 'ordinary people' with fear, but also provide laughter and amusements, which is seen as an imperative tool in the process of social control. At one stage their discussion became passionate and as one of the men spoke of the history of crime, punishment and social control he slapped one hand onto the other as he said, 'God decides, man decides, trials in public, the common man participates in punishment, ordeals by fire, torture, prisons, therapy, education, understanding the reasons why there is crime...'

Another film was shown, but this one was made by the state. It dealt with surveillance and how in the past the 'liberals' used technology, such as cameras, tags, swipe cards and numerous other devices to destroy human relations by victimising the average person, who felt he or she was constantly being watched and monitored, and although not having done anything wrong it was essentially because they were the only people who paid fines. They were easy bait for governments to tax and impose financial penalties and fines upon for what were often petty misdemeanours, and so found themselves trapped and squeezed further with the authorities justifying their actions as necessary to address crime. Yet the 'hard working' person saw the criminals going about their way with liberty and ignoring any government measures as they were outside of its net. The 'normal' hard working people were punished further by curfews that were put in place, ostensibly to deal with violent crime, and so the law-abiding people came home from work and were prisoners in their homes until morning when they went back to work, with their personal creativity limited and freedom to go out and about restricted because criminals would attack them.

The film portrayed the run-of-the-mill person as nothing more than a product for a tax collecting system under the 'liberals' who veiled their actions with 'progressive' language, while in reality citizens were financially besieged by unscrupulous companies which the state allowed to rifle though their personal bank accounts as credit cards and insurances of many variants squeezed and further harassed the average tax payer.

The group discussed the film and of how the state uses different propaganda techniques. They then spoke about the average person having what they called a false consciousness and of not being aware of their position within the situation they exist or of their relationship with the state. Bill Copley showed another film that had a severe looking man staring into the camera; Bill told Chris the man is head of intelligence in state security. They all watched intently and listened to what the man was saying as he narrowed his eyes and began to speak. 'Don't tell me a system that promulgates an entity called 'free will' is being honest - decisions are not made 'freely' by an individual. An idea or opinion - and all thoughts, are restrained by socialisation, and the supposed individual's personal idea - his or her original thought, is only part of that making up dominant ideas

170

at the time that he or she is alive. It is a lie, as it has always been. There is no such thing as pure cognition - the 'will', of an individual? It is a childish concept, but then it is accepted by children, although devised and disseminated by those with cynical intent - who go about their way disregarding rules of societal standards - and at what cost?'

Chris could not follow what the man was saying because he could not maintain concentration, so he just sat there watching the man and the people in the room staring at the screen as if hypnotised by what he was saying.

After that film there was another one and the group discussed theories of mind control and brain washing. One of the group spoke of how in the past there had been a machine called an Air Loom that had invisible magnetic rays, and although its creator was ridiculed, why should not there be an advanced machine today, a more sophisticated method where sound waves wipe out parts of the brain that deal with memory so specific questions are forgotten, and a vague feeling of once wanting answers to matters become mixed up and confused. The group spoke about how ideas are seemingly just formed in the mind with no knowledge of how one came to decisions about preferences such as why one feels an aversion towards a person or idea. They discussed the use of mind-altering methods such as electronic waves, subliminal messages, hypnotic suggestions that are embedded in music, and the use of chemicals in food and cigarettes. One of the men began to talk about sex and other urges and how they are used as strategies to distract from one's actual personal experience, and how a person actually feels about the way he or she is told by the state how their life is. He spoke of a paper he had written called Repressive Desublimation and Social Control.

Chris thought of The Offender's Nemesis and Mistress T, among other things, as the man explained, or gave a lecture, on how desires, our innate urges in relation to sex and aggression, are manipulated and how feelings of satisfaction are expressed publicly, and personally, yet the actual desires have not been addressed, but only transferred by being satisfied through an expression deemed appropriate by the state and others and therefore socially acceptable, which ultimately leaves the individual with unconscious feelings of inadequacy and frustration.

And then the lights went out. As Bill lit candles he told Chris power cuts were a regular occurrence. They resumed talking, sitting in the light given by the candles with their shadows shifting on the wall. Chris spoke of people who consider themselves to be informed and aware, but underestimate the means it takes to control the mass of society and the lengths the state will go to, and he gave an example of the power and influence television shows have in this process. The group discussed the fickleness and superficiality of celebrity culture, but Chris pressed his point that Alan Manville is an important person for the state.

Finally, Bill Copley spoke to Chris about arranging meetings with contacts that would help Chris with his plans for Steven. It was apparent the other people in the room knew about it as Bill told him of a contact in Holland he had been in touch with who is connected with a group that gets people like Steven out of the country and settles them in the 'colony'. The group that the contact was part of had specific details of routes, methods of transportation and the times of flights and shipping when the human cargo takes place.

When in Holland he would be met by the contact, or members of his group, and taken to a 'safe house'. Chris became confused, there were too many vague aspects to the trip and unanswered questions about the whole thing. The 'colony' was discussed as a sanctuary that is friendly to the aims and feelings of those disenchanted with the system in this country. It is a place 'refugees' can settle in safety and have a family, and it has a growing population, but because of this it is said that it may one day be clamped down upon by the powers of international forces to stop it becoming a threat, with this country having a main influence in doing so. Chris had heard the 'refugees' that had made it to the 'colony' often refer to this country as 'Angerland.' Chris felt this name to be immature and the 'challenge' to the 'system' can be seen as not much more than a hobby for those coming from the professional class who feel guilty at having acquired a knowledge of things, but perpetuate the running of society by doing the jobs they do and by following a course set down for them to follow. 'Empty rebellion,' was a term that came to Chris's mind and he thought of the 'dissidents' as ineffectual.

Twenty-Six

Chris was looking at the television with the sound off while lying on his bed. Rosie and Nina were in the living room watching a programme which they interested in, so Chris went to the bedroom because he wanted to be alone. Chris was deep in thought about the following day when he was going to see Roger Edgebury. It had caused an argument between him and Rosie, she had found out, which was not difficult for her to do as Chris was not good at keeping things from her. Rosie did not like the idea of Chris visiting a man who he had no idea about, and she warned him again to be careful of who he is talking to. His thoughts were displaced by the smiling face of Alan Manville on the television, but it vanished after a couple of seconds as the opening titles for a show began to run; Chris pressed the button on the remote control that instantly delivered sound into the room.

A voice-over introduced two girls of about fifteen or sixteen years of age dressed in their school uniforms onto the set; they were self-conscious and nearly breaking into giggles. The voice told of how the two girls had won an inter-school competition with their project about law and order, and the lights on the set changed to show a couch at the rear of the studio with the silhouette of two people sitting on it. The studio lighting increased to show Alan Manville sitting next to a middle-aged man wearing a suit as props were wheeled onto the set that included a computer, a large screen and various replicas of appliances of torture. A man walked onto the set and shook hands with the girls.

'Okay,' the man said, 'this is Dawn and Katy, the worthy winners of a competition run by the ACC, and they are here to show us their project they did not only during school time, but also in their own time away from school - welcome.'

The girls representing the Anti Crime Crusaders smiled at the man and became more nervous as he, in a rather over-gentle manner that caused Chris to take notice, took one of the girls by her arm and guided them to where they were meant to stand.

The man continued, 'Now, the subject of your project is law and order, and you two chose to research methods used from many, many years ago - would you like to take us through some of the things we have here.'

The girls went to their pre-rehearsed positions and in tandem explained how criminals were dealt with years ago and the medieval forms of punishment, humiliation and execution that existed. One of them turned the computer on while the other girl showed the man different appliances and explained what their function was, and every now and then the

173

camera showed Alan Manville watching attentively. The girl explained what the Rat Torture was, and how a rat would dig its way through the stomach of the 'offender' to escape burning, and then she broke into giggles as the man made a comment about how it would get rid of indigestion. The other girl who was operating the computer showed a film they had made that had graphic re-enactments of punishments and tortures. She explained how torture and punishment was what the public wanted at the time and people did not see anything wrong with it.

The man broke away from his faked interest in the film and pointed at a sandal with spikes protruding from the insoles. 'Cripes,' he said, 'I wouldn't want to do a fun run wearing a pair of those!' The girls folded in nervous laughter. 'What is it?' the man asked, 'besides being a style of shoe made by a cobbler with a very strange sense of humour.'

Both girls giggled and tried to stop laughing out loud at the man's remark, and enjoying the effect he was having on the girls the man picked up the sandal and asked them to tell him about it. One of the girls tried to tell him, through fits of giggles, that a criminal had to wear the spiked sandals as a punishment for committing a crime, and all the while as she spoke the man made exaggerated facial expressions of pain and discomfort. The girls showed him other appliances of torture and described different methods of punishment and ordeals between giggling at the man's antics.

Alan Manville watched the presentation, and although he smiled at the man's behaviour he retained a pose of having a serious interest in what the girls were saying. When the girls had finished Alan Manville spoke to the man sitting next to him, who was the head teacher at the girl's school. Manville said how proud the man must be and that he was honoured to present them with an award on behalf of The Offender's Nemesis for 'positive and imaginative work.' He went on to talk about how different methods from years gone by had been featured on The Offender's Nemesis and of how they will continue to do so because it is popular with the public, and looking over at the girls he asked them if they had got some of their ideas from The Offender's Nemesis. They both nodded, and this pleased Manville as he stood up and walked towards the girls carrying two medals on ribbons. The girls held their faces in delight as Alan Manville praised them and said he would organise it for the girls to show their exhibition on The Offender's Nemesis.

As the programme ended, and the titles began to stream down the screen, Chris thought about the time he was round Brendan's flat a few months earlier when a programme came on the television about torture and the history of punishment. Chris spoke to Brendan about how they live in a society obsessed with torture and retribution, and they discussed how humiliation plays an important part for the ordinary person to make the criminal suffer. They talked about the function of torture, of its basic simplicity and how it satisfies the minds of the populace. The programme was introduced and presented by a smarmy man who explained in condescending, easy-to-understand language that the programme was historical and educational and would take an 'intelligent in-depth understanding' of torture and punishment throughout history.

A series of different forms of torture and punishment throughout the ages were shown, and there was a brief and oversimplified explanation of how in those days God played a role in these 'tests' because the criminal had violated His decrees and it was Him that punished the 'sinner.' It showed examples of the different ordeals involving fire, water or trials by combat, and the man explained how communities were not prepared to pay for imprisonment so execution was preferable, and having it sanctioned by God took the onus from the people to feel responsible in dealing with the criminals and their future. They would hang the dead body in a gibbet at the entrance of the village so the sight of a decaying body hanging from a tree gave a stark and clear warning that criminal activities would not be tolerated. It acted as a deterrent and was also a public display of retribution.

Brendan and Chris talked about how parallels drawn with today's society since the 'big change' is obvious in how criminals are viewed, and that execution and public disgrace is seen by many as the best way of dealing with crime. This led Chris and Brendan to talk about The Offender's Nemesis. They spoke about the act of torture and control, the sexual factor involved in it all and the role of Mistress T, of what the T stands for and who Mistress T really is.

Chris and Brendan joked as they went through the possibilities of her being a police officer, or an actress who Alan Manville spotted and signed up, or that she could even be a friend of Manville and they might be lovers, and they could possibly be involved in a relationship where deviant sex plays a big part, and maybe Manville enjoys sadism and Mistress T really is a dominatrix, and maybe she is blackmailing Manville. They spoke about how, for many people, there is the element of sexual excitement and stimulation in witnessing torture and punishment and how those feelings can be sublimated and transposed onto the state itself.

Chris lay back on the bed and thought about the meeting he went to a few weeks earlier when the man was talking about repressed desires, sexual urges, fantasy and the frustrations felt because there is simulation of release yet the innate urge has not been addressed. He broke from his thoughts and looked up at the television as his attention was taken by quiet relaxing music, which was very uncommon as most of the time soundtracks and music is fast and loud.

Gentle music flowed lightly over a peaceful setting of a lake set in a forest, which was filmed in soft focus. A young woman dressed in a light elegant robe was walking by the edge of the forest looking across the lake with a serene smile on her face. She is the seventeen-year-old daughter of a man occupying a powerful position in the military and is a director of a company that has the major contract in supplying the country its arms. The young woman is gaining the status of a higher, other-worldly figure as stories appear of her having the ability to heal. One such story that has been popular with young girls is of how she was able to cure her sick pony when the world's leading vets failed to do so. Her talents and remarkable relationship with nature, along with an 'unexplainable gift for healing,' has created the notion of her 'specialness' and that possibly she is connected to a greater force that separates her from mere mortals; the validity of these claims of her outstanding and fantastic abilities are never questioned. There is an emerging story of her using her powers to help the 'people' in the country because she is so upset by their plight of having to 'make the best of things' before, apparently, 'things' are going to get better. It is said that since she was a young child she has cried herself to sleep at night when thinking of the suffering that exists in the world.

Her affinity with animals is expressed with heavily embroidered sentimentality, and there is a well known story of how as a child she felt their pain and fear so acutely, because of her deep sensitivity, she would often seek out small animals in her garden and develop a close relationship with them. This, it is said, continues to this day as small animals perch on the windowsill of her bedroom at night, as if looking over the young woman, and birds whistle the softest of song.

In the last two years there has been a book published about her that is now on the school curriculum for children to learn about her 'virtuous' ways. She is becoming known as a saintly figure and is referred to as 'the great protector' and the 'special one' with her birthday set aside as a day of celebration. Small children are seen on television praying to her to bring relief from ill health and poverty, or maybe just for luck when doing exams or something to do with a sporting competition. Chris thought about her iconic status, and how that kind of worship of other worldly figures exists in a society where superstition is the dominant value instead of reason. The widespread belief in her supposed abilities would have been inconceivable only a few years earlier, although in recent times there has been a style of presenting state leaders in a quasi-superstitious way.

Chris mulled over these thoughts, and of how the propagated myths regarding their 'greatness' help to create an illusory notion of reality that is of use in applying methods to control the populace.

Chris looked at the television guide and saw that the whole evening was to do with respect and celebrating young people. There were the girls with their school project, the daughter of a powerful state figure and the programme just starting was about how adults can learn from their children, especially the older generation. The reason for this, according to what he was reading, is because older people were indoctrinated by the delusory ways existing in the system before the 'big change', while young people who were born or have grown up since have a more realistic view of the world and their place in it.

Chris turned the television off and sat in the quiet, although he could hear Rosie and Nina laughing in the living room, and when their laughter melted away it then returned to the soft mumbling sound coming from the television they were watching. He thought about how they would not be watching what he just had been looking at, and their minds were not occupied with the thoughts his was, and as he listened to the sounds from the living room he became aware of how at times he felt separate from them, from his wife and daughter, the two people he loved more than anything in the world, the two people that should have given him a feeling of solace and warmth, but the sense of detachment he felt from them grew until he thought he was going to cry. It was an awful feeling, and Chris reminded himself that the next day he was going to visit Roger Edgebury at his home, out of town in the country.

Twenty-Seven

As Chris sat on the train thinking through what he had been doing to help his brother he could not shake off a sense of doubt that it had all been in vain. The meeting with 'X', that never happened, was six months earlier, on a cold and overcast damp day in an environment of hostility and decay with people wearing a defeated look that had gone beyond despair. Chris looked out of the train window and contrasted the sights and mood of the project with the countryside he was passing through. Rays of sunlight made contact against the window, sending a shattered spray of blinding light through the carriage and bringing satisfying warmth. He looked out at small gardens spread behind houses like neatly woven tapestries as the wild woodland seemed to be smirking at its neighbouring coppice, and small ravines cut through forests to show a stream blinking contentedly at a perfect day.

Chris walked out of the small railway station and was met by an intense heat from the afternoon sun, but what was foremost in his mind was the thought that he had entered a coexisting society, which was nothing like the one he had left only just over an hour before, and it occurred to him he had not been to an area like the one he was standing in for many years. Everything had a slower pace from what he was used to and the sounds had their own distinctness. While standing at the bus stop Chris watched the people passing through the station area that had a little shop, two bus stops and a small hoarding with advertisements on it for shops in the 'village centre' that was, 'less than a kilometre away.' Chris assumed there must be a school nearby as young girls wearing their school uniforms came in ones and twos, usually visiting the shop before going on their way. They looked different from the school kids he saw around the edges of the housing projects. Dressed in a uniform symbolising they were part of an elite band in society, they seemed to walk with free abandon, displaying confidence that was in contrast to their peers in poorer areas, who at their young age seemed inhibited and burdened with self-limiting thoughts, and, fully aware of their dull prospects, they exhibit hostile behaviour as a defence.

A car pulled up in the allotted area for parking, and as the driver stayed in the car Chris assumed she was probably waiting to pick someone up, and then it was quiet again.

It was a fair wait for the bus that would take Chris close to where Roger Edgebury lived, but he did not mind hanging around the station area because he found it enjoyable just to watch a sedate part of society go about its day. He decided to go into the little shop, and as he entered he was suddenly hit by a feeling he had not sensed for years. The shop in its peaceful surroundings reminded him of when he was a child on holiday. It had a smell from that time, so very different from the shops where he lived, where the owners stare at anyone who enters with eyes filled with suspicion and glaring at the 'intruder' as they check for any likely trouble; it is an experience bound in aggression and, of course, fear.

It was not like that in the little shop by the station. The man working there hardly looked up when Chris entered as he continued to check items of stock on a delivery sheet. There was a calm atmosphere, and the first thing Chris noticed was that there were none of the lottery cards with the faces of 'offender's' on them. They were not on show if the shop did stock them, but Chris doubted if they were to be found in this peaceful nugget of civilisation with its genteel order. Chris bought an ice lolly and a local newspaper and as the man served him he said, 'It's a warm one today,' and he spoke about how they needed some rain for the garden. Chris felt like a foreigner as he said in a dull tone, 'yes.' It was as if the man came from a completely different world. 'Different,' Chris said the word aloud when he left the shop, feeling it was the only word that described it.

There were only a few people on the bus and as it made its way down lanes Chris closed his eyes, leaving behind the shadows of branches, thick with leaves, and the intermittent flicker of sunlight creating a kaleidoscope of flashing so bright it made it difficult to see clearly. Chris was enjoying himself, he loved the feel of heat penetrating through the window and warming the side of his face, and the smell of fertiliser spread on the fields they were passing by triggered sensations and emotions that had not been lit for a long time. The area Chris was in, or the zone, is predominated by wealthy people; this is where they live and where they enjoy themselves. They live in large houses set back from lanes and roads, often immersed in a maze of trees and their cars travel on roads at liberty while others require the correct permit to do so. It is not uncommon to come upon a rolling roadblock where heavily armed guards check permits, IDs and other relevant papers that give a valid reason for being in the area.

Chris was fortunate in that he could apply for a permit to travel through most of the zones, including the one he was in, without having to give detailed explanations for doing so, and could get it almost immediately at a main railway station. The reason he could do so was because of his family background, his father was a qualified person and Chris also had qualified status as he had been to an academy of higher education and gained the relevant qualifications that enabled him to work in a 'profession.' People who do not have a qualified status and travel into that zone for purposes of work need to have a permit or they are breaking the law. To be in possession of a permit and to have an explanation for being in the zone is stringently monitored, and those who break the law are dealt with most severely, with hard labour being the usual punishment. Offenders are often put to work on building projects that require a lot of labour, which is hard without any rights to one's conditions, and it is not unknown for a person to get many years for a first offence.

Chris got off the bus at a fork in the road where there was a house, which at one time was a pub; the road split into two lanes, the bus continued down one of them and Chris walked down the other.

There was no traffic noise and the smell of bark and plants in the woods was so strong and clean it stopped Chris from lighting a cigarette and ruining it all. The lane climbed into a clearing and the sun was hot, which prompted Chris to take off his jacket and dab the sweat on his forehead. As he walked along he watched ponies in a field by a large house, a girl of about fifteen years of age looked over at him and he saw two men who were probably labourers. Another girl came out of the stables and walked over to the first girl Chris saw, she adjusted the saddle on one of the ponies and then an elderly man came out of the stables and held the pony as she climbed upon it. For a few seconds the whole scene seemed to give way to an unusual image and feeling. It was as if Chris's senses had altered and he saw things he had seen many times before as different. The rays of sunlight magnified the yellow landscape and ripened the strawberry coloured floss that held onto trees and bushes. Dragonflies took aim before darting purposefully in a direction out of Chris's sight, and the throaty nasal choir of insects rose to agree on a collective pitch that was in harmony beneath the heavy sun that had settled itself in the mid-afternoon. A pleasant tired feeling of heaviness came over Chris and he gave into the feeling, accepting it and enjoying his relaxed state he noticed how he had slowed his pace of walking.

Twenty minutes later he reached the turning he was looking for. A gate was set back from the lane in front of a track that was large enough to drive a vehicle down to the house where Roger Edgebury lived.

Chris spent a short while trying to open the gate before seeing an electric security system. He pushed the button and within a few seconds a metallic voice, which was female, sounded through the small speaker, asking who it was. As Chris gave his name and explained he had arranged to visit, the gate slowly and silently swung open.

Chris walked down the track, and looking back at the gate for a second he thought about the electrical system that operated it. He did not like it. It ruined the feeling he had of being away from everything mechanical and ordered. He saw it as a bit of a sham, what with the gate looking old and rustic, fitting in with its surroundings, but having the sophisticated trappings of urban security changed its image for Chris and turned his thoughts to wonder if everything was really nothing more than a facade and delusion.

It was at least a minute's walk down the track until it broke into a clearing where a farmhouse stood proudly before him. There were stables at the side of the house and a field that had been prepared as a practice area for show jumping. A woman was standing in the open doorway waving to Chris. She was smiling and waved her hand more vigorously in an effort for Chris to notice her.

Chris waved back and walked towards her, feeling uncomfortable as he had never met these people before and was in an environment that was their home, and one very different to what he was used to. The woman had deep lines on her face and was dressed in clothes Chris imagined peasant women might wear who make a meagre living from hard toil on the land.

Chris shook her hand as they introduced themselves to each other. The woman's name was Maddy, she was Roger Edgebury's wife and as they went inside the cottage she told Chris that Roger was not in but would be back soon. Maddy made a hot herbal drink and told him what he could smell was the soup she was making. Chris looked around their living room as he sat in a chair by a large open fireplace, which considering the weather was obviously not lit. Chris liked their home. He noticed the stone floor in the kitchen and the old furniture that comprised of oak tables and a Welsh dresser. Chris knew it was a Welsh dresser only because Maddy had told him the history of much of what was inside the house.

The ambience was, for Chris, from a time gone by. It reminded him of a distant feeling from his childhood. A time before the way things are now. 'Before'. The word seemed apt. As did 'different', although the electronic gate was a security system from the present, and Chris felt although it might be unduly critical to think it, Maddy did seem to be acting a part in that the image of unconventionality she presented was a fabrication. He did not know why he thought this. Why should he? All she had done was open her front door, invite him into her home and make him a herbal drink.

Chris reproached himself for making unpleasant assumptions as he listened to Maddy tell him about her family. They had three children, two had left home while the youngest, their 'treasure,' was a fourteen year old girl called Petunia; the show jumping accessories in the field were for her.

Maddy told Chris how Petunia had won many show jumping competitions and had a, 'Special relationship with horses that was uncanny.'

She pointed out photographs of Petunia and told Chris how 'gifted' and 'talented' her daughter was.

An uncomfortable feeling filled Chris as he felt there to be a contradiction with the modest surroundings and way of life she was keen to tell him about and her feelings of withdrawing from a competitive and materialistic culture, yet she unashamedly boasted about her daughter's achievements and personal attributes.

Maddy was surprised that Chris did not have a bag with him, thinking he would bring a change of clothes as she assumed he was staying for the night. This took Chris by surprise as he had not expected to stay overnight, and this must have shown on his face as Maddy said they would be having a drink and conversations can go on late so it would be too late to get back home. Chris felt even more uncomfortable as he did not relish the thought of staying overnight, although knowing he should not be so judgemental and to dismiss people so quickly, but there was something he did not like about the situation, and he had only been in the house about an hour.

It was not long before Roger arrived, and although he introduced himself in a friendly manner his handshake was so firm it not only surprised Chris but also hurt his hand. He thought it unnecessarily hard, and wondered why Roger had gripped his hand so tightly his knuckles actually compressed together to an extent he thought his fingers might snap. Roger was a short man and of small build, and Chris felt he was conscious of this as he looked up at Chris who was a lot taller than him. Roger was over twenty years older than Chris, and he reminded him of it a couple of times as they talked about music while he was showing Chris around the outside of his house.

They went into the stables and as Chris was nervously patting a pony Roger told him it was obvious to see he was a city person. Chris did indeed feel like a fish out of water, and he felt Roger was overemphasising it and that his presentation of an individualistic, alternative lifestyle with an easygoing manner could not belie a fierce ruthlessness he had in pursuing his aims. He asked Chris how long he had known Bill Copley, Karena and Roy, watching Chris closely as he answered and then telling him he knew about Steven, and just as they were leaving the stables he stopped and looked at Chris, his voice taking on a serious tone of warning as he told him what he was pursuing was a dangerous thing to do.

They returned to the house to have the soup Maddy was making earlier, and as they did so Roger and Maddy told Chris about the food they ate and of how the vegetables they used were organically farmed. Roger told Chris of a 'supplier' they bought their meat from, all of it reared without the use of harmful artificial chemicals, and just as they were finishing their soup Petunia came in from school. She was a friendly self-confident girl, and it was obvious by her manner she had been regularly told how attractive and talented she was. The proud parents told Chris of how proficient she was at music, yet more than competent in the sciences she excelled in art and literary subjects, and although having an ability to initiate original creativity in the arts, and having a gift for languages, her precocity as a horsewoman was so evident it had been picked up on by a coach working for the national team, who coincidentally Roger happened to know.

Chris felt she responded to what her parents were saying about her with an act of rehearsed modesty. He noticed the ease she felt in how she spoke and explained her clearly defined ambitions, and Chris thought about people he knew who were intelligent and creative, but just too sensitive to make a mark upon the world, people like Paul the artist and his brother Steven. They, and others like them concerned themselves with what they believed were the big and significant matters affecting the lives of people, and here was a person, who was little more than a child, expressing herself in such a positive self-assured manner, telling him what kind of person she saw herself as being and where she was going, with, ostensibly, little or no regard for people or matters that might impede her personal quest.

She said, 'Life is a balancing act, and one has to be aware of the negative facets that impact on our lives,' and she went on to say, 'They can't control everything all the time - it's your life, enjoy it, take advantage of what you can and create opportunities that can give you what you want.'

Her eyes settled on Chris with a look that might have been saying there are many options out there and I'll choose what I want and when I want. The girl's knowing look and self-belief made Chris feel even more uncomfortable and he thought of Nina, only a year younger than her, but so different with her naïve and open view of the world. The young girl's proud parents looked on, her mother watching Petunia with a satisfied expression, content in the way her daughter is turning out, and Roger looked at Chris with what Chris thought could be a smile bordering on smirking at his and other people's shortfalls when contrasted with the confidence and astute bearing his daughter possessed, and then with his sneaky smile remaining on his face Roger said, 'Our meal is ready.'

While eating their meal Petunia asked Chris some questions about where he worked, but her inquiry quickly gave way to talking about herself, which Chris was pleased about as he was beginning to tire with her precociousness. After they had finished the meal Roger and Chris went into another room and quickly got onto the subject of the system, and how things are organised. Roger spoke in a way as if it was common knowledge that innocent people are utilised for the state's preservation. Roger spoke about the state's security system and of how it is incredibly tangled and is made up of separate cells, often working in ignorance of what the others are doing. He told Chris that they do not even know of their existence let alone the other agents who work in them. Roger said, 'Sometimes their wires cross, so to speak, and they blow each other away, but that's a chance they take - all in all the system works.'

They spoke about Steven and the possibility of him going to the 'colony,' and Chris talked about his obsessive concern with how people who have done nothing wrong are used as scapegoats and that he had heard how innocent people are killed on game shows and the state often gets more of the so-called 'offenders' from abroad, more innocent people who are vulnerable and exploited by rogue head of states for profit and to build strong relationships with this country for their own purposes.

Roger told Chris how people are flown in to remote airports where high security is in place, and to get within five miles of them is impossible. They are not only fodder for the game shows as the majority of them are used for purposes of security, such as measuring the effects of bomb blasts, bullet wounds, chemical and gas use, methods of mind programming and torture.

'Some of these things have been tried out in the past on one's own people,' Roger said, 'Like those in the army, or people from very poor areas.'

'And artists,' Chris said.

Roger looked at him, considering what Chris had said. He then nodded slowly and deliberately before speaking in a quiet tone, 'Yes, indeed, and artists. Luckily, us musicians, generally, have always been more adept at presenting, in public at least, an acceptable face - what we really think remains hidden.'

Chris did not want to discuss what he actually thought, which was how some musicians compromise to such a degree and produce work to be used by the system so they can live a comfortable life.

They went back into the farmhouse and Chris asked Roger for a lift to the station so he could get home while there was still time. Roger and Maddy insisted he stayed the night, and for him to spend the evening with them having some wine and conversation, but Chris had not relaxed since the moment he arrived and he could not connect with Roger. His excuse for not staying the night was because he did not realise how long it took to travel there and that he had an important appointment in the morning concerning work. It was a lie, and lying was a thing Chris found very hard to do, and it was something he had been told many times he was not good at all. Roger agreed to drive Chris to the station and said if he caught the last train back he would be able to catch the connections in order to get home. For the remainder of the time Chris was there Petunia was in her room talking to her friends on the computer, while the three of them discussed history, politics and the prevailing regime.

Chris brought up Kim Blakely's name and spoke about his ideas and how his identity had to remain hidden because it would mean certain death if the system got hold of him.

Roger looked at Chris before speaking, and then told him he knew Kim Blakely.

Chris could tell that even though Roger was blasé about his relationship with Blakely there was a great sense of gratification beneath what he was showing, and when Chris asked Roger where he met Blakely he told him he could not go into matters like that.

Chris did not find it intriguing, as he felt Roger thought he should do, in fact he found the bluff and secrecy to be frustrating.

Roger asked Chris if he had seen a film called Corporations Rule. Chris had not, and so Roger gave him the background to the short film, which was overseen by Kim Blakely, as he took it out of a drawer and placed it in the player. It was a documentary that gave an outline of the interrelationship between the government, the ruling elite and corporations. The film explained how the different parts making up the triad fed off one another in a relationship that is reciprocal in order to pursue the interests of each part. Legislation is passed by government that had been initiated by the ruling elite to benefit corporations and those connected with them who are members of the ruling elite and in government. The film named individuals, revealing what connections they had and what positions in government they held, and explained the practices that exist as trading laws had been swept aside in recent years and that legislation protecting employment rights, wages and working conditions have been totally scrapped.

The film told of how government legislation had whittled human rights to a state of virtual non-existence and pushed the point that the individual is no more than a product for corporations to own and utilise at their will.

Roger went on to say how he and Maddy had met Kim Blakely on many occasions and were quite close to the esteemed significant figure, and as Roger spoke Chris became conscious of the cosy little room he was sitting in, the renovated old farmhouse set in peaceful countryside and their high achieving children Maddy and Roger were only too willing to brag about.

He felt the situation to be absurdly perverse - that people like Roger could have an influence in bringing about progressive change and challenge the system in any meaningful way whatsoever and what Roger and Maddy were doing was merely a lifestyle choice. They could have chosen another one and been a member of an exclusive golf club and took holidays in expensive places where only the elite can go because it is too expensive for the average person to afford on their wages.

Roger spoke for a while longer before noticing the time and telling Chris he would drive him to the station. Chris said his farewells and Maddy said how pleased she was to meet him and that he had to visit again and stay over, but when Chris asked if he should say goodbye to Petunia he was told she would be far too engrossed in her work or communicating with friends to bother her.

The station area was quiet, as it was earlier in the day when he was waiting for the bus, which for Chris seemed a lot longer than seven hours before. Those seven hours could have been weeks, or even months. It seemed to Chris that even time was different in a place of peace and cordial routine, although a place that was probably monotonous for some young people who craved more lively stimulation.

Chris stood on the platform, aware of being the only person in the little station and the immediate area. There was an eerie atmosphere and he could not stop thinking that something was going to happen. Exactly what it was, he did not know, but it would be sinister when it did happen. He considered two words in his mind, sinister and different, and he would not have been surprised if two men in uniform carrying machine guns appeared on the platform, grabbed hold of him and dragged him out of the station to an armoured vehicle where a salivating dog was straining at a leash wanting to attack him.

Chris suppressed these unnerving thoughts and concentrated on the quietness, listening to sounds he had not heard for years. One was the yawning sound of space punctuated by random noises made by wild animals as they called and rustled in nearby hedges and undergrowth, and there was the sound of just one car in the distance, solitary, as if it was the only car in the world. It evoked feelings that reminded him of his childhood and he thought back to holidays he had with his parents and of the long summer breaks from school. Chris remembered film his father had taken during childhood holidays, and he wondered what had happened to it.

And then his mind came back to his present situation and of how he felt. Not only of feeling anxious in the deserted station, but of what he had embarked upon in relation to Steven. A bitter taste broke in his mouth and disappointment filled his mind as a feeling of loneliness suddenly overwhelmed him. Troubled emotions clouded his thoughts and any positive focus gave way to past memories that carried doubt and apprehension about what he was doing in the future.

He thought of Rosie and of what he was putting her through. Chris went over what she had said to him in either impatience or anger about Steven, and people like him, of how they are not able to change the world, and she did say a while ago that there are people telling others what to think when they cannot even sort out their own lives, because they project feelings of dissatisfaction they feel about themselves onto society, which is easy to do, to blame something they have no personal influence over for causing them to feel the way they do. Rosie had turned away when she had said that, and Chris could see she regretted saying what she had; but she did say it and Chris realised it could be something that might just break them apart, and that was something he feared terribly and upset him to think about.

Chris did not share the stillness of the nightime quietness as he sat on a wooden bench on the platform as his mind was swimming with conflicting thoughts. The soft breeze had a sharp edge to it, which was surprising considering what a hot sultry day it had been, but it was the only refreshing thing Chris felt as he looked down the railway track that vanished into darkness.

Twenty-Eight

Chris entered his house quietly, as he always did when it was late. The day's events of visiting Roger Edgebury had been tiring, but Chris did not want to go to bed, he wanted to sit down for a while in the living room and have a hot drink. He thought about Roger Edgebury, his way of life, his daughter Petunia, of how confident she was and the way Maddy is with her fashionably austere rustic life-style, complete with an artificial fabrication of peasant clothing. He also thought about what real weight people like Roger Edgebury and his type actually had in challenging the system. Chris was tired of thinking about it all, so he picked up the remote control, pointed it at the television and pressed a button, knowing what was going to be on, but it would take his mind off what he was thinking, for a short while at any rate.

Chris looked at the screen thinking how the incessant flow of music shows, information films, quiz shows, talk programmes and the comedy shows, which, for Chris, came across as surreal, fused together like a mental battering ram intruding into one's personal senses. He went through the channels and stopped on a news programme that had an item about terrorists in a far off land sabotaging essential commodities destined for the part of the world where Chris lived, and that was followed by a news 'special' to do with people taking the law into their own hands.

There were stories from around the country about members of the public carrying out punishments on alleged criminals and people suspected of sexual crimes, often based on the style shown on The Offender's Nemesis. It is a common thing for people to do, some of them say they are frustrated because they cannot get on the show, or their requests for dealing with an 'offender' have not been taken up. They enact gruesome punishments and feel aggrieved when the authorities arrest them, although, as the programme showed, the police look the other way in certain cases. One such case was of an elderly man who took action against a group of young men who congregated on a street corner near to where he lived. The man lobbed a petrol bomb from his car window at them as he drove by. He spoke about how he remembered the 'bad old days' when people's lives were ruined by young louts, and he said, 'I just thought I would let them know if they have any ideas of causing bad behaviour it will be countered with more force than they can muster.'

And there was the case of a young man whose family said their questions have led nowhere after continually asking the police to investigate his death. The young man was accused of stealing from a woman's handbag in a shop and the staff and members of the public pounced on him and enacted what they jokingly described as a 'sit in.' The man was dead before the police arrived, his ribcage crushed by the enormous weight of people sitting on him.

Chris thought about the man in the college refectory and how he spoke to him in an accusatory manner, and of how he pushed his point and how he supported members of the public getting together in numbers to challenge, beat and even kill criminals and those suspected of doing wrong. Chris felt unsettled thinking about the man as it worried him he would make trouble for Steven, so he pressed a button on the remote control in a hope of shifting his thoughts away from persecution and suspicion.

There was a news programme about rioting taking place in a far-off land. It was difficult to say where it actually was because the reporting was so imprecise, but it was, apparently, a country somewhere in the Far East. The commentator explained how the country had once enjoyed a good quality of life afforded by a strong economy, but that had now all changed and austerity measures had been introduced by the government, although the effects of poverty had opened old regional rivalries that had culminated in bloody wars taking place.

The commentator spoke of how life was now cheap for the people living there, as it was in other areas of the world, and bloodshed was a common experience of daily life. Chris noted how old the film footage was, probably years old and the whole presentation was unconvincing, with no clear identification of who was being interviewed, just improbable titles, such as, Government Minister For Food with what was supposed to be the person's name. The images jumped from what was obviously one country to a different country altogether, yet the dialogue led one to believe it was happening in the same place.

Chris changed the channel and watched a documentary about a group of popular comedians who were on tour around the country. There are people who go to see them that become so excited when seeing their 'idols' and in some cases the excitement spills over to violence, so armed guards have to be present in the large arenas where the comedians are appearing.

Pressing a button on the remote, Chris gazed at the screen phlegmatically as yet another news and 'debate' programme was showing scenes of an arrest taking place in a project housing 'foreign nationals'. A spokesman for the state's security said how parts of some projects are 'infested with illegals.' He told the presenter, 'It is a multi-parallel society, at odds and contradicting the host country's beliefs and way of things, and inevitably it results in friction.'

The man went on to explain how there are many illegal immigrants whose primary aim is to inflict destruction upon the country, and as the man spoke footage was shown of state security officers breaking into flats, pistol whipping people, using batons and firing live ammunition into crowds that gather around the scene. The programme is billed as being news, but it is in essence entertainment, and the more violence is shown the more popular it is.

A well-known female celebrity was interviewed and asked for her opinion on law and order and the way criminals are dealt with. Chris remembered she is signed up to a company owned by a consortium headed by Alan Manville. She smiled and giggled her way through the interview and was thanked by the presenter for her, 'interesting insights and comments.'

Chris had seen enough and decided to call it a day.

Twenty-Nine

Over the following weeks Chris had made a visit to Bill Copley's flat. It was the same old thing, people reading out articles they had written that had been published in the 'underground' journals. Karena and Roy turned up later and as Chris was leaving Karena approached him. Speaking in a quiet tone she told him to be careful and consider the next step he makes as he goes further and deeper into his plan to help Steven. She leant close to Chris and asked him to come round to her place as she thought he would interested in seeing film she had, and also she wanted to talk to him about what he had been doing to help Steven. Chris gave her his number and Karena said she looked forward to him coming round, and then she did something that surprised Chris, she pressed two of her fingers against the back of his hand, and he noticed how cool her fingers were and how firm the pressure was. Chris looked into her eyes, and for the first time he noticed the green shade in them, and how they were fixed onto his.

Chris kept a lot of what he was doing, in terms of contacting people and what he spoke about, from Rosie. She was making it very clear how she did not like him doing what he was, and although she would support Steven to the end she felt Chris was going to bring trouble to them all, and one thing Chris especially did not tell Rosie about was his intention of going to see Karena. Chris contacted Karena a few days after she had asked him to come round to her place; it was difficult for Chris to keep spending time away from his family, but he told her he could come round the next day as he was able to get out of work a couple of hours early, and she agreed to that.

As Chris rang the bell to Karena's flat he was aware of feeling slightly nervous, and just as he was thinking about why he should be feeling the way he did the door opened, and there was Karena smiling at Chris in a way that was different to how she usually did. Karena guided Chris into the living room and as she directed him to a chair she told him Roy was still at work. She placed her hand on Chris's shoulder and looked down at him as she spoke, telling him about the film and that the words were Kim Blakely's, but another man was reading them. Chris was offered a cup of coffee and when it was made they sat back to watch the film, which started with a narration over various images, which at times related to what was being said while at other times seemed unconnected with what the narrator was saying. There were scenes of desolate terrains, which changed into images of hardship suffered by those working in mines, and images of unashamed opulence contrasted with the meagre living conditions of people who worked in the mines.

Chris sat back and listened to what the narrator was saying.

'*Those people who have no desire to please authority and do not feel the need to be given a reward for exhibiting certain behaviour – the people that refute general consensual belief and refuse to be compliant – these are the people that do not incur measures and penalties that limit self-expression, but their lack of co-operation does not mean they will be left in peace to enjoy their independence to explore, unhindered, latent knowledge and personal attributes.*

'*The individual has a lack of confidence, wandering lost like a child seeking reassurance. Like a desperate man confessing inner feelings to a stranger, resulting in being led by the hand just as a scared five year old child might be. A lack of strong, positive self-identity arises as a person's fears and causes of insecurity are targeted. This creates a state of stress so that thoughtful responses and reason are not drawn on, but rather the individual responds by exhibiting irrational behaviour. Fear and anger are emotions constantly induced through mind persuasion strategies. The individual becomes imbued with a personality that is practiced unconsciously. So intoxicated is the person through over-stimulation, that his or her mind is open to instruction and does not question with logic.*

'*The successful outcome is an individual deprived of independent will. It is the intention to bring about a condition where the individual believes in the validity of what he or she is presented with on a daily basis. It is nothing other than torture, similar to strategies used by interrogators in the Inquisition as a method to bring about desired results.*

The resistant mind is dismantled and kept in a perpetual state of anxiety and insecurity. The demands of the state are pitched persistently in a series of contradictory and conflicting messages that change daily. Its content changes meaning and is presented without comprehensible order, which renders the individual to be vulnerable and confused.

Feelings of guilt are instilled, as are other emotions such as despair, depression and a need for consolation. The individual is fatigued, needing approval from established authorities in order to kindle a sense of relief and accomplishment. Yet this feeling of achievement is transitory as the condition of uncertainty continues, seemingly, forever.

'*Alienation is a condition the state encourages every individual to feel. To be estranged from those who are perceived as other and a possible threat. Although they are in fact just friends, family, associates and neighbours. They are just people who share and participate in one's community. People who could, and should, be seen as people one shares everyday experiences with, rather than people to be feared and treated with suspicion. Emotions are united in cases of hatred, as in the example of punishing criminals - or supposed criminals.*

192

'A sense of felt loneliness is a perfect condition to manipulate, because a person who is lonely is often vulnerable and likely to be desperate for relief from the unpleasant or unbearable feelings suffered. The lonely person will often grasp at anything that, or anyone who, offers sympathy and reassurance, even if that relief has negative consequences. Those consequences can be dangerous as they could further limit a person's independence as the person offers his or herself to be controlled and placed deeper within the grip of a power and authority that oversees everything in his or her life.
One relinquishes one's responsibility for oneself because one cannot bear the pain one feels when addressing one's own situation.

'It can be understood as a conversation between the state and the individual. It happens daily and occurs in all situations to bring about the transformation of minds that might offer resistance to the desired response wanted by the state.
One method employed by the state can be described as being similar to the bad cop/good cop routine used in the process of forcing a confession from an offender - or a supposed offender. The method is to alternate between kindliness and aggressiveness. Under the extreme pressure, during this type of interrogation, the person being interrogated will like one policeman and be scared of the other. An attachment is made with the kind one, who seems friendly and understanding. Affection develops as the recipient of the interrogation seeks relief and the good feelings that come from the compassion shown by the kind interrogator. A perverse relationship is formed out of desperation and limited within the conditions established by the interrogator towards the offender, or suspected offender.

It is similar to the sense of loneliness felt through alienation in the case of the state cajoling people to comply with its demands. Those that resist are pressurised and often acquiesce to avoid feelings of difference. Their resolve is broken by the negative effects they feel because of alienation.'

The film went on for a while, longer than Chris would have liked it to really, and he noticed how the relentless monotone narration that seemed to accompany 'underground' films was not dissimilar to the voice used in the state information films. Every now and then Chris looked over at Karena and they smiled at one another, and when the film finished Karena changed her position in her chair and asked Chris what he thought about it. They discussed the film and Blakely's ideas, although Chris felt it was like a teacher and student conversation, with Chris being the latter. Karena, quite suddenly, said that Chris looked tired, and as he told her he had not been sleeping well she arched one eyebrow and a secretive smile danced on her lips, which accentuated her highly defined cheekbones, and Chris thought that was another one of Karena's features he had not noticed before.

A strained silence came upon the room, although it was not completely silent as Chris became aware of what could be described as background sounds he would not normally have noticed. Slight creaks in the building caused by the wind outside were now heard as deep grating sounds, the footsteps of people walking outside were distinguished from the passing traffic, and a voice raised in the distance held a resonance that Chris tried to decipher, and he realised Karena was just looking at him. He shifted in his chair and started to speak, asking Karena about her connection with Blakely. Karena spoke in a way as if she was allowing Chris an insight to privy information and emphasised her close relationship with Kim Blakely. Chris felt that maybe she was having an intimate relationship with Blakely by the way she spoke about him, who she obviously saw as sensual, besides admiring his other attributes of intellect, bravery, commitment and passion, but then maybe she was just infatuated with the man, in a way a teenage girl has a crush on someone.

Karena looked at Chris for a while before saying, 'I have a passion for politics, campaigning and justice - strong, intelligent and passionate men turn me on.'

She then regarded Chris coolly, but not in an unfriendly manner, and although not deliberately inferring anything, Chris asked where Roy was. Karena smiled at Chris, but did not answer him and she looked across the room as if considering what he had said. Chris had not meant anything by what he asked her, but realised it must have been subconsciously prompted, because he was wondering if Roy knew about Karena's intimate relationship with Kim Blakely. As Chris mulled over these thoughts he was unaware of Karena watching him, concentration showing on her intelligent face as she studied Chris as if he was easy reading matter. 'Don't worry,' she said, 'Roy knows, we are very adult about our relationship.'

Chris asked Karena how long she had known Blakely, and she told him she had met Kim Blakely many years ago at covert meetings that were open only to those by special invitation, but it had only been in the last four years their relationship had developed, and Chris thought she stopped herself just as she was going to tell Chris what Blakely looked like. Karena looked down at the carpet, and a look of self-reproach came upon her face for telling Chris what she had, and shaking herself from her mood she continued to talk, although not about Blakely. She spoke about the inner sanctum of the 'underground movement' and how meetings are held at short notice, and the places where they met varied and were

194

changed at the last moment. Karena told Chris how Blakely would always come alone, delegate tasks to others and discuss plans with the people there. She told Chris that none of the people he had met who were connected with the 'underground movement' had attended the meetings she was telling him about, and neither did they know anything about them, and the one's that said they had were lying. This made Chris think of what he had been told round Bill Copley's flat, and Simon the supposed health worker, and Roger Edgebury, but he did not say anything to Karena, although he did ask her if Roy knew about the meetings. She told him that Roy did not attend the meetings with Blakely, and also he did not know about the existence of most of them.

Karena stopped speaking and looked at Chris in a way that was hard and resolute.

Chris was surprised how easily Karena had divulged such important and personal information to him, and then as if answering his thoughts she said, 'I shouldn't have told you, but I wanted to share it with you - and now I have no alternative, but to trust you with my life.'

Chris was stunned as Karena continued to talk, telling him how the secret police and the various security agencies are working to catch Kim Blakely, but he is an evasive character and as much as they try they had not been successful in their endeavours. She said that it sickened the state how he operates and there had been a high priority file open with his name written across it for a very long time and that it is an embarrassment to them as they have such confidence in nailing anything, or body to the floor they consider to be out of place. Karena repeated herself as she implored Chris to remain silent and to never say anything about what he had just learned.

Chris was bewildered. He moved carefully in the chair he was sitting in, like a person coming out of general anaesthetic.

'I better go,' he said as he stood up. In one way he could not wait to get out of the flat, but he also wanted to stay because he was intrigued to find out more about her relationship with Kim Blakely and the inner workings of the 'underground movement.'

Karena saw him to the door, and for a second he thought she might give him a quick affectionate peck on his cheek, but that did not happen. She stood a little distance from Chris, repeating in a formal manner that he had to give his word he would not say anything to anyone about what she had told him. She waved goodbye and said, 'Bye Chris,' in a manner he imagined a medical consultant might use when talking to a patient.

As Chris went home he thought about Karena and what she told him about Blakely, and of her relationship with him, and he thought about the 'underground movement,' the people he had met who were in it and what they had told him. At best it was similar to the state, in that it had different people working for the same aims yet were unaware of one another's activities, or even existence, and at worse it was just something that attracted fantasists, but Chris reminded himself one has to be careful because 'underground movements' are taken seriously by the authorities, that is why they are infiltrated by state moles. It is a major concern for people engaged in what is sometimes described as 'nonconformist conduct,' even if they are involved in the most minor way, because the state is known for monitoring every kind of activity. Anything related to politics is scrutinised and those involved are dealt with in different ways. If found to be harmless they are either bought off or lose their qualified status, which results in the person, and his or her family, having to live a life without the trappings and opportunities they once enjoyed, while others are 'despatched' if judged to be troublesome.

And then a twist of fear turned in his stomach as he considered how he did not know the people in the groups he attended, neither did he know if some of them were actually who they said they were. It was all so potentially very dangerous. He thought of Karena and that even Kim Blakely, the underground's messiah, could be a spy and was an elaborate manifestation created by the security services. Chris told himself to present an affable presentation when he got home and not show how troubled he was, Rosie had been telling him more and more how she did not want Nina to become upset by what he was getting into.

Thirty

Chris went round to see Brendan on a weekday evening. He had a smart, but basic flat in an inexpensive area that was okay although quite near a housing project. Brendan could have found work paying far better money than he earned in the job he did, but he settled for a very modest lifestyle working as a manager in a large home for people with physical and mental disabilities. He applies his skills in electronics to improve the quality of the lives of the people who live in the home, and as the budget is extremely slim, Brendan uses his initiative to devise mechanisms that aid and support everyday living, such as inventions to open doors, lifts on staircases and heat sensors when cooking. Steven had told Chris that Brendan was a near genius in electronics, but the state 'acquires' people with talent in this area to serve its interests, so he settled for work that gave no real advantage to an authority that would utilise his abilities for purposes of military conflict.

Brendan's family was destroyed by the 'big change', as were many others, his father could not cope with the transformation and took to drinking heavily and in doing so became abusive to his mother, a meek woman who died far earlier than she should have done. His father died from liver disease and two of Brendan's bothers were affected badly by what had happened to their family, one becoming an alcoholic and the other committing suicide over ten years ago. Despite all that had happened to Brendan he remained a kind man and applied himself to helping people, especially people who can not help themselves, and he is a person who Chris values greatly as a friend.

Chris spoke to Brendan about who he had met and what they had been talking about, and although talking about Karena and what she had told Chris he did not mention how he found her attractive. In the past Brendan told Chris he had never been involved in any way with dissident groups, and although supportive of Chris in wanting to help his brother he thought the activities and plans of most dissidents to challenge the system was completely ineffective. He did not like the sound of Roger Edgebury at all and he told Chris to be very wary of Simon the health worker.

A few weeks later was the first day of November and winter had set in. As Chris made his way into the college to do his day of tutoring he hoped to see Steven as he knew he would be working that day, but he could not find him during the lunch break and his phone was switched off. When Chris had finished for the day he went in search of Steven until eventually he bumped into Steven's Tutor Manager, an officious looking woman who dressed very plainly. Chris asked her if she had seen him, but she did not answer and she studied Chris, staring into his face before speaking without any expression in her eyes, other than disdain. She told Chris that Steven had been reported by a number of students for expounding 'unusual views,' and a female student had made an allegation that Steven was always staring at her. The head of his department wanted to see him, and until he did, which had been arranged to happen the following week, Steven was suspended from work while investigations took place. Chris looked into the women's eyes, hoping to find something to establish if what had been alleged was really true, but there was nothing in the way of sympathy or wanting to help Chris, on the contrary, she looked as if the matter was closed, Steven was guilty and he should be punished severely.

As Chris made his way home his mind was ablaze with conjecture, all of which was negative. He imagined how Steven's flat was under surveillance and state security agents were monitoring his activities. Chris thought about the lecturer who had spoken to him in the refectory, thinking through what the man had said word for word, and playing over and over in his mind the way the man looked at him and how he spoke in what Chris felt to be a condemnatory manner. There was also the matter of money, Steven did not get paid that much, but it was a wage and one that he needed. If things went against him he would never get a job in a college again, or in any qualified capacity. It would be labouring work and he would lose his flat. Images flooded though Chris's mind of the people he had seen that had lost their qualified jobs, their faces gaunt and burned with worry and fear.

Chris phoned Brendan and told him what had happened, and as usual Brendan spoke in his logical manner, telling Chris to take one thing at a time. He then phoned Simon, but all Chris heard was a recoding of Simon's voice sounding calm and professional, saying he is not available, to leave a message and he will get back.

Rosie listened without saying a word as Chris told her about Steven being suspended, her hands folded gently in her lap as she looked down at the floor deep in thought. She tried to placate Chris, but the worry in her face told that she thought more trouble was on the way. Chris had no luck trying to contact Simon that evening, and it was not until the following afternoon that he spoke to him, and immediately Chris detected something different in his voice. He was very matter of fact and distant as he told Chris that Steven had not contacted him, but however, he would not be looking into the matter until Steven tells him about it at their next appointment, which was not for a couple of weeks. Chris asked him if he could get in touch with the college and try to find out more about what was supposed to have happened, but Simon's manner remained detached as he said, 'that type of action was not his area of responsibility.'

Two days passed and Chris had not been able to contact Steven so he went round to his flat, cursing the fact he did not have a key to where his brother lived, he asked Steven enough times, but although saying he would give Chris one he had never got round to it. Steven was not there, and it felt to Chris like he had not been there for some time. He phoned Brendan who told him to ask the neighbours if they had seen him, or had seen something. Chris was now very worried, the people living next door or near to Steven had not seen him or anything out of norm. 'Keeps himself to himself,' one of them said, 'bit like a ghost', and then eyed Chris with suspicion as he shut the door.

It was as if Steven had vanished, and the frustration of not being able to find anything out grew in Chris's mind as he stood outside his brother's flat looking about himself at a hard concrete world that appeared as hopeless as he felt.

Over the following few weeks Chris still had not been able to contact Steven, it really was as if he had disappeared without trace. Chris had gone through endless possibilities of what might have happened to him, suicide being the main one. He reported it to the police, going to the station and filling out a form with all his details and of his brother's, and while doing it imagining what Steven would say to him if he turned up unscathed. Chris asked the police if they could go round to Steven's flat and break into it, as he might be lying dead on the floor. Their response was not friendly and although they thought he was making a fuss about nothing they promised to go round and check it out. Chris heard from them the day afterwards, they had entered the flat and had found it empty, but found 'nothing suspicious to report.'

Chris could not concentrate at work and it was brought to his attention that it had been noted. He told them he was going through family problems, but did not go into detail or tell them about Steven. Chris kept an eye out for Paul, the artist, hoping to see him, feeling he might gain some comfort by telling him about Steven, but Paul was not to be seen. Chris found it difficult to contact Simon, and when he did the health worker was businesslike in his manner, telling Chris to be patient and that Steven is a grown man and maybe he had just gone away to have a rest from things, considering the worry he must have over the matter at the college. When Chris asked why he did not seem that concerned, especially since Steven had not turned up at the appointment they had arranged, Simon ignored what Chris had said, saying Steven was a complex man and it was not a legal requirement to attend the appointment.

199

Chris contacted Karena who told Chris not to worry and went into a convoluted theory of what might have happened, so much so that Chris found it irritating. He went to a meeting at Bill Copley's, having contacted Bill and telling him he wanted to come along and talk about his brother. The people at the meeting, including Bill Copley, appeared indifferent as Chris told them about Steven being suspended from college, as if they did not want any trouble brought into their lives. Their apathy, or distance, remained when Chris told them about Simon and that he had not seen Paul the artist, and Chris felt it was either frightening to them because it was real and not a game of theorising from a safe distance, or it could be something else, something Chris could not put his finger on, but it felt dark whatever it was.

Thirty-One

On a Saturday evening in the middle of December, Chris was sitting in the living room at home watching the television. The volume was turned down low and Chris was not really watching what was on it, but just looking in its direction. He looked from the screen, which was showing fish swimming in the depths of the sea, to Rosie sitting next to him on the sofa reading a book with her legs curled beneath her. Chris looked around the room with a thoughtful expression on his face before finally speaking.

'Nina's friend will be arriving shortly then?'

Rosie was immersed in the book she was reading and just nodded without looking up. Chris watched her for a few seconds before continuing. 'They're not going to be up all hours this time.' It was a statement, not a question and he watched Rosie waiting for her to respond, but she did not, so he carried on, 'They can go to bed late, of course they can, but I don't want them chattering down here in the middle of the night.'

Rosie barely nodded as she shifted a little in a lazy and comfortable manner.

Chris realised he was not going to have a conversation with her and looked at the television, although what he was looking at did not enthuse him, he spoke quietly, nearly under his breath, 'I might as well talk to these fish - trying to talk to you.'

'What?' Rosie said without looking from her book, and she gave Chris a little kick as a signal to leave her alone.

The house was quiet and peaceful, the only sound was the soft music coming from the television, which added to the stillness of the room, and as Chris began to stretch tiredly his mobile telephone rang and made him jump. He went to answer it, but before he could say anything the rush of words that spilled out of the phone caused him to hold it away from his ear, and then he leant forward, stunned as he listened to what was being said to him. He sprang up from the sofa holding the phone to his ear, his eyes staring in shock as he repeated the word, 'what?' And then he shouted into the phone, 'What? Where? When? Tell me, where? When? How?'

Rosie stared at Chris as she dropped her book, stood up and asked Chris what had happened, but he did not answer her.

The door opened and Nina was standing in the doorway, her eyes showing a fright that would stain her memory for the rest of her life. Rosie and Nina watched Chris crumple to the floor and burst out crying as he repeated the word, 'no, no, no, no, no, no.'

Nina was scared, never having seen either of her parents in such a state. Rosie kept asking Chris what had happened and then turned to Nina telling her to leave, but the young girl stayed where she was looking at Chris.

'They've killed Steven,' Chris blurted out, 'they've killed him, killed him - he's dead, they murdered him, on that show,'

Chris began to wail and Rosie stared into a space that was light years from the room she was in. She snapped out of it and tried to comfort Chris, placing her arm around his shoulders and speaking softly into his ear. Nina continued to look at Chris, tears breaking in her eyes and tumbling down her clear smooth skin, but she could not speak because the sight of her father in such distress had shocked her into silence, but then she did open her mouth, and although wanting to scream all that came was an inaudible hollow cry. Rosie looked up at Nina and holding out her hand spoke in a voice she intended to sound controlled and calm. 'Go to your room Nina, it's okay, don't worry love,' but Nina did not move, she was rooted to where she stood, standing rigid and staring at her father.

Chris cried out the words, 'Hunted down like a scared animal and beaten to death.'

He threw himself at the sofa, snatched the remote control, pointed it at the television and desperately searched through the channels. Rosie placed her hands on his shoulders, telling him to calm down and that she would contact the relevant people to get information, she then turned and shouted at Nina, telling her to go to her bedroom, and immediately regretting having raised her voice she said, 'Please darling, I'm sorry I shouted, but please darling, not now, just please go along.'

Chris finally stopped pressing the button on the remote control as Alan Manville appeared on the screen pointing into the camera. The forced smile on his face contrasted ominously by the hard edge in his dark eyes, and an underlying smirk seemed to say he will find out if anyone is up to something they should not be as he said, 'Where have you been? And what have you been doing, good people of this fair land?'

His look and tone became sinister as he delivered his next line. 'Let's hope it wasn't anything bad,' and his smile broadened as he dropped his finger, 'Welcome back and join us as we deal with people who have been very bad.'

The theme music of The Offender's Nemesis sounded quite separately from the dead atmosphere in the room where the only other sound was of Chris breathing hard and uttering pained cries. It was as if the room and the world itself had been struck down with a thunderbolt and the only life was of that being shown on the television with three people staring at it, as maybe condemned people do when looking in the face of impending and irreversible doom.

Thirty-Two

The following hour was torturous as Chris telephoned everyone he could think of in a frantic plight to find some information about Steven. He tried to contact the television company, but there was only an answer phone, and then the police said he should go in person to his local police station. Before leaving to go to the police station Chris rang Simon, knowing it would be pointless, which it was. He felt so helpless and just wanted to speak to somebody, but was confronted by what felt like an impenetrable wall.

A knock on the front door silenced the three of them as they stared at one another, fear showing in their faces as they wondered who it might be. And then Nina said it was her friend, the one that was going to stay the night. Chris dropped his head into his hands as Rosie told Nina to stay in the living room and she would tell the girl there has been a change of circumstances; fortunately the girl's mother was still outside in the car, otherwise Rosie would have had to drive her home.

Chris drove, against the wishes of Rosie, to the local police station. She told him he was in no fit state to drive, and she was not going to leave Nina alone in the house, but Chris set off, his distress blinding him from any danger or his surroundings. While driving to the station he had a call from Brendan telling him that he was at Steven's flat and there was police tape over the door barring entry. Brendan told Chris he had asked the neighbours about it and they said there was a police investigation taking place and that they had come round earlier in the day and taped it up. Chris told Brendan to wait there for him and he would drive over after going to the police station.

The police officer in the station eyed Chris with suspicion as he explained about Steven, and then gave him the kind of look a person in authority can give to a person they consider to be wrong about something. Suddenly a door opened by the side of the reception desk and a man appeared, only a year or so older than Chris. The man's manner was that of an adult speaking to a child.

'Can you verify who you are?' the man asked Chris in a flat neutral tone as he sat behind his desk, and leaving Chris to stand with no intention of asking him to sit down. Chris thought about the word 'verify,' it had connotations of a military type of language, the police simply ask for one's ID, as was the case with the police officer behind the desk earlier on. He showed his ID, not telling him he had already produced it because Chris wanted to stick to the reason why he was there. The man looked from the photograph on the ID to Chris, as if it was a difficult match and he was undecided if Chris was who he was claiming to be, and when Chris went to speak the man stopped him by quickly raising the flat of his hand.

'What exactly do you want here, Mr Kirby,' the man asked, looking down at the ID and feeling it in his hand as if it was not genuine. Chris told him, trying to remain calm enough to be articulate, and at one time when he asked if he could sit down the man shook his head in the negative without taking his unrelenting stare from Chris's face. When Chris had nearly finished what he wanted to say the man stopped him, again with the flat of his hand and spoke while staring into his eyes.

'What you have just told me does not make any sense. If only you could hear yourself - it sounds like the demented delusion of a person who has gone mad,' and he continued to stare at Chris, challenging him to defy what he had said.

Chris exploded, but in the time there was for him to shout, 'What?' the door to the room was thrown open and two security officers appeared, dressed from head to toe in riot control clothing. They stood in the doorway holding their weighted truncheons and probably watching Chris for a sign to attack him, but it was impossible to see their eyes behind the visors of the helmets they were wearing.

'Behave yourself, Mr Kirby,' the man behind the desk said, 'remember where you are and that you can't just go around making up stories and attacking people who are trying to enforce the law of the land because they might doubt such a fantastic tale,' and instantaneously a feeling of total isolation and powerlessness engulfed Chris as he looked from the man behind the desk to the two men in the doorway. Nothing was said, Chris remained where he stood until finally the man behind the desk said in an unemotional manner, 'I think, Mr Kirby, because of your behaviour and present state of mind, it would be best for everyone if you stayed here in the station tonight.'

What the man had said shocked Chris, and he looked at him, confused and wanting to know what he meant. 'I think you might be a danger to yourself, if not to others, Mr Kirby,' the man said, 'and I would not be doing my job, which has given me the responsibility to protect the public, if I allowed you to leave this station in your present condition.'

Chris heard himself saying, 'what?' but it did not sound like it was him saying it and two police officers, dressed in normal clothing, entered the room.

'If you please, Mr Kirby, this way now', one of them said as he placed his hand on Chris's arm, and as Chris went to pull his arm away, so dumbfounded he was not aware of what he was doing, the two security officers in riot clothing stepped forward and the police officers moved quickly to stand either side of Chris.

'Don't make matters worse Mr Kirby,' the man behind the desk said, his voice rising slightly to a patronising tone.

'What the hell is going on here?' Chris shouted, and in that instant he felt his feet leave the floor as he was propelled towards the doorway. Chris was unable to resist the force that virtually carried him through the door, down a corridor and into a cell, all the while shouting and screaming as he released years of suppressed pent-up tension, yet even in the state he was in Chris was conscious that the black cloud he felt to be constantly above him had now descended, and with it his worst fears he had about the establishment were now to be confirmed.

Chris did as many other people have done when in an extremely dangerous or urgent situation, which is to think of the most routine things. He thought about whether he had parked his car in the correct space in the car park, and then it was Rosie and Nina with Rosie telling him to be careful and think things through before reacting, and of course there was Brendan, who would be waiting at Steven's flat.

The door slammed shut and a metal cover slid over the peephole. It was quiet in the little cell and Chris looked around, first at the bed and then back at the door, and he did it again, because they were the only things to look at, besides the floor, ceiling and four walls. He stood in silent reflection, not believing what had just happened, the shock of it beginning to fan through his mind and body, but all that evaporated, because his brother was dead, killed on that show, and he broke down, crying, on his hands and knees, filled with thoughts of his poor brother, and he wailed uncontrollably - he knew was helpless and the frustration tore through him.

Chris remained on the floor for a while after he had stopped crying, just sitting there, his mind numbed and his heart breaking. A sudden realisation that he did not have his wallet in his pocket froze his mind as he panicked and patted his pockets, and his phone, that too had gone, and also the keys to his house and car. He stared at the bed and the word 'no,' came involuntarily from his mouth. Chris repeated the word, louder each time he said it, the sight of the bed and thought of staying in the cell overnight was too much for Chris, and he began to scream in a horrifying pitch and tone he had never heard before. Chris continued to scream and cry out until he exhausted himself. He stayed where he was on the floor, not looking at anything, his eyes were open, but his mind was shutting down with shock.

Rosie had been ringing Chris, as had Brendan, but all they got was a message with Chris apologising for not being able to answer his phone and for the caller to leave their name and number and he would ring back. Rosie had left three messages, the last one becoming increasingly concerned as she asked him to ring her and explain what had been happening. Brendan had also left messages, the last one telling Chris he had rung Rosie and they were very worried, and for him to, 'be careful of the bastards, they appear as being thick and stupid, but they're devious fuckers...'

But it was not Chris who had first listened to the messages; it was Garman, in the police station where Chris was in one of the cells. His strong, heavy features concentrated and his lips curled slightly to show his dislike as he listened to what Brendan was saying. He leant over the phone, which he had placed on a table, staring at it for a while after the last message, as if studying it and the man the phone belonged to. After going through a process of thought he picked the phone up and handed it to a man, telling him to give it an 'FT examination,' FT meaning 'fine toothed.' Garman left the room and walked down a corridor where the cells were, and then stopped outside the one holding Chris. He stood close to the door and stared at it as if the door was actually the man he wanted information from.

Thirty-Three

It was over three hours after Chris was put in the cell when the sound of the electronic lock releasing in the door caused Chris to turn and stare at it. A police officer stood in the doorway holding Chris's phone, wallet and keys, and with what might be described as a smirk on his face he said, 'You dropped these in your hurry to get in here.'

Chris stood up, slowly, distrust and confusion limiting his thought and physical movement. Another officer edged past the one in the doorway and said he wanted to search Chris, saying, 'Just to see you're not running off with police property,' which caused the one in the doorway to smirk even more, but the irony and sarcasm did not register as Chris had more important things flooding his mind. The officer searched Chris, very thoroughly, looking into his mouth and exploring with a utensil and then telling him to drop his trousers and pants for an anal inspection. After the body search Chris was led to the charge desk where a different police officer from before was standing. He asked Chris to sign a form, and as Chris began to read it he asked him why he was put in a cell and had his personal things taken from him.

'For your own safety sir,' the man said in a breezy manner that was totally incongruous with the claustrophobic atmosphere of the police station, and he added, 'you were in quite a state by all accounts, we couldn't take the risk of you harming yourself or anyone else - our job is to protect all members of the public sir, not only you,' and he smiled as though he was delivering a piece of surprisingly good news. But Chris was too exhausted to consider what the police officer said and his mind was in turmoil, so he rushed through the small print on the form, which in essence said the person signing the form agreed with the decisions made by the police officers at the station and did not feel 'aggrieved due to unfair treatment' while at the station.

Chris was walked to the door by one of the police officers, and as he opened it he said, 'be careful out there.'

Chris stumbled to the car park thinking if his car was not there he would not have been surprised, but it was, although if it was just as he had left it was another matter. He sat in the car, going through the calls and messages he missed, and he looked at the time, it was ten to midnight, but Chris found it hard to believe everything that had happened had happened all in one day. After calling Rosie and explaining the situation he rang Brendan, who was now at home. Brendan told him he had spoken to Rosie and if he wanted he would come over to his place, just if he needed support. Chris told Brendan they would meet the next day and that he was thankful he had him as friend, and together they would find out about the whereabouts of Steven's body, and get some information about what had happened.

Chris was barely able to drive, having to concentrate on the most simple of actions because his mind could not focus on what he was doing. He cursed himself for not listening to Rosie, and if anything he had made matters worse by rushing into the police station, and then he thought of how the security people would be monitoring everything he did and the people he was close to, probably with bugs and other methods of spying. Chris looked around the inside of the car, knowing it had been searched by the security services and there would be a bug, camera or some other device hidden somewhere, and a person in a building maybe close by or in the other part of the country is listening and watching everything he does.

Thirty-Four

Brendan came round to Chris's house the following morning and the three of them, Rosie, Brendan and Chris spent the day trying to contact people and find information. Chris wanted Nina to stay with Rosie's sister for a while, but Nina was adamant she wanted to stay at home, the trauma of what had happened had taken the youthful spark from her young face and it had been replaced with a shadow of doubt and fear of the world she lives in.

Chris knew things were not right with the people he had been ringing, such as Simon, Bill Copley, Karena and Roger Edgebury. In desperation to find something that might help him he rang each one of them several times, but they were not answering his calls, and although not saying what had happened it would be obvious it was an urgent matter by the tone of his voice when leaving a message. Not one of them got back to Chris for the whole of the day, which was filled with thinking of whom they could contact. There was the matter of Steven's body and what happened to it; what does happen in this situation? These were questions they asked themselves, and would there be a funeral, but then maybe people like Steven were not given one and their bodies were just got rid of, and the thought of Steven's battered body being thoughtlessly thrown into an incinerator was too much for Chris to bear.

Rosie persisted in attempting to speak to someone at the company that made The Offender's Nemesis, but only to be told the regular working week started the following day, which was a Monday, and there might be someone then who could answer her questions. Chris was stopped by Rosie and Brendan from contacting the police and then the remainder of the evening was left in frustration as it became blatantly apparent there was not anybody to speak to, and it was as if Seven had had just vanished without trace and all roads that one would think might lead to an answer were blocked.

Chris told himself he should contact his sister, Helen, he had her address and phone number stored away, and there were a couple of cousins as well as an auntie and an uncle, but he did not have their addresses or phone numbers. There was not anyone else, the family had broken up and they were not close to start with. Chris had to look for his sister's number, the contact they had was so rare he did not have the number to hand. He rang it and listened as his stomach tightened, but there was no dialling tone so he rang the phone company and was told the person at that address had moved a while ago. He had no way of contacting her, and this thought struck him so hard he had to sit down and think about it. His sister did not want to have any contact with him, the realisation sunk in and Chris went over childhood memories of the little he remembered of Helen, and he started to cry.

There was an eerie atmosphere in Chris's house the next morning, Nina refused to go to school and Chris and Rosie phoned their places of work to tell them they would not be going in. The frustration at not being able to find anything out about Steven was unbearable, and it continued throughout that day and into the next when finally Rosie had two numbers to ring. One was for a company associated with the production company that makes The Offender's Nemesis and other number was for the locally elected politician. Chris rang the politician and asked for an appointment, but was told by his secretary he was fully booked up seeing other constituents for at least two weeks, and when Chris explained what it was about the secretary's voice lost its former timbre as he told Chris how a case as important and exceptional as this one needed some research before they meet. Chris asked him if he had any experience of this before, but he told Chris it was a matter that he could not possibly talk about over the phone, although he would take all his details and arrange a time for them to meet.

Rosie did not have any more luck with the company who told her that even though they are a private company the matter she is talking about was dealt with by a particular government department. When Rosie asked for some details of who to contact she was told it was up to her to find out for herself in cases such as this, and was then given numbers for departments she had already rung. And that was it, as painful as it was to accept, there did not seem anything else they could do.

Brendan came round in the evening, offering support and ideas, but just finding the most basic answers to their questions had been impossible. Chris and Brendan spoke of how it had been six weeks after Steven was suspended from his college job that he appeared on The Offender's Nemesis, and during that time Chris did not have any contact with him. Chris thought about when he went to Steven's flat and reporting it to the police, which was at a different police station from the one he was in a couple of nights earlier.

A few days later Karena left a message on the phone Chris used to contact her, it was a short message asking if he was okay, but it felt like a lifeline to Chris, even though he kept it secret from Rosie. Chris was so relieved when hearing her voice that he rang her, and he was even more relieved when she answered. He told her what had happened and she listened carefully without interrupting him. When she spoke her voice was calm and professional, although Chris could not help thinking she sounded objective to the point of sounding clinical. She arranged to meet Chris at Bill Copley's flat, but when Chris told her Bill had not returned his calls and he was getting worried because he thought everyone had shunned him, even her, Karena told him he was anxious and that she had been busy, but she could not speak for Bill Copley or Simon. Her voice then took a serious tone as she said she wanted to speak to Chris about Simon, and when Chris asked what it was about she would not say, only that Chris should be careful of what he says to Simon and she would talk to him when they met.

After speaking to Karena, Chris phoned Bill Copley, but again there was no answer, so he left another message, this time asking if it was okay to come round on the date Karena had told him. Chris looked at the phone in his hand after leaving the message, over two minutes had passed, but he continued to look at the phone as if it was a key that might help him open a door and shine a light into the tangled dark mess where there are no answers to simple questions, and all the while time was going by and his frustration was growing, because he knew how helpless he was against frightful powers wielded by the state; and once again, Chris felt a sense of trepidation at how he had exposed his family to those powers.

Later that evening it was only Chris and Rosie sitting on the sofa in the living room. Rosie had grown very quiet as all avenues to finding out information had been explored. Chris was talking about the whereabouts of Steven's body and the matter of a funeral, and as he was speaking he let out a cry like a wounded animal and jumped to his feet.

'If I hadn't have got involved - snooped around, stirring things up and probably highlighting Steven as a character to monitor, even, get rid of - for Christ's sake - if I hadn't stuck my stupid bloody nose in he could well be here today - but no, he's gone - my brother - dead, and it's my fault,' and he began to sob.

Rosie stood up, watching him before starting to speak. 'Don't, Chris, don't blame yourself - you did what you thought was the right thing to do, because you cared about Steven - you were concerned - because you were a good brother - you defended him, like you did throughout your lives together - he was a large part of who you are, and still is - he had a profound influence in shaping you into the person you are Chris.'

Rosie stepped towards him holding her arms a little to her side as she said, 'Into the person that I love.'

She wrapped her arms around Chris and closed her eyes as she spoke.

'You're a sensitive, brave man Chris, unselfish and kind, please see that whatever pain, upset, embarrassment and hurt you felt about Steven during the course of your life was because you loved him, and it has made you into what you are - and Steven was a decent, intelligent man with good intentions - with insights and capacities,' and she stopped speaking as tears filled her eyes.

As Rosie and Chris held one another they were not to know Nina was standing outside the door listening to the muffled cries of her father, quietly crying and with a burning feeling in her stomach, a feeling she had never felt before; it was fear and anger, she was scared of what was happening to them and angry that it was.

Thirty-Five

Chris went back to work at the end of the week, but finding it difficult to concentrate he decided to leave early, and of course he did not tell anyone at work about Steven, although he was nervous someone would find out. Neither Simon nor Bill Copley had contacted him and he had not got any further in gaining information about Steven's body or about anything else. It was a wall of silence, a term he had heard before and now knew what it felt like to be up against.

Chris took a different route home and decided to take a walk in a shopping precinct, and while walking he saw Paul, the artist, which caused him to stop suddenly. He had to take a second look to check to see if it actually was him, because his appearance had significantly deteriorated. Paul backed quickly into a shop doorway on seeing Chris and waved for him to come over.

'They're doing it to me, Chris, I know they are,' he said. The fear showed clearly in his eyes as they darted in all directions. For Paul, every person that passed was a suspected threat. His desperate stare scanned Chris's face, searching for hidden messages and clues that might give him answers to his sense of torment. Chris tried to placate him, saying he needed to relax and keep quiet, but Paul would not listen, and he told Chris how the state security had been in his flat on a few occasions when he was out, and they had taken some of his belongings on their last visit.

Paul said, 'They don't care I know they've been nosing around my flat - they're so blatant about it they smile in your face,' and he told Chris he had complained and a health worker came to his flat with a state official who told Paul he was going to assess the situation to see if Paul was capable of living in the community by himself.

Paul started to rant about the state official, of how he was wary of him and could never contact him and when he rang up nobody knew of him. He told Chris, 'He's a hulking bloke, looks like a character from an old gangster movie, but makes out he's friendly - but his mean eyes give him away, he's nosing around to cause me trouble, I know that much - I'm sure of it.'

He stared at Chris and told him it was not paranoia as his nurse and doctor kept telling him, he was sure the man had been put onto him by the state and was out to get him in some way, and he shouted out loudly, 'They'll finish me, extinguish me like a light that has to be turned off in a disused building.' Chris tried to calm him down, asking Paul to go for a walk with him and have a cup of coffee. Paul declined the offer, his eyes wild as he looked around the precinct and the people in it, saying nothing, but just staring. After a short while Chris asked Paul if the health worker's name was Simon, and he told Paul he had spoken to him before about him being his brother's health worker and of how he was involved in a plan to get his brother out of the country, but it was useless. Chris gave up as he could see Paul was too far gone to take anything in he was telling him. It would be hopeless telling Paul about Steven being on The Offender's Nemesis, and although frustrated because he wanted to tell him, Chris decided not to bother.

Chris patted Paul on his shoulder, which alerted him to Chris's presence, and they shook hands, and as they did so Paul shook Chris's hand vigorously and warned him of how the state tracks down and 'despatches undesirables' before turning and walking off, looking around himself as he went, staring into the faces of anyone walking close by to him. Chris watched him walk away, remembering how Paul used to look, seemingly at ease, with Dee Dee looking up at him as he exhibited his eccentric personality when stopping to speak to someone or pass a comment and point a walking cane he often had with him at a person, shop or car, but now he looked very much alone and extremely troubled. As Chris watched Paul flail his arms in sudden frenetic movements his attention was drawn to the sound of raised voices, and as well as the shouting there was also a noise that sounded like a cabbage being hit with a bat; Chris knew it was the sound of a person being beaten.

Chris looked in the direction of the noise and saw a small gathering of people, and as if by remote control walked towards the incident that was taking place. He stood among the group of people who were watching a man being beaten by a security officer with such ferocity Chris found it difficult to breathe or swallow. The faces of the people watching were ashen and troubled, but there was a man in is thirties who stood with his legs apart and a smile of deep pleasure filling his face. A woman, who was probably his wife, pulled at his arm to move him away from the scene.

The security officer pushed back the visor on his helmet in order to shout clearly at the man he was beating, and in doing so showed his face, which is not the done thing as anonymity is the usual practice. He snarled words at the man who was on the ground and in the last throes of consciousness, but in a useless and pathetic action he raised his arm to protect himself against the battering he was receiving from the weighted truncheon. The security officer shouted with such anger spittle showered the words he screamed, which were just a repetitive string of expletives and curses. Two other security men looked on, watching their colleague administer the immediate justice.

The man being beaten was not going to be taken away for interrogation, further punishment or to be arrested. This was merely a warning, openly demonstrated for the public to view and to remember this is what happens when you step out of line. Chris was sure the security officer doing the beating was fully aware the other security men were watching meticulously the way he beat the man and noting his verbal tirade. They were monitoring the manner in which he was going about his work; his work colleagues were assessing him

Chris noticed the expressions on the faces of the people who were standing and watching those passing by. He felt that although they did not say anything, beneath the facade of neutrality was a deep questioning as to whether the man on the ground was guilty of any crime and if the level of brutality used was necessary, but those thoughts and feelings were hidden because fear forced a public presentation of blind acquiescence to the practices and methods of punishment metered out by the authorities.

Chris often thought about the security people and how they carry out the things they did. He thought how they must be pretty desperate people if they did it just for the money, because the wages were not that good so there must be other reasons, or a motive such as a desire to wield power over people having little means or support in order to defend themselves. As Chris stood in the precinct he thought of how the security people are not the homogenous group one might at first suppose, there is more than just speculative rumour that shows how members of the security turn on each other and it is fear of their colleagues that maintains their brutality and makes them act in an ostensibly blind manner to order.

The more Chris looked at the security officer the more he believed he was motivated by fear, fear of the other, even of his family and of course the system, which provides the power that sanctions his actions, such as vigorously delivering blows to the man on the ground. Chris often wondered how the security men saw themselves, if maybe they saw themselves in a special way, like the chosen ones in upholding the protection of the state's values. They are men who are involved in work where they beat people who have often done nothing wrong, and sometimes they kill them.

Chris had asked himself, and others, on many occasions how the security men could possibly feel part of the general population when considering what they get up to in the name of their work. He had always thought of the security men at home with their families, buying a birthday card for a young daughter after just beating an innocent man into an irretrievable coma. Chris stood in the crowd thinking what the security man's beliefs and principles actually were, and he remembered a photograph he once saw of a British policeman saluting as he held a car door open for a German Nazi officer. It was taken in the Channel Islands, that part of the United Kingdom occupied by Germans during the Second World War. And maybe that is what would have happened if the Nazi army had invaded the country and occupied it, the security officers, or police staff, would have responded by capitulating with the incoming power and working for them. It might have been just business as usual, only with a different boss; and that is how easy it all is. Theoretical consideration, conjecture, conscience and ethical values had about as much substance as sugar dusting on a birthday cake for a three year old girl. Just doing their job. And scared not to.

The man on the ground did not suffer any more strikes with the truncheon, but the security officer kicked him so viciously it caused Chris to wonder how a person could muster such anger against a person who had not done him any personal harm. The deep hollow thuds echoed as the heavy boot made contact with the man's body. And then it was over.

The man was still conscious. Chris was sure he saw some teeth and a piece of gum on the concrete, but averted his gaze, not wanting to see if it was what he thought it was. The two other security officers dragged the man to his feet and one of them spayed a solution into his face. It was a mix of ammonium carbonate and water, used to revive people that had been beaten. The man's face was swollen and red, and there was blood coming from weal marks. His eyes were filled with shock, like a person looks after being in a car accident. Chris noticed bruising was already beginning to show and the skin on his hands was scuffed showing blood seeping through. A few fingers on one of his hands were bent at an angle and the knuckles massively swollen, a sign they were broken. And as Chris was thinking what a bad state he was in, a man standing near him said the man who had been beaten worked in the warehouse at the back of one of the stores. Chris looked at the beaten man, who was wearing industrial trousers and boots, and Chris thought how he looked to be a hard-working type of person. A woman in the crowd said the man had argued with his manager about working conditions and something to do with overtime money. The man had stuck to his point of view and this riled the manager who called in the security officers, and he told them the man was threatening to attack him. So they dragged him away from the store into the middle of the precinct and gave him a public beating, which was not an uncommon thing to do. The woman who said this was in her sixties, she, and a lot of people of her age, found it difficult to easily accept what went on in certain situations. She shrugged her shoulders as a few people gave her cautionary looks.

Chris turned away, no longer wanting to walk around the shops he made his way back home, but he could not stop thinking about the man, the way he was beaten and how he looked afterwards. He would now be unemployed, and because of the way he lost his job, medical treatment at the hospital would be minimal, and he would have to wait a long time to receive it.

When Chris got home he was relieved to see Rosie; she had got off work early herself. Nina was in her room and although not going to school that day they agreed she would return the following Monday. Chris sat next to Rosie on the sofa and they talked, holding hands and listening to one another. Chris told Rosie about Paul, how he had deteriorated and living a life fraught with threats, fear and suspicion. He then told Rosie about the beating of the man he witnessed in the shopping precinct, he did not intend to tell her, but he could not shake the terrible image and sounds from his mind.

Rosie told Chris he should try and remain quiet as his nerves and emotions are so tangled and he will get easily upset. Chris spoke about the society that has been created and how people are desensitised and do not think, 'They can't have empathy for anyone else,' he said, 'because they haven't got any for themselves. They're too scared, that's what our society has become, a place where people are like slaves on a ship, or prisoners who are part of a chain gang - living with a constant fear they will be the next one to be picked on - maybe they've given up looking at the reasons why, and they're just glad it's someone else who is being picked on - and it goes on every day - day after day - existential fear, and it's all consuming, it renders the inmates of this sick experiment as vessels who have their senses muted, anything other than the primeval sense to survive doesn't matter - any capacity that might lead to feelings that form discerning thoughts to challenge what is around them is repressed to a point where we have the situation of the average person no longer knowing what to do with those feelings when they do arise.'

As he spoke Rosie watched him, nodding slowly, waiting for the time when finally she could say something in a calm manner and change the subject. Chris sat back on the sofa, closed his eyes and sighed deeply while Rosie watched him as a mother looks at her baby when there is cause for concern.

Thirty-Six

The following Thursday Chris visited Bill Copley at his flat on the date Karena had told him. It was three days before Christmas day, a fact that was very clear in Chris's mind as he thought of his family and what had happened since he was a child. Bill Copley had not contacted him, but Chris decided to go along all the same, especially as Karena said she wanted to talk to him about Simon, who also had not got back to him and neither had Roger Edgebury, although Chris had given up on him. As Chris walked towards Bill Copley's flat he felt the project took on an ambience the architects and designers of the monstrosity had envisaged and wished to bestow on the poor and powerless in society, which was an unremitting grimness set in fear. The smell of chicken urine burned the hairs in his nose, and the shouts in the darkness coming from coarse voiced adolescents echoed around the concrete living quarters of the damned, which at that moment was veiled in a cold damp coating ready to freeze into ice.

Bill opened the door and invited Chris inside, making clichéd remarks about the 'inclement' weather, but not mentioning he had not returned his calls, and such was his manner it led Chris to think he was being evasive and he was not very good at it, or just did not care. As they walked into the living room Chris told Bill he had rung him and left messages on more than one occasion, but Bill's response was to raise his eyebrows while pointing at a chair for Chris to sit in and said he was intending to do so and that he had only seen his messages the day before as his phone has a tendency to 'malfunction.'

It was frustrating for Chris as he could tell Bill was not going to talk about it. He could sense things had changed, which added to his feelings of continually running into a brick wall. There were two other people in the room, a man and a woman, and about half an hour later Karena arrived. She was greeted as if she was a hero returning from battle; Chris learned the excitement was because of a speech Karena had made at a meeting a few days earlier. Chris watched as the women stood up from the sofa, took Karena's hands in hers and congratulated her in a reverential manner that was similar to the way Chris had seen theatrical people behave.

Chris brought a bottle of wine with him and there were other bottles on a table, which Chris was pleased to see because he felt he needed a drink to help him remain in the flat, otherwise he would follow his wanting to leave. When there was a pause in the conversation taking place (about conspiracy theories), Chris told the group about Steven and what

219

had happened since with his efforts to gain information. Chris looked around the faces in the room and felt that what he had said had ruined their party. He wondered if their response was because they were too shocked to speak or that they felt powerless to do anything about it and were scared because of their impotence. Karena nodded and smiled sympathetically, but the others avoided eye contact with him and shifted uneasily in their seats. Chris then told them about Paul and the last time he saw him in the precinct, and the beating that took place with people watching on in a state of helplessness. Chris then became upset and with a flash of anger he told them that the people in the precinct watching the man get beaten had looks on their faces just like theirs.

The room remained silent for a while afterwards. Karena kept looking at Chris smiling encouragement, but Chris had made his mind up about the 'dissidents' in the room and all the ones he had met. Eventually Bill Copley began to speak about Paul in a very matter of fact manner, saying that was the way of things and one does not have to stray far from the beaten route before discovering that the designated path is closely monitored, and the state will come down extremely heavily on those that do so, and while they do so their actions are covered by duplicity. Chris was annoyed at Bill Copley's insensitive manner, seeing him as just bleating words from a script without feeling.

Chris sat back in the chair he was sitting in, becoming separate from the other people in the room. He was listening and watching them with a feeling he was not part of what they were, because he had become merely an observer of their mannerisms and language, although initially having set out to learn and discover something of importance that would be of help to his needs, but only to come to the realisation it had all been futile. Rosie had told Chris about the naivety of people involved in dissident groups and that the vast majority were not activists in terms of doing anything practical. He knew people like himself, Rosie, Brendan and of course other people were conscious of the situation, but accepted there was not much they could do about the state of things. His experiences had really brought it home to Chris how the state needs just a proportion of the population under its guidance for it to function as it wishes and there will always be those that deviate from the authority's planned route for people to follow, but that is manageable.

The group were talking about Kim Blakely, and the man sitting on the sofa next to the woman asked Chris if he had met him. Chris told him that he had not, and the group discussed some of the things Blakely had said and the influence he had in the underground movements. Chris was finding it difficult to follow what they were talking about and just nodded when something was said to him. He was barely able to keep his eyes open as they talked about security and of how it is of vital importance for the system, as it is for any system, large, small, complex or simplistic, otherwise the system will break down. They went into detail discussing how methods of security differ, whether it is to alter states of mind by sophisticated means of conditioning through education, the media and the psychological, to the use of threats and a cudgel. The woman looked at Chris as she said, 'Fear doesn't only exist among the ordinary people, it's also felt by the agents of security - it's everywhere, keeping the system together and us all apart - it is total fear.'

Chris nodded and offered a weak smile, not only had his patience run out, but he was having a hard time focusing on not only what was said, but he was finding it difficult not to drift off. He sat upright and asked Bill Copley if he could go to the kitchen and get a glass of water. Bill said he would get it for him, but Chris insisted he would go himself, because not only did he want to stand up, he also wanted to get away from the conversation that was taking place. He had drunk quite a lot of wine and vodka and was feeling the effect quite strongly.

Relieved to be in the kitchen, Chris picked up a glass from the draining board and held it under the tap until it was full of water. As he turned around he saw Karena standing in front of him. Her eyes fixed into his as she told him how sorry she was about Steven and if she could help in any way he could always get in contact with her. Chris told her he had tired of the people involved in the underground movements, even though many of them might be well intentioned it was little more than a hobby. Karena watched him closely, and very slowly she reached out her hand and stroked the side of his face with the back of her hand and said, 'I only wish I could help you more than I can.'

It was the way she touched him that startled Chris, it was not just affectionate, there was a sexual element he had felt from the first time he met her.

Karena asked Chris if he minded her talking about Simon. Chris shook his head and said he did not mind, but he had a feeling he would never see or hear from him again.

Karena told Chris to be careful, as it is common practice to have state security agents working in the area of mental health posing as nurses when really they are gaining information on a person and passing it on to their department. Chris told her that he had been told that before, and Simon had not got back to him, not that he expected him to as it is obvious he was involved with what happened to Steven. Karena said he was correct to think that and the man calling himself Simon would disappear as his, 'piece of work with Steven had been completed.'

Karena went on to tell Chris about a state agent called Garman who works in the area of mental health. He gets to know mental health workers, psychologists and nurses, those having contact with 'patients' and know their personal details. They set out to form a trustful relationship so that the patient reveals intimate feelings, personal histories, information about their families and matters that are of interest to them. Garman is looking for patients who offer a potential threat to state security, and some of those deemed as a risk are 'despatched' in various ways, although a 'tiny percentage' can end up on the television show The Offender's Nemesis.

Chris spoke about the health workers and how they are directly involved in vetting their patients for the state's security, even though they profess to have a commitment to safeguarding confidentiality, as if they were honestly working on behalf of their patients.

Karena told him he was right not to be naïve, although there are mental health workers that accept they work for the state and believe they are doing the right thing by colluding with state agents like Garman; who looks what he is, a powerful man with grim features and a feared reputation that has given him notoriety. She told him Garman is an assassin, and he tortures people, an ex-military man, he is a soldier for the state who does what he is asked to do without question or moral consideration.

Karena continued to speak, but Chris could not hear what she was saying because his mind immediately flicked back to the conversation he had with Paul the last time he saw him in the shopping precinct, remembering how he had described a man who was a 'state official,' describing him as a 'hulking bloke'. Chris recalled what Paul actually said. 'He's a hulking bloke, looks like a character from an old gangster movie, but makes out he's friendly - but his mean eyes give him away, he's nosing around to cause me trouble, I know that much - I'm sure of it,'

Paul was suspicious of the man, and said he did not even work for the health authority because when he rang them about trying to contact him they did not know who he was talking about.

Karena was still talking, but was watching Chris carefully, as though she had been reading his mind as he went through his thoughts. Chris told Karena he wanted to go back to the room and sit down and that he did not feel well, and the drink had not helped him in any way as the tiredness, stress and upset began to mount inside him. Karena stepped towards Chris, placing her hand on his arm she kissed his cheek and when

Chris looked up he saw her eyes were fully focused onto his, but he was not in any mood to read what her eyes were conveying, because he was quickly seeing Karena as a person like others he had met in the 'underground movement' who were playing at it, while he had real problems to deal with.

Chris gently shrugged her hand from his arm and walked into the room carrying the glass of water, and as he did so he did not see the look Karena gave him; it was a mindful gaze, as if monitoring a piece of work in progress.

The evening continued with discussions of state security and collusions. Karena watched Chris and smiled at him when he looked at her, and he drank more vodka and wine in an effort to block his distressing thoughts. Karena was the first one of the group to leave, and on her way out she stood next to Chris, squeezed his hand and in a whisper asked if he was okay. Chris nodded, and not wanting to talk to her he just muttered he was okay. The others left a short while after, leaving Chris to be the only member of the group remaining. He felt so tired and drunk and did not feel like making the journey home. Getting a taxi from an orthodox company would be impossible as they did not venture into the projects when night fell, and he did not like the idea of using one of the firms that had set themselves up in the project that served the local residents.

He was unable to keep his eyes open and drifted in and out of sleep as Bill Copley continued to talk, and then when looking up he saw Bill standing over him and asking if he wanted to stay the night. It was of great relief for Chris, because the thought of walking down the stairwell and across the open space in the middle of the housing project, with the lights out, had been on his mind for the past hour. He had to let Rosie know and she would not be pleased, and although intending to go into work the next day he already knew he would feel differently about it in the morning. Chris rang Rosie and told her what was happening, she was not so much bothered by his staying out, but was worried about the way he was acting and felt things were coming to a head.

Bill Copley told Chris the flat had two bedrooms, but as one of them was used as a storeroom he asked Chris if he minded sleeping on the settee. Chris did not mind, he knew he should not have drunk so much in his present state and was grateful to just lie down and rest. Bill gave him a blanket and a pillow, and he settled down on the 'settee' as Bill called it. Chris was only awake long enough to hear Bill use the bathroom and a lone voice from somewhere in the project shouting a name over a few times, a name Chris could not discern, and then he was asleep.

223

Thirty-Seven

The morning broke for Chris over several short spells of consciousness as he left behind a heavy, although not restful sleep. During those waking periods he saw objects in an unfamiliar room, and then realised he had slept somewhere other than his own bed. The room smelled of damp and stale cigarette smoke, a mixture that affected his sinuses, which were swollen because of the alcohol he had drunk. Bill Copley was not up and about and, accepting he was not going to get any meaningful rest, Chris got off the settee and folded the blanket he had been given. He knocked on the door of Bill's bedroom, called his name and waited for an answer that did not come. Chris walked into the kitchen and looked at the unwashed cutlery, the stained tea towels and the mould on the walls. On the draining board was half a loaf of bread next to a glass containing liquid the colour of dirt and there were cigarette butts floating on the unwholesome concoction. Chris wanted to leave. He felt terrible, but did not want to go without saying anything to Bill.

Chris knocked on the bedroom door again, waited for a few seconds and called out his name, as he did before, only this time louder. Feeling he ought to tell Bill he was leaving, Chris slowly opened the door. Bill Copley was not in bed, but a woman was. She looked over in a dreamy state and said, 'Hi – Bill's not here, he's gone to work.'

Chris apologised, telling her he did not know she was there. She told him that it was okay and smiled at him before turning over and closing her eyes.

Chris left the flat, thinking about the woman he had just spoken to. It puzzled him, he had not seen her before and he wondered whether she was there the times before when he had visited the flat, staying in the bedroom all the while, but then maybe she came in very late at night or early in the morning. Chris exhausted possible options and looked across the housing project as he stood on the balcony. He felt nauseous as it was, without the smell of chicken urine, and he retched, although was not sick, and as he was doing so remembered to phone in work to tell them he was not coming in, again. The effects of cheap wine and vodka had left his head muzzy and a thick sickly taste in his mouth. The alcohol had heightened his senses and frayed his nerves. It made the scene he was looking at more depressing. Chris stood on the balcony thinking how on earth could a person like himself, or people he spent the previous evening with, have the power or influence that could possibly impact in any positive way on a place that was so squalid, hostile and hopeless.

He walked down the stairwell and across the grassed area listening to the sounds of the project playing to a backdrop of noise from the chickens. His intention was to go over to the three shops, but he decided to walk in the direction of the road encircling the project that would take him to an area where he knew he could catch a bus.

It was a longer walk than he anticipated and Chris counted every step taking him away from a place he did not want to be. As he neared the edge of the project, Chris noticed a small shop that appeared hidden behind a concrete arch leading into a square between a block of flats and a row of maisonettes. He tossed around the idea of walking over to the shop, and after some deliberation decided to do so, although telling himself to make his way out of the project as quickly as possible when he had left the shop.

The shop was tiny. There was really only enough room for about three customers to stand in front of a counter and be served by an old lady who was standing behind it. She had a look in her eye that said she had seen and heard every conceivable trick in the book. The shop was spilling over with sweets, cigarettes, everyday bits and pieces - jokes, magazines, newspapers, the cheapest of little toys and crates of candles, and of course there were lottery tickets and scratch cards of every description. Chris bought a packet of cigarettes, a type of chocolate bar he had not had since he was a child and three scratch cards that gave the chance to win money and nominate a 'criminal' to appear on The Offender's Nemesis. The old lady thanked Chris with a curt nod while her eyes stayed on his face in a way that made Chris think she might have to remember what he looked like at a later date if asked by an agent from the security services.

As Chris left the shop he took a bite of the chocolate and was immediately disappointed, because it did not taste as he remembered when he was a boy. It was not his imagination, the chocolate bar would not have tasted as he remembered because the ingredients are not the same as they were years ago.

He left the housing project behind, crossed the road and walked to a bus stop. Chris took the three scratch cards out of his pocket and examined them. The prize money for winners was written on the front of the card next to the face of a 'criminal.' And then Chris's heart stopped beating. The face on one of the cards was Paul, the artist.

Chris looked about where he was standing, wanting to shout out and scream that it was wrong and that everything was wrong. The effect of tiredness, alcohol and the stress of Steven exploded inside him and he began to cry and shouted out, 'No, no no,' very loudly. He forced himself to keep walking and even in his present state he was aware of attracting the attention of people in the street. He focussed his mind on getting to the bus stop and getting to Paul's flat, although not having been there before he had the address in his pocket; Paul had given it to him in the café and Chris had kept it in his jacket pocket. At the time, when Paul wrote it down on a piece of paper he had torn from the corner of a page from his pad, Chris noticed the way it was written so artistically with a pencil specifically made to draw or sketch, all performed by a tutored hand in a meticulous style, an act in itself that was contrary to the norm of just adding an address or number on one's pad or phone. There was something old fashioned about it that interested Chris, as it evoked a time when things had substance and individual worth.

Chris staggered rather than walked towards the bus stop, his mind filled with conflicting thoughts about people he had met and the duplicity that exists everywhere, in the underground movement, the state, the media and among all people in every interaction that takes place, whether it be at work, at home or in places of leisure. Deception was everywhere. And then Chris stood still, his mind so inflamed he could not form a single clear thought, but what stopped him walking was a poster on a large board secured to the wall of a shop next to the bus top on the main road. It was a poster of Colette, the female presenter on The Offender's Nemesis, produced in the same style as all posters of that type are, crudely drawn in bright clashing colours showing effervescent celebrities smiling in a blurred airbrushed presentation of reality, yet only existing in a never-never land created by cartoonists. The young woman's joyous face beamed an exultant expression, celebrating the content of the television show she presents. Her long hair framed her broad face, and perfect teeth dazzled a brilliant whiteness that was matched by the shine in her eyes that, quite eerily Chris thought, penetrated anyone who looked at her face, which was a demonstration of beauty, strength, rectitude and, ominously, a power to reap retribution.

Chris felt a lump subside inside his stomach and a crushing sense of defeat bore down upon him. He felt helpless because he was unable to offer any kind of challenge to what she represented, which was the all pervading power that controls a weak and malleable populace.

Although finding it difficult, Chris drew his eyes from the poster, and as he did so was conscious of the damp air, the wind swirling under heavy clouds the colour of dirt, the rejected lottery tickets that told those who bought them they were losers, the traces of synthetic tobacco smoke, the worried faces of the elderly people he passed, each staring through eyes ringed by dark lines, the shabbiness, the forced poverty, the hurrying, the fear, and how it was all so cruel when contrasted with the smiling face of

Colette. And he began to cry as he walked towards the bus stop, burying his face in his chest with his fists clenched in the pockets of his jacket.

As Chris got on the bus he looked at the driver and the people sitting in the nearby seats, and a thought flashed across his mind that they were going to physically attack him. He walked to the rear of the bus and sat in a seat next to the window, and as he sat down he was overcome by an intense feeling of impotence. He asked himself over and over how could he possibly do anything about Steven and Paul, and then he had to stop himself from shouting at the passengers on the bus that his brother was dead and he had been killed by the state on that vile television show they like to watch, but then his thoughts were diverted as a man sat next to him, pressing Chris against the window. The man's heavy bulk was hard and a sour smell of stale alcohol wafted around the man as flies buzz around faeces. Chris looked down at the card, and with his fingernail scratched at the strip beneath Paul's face to reveal the criminal's name.

The name Nick appeared, and Chris dropped his head onto his chest in an involuntary action. When Chris looked up he was aware that the man sitting next to him was watching him slyly through the side of his eye. On realising Chris had caught him looking he averted his gaze straight ahead, and momentarily Chris looked at the man's face, noticing the strong features of his nose and cheeks, but only for a few seconds before looking away and thinking of Paul and wondering what crime he was accused of, and that they had not given him a foreign sounding name. Chris stood up as the bus approached the stop he was going to get off at, and as the bulky man made room for him to pass, he turned his head away so that Chris could not see his face.

Chris approached the block of flats where Paul lived with trepidation, thinking what he might find and that the security people might have put tape across the front door, with maybe even a police officer standing outside. He asked himself why he was going the flat, because he knew Paul would not be there, and his mind flicked through what he could do and who he could tell about what happened to Paul. He was desperate to find someone who might be of help, someone who could answer some questions and give some guidance, but it was hopeless.

Chris knocked on the door of Paul's flat and waited. He was surprised to see no tape across the door, and just as he thought nobody was going to answer the door began to open and Chris became frightened. A woman, who was probably in her late twenties, but looking a great deal older, stood in the doorway and before he could speak she asked him if he was from the authorities. Chris told her he was a friend of Paul's, knowing he should not be doing what he was because he was implicating himself, as all associates of Paul would be monitored. The woman looked at him with a blank stare and asked who Paul was. She told Chris she had only moved into the flat a few hours earlier, just her and her daughter. They were waiting for what is called a subsistence package to arrive and thought it had turned up when she heard the knock on the door. Chris asked her if there was anything left in the flat that had something to do with Paul. The woman shook her head rather sadly as if understanding the plight of Paul and told him the flat is cleaned thoroughly after they move someone out, leaving nothing, as if the last person who lived there had never existed.

Chris remained at the doorway knowing he could not stand there gawping at the woman and asking the same questions, but he was not sure what to do. He wanted to go in the flat to gain a feel of the place where Paul had lived, having not been in there before it would have given him a chance to connect with Paul, but it was not to be. He thanked the woman for her time and walked slowly down the stairs, and as he was leaving the block of flats he nearly walked into a man who stood back and stared at him; it was a hard stare filled with malevolence. Chris broke eye contact with the man and looked away, but as he was about to turn the corner he looked over his shoulder to see the man still staring at him.

The incident made Chris feel uncomfortable, and even after physically shrugging his shoulders he could not free himself of the bad feeling the man's presence had on him. As Chris walked away from where Paul lived he was unaware that standing in the entrance of another block of flats was the man who had sat next to him on the bus. He was watching Chris; the man was Garman.

Thirty-Eight

Christmas day in Chris's home was downbeat, it could not have been anything else, and as much as he tried for it not to affect Nina he could not help feeling the way he did. Brendan came round and stayed for a while. They exchanged presents and had a few drinks, but the mood did not lift and the conversation kept returning to Steven, Paul and the frustration of not being able to find information or someone to talk to. It was excruciating, and Chris could not wait for the day to come to an end, although he was very much aware he had his family with him and that they loved one another.

Boxing Day has its own feel, different from the big day preceding it, but one that is commonly enjoyed more because of it having a relaxed atmosphere. Chris remembered it as a young boy, the excitement over and then the warm glow; happy days, but things felt different to him now.

The sound of glass smashing caused Chris and Rosie to stare at each other as they sat in the living room on Boxing Day afternoon. His immediate concern was for Nina, she was in her bedroom, but because of the sound she had run into the living room asking what it was. As Chris rushed to the front door he was too intent on finding out what had happened to hear Rosie telling him to be careful. A brick wrapped in a sheet of paper had been thrown through a glass panel next to the front door and was lying on the hallway carpet. Chris opened the front door, stepped outside and looked around, but could not see anyone or hear a car driving away. It was as if nothing had happened on a Boxing Day afternoon, everything was perfectly normal, nothing untoward, just as it should be, except Chris had a brick lying just inside the doorway of his house, his brother had been murdered on a sick television show, and there was nothing else to be said on the matter because things would carry on as if nothing had happened.

Chris went back inside, picked up the brick and did not answer Nina and Rosie who were calling out and asking what it was, because he was concentrating on the sheet of paper the brick was wrapped in. There was something scrawled on the paper, and as Chris read it his breath left his body and a tight band constricted around his head to a point that the pain exploded and he screamed out loud. Rosie and Nina ran into the hallway and held onto Chris, asking him what it was. Chris handed Rosie the sheet of paper and she read what was written on it as Nina clasped onto her father, her eyes shut in prayer with tears running down her face. 'One less weirdo on our streets,' was written on the paper. Rosie looked at Chris, his eyes were screwed up tightly and an agonised torture showed in his face. His mind was flashing back to times when he was young and had people shout at him that his brother was 'spaz' and 'not right in the head' and even, 'should be put down.' Well they got their wish, he had gone now, killed for being innocent and well meaning, but the aftermath of hate and ignorance continued.

'When will it end?' Chris repeated as he stared up at the ceiling as if looking for an answer. Rosie tried to calm him, saying it was a one-off incident by irrelevant thugs and that she would clear up the glass and Nina will make a hot drink. She led him into the living room, fearful he was breaking down.

When the shock subsided Chris wanted to inform the police about what had happened, and if not going to the station he would ring them, but Rosie told him not to, explaining that it would be best to not have contact with the police at the present time.

The following evening, Nina was in her room and Chris left Rosie in the living room telling her he was going to have a rest and lie down on the bed. He switched the television on and saw there was a 'special' edition of The Offender's Nemesis. Chris turned the volume down, knowing Rosie would not like him watching it, but he wanted to just in case Paul was on it. The theme tune introduced the show and as the 'offenders' faces spun on the screen Chris held his breath, hoping he would not see Paul on the show, or *Nick* as he was called.

'It's *crunch* time, for the guilty, ladies and gentlemen, boys and girls,' the presenter said as his tan-blasted face creased to display bleached teeth.

'Okay - it's a Christmas special treat for all you lucky people out there,' he announced and the camera turned on the audience. They cheered their appreciation as different voices of the presenters shouted out, 'Crush the crud'. 'Squeeze to please'. 'Pulp the prat'. 'Squash and squelch'. 'Flush that turd'. 'Trample a toe rag'. 'Squish wish'. 'Squash a subversive.' And as the titles were announced the audience cheered all the more.

The presenter smiled his way through his script as cartoons relating to what he was saying appeared on the screen, and as they did so Chris controlled his breathing and tried to relax. The relief Chris felt because Paul was not on the show drained him, and he choked up, nearly starting to cry - he was not taking notice of what was happening, which was the female presenters of the show parading themselves dressed in an army uniform. A song blasted out and the girls marched in a line saluting the camera. 'Remember,' the presenter shouted out, 'support our boys in far flung lands who risk losing their lives so you can have Christmas dinner with your loved ones,' and the bedroom door opened.

Rosie entered and she was not too pleased with Chris as she said, 'What's wrong with you Chris? You're obsessed with that horrible show and all this violence - don't look at it, especially when Nina is in the house.'

Chris stood up and told her how he could not get the show out of his mind, and he was checking to see if Paul was on it, and that they had killed his brother and he could not rest until he had done something about it.

Rosie looked at him. 'But watching that terrible show isn't doing anything about it - you're just wallowing in it - and it's sick and depraved.'

She stepped towards Chris, holding out her arms for him to embrace her. Chris wrapped his arms around her, nearly greedily and pulled her close, so tightly that as she spoke her words were laboured. 'Oh love - I'm here, and always will be - and Nina - she loved Steven, it's been really hard for her - don't do anything stupid Chris, don't let them ruin what you have - what we have.'

Chris gently stroked her hair as they rocked slowly in each other's arms. Resting his cheek on top of Rosie's head his eyes softened, tears were forming, but he continued to look at the blank screen of the television, into the place where The Offender's Nemesis resides and dominates.

Thirty-Nine

There was a time when anyone could go on the internet and find information to make explosives, which, although not sophisticated could be extremely destructive and were used successfully by urban guerrillas, freedom fighters, terrorists and the disaffected when fighting against a state's highly powered armies, but the opportunity of finding such information no longer exists. It is now impossible to buy the ingredients, let alone weapons, and ex-soldiers, or anyone connected with the military, cannot supply arms as they are scrutinised, and the punishment for doing so is death or hard labour until you die. There is rioting against the state, which is always unreported, unless it is in the interest of the state to make it publicly known, and the weapons concocted by the rioters are pitifully pathetic when considering whom they are up against. Chris was seriously considering the idea of getting hold of explosives if anything happened to Rosie and Nina, and just how he could get it was beginning to take up most of his thought. He asked Brendan, who told him to put the idea out of his mind as it would be impossible for someone to do such a thing even if they had not drawn the attention of the authorities to them, which was something he had done.

It was the end of the first week in January and the authorities, or anyone else, had not come back to Chris with information regarding Steven. The pain and frustration was building inside him to a point where he had to do something. Rosie gave him warnings every morning and evening to remain as composed as possible and that eventually someone would be contacting them about Steven. As he was leaving for work Rosie told him to accept the way of things, but not to give up and she would always be there for him. But it was not enough, the agitation Chris felt stopped him concentrating on his work and his managers noticed it. On leaving work Chris phoned Brendan to see if he wanted an early evening drink before going home, but Brendan had commitments at work to attend to, so Chris went for a drink by himself, intending to have just one or maybe two drinks in an effort to lift his mood a little.

The bar he selected to go in was quiet, in an expensive area and frequented by those in professional occupations. The atmosphere was polite, but Chris felt it to be distant, sterile and predictable, and staffed by people who adopted an overbearingly toady manner. Chris had gone beyond the two drinks he told himself he was going to have, but on finishing his third he made himself walk to towards the door and exit the bar, leaving behind an endless sound of chatter where it was impossible to distinguish a single word that anyone was saying. Chris was making his way to the police station - he rang Rosie, telling her what he was doing, and she shouted at him, pleading with him not to go and to come home. But he would not listen, Chris was set on a course and he had to follow it, because there was too much in his mind for him to not do something about it, even if it meant causing trouble.

It was just before seven in the evening when Chris walked into the police station, a different one from where he went before. He jabbered, at times incoherently, to the officer on the desk, which caused him to think Chris was unstable or had been drinking too much, or both, having smelt alcohol on his breath. The officer took his name and address and asked Chris to walk down a corridor and go into a room, which Chris noted as being an identical corridor and room as in the other police station, and the officer then asked Chris to wait and told him a person would be along in a short while to speak to him. Chris felt it had gone quite well, in that the officer seemed friendly, and he sensed a feeling of excitement as he thought he might actually be getting somewhere in finding out about Steven.

Twenty five minutes had passed before a man wearing a black coat over a dark suit entered the room, stopping for a second in the doorway, his cold eyes looked at Chris in a way as if checking points off about him on a checklist, and then he closed the door and sat on a chair on the opposite side of a table from where Chris was sitting. The long wait in the silent room was beginning to dim the feeling of excitement Chris had felt, and the attitude of the man sitting opposite him made Chris feel like a heavy weight had returned and his stomach tightened.

'Been drinking, Mr Kirby?' The man said as he regarded Chris with a disparaging look that quickly turned to one of disapproval. Chris told him he had stopped for a few beers after work, but had not drunk much and was certainly not drunk, and as he began to talk about Steven and the whereabouts of his body, the man stopped him and told Chris he was not going about what he wanted in the correct manner, and he could not just 'crash' into a police station making demands in an aggressive manner. He told Chris his behaviour was bordering on the disorderly and he should be careful or he would be arrested and charged. The man, who did not introduce himself, told Chris to write a statement and to put in it all of what he wanted to say, he then just looked at Chris without saying anything else. Chris spoke so quietly when saying he would like to make a statement that the man asked him to speak up.

Chris was broken. It had all been in vain and the raised hopes he had were now seen as laughable. All he had done was to further implicate himself and make himself known to the authorities, and he cursed himself as he thought of Rosie and how she was right. The man left the room, telling Chris that an officer would bring in the 'correct' form for him to make his statement. At one point Chris was going to ask the man what his name was, but thought better of it as he would only have twisted round what he said and accused him of something.

Over half an hour passed before an officer came into the room. He gave Chris the form and told him to hand it to the officer behind the desk when he leaves. When Chris had finished writing he gave the form to the officer behind the desk and asked if he could use the toilet, but was told the toilet he would normally be able to use was out of order and the officer gave Chris precise details of where he could find a public toilet, which was about a mile away.

Chris left the police station in a terrible temper; he felt there was nothing he could do and for the first time he thought he would never find the information he wanted to know about Steven. He rang Rosie, but before he could finish what he wanted to say she exploded and took Chris to task, telling him he should not drink if he loses a sense of reality with things that are important. She then quickly apologised and told Chris she was angry because she was worried sick about what he was going to do. Chris told her he was on his way home and for her not to worry about him as he could now see things as they were. When Chris hung up, Rosie kept the phone to her ear and she tensed up, because what Chris had said about seeing things as they were stood out as a strange thing to say and she just hoped he would get home safely.

Chris took a different route from the police station than the one he had taken to get there, thinking it would lead him to a railway station, but his knowledge of the area was not as good as he thought it was. He caught a bus to a railway station and went into a bar nearby in the high street to use the toilet, telling himself he would not have a drink as he had told Rosie he was on his way home and he knew she was worried.

As soon as Chris entered the bar he was sorry he had done. It was a rough looking place and he ordinarily would have checked and taken a look first before venturing in a bar he did not know. But, he was already in there and people had turned and looked at him, so he did not want to turn round and walk back out. He kept walking, and on seeing the sign for the toilet made his way in that direction, noticing the bar was quite small and about half full; the clientele were all men except for three women. The walls of the toilet were covered with different stickers advertising services and products, the vast majority being a type one would not see in the mainstream media. They were to do with companies offering 'no questions asked' loans to buy a car, and Chris felt an inordinate amount of companies offering a service to do house clearances, as well as adverts for second hand furniture and lottery tickets that can be bought in bulk. The stickers looked trashy and symbolised a culture with no substance, its values being only that of monetary worth in a desperately competitive world overshadowed by poverty. And as Chris looked around the walls he became acutely aware of how fortunate he was having Rosie and Nina and a good job to support his life, and the pleasant home they all lived in.

When Chris came out of the toilet he stopped for a couple of seconds and took the decision to have a beer, not that he really wanted one, but he felt it impolite to just use the toilet and leave. He was also aware of people watching him and thought if he left without buying a drink it might draw attention to him; in fact Chris did not know what to think and he found himself walking up to the bar counter. As he stood waiting to be served a man entered and stood near him, taking a note from his pocket he waved it at the man behind the counter, who walked towards him, but then stopped and pointed at Chris, 'He's first my friend,' the barman said to the man, 'got here before you he did, just relieving himself of a troublesome burden in the little boy's room, weren't you mucker?' and he looked at Chris as he said this.

Chris nodded, and said that was so.

'Okay squire, that's all good by me, 'the man said to the barman, who shot the man a look that said he did not trust him, and he said, 'Good, I'm glad it is.'

Chris turned and leant back against the counter, the cold beer frosting the glass in his hand; all he had on his mind was Rosie and that he wanted to leave the bar and get home. A sign up on the ceiling caught his attention and diverted his thoughts as he read what was written on it. JUST DO AND DON'T THINK. It was a relatively new sign and one Chris had seen before in other public places, which made him think it must be a new initiative by the state, which along with other methods adds to the objective of creating a populace that does not think too deeply about things.

'Mind yourself there, friend, you're spilling good beer,' were the words said by a man to Chris that jolted him from his thoughts. A tough looking character was looking at Chris with a smile that was more than countered by a look of deep suspicion in his eyes.

'Thanks,' Chris said, 'in a world of my own,' and the man nodded at him thoughtfully as he turned and resumed his place with the group of men he was with.

The man who had entered just after Chris asked the barman if there was any football on the television, which was chained to the wall in the corner of the bar above the door to the toilets. Chris looked up at the television, a programme about the military was on, but the volume was turned down. The barman picked up the remote and flicked through the channels, but then one of the men in the group next to Chris told the barman not to put the sound up and just show the results and scores. It was plain to see the men in the group pretty well ran the way of things in the bar, and the man who had asked for the football to be on realised that was so very quickly and nodded his acceptance of the ruling made by the group.

The man who told the barman not to put the sound on said in a loud voice, 'Load of noise all the time, pisses me off.' Chris understood the man's displeasure was directed at the man who had asked for the football to be put on, and again he nodded, but this time he looked down at his beer as if feeling he was not being welcomed by the men in the bar.

The other man who had told Chris about spilling his beer looked at Chris and said, 'Crap, ain't it me old china.'

Chris nodded, 'Totally,' he said and took a large swig of beer.

The man turned and looked at Chris with a roguishly good humoured smile filling his craggy face, 'That so?' he said, 'You look as if you need a drink to give all those troubles a swerve that have filled your bonce.'

'Shows, does it?' Chris said, attempting to reciprocate the humour. The man nodded, and taking a step towards Chris he leant on the counter, looking at him with his head cocked to one side. 'Trouble at work? Home? Or both?' he asked, and Chris finished his beer before answering, and when he did he could not believe what he said, the words just tumbled from his mouth.

'It's all crap, everything we see and hear - we're told crap and conditioned to hate ourselves,' and he went on, saying how the media, the television and just about all outlets spread information that is false and socially divisive.

The man nodded and watched Chris as he ordered another beer, the alcohol hitting him because of lack of food and tiredness, which caused him to not be alert to the danger that could happen to him in the bar. The man gave a final nod at Chris as he returned to his group; thoughts he had about Chris were now confirmed.

Chris drank the beer quickly with an overriding thought to have another one before going home. He wanted the alcohol to block out what he felt was a house brick in his head that was increasing in size and driving him to a point of distraction, and as he drank he gazed down at the floor unaware of the man who had entered the bar not long after him, he was watching Chris closely and monitoring every detail of his

236

mannerism as Chris finished his beer and ordered another one, his mind now steeped in the depths of despair.

Chris stood with his back to the bar looking up at the ceiling and around at the tattered furniture, languishing in depressing thoughts he did not have any interest or concerns about the people in the bar, but then his thoughts were broken by a woman's voice. She cackled on about a media celebrity and of how he was not only handsome, but also did so much good work for ordinary people who are in need. Chris muttered derisively to himself, but not quietly enough as not to be heard by the tough looking man who had spoken to him earlier.

'What's that friend?' he said, turning towards Chris, his face hardening as his eyes narrowed, 'What is it the lady said you don't like then, friend?'

Chris shrugged, and glancing over at the woman he shrugged again and mumbled that he had not heard what she said.

'Yes you did, don't come the old innocent with me - I don't knows who you are, but you have a habit of sneering, I knows that much,' and he nodded up at the sign on the ceiling before saying, 'I saw you giving that a real old sneer earlier on and you looked at the lady like a dog had shit on your top lip.'

Chris protested, while being mindful to be tactful, saying it was not the case, and that he was tired and had not meant to be looking at anything or anyone with disdain.

A voice from behind Chris made him turn, it was the man who had entered the bar after him, 'Yeah, I make the lady right, what's wrong with him and what he does, like Alan Manville aint he, but not as big - they do a good job if you ask me, and it's in good fun, gives people a laugh.'

Chris turned and looked at him, and knowing the man was aware of far more than he was making out, Chris launched into a volley of criticism against the system, 'Those shows contribute to the destruction of a decent society, making millionaires for morons who are used as lackeys that patronise the powerless - all to maintain the power for a cruel band of people who for them having a laugh is the last thing on their perverted minds.'

'And what's wrong with having bit of a laugh?' the man said, 'You're a long time doing the vanishing act,' and he looked over at the group, 'Aint that right boys?' he said while looking questioningly at Chris before continuing. 'Oh, I see you're one of those who thinks he's got it right and everyone else has got it wrong,' and he forced out a laugh as he looked at the group for support.

Chris looked at him, his anger and frustration ready to boil over, but he struggled to keep from losing his temper as he began to speak. 'Most

237

people don't like that show, or all the other things that are forced upon them that ruin their lives, but they're too scared to do anything different but toe the line,' and then he lost what composure he had as he shouted at the man 'And you know it.' Chris went on, saying that shows like The Offender's Nemesis are rigged and innocent people are used as props in stunts and that it is nothing to do with law and order, 'It's crass entertainment for cretins,' Chris shouted out loudly, and, now completely upset, he told the man and the people in the group next to him how his brother was killed on the The Offender's Nemesis and of how he was innocent of the disgusting things he was accused of, and that he cannot find out any information about what happened to his body, and his life has been ruined, as are the lives of others, and that the world cannot be made into a better place because of the 'horrific greed mongers that control everything,' and he cursed the system, Alan Manville and the crass way the state keeps people in bondage and fear.

The tough looking character who appeared to be the dominant figure in the group watched Chris closely, as though maybe one part of him agreed with what he said, but he had never really thought it through because he knew it would do no good.

The man who had entered the bar after Chris, and was stirring up trouble, continued to speak, looking at the group for support as he did so. 'The man's a trouble maker and a grass - he goes round different places making trouble - he's an agitator who incites bother and only brings grief to good people who don't need it and do an honest day's work - looking down his nose, thinking he's the Big I Am, with his professional job, like he knows better than the rest of us.'

The tough looking character took a step towards the man and said, 'I make you right, but we don't know who you are either, cock - you haven't been in here before.'

The man looked at the faces of the men in the group who looked at him, one of the mistakes he had made that caused further suspicion about him was the use of the word, 'incite'; it was not in keeping with the accent and type of character he was pretending to be. The man looked at the men in the group who were all now staring at him, and taking a step backwards he held his hands to his sides in an act of having nothing to declare before speaking. 'And I make you right for saying what you have, squire, but I'm only pointing out that the man is a wrong'un.'

'We can see that, me old cock sparrow,' the tough looking character said, 'and although you're doing the old, I'm brand new and straight up act, we still don't know who you are,' and he glared at the man, making it evident that what was going on between Chris and them was their

238

business and had nothing to do with him. The man retreated, and continuing to walk backwards towards the door he said, 'Easy up boys, I means no harm to any man in this bar, and I'm on my way, knowing only what a blind baby does,' and with that the man turned, pushed open the door and left the bar.

Chris looked from up the television to the grim faces in front of him, and then everything seemed to drop into silence.

It felt to Chris as though the room was pulling away from him, but what was actually happening was that he was being pulled from the back of his shirt collar and jerked with such force his feet left the ground as he was dragged across the floor and through the doors exiting the bar. As Chris was bundled through the door he was conscious of the cold night air and of blows thudding into his head and body. Chris could make out at least two men punching and kicking him, but was helpless as they beat him and swore at him, and made threats of how he would be killed if he returned to the bar or was seen in that area again.

The pavement took his breath from him as it slammed against his back, and then there was nothing, no shouting, no blows into his body or head, and, quite perversely, the cold concrete against his face felt comforting, but this sense of relief was short-lived as the door to the bar opened and he was hit in the face with something hard. On opening his eyes and feeling around he saw it was his case he took to work that had been thrown at him. It was torn open, the contents still intact, but obviously gone through by the men in the bar. For them, the incident would be nothing more than bouncing out an irritating middle class 'professional' who had strayed from his route and opened his mouth, but for Chris he felt it to be the final straw in the hell that was consuming his life.

People looked at him as they walked by, but only briefly, most hardly averting their eyes to take in what he looked like. Nobody wants to be involved, it is unsafe to do so, and Chris was fully aware of that as he stood up. Having to steady himself against the frame of the door of the bar before walking off, he did not even check to see if people were looking at him. He could not care, because his phone was in his pocket, as was his wallet, he was still alive and he had a loving family to go home to; although having to explain to Rosie what had happened was a thought that began to dominate his mind.

As he limped away from the scene, Chris did not see the man who was in the bar causing trouble, he was now standing in the shadow afforded by a shop doorway on the other side of the street watching Chris with an expression on his face that said a job had been well done.

Forty

Chris had not been badly injured in the beating he took outside the bar, just a few bruises and grazes, although his nose was swollen and very tender, which caused Rosie to think the bone had been fractured, but Chris did not go to the hospital. As for Rosie, she was too worried about Chris to rage at him for going to the police station and being stupid by drinking in places he should not have been going into. She and Chris shared a growing sense of doom and that something was going to happen, that it was going to be imminent, and that it was going to be bad.

Chris went to work the day after his altercation on the bar, the bruising and cuts on his face did not go unnoticed, and his excuse for getting them - as a result of falling over at home while doing some decorating - was not believed, and only confirmed his manager's feelings that Chris was sliding downhill and might become a liability.

The following weeks went by as before, with Chris trying to find out about Steven's body, attempting to contact Simon, a pursuit Chris had really given up on, but continued to do so out of habit. He did speak to Bill Copley on the telephone, telling him about Paul's face on the card and how he went round to his flat, and that someone had thrown a brick though the window of his house and what was written on the piece of paper, but he did not tell him about what happened in the bar. Bill Copley's response was cool to a point of disinterest, and so much so Chris ended the call saying he had something to do. Karena had not returned his calls, and Chris imagined state agents listening to the messages he had left on her phone, sitting in a room with Karena watching on; Chris now believed all significant 'underground dissidents' were state agents, which went towards creating a frightening sense of isolation and helplessness.

It was a Sunday in the last week in January and the days and weeks had passed quickly, even though time had felt to be agonisingly stagnant in terms of trying to get information from different agencies and departments. Six weeks had passed since Steven was on The Offender's Nemesis, and nothing had changed in regard to finding anything out about him. Not long after Chris, Rosie and Nina had their meal Chris decided to get a case from his car that had stuff in it to do with his work. As he was lifting the case from the boot of the car Chris heard raised voices, and being a quiet road, the voices stood out. Chris looked around to see where the shouting was coming from and saw a small group of youths and men gathered on the opposite side of the road, and then Chris realised they were shouting at him.

'Fucking kiddie fiddler,' one of them shouted, 'got what he deserved - look at you, you prick - it's not like it used to be, they're not allowed to do what they want now - their handlers have also gone, thank God.'

Chris just looked at them, he wanted to say something, and even remonstrate with them, but they looked as if they were on the brink of becoming ugly so any form of talking would have been useless, and probably dangerous.

Chris turned and looked into the boot of the car and heard another member of the group shout out, 'Got to be in the family - they're all at it, or knew what he was up to - fucking liberal perverts.' Chris closed the boot with intentions of getting into the house as quickly as possible, but just as he turned a loud thud caused him to jump. A brick had been thrown by one of the group and had hit the side of the car. Chris looked down at it, and seeing paint from his car on the brick he looked at the damage it had done, which was a deep gouge in the side of the front wing. He turned round and shouted, a spontaneous action, and it was the reaction the group wanted.

'What the hell do you think you're doing...' Chris shouted, but he stopped himself from saying anything else because they had spilled onto the road and were moving towards him, their faces twisted in hate and anger, and although it was an odd time to think such things, Chris thought about the expressions on their faces, an appearance now so familiar, hate and anger, an image, a response to one's environment, feeling powerless so destroying what they can, and at that moment it was Chris they wanted to destroy.

'You must have known he was a kiddy fiddling scum cunt,' one of the younger members of the group shouted at Chris, spit spraying from his mouth and expelled with such force and venom the words were barely understandable.

'What you getting out of the car? Paedo stuff? Photos and stuff? Eh?'

Chris had to think clearly, although it was difficult in the circumstances it was imperative that he did, because the situation was inflammable, and they would attack him if he said the wrong thing or made the wrong physical movement. They crowded around Chris, all shouting at once as they pointed into his face, accusing and cursing him, and Chris backed up against the car with his free hand extended towards the group as he tried to placate them, repeating that they ought to think what they were doing and to calm down, but one of them bashed his fist down on the bonnet of his car, denting it, and that was followed by other punches and kicks to the car. A weapon of some kind was pulled from a jacket and smashed repeatedly onto the roof and finally thrown through the windscreen, showering glass inside of the car. Chris knew it was too late to save the car, he thought they were going to completely wreck it before setting it alight, so he concentrated on self-preservation, knowing it could be fatal if they started to attack him. His mind filled with thoughts of his daughter and Rosie, of the trouble that was entering their lives, and also he did not want to draw the attention of the authorities to him and his family.

'Let's fucking do him,' one of the gang shouted, and an arm was thrown around Chris's neck. Chris attempted to stay on his feet, but almost immediately the ground appeared to zoom up and smash into him. He panicked, thinking of his brother, of how he was beaten to death and the common proclivity to stamp on people; he could be left with brain damage, and what good would he be to his family then? This was one thought, another was that at best he might be just seriously injured, a fractured skull, broken bones in his face, ribs, back, arms, but then again he might be killed. A few kicks thudded into him, but, wrapping his arms around his head, he managed to roll across the ground and into the middle of the road, and this gave him hope because the group had allowed him enough room to roll away, and he realised some of them were shouting at someone else. Chris got to his feet and saw Nina and Rosie at the front door of his house and he shouted at them to stay where they were and not to come out to the road. Some of the men were shouting vile obscenities at Rosie and Nina, and accusing Rosie of harbouring paedophiles. Chris was petrified, one of the gang shouted threats at him while two of them wrestled with his case, until they eventually ripped it apart and threw its contents on the floor.

'What's this?' one of them shouted, 'Paedo stuff, you fucking liberal cunt,' and some of the others were making baboon noises and hopping from one foot to the other, as if aroused at the prospect of witnessing or taking part in an act of violence. It was the same as when he was in the bar, those were the same noises he had heard when the solitary man was picked on.

Neither Rosie nor Nina were addressing the gang, they were shouting at Chris to come inside, 'Run dad, run,' Nina was screaming, but she then held her face in her hands and broke down in tears. Rosie was also telling him to make a run for it, either back indoors or to get away. One of the gang walked down the path towards them, his arms held out to his sides and making what were meant to be baboon noises. Chris ran towards the man, shouting at him to leave them alone, while aware the others were now concentrating on smashing up his car. He reached the man who had made it half way down the small path to his house, but as Chris took hold of his arm he immediately realised, with a heavy sense of defeat, that the man was too strong to pull away. He did not move, his body was hard and not giving at all.

The man laughed, and stepping quickly into Chris, he head-butted him in his face. Chris saw stars and for a couple of seconds was made deaf by the blow, but when his consciousness returned he heard Nina and Rosie screaming for the man to leave him alone, and then it was too late for Chris to react as he saw the man had a piece of wood or pipe in his hand and it was raised. The man set about Chris, beating him with the weapon, swearing and cursing as he did so. One blow caught Chris on the side of his head and triggered a feeling of sickness. He heard more than felt the blows on his body and legs and tasted bitter bile and blood, and through it all he could hear Nina and Rosie screaming, especially Nina, her screams so desperate they reached a terrifying pitch. Shock had caused faintness and a cold sweat, but the faint feeling grew and it was at that point Chris lapsed into unconsciousness.

Chris was not aware of Nina holding onto the man's arm as she cried out and frantically pulled his arm in an effort for him to leave her father alone, but the man ignored the young girl and continued to hit Chris as he lay unconscious on the path to their house. The man's face was heated with pleasure as he struck Chris, gone was the snarling anger, his expression now showing his enjoyment, gorging on a desire to feel this form of satisfaction; it was as if this is the way he found a release from the restricting emotions that is the norm for people like him and many others in society.

The gang did not set fire to the car, but it was completely smashed up with personal belongings strewn across the road amongst the glass and different parts of the car. A few kicks were delivered into Chris's body by two of the men as they passed him, having just sprayed on the wall of his house, 'paedo scum,' and 'paedo's off our streets.'

Rosie had phoned the police, although not immediately, she had not thought of it because of the shock of what was happening, it fully consumed her and she was too occupied with Chris being hurt. She did try to get Nina to go into the house, but she would not leave her father's side. Nina was hysterical and she would not let go of Chris as he lay unconscious, bloodied and beaten on the path to her house, her home, a place she felt was safe and away from what might happen in the world. A place her parents had created and provided for her to live, that blissful feeling of belonging, a place of safety and her father representing a feeling of stability, even if they did have disagreements and he did not understand her at times. These were feelings she had not really thought of before, but in that instant, while holding her father on the path to her home she knew she would never have that feeling of being safe in her home again, because it was not that impenetrable sanctuary she always thought it was, from the threats and evils that might exist around her. Nina was a little girl again, no longer the young woman comparing and contrasting her values and beliefs with her father, no longer caring about how she looked or might appear to boys or anyone else who might see her, she wanted her daddy so badly to be well and for things to be normal again, and she prayed that she would be so grateful if her dad was not badly hurt, because she loved him so much in a way she could not put into words.

Rosie knelt next to Nina, her arms spread over both of them, the debris in the road lay discarded and the words sprayed on the wall of their house were clear for all to see. Their life had been intruded upon in the most grotesque and frightening way, torn apart in public and sullied for all to see, and Rosie knew as she looked at the car and the graffiti that those in authority had instigated what had happened to them.

After a short while Rosie got on with phoning for an ambulance and contacting the police. She saw movements behind curtains in the houses opposite, people had been looking, but they did not want to get involved. Rosie shouted at one of the windows, seeing a head pull quickly to the side. 'Come on - come out here and look - we're all meant to be in it together - the days of shying away from thugs are over aren't they? Look how "empowered" we are - great isn't it? Now that we, the ordinary people, are dealing with bullying and intimidation, now that common sense and reality is here - makes you really happy to be part of it all…'

Rosie broke down, she could not keep shouting, but when she looked up she saw an elderly woman standing at the end of the path holding a blanket, which caused Rosie to think how stupid she was not get a blanket; and Rosie felt a pang of optimism and hope when looking at the lady, because beneath her caring look and quiet presence was a great strength. She did not know her name, although they always said hello to each other when passing in the street. The lady lived just down the road and was often seen walking her little dog, who, when it was cold, wore a warm coat on his small body.

The lady put the blanket over Chris and asked Rosie if she had phoned for an ambulance. Rosie told her she had, and for the police, which at the mention of their name the lady gave her a knowing look, and in that instant a feeling came upon Rosie, a foreboding weight that said this is just the beginning of what was to come and their lives are now changed and would never be the same. The lady placed her hand on Rosie's shoulder, it was soft and although having lost its physical strength over the years its frailness was contrasted with the fortitude in her eyes. She suggested to Rosie that she might want to take Nina inside, but, hearing her words, Nina let out a squeal and said she wanted to stay with her dad.

After a while Chris emerged from unconsciousness for short spells, in which time Rosie had phoned for the ambulance another two times, all they could do was comfort him and hope his injuries were not going to be fatal.

The waiting became unbearable, and the more Rosie looked at Chris and the damage around her, the more she thought of their future and what might lie ahead of them. The lady said she would get them a hot drink, and when Rosie said to make it in her house, the lady told her she would go home and do it as she lived just a few doors away. Rosie did not realise she lived so close to her, and it made her think how they did not really know their neighbours. She thought this as she watched the lady walk away, noting her small frame, a neat and proud woman, modest, making the most of what she had and could afford, decent and principled. Her manner of walking was rather stately, and a sudden thought hit Rosie that the lady represented the past, a time when she was young and used to visit her grandmother, a time, she felt, when things were better than they are now. But then she saw a curtain move in the house opposite and a head withdraw quickly from view, and a different sickening feeling replaced what was in her mind and brought her back to the present, a feeling of presenting a front to the world, and suspicion.

Forty-One

A police car came round the corner with no urgency whatsoever and parked at a leisurely pace next to the remains of Chris's car. There were three policemen in the car, the one in the front passenger seat was older and looked to be senior in rank to the other two. Rosie watched as they got out of the car, how they were unhurried and the way in which the senior policeman adjusted the hat on his head and methodically surveyed the scene before finally looking at the three of them on the path, as if just noticing they were there. He nodded at Rosie as he sauntered up the path leaving the other two by the car, one of them chewing gum as he looked lazily at the debris in the road.

The policeman looked down at Chris and pursed his lips before saying in a detached manner, 'My, we have had a bit of trouble here.'

His attitude, how he spoke, everything about him, the lackadaisical manner of the other two and the way they pulled up and got out of the car bewildered Rosie. She looked down at Chris, he had uttered a few incomprehensible words, but that was a couple of minutes earlier. She suddenly felt lost, pulling Nina close and hugging her tightly, she told her things were going to work out, that Chris was going to be fine and everything was going to be as it was before. Her words fell onto the hard concrete of the path they were crouched upon, because the look in Nina's eyes told of a different sentiment to their predicament and future.

The policeman asked Rosie what started the violence, who was involved, did she know any of the people involved, what was her relationship to the man on the ground and was there anything stolen from the house. Rosie felt he was too offhand and disinterested considering the situation, and it took her a few seconds to respond to what he had asked her. She told him what had happened, at times pausing and nodding at the policeman, to see if he was taking in what she was saying, and if he was really interested, but as she began to repeat what she had already said in an effort to get through to him Rosie broke down in tears and asked him why the ambulance was taking such a long time to get there. The policeman told Rosie the emergency services were under strain, his cold eyes evaluating her as he said, 'Because they're dealing with the sick and needy.'

Rosie looked up at him, she was stunned and his attitude had totally confused her. She asked herself why he was acting in such a manner when her husband had been brutally attacked, their car was completely ruined and defamatory slogans were painted on their house; all in front of a child.

She stared at him, trying to understand him or what it was that was happening.

'You got a broom, and bags to put the bits in,' he asked Rosie as he nodded at the car. Rosie continued to stare at him as a mixture of shock, amazement and incredulousness gave way to anger. She shouted at him with such force it tore the membrane at the back of her throat.

'What the hell are you asking me that for?' she screamed, and she asked him why he was acting in such a flippant manner when a serious crime had been committed against innocent people and her husband might be suffering injuries that are life threatening. Everything Rosie said, the manner in which she said them, her anxiety and sense of helplessness appeared to feed his indifference and air of arrogance, and a sneer began to show itself beneath the surface of his facial expression. Standing squarely in front of Rosie he pushed his gloves tightly onto his hands, and it was easy to see he was revelling in feeling a sense of power and gratification.

'Oh, is that right, madam? He said, and Rosie saw he was enjoying the situation. 'As I said, the services are stretched, what's happened here is important, but you're not the only people we have to deal with - there's some much worse off than yourself, we only had one earlier this morning, fire in a flat, was it started deliberately? We don't know, but the body of the five year old boy we dragged out of there had injuries that wouldn't have been inflicted by the fire, not even if he flung himself though a window and against doors and walls in a desperate effort to get out of there - not with a cut throat, one of his eyes missing and nearly every bone in his body broken.'

Rosie looked at Nina who was staring at the policeman, and he very nearly smiled as he said, 'I'm sorry to say this in front of the girl, but, it does make you wonder what goes on behind closed doors - it can make you very suspicious of people,' and as he said this, he looked around at the scene where he was standing in an unperturbed and philosophical manner. Rosie was caught between thinking of Nina and what he had just said as she began to speak, but only a babble of words came from her mouth in incomplete sentences that were attempting to articulate uniformed thoughts.

'What are you trying to say? Just what the hell are you insinuating, for Christ's sake,' she said as she walked up to the policeman and stood directly face to face with a man who looked as if he was going to work on an area of activity he really took pleasure in. A superficial smile drained from his cruel face as his mouth turned downward and any light there may have been in his eyes went out, leaving them lifeless and devoid of emotion.

He spoke in a flat tone. 'Did your husband have any enemies? Was he aware of upsetting or antagonising people and possibly making trouble for himself?'

Rosie was becoming increasingly confused and feeling helpless to the point of exhaustion. She did not answer, but she looked at him, and as a thousand fragmentary thoughts rushed through her mind she saw the elderly lady approaching holding a tray with cups and a plate with biscuits on it. The policeman looked at her with a distasteful expression showing on his malicious face.

'Okay dear,' she said to Rosie, 'here's a little something, it's not much, but the sweet tea will help.' The policeman looked from Rosie to the lady, and placing his fingertips on the tray to stop Rosie taking it he spoke in a firm and officious voice.

'There's an investigation taking place here madam,' and he looked over at the two policemen by the car, in a way that said to them how was she allowed to be standing where she was? One of them shrugged while the other walked over, adjusting the hat on his head as if having a pressing matter to deal with. The benign expression began to dissipate from the lady's face as she regarded the senior policeman with not so much puzzlement, but annoyance at his attitude. Her voice began to rise in pitch as it weakened, although her resolve and intention remained strong.

'Excuse me officer, but all I am doing is offering this young woman and her child a cup of tea, and considering the circumstances I feel a little…' but she was not allowed to finish what she was saying, the policeman cut her off by gripping the tray and guiding it away from her until she finally let go of it.

'What is your involvement with this incident madam?' he asked the lady, his hard eyes remaining on her face as he handed the tray to the other policeman.

'Well, I…' and her voice faltered for just a second, but that was long enough for the policemen to interject. 'What I'm trying to ask you madam, is what exactly is your involvement with this incident? Did you see anything?'

The lady looked over at the policeman putting the tray on the bonnet of the car as the other one leant on the car, nonchalantly watching him. The senior police officer continued, 'If not, can you kindly leave because you are holding up the police with their investigations.'

Rosie looked on, feeling her powerlessness as she held on to Nina who was holding Chris and not looking at anyone else.

The elderly lady began to speak, her face filled with shock, 'I am absolutely flabbergasted - I would never have thought...' but again she did not finish what she was saying because the policeman spoke over her, his attitude now aggressive and his voice raised. 'Madam, what you are doing is illegal - vital evidence might be interfered with by you being here - so go away - leave the scene of an incident where there is an ongoing police investigation - now!'

The lady suddenly looked older, her homely efficiency and pride had been knocked out of her by the policeman's belligerence.

'How dare you - how dare you speak to her like that,' Rosie said, and standing right in front of the policeman she pointed into his face as she began to speak.

'Oh, you love all this don't you? Pathetic examples of inadequate individuals like you are replicated throughout history - given the right conditions, like the one we unfortunately live in now - a uniform and power - were you always afraid of things when you were a little boy? Eh? Did fear make you hurt what you were able to? Eh? Like some smaller person or an animal that couldn't fight back and cause you harm? Then finding a place in a system that sanctions a function for your dysfunctional personality.'

Rosie began to stammer as she fought back anger, but she managed to deliver her words with force and emotion. 'Your face, your stance - everything abut you symbolises fear, and the system has done its job well because your face is the perfect image, it is the embodiment of what our society has become - the fear you instil in others, fear of an immensely powerful and impenetrable state, and the fear you feel as an insubordinate within that power which you represent, and you're fully aware of the position you hold, that's why you wield your club and what authority you have with as much might and spite as your pathetic mind can muster in a repressed act that reveals your feelings of self-hatred and frustration.'

The policeman looked at Rosie, letting her speak, biding his time in the confidence of knowing he is going to have the last word and will enact retaliatory action against her.

'But then cowards and bullies are scared aren't they officer?' Rosie went on, 'Just as you're scared of your colleagues and nearly every face you see in the street, you have a conscience, but its been hidden for so long behind a cover provided by the system, but you know there are those people within that order that will expose you, denounce you, so you can never be at rest.'

Rosie looked from the policemen to the other two by the car, and then from the elderly lady to Chris and Nina, before finally looking back to the

249

policemen, 'And this, it is in situations like this where a man like you can show what you really are.'

The words remained as if suspended beneath the dark clouds that drifted across the scene in the street, which was silent except for the quiet moaning coming from Chris, but then Nina cried out holding him tightly in frustration at seeing her father in the way he was and nothing was being done.

Rosie suddenly screamed, and as she shouted she was shaking, and with tears breaking down her face she took hold of the policeman by the front of his jacket, 'Just get the ambulance, where the hell is it? And what the hell are you playing at you, you absolute,' but that was all she said, for next thing she knew was a sudden blackness as something incredibly hard impacted against the side of her face and head. Her consciousness lapsed only for a second and her sight changed from being blurred to focused and she was aware of a voice, at first distant but becoming clear, it was the elderly lady's, 'What on earth have you done - you beast, you absolute monster - this poor girl.'

Rosie had been hit by the policeman, using the heel of his hand and the elderly lady was confronting him, but he was becoming increasingly aggressive as he turned on her. 'Back away madam, step back now - I have already told you to leave a scene where a police investigation is taking place.'

On realising she had just been hit, Rosie exploded in a fusion of shock, anger and desperation. She grabbed the front of the policeman's jacket, but before she could say anything, he took hold of her wrist and twisted it, causing Rosie to drop to her knees and scream in pain.

The policeman's face was now stern, he was at home with the way the situation had turned out, having no need to present a façade of professional authority, this man could indulge himself in what he enjoyed as he shouted at Rosie, 'You have just assaulted a police officer, if you carry on in this manner you will be taken to the ground and cuffed, as it is you are going to be taken to the station and charged with assaulting a police officer, and if you continue you will also be charged with causing affray and inciting public disorder with intent of breaking harmonious relationships between the police and the community - and that, madam, carries a hefty prison sentence,' and with his final words he twisted her wrist sadistically, and got what he wanted, or some might say what he needed, which was a squeal of pain.

It was an upsetting sight as the elderly lady instinctively took hold of the policeman's arm, in reality a totally futile action, but her intent was powerful as it was poignant, and Nina leapt from her prone father to help her mother, she too was holding onto the policeman's arm in an effort to make him let go of Rosie.

One of the two policemen by the car looked over at what was happening while the other one was looking through the contents of Chris's case.

Rosie was pushed to the ground by the policeman, who then shoved Nina away, which caused her to stumble backwards and fall over.

Rosie screamed at him to leave Nina alone, but the policeman was now in beat-and-arrest mode.

'How old is she? He shouted at Rosie, 'How old? How old? Answer me, now!'

'She's thirteen,' Rosie sobbed.

'Move her, move her away from here - thirteen year olds stab people and plant bombs, she's old enough to be arrested - move her now,' he shouted at Rosie.

One of the policemen by the car spoke into a microphone in the lapel of his jacket as the other one ambled over and helped Rosie up from the ground.

'Careful,' the senior policeman snapped at him, 'she's proved herself to be violent and she might resist arrest.'

On hearing his words Rosie went to protest, but the policeman holding her applied a lock on her arms, and then forcing her forward he walked towards the police car. As this was happening a police van and an ambulance pulled up at the scene, the timing was very convenient; it was as though they had been waiting around the corner for the call to make an appearance. A police officer got out of the van and walked towards Chris's front door pulling at a roll of tape that is put up at scenes where a crime had taken place, and as soon as he reached the house he began taping over the open doorway.

'No one's allowed in the house,' the senior police officer barked out the words, now fully and happily engrossed in the chaotic scene that had developed.

'Those two,' he said, pointing at Rosie and Nina, 'put them in the van - I can only take so much of these people, and let the paramedics deal with him on the ground - he's still breathing, we'll question him later.'

He turned to the elderly lady who was visibly shaking with shock, and lowering his voice he said in a gruff, offhanded manner, 'And you, madam, take your tray back home, you are holding up our enquiries and our dealing with a police matter - now if you would be so kind, and I do mean now, as of this moment.'

He stared at the lady and added, 'Come on, come on - get the tray please madam, you don't want to be joining your friendly neighbours down at the station, now do you? Especially at your age, madam, I don't think it would go down very well with the morning coffee circle, or whatever it is you demure people get up to during the course of the day.'

It might have been his manner, but it was probably the word, 'demure,' that caused one of the other policemen to look up at the senior police officer with a furtive smile.

The police officers went about their work, one of them taking the tray from the bonnet of the car and handing it to the elderly lady, while the other one hurried her along by holding her arm. She offered some resistance by attempting to shrug off his hand, which brought a stern warning as she was told if she did that again she would be taken down to the station. As she walked away the lady told the senior police officer she would be making enquires into who his superiors were and she would be writing a letter of complaint to the local authorities and the local politicians. She was dismissed by the senior police officer as an irrelevance before he took an interest in the two paramedics who were attending to Chris. He asked them how Chris was, and when told he looked as if he was going to spend some time in hospital, but his injuries did not look life threatening, the police officer immediately lost interest and said Chris would be questioned later at the hospital, either by himself or by someone else.

As the van drove away with Rosie and Nina inside it, and Chris was being carried into the ambulance, the senior policeman looked about himself and nodded at a job well done. Looking from the taped-up front door to the debris in the road he told one of the officers to get someone to, 'Clear up this mess in the road,' and looking into distance he said to himself, 'they've got big ideas these people, who do they think they are?'

Forty-Two

The room was fairy small and had a utilitarian feel. There were not any artefacts or objects denoting a place of personal identity; it was a space kept adequately clean and utilised for its relevance. The blinds on the window were closed, although there was enough light for Chris to see clearly and look around the place he had woken up in.

He was in bed, a rather ordinary one, not a hospital bed, and there was nothing to indicate it was a medical setting, even the sounds, or lack of them, outside the room did not sound like what one would expect the noises in a hospital to be like. As Chris made an effort to sit upright an immediate pain in his head and stomach stopped him abruptly, and as it did so his mind sifted through pieces of a jigsaw, which began to fit into place and gave him a picture that explained what had happened to him, but where he actually was remained a mystery. He began to panic, even through the effects of the sedative he had been given, as Rosie and Nina came to his mind. He saw them outside his house, screaming, and the men, and they were shouting and then he was getting beaten, and now he was in a bed, in a room. He tried to move again, but as before the pain and discomfort was too much and so he remained where he was.

Minutes passed by, and Chris noticed there were no machines monitoring his progress, no charts and no glass of water on the small table next to the bed. There was nothing, it was just a room, and he began to panic even more, but the more he became anxious the more pain he felt in his head and body. After a while Chris called out, or he intended to, but the weakness and his parched mouth made it sound like a feeble croak, and the sound he made felt significant to Chris, as if symbolising any strength he had to challenge those that had put him in the situation he was in.

Nothing happened, nobody came into the room and Chris could only hear vague sounds of activity every now and then from outside the room. He tried to think where it was that they had taken him, but his thoughts were broken by the worry of Rosie and Nina, and every time his anger tried to take hold of him it was repressed by weakness and chronic fatigue. It went on for over an hour, until Chris fell into a deep, artificially induced sleep where there were no dreams, but only the imprint of unpleasant feelings.

When he awoke he felt worse than before. His mouth was so dry and the pain in his head throbbed, a sick feeling pushed from his stomach into his chest and he thought he was going to vomit, which frightened him because of the pain in his body. But he was not sick, and a feeling of dizziness caused him to close his eyes and hope that it would pass.

To his relief the feeling did settle, leaving Chris more tired than before, and he felt as though he was sinking, deeper and deeper into a well, crowded with faces of aggressive men who were shouting, but there was no sound, just their mouths forced into mean slits, angry and vicious.

It seem as though time had lapsed, and the aggressive faces of the men had returned with their mouths twisted in hate and eyes dark with violence, but some of the mouths were making sounds. They were speaking, and the mouths became as one, and just the one face, the face of a man, and he was talking; he was talking to Chris.

'Mr Kirby - Mr Kirby - can you hear me? Are you with us Mr Kirby?'

It was a man, a real man, standing by the bed talking to Chris. His face looked familiar to Chris and he was sure he had seen him somewhere before, and then he realised it was the face of the man in the sleep he had just come out of. He then realised there was a man standing in the corner of the room; it was the senior policeman who had attended the scene outside Chris's house. He was looking at Chris as if disappointed he had regained consciousness and survived the attack.

'Mr Kirby,' the policeman said, as he looked at the man standing by the bed who stepped back and nodded, giving his consent for him to speak to Chris.

'You've been in the wars, Mr Kirby,' the policeman said as he walked up to the bed, and holding his hat between his fingers in a way one might do when reverently standing by an open grave he raised his chin in a contrived act of politeness as he said, 'Can you remember what has happened to you, Mr Kirby? Have you any recollection of what happened outside your house yesterday? The men who attacked you? Eh?'

Chris looked at him, but his mind was elsewhere, in a place of smudged images and where voices were raised in anger, but sounded to be very distant, and then he remembered, and he gave a sudden, violent jerk that was so powerful his body actually raised itself from the bed.

'Where are they? Where are they?' Chris tried to shout the second time he said it, meaning Rosie and Nina. The panic in his face was completely in contrast to that of the policeman's, who smiled in an affected benign manner as he shook his head and asked innocently who Chris was talking about. The man who had stepped back from the bed looked on, having witnessed what was happening many times before his seemingly emotionless expression did not alter as he looked from the policeman to Chris. Again, Chris attempted to raise his voice as he asked, and pleaded, wanting to know the whereabouts of Rosie and Nina and if they were safe. The pathetic feebleness of Chris only gave more strength to the policeman as it fed his need for power, and it was all he could do to stop a smile breaking on his face.

'You've been having a good old talk to me, Mr Kirby, yes, you have a lot on your mind that you want to say,' the policeman said as he leant his face closer to Chris. 'Telling me all about yourself you were - about your family, what you've been up to and what you want to do,' and he paused for a couple of seconds as his stare intensified before saying, 'and about your brother, Steven.'

Chris gave an involuntary gasp as he struggled to say, 'What? What did I say about him?' The urgency in his eyes showed how desperate he was for an answer, but the policemen feigned an air of it not being important and sighed as he looked across the room. 'Oh, you know,' he said, 'just things - things you said to one another, as brothers do, little things, big things,' and looking down slyly at Chris he added, 'secrets.'

Chris was confused, and it was visible on his face; it was not the response the policeman wanted.

'Secrets,' Chris said the word softly, as if examining its meaning while looking through the policeman as he did so.

The policeman let Chris have a time to think, but his impatience was getting the better of him and the tone of his voice hardened considerably as he said, 'Yes, Mr Kirby, secrets - we all have them, and it appears you certainly shared a few with your brother,' and he watched Chris shake his head slightly as he continued to look into space.

'Yes you did Mr Kirby,' the policeman said, pushing his point more firmly, 'so it's no good making out you didn't.'

The tone of his voice and manner caused Chris to look up at him, his head was clearing and he recognised that the policeman wanted information and he was not a pleasant person in anyway whatsoever.

Chris shook his head slowly as he told the policeman he did not know what he was talking about, and continued to maintain he did not know when the policeman questioned him about whether his brother had confided in him about any matter or problem he had on his mind.

'Where am I?' Chris asked him, ignoring a question the policeman had asked, which annoyed him, and it showed as he pursued his line of inquiry.

'Come on, Mr Kirby - just tell me about what you and your brother talked about - we know you did talk to each other about important things, and if you don't talk about it now it will be worse for you at a later date, which will probably be sooner rather than later, I should imagine.'

Chris just looked at the policeman, the realisation of his situation hitting him; it was terrible, but it was true.

'Come on, you've been through a bad time as it is - we're only trying to help you, but you can't see it.'

It was a long while before Chris spoke, his voice weak as he said, 'I don't know what you're talking abou...'

'Come on, Mr Kirby,' the policeman cut in.

'No, really, I don't - please, you have to believe me,' Chris said.

The policeman took a deep breath and, leaning over the bed, he said in a low voice, 'But I don't, Mr Kirby, but I don't,' and then he stood upright before turning and walking towards the door. Chris asked again where he was, but the policeman did not turn or pause as he said, 'That is not your concern, what is significant is that you tell us what your brother has said or given you - something, which you know to be important.'

Chris shouted, or intended to shout, 'Where is he? Where is Steven?' But the policeman ignored him and shut the door as he left the room.

Chris tried to scream, but the pain in his ribs and head stopped him, and when he struggled to sit upright pain and weakness pushed him back down. All he could do was stare at the door the policeman had just walked through, stare and shake his head as he formed soundless words, and all the while the man standing nearby watched him, passively, as if reading a timetable at a railway station.

Forty-Three

The police tape sealed the front door of Chris's house, even the windows were taped over and at the back of the house the door and windows had metal frames screwed into the doorframe and windowsills. A sign had been nailed to the wall with the words on it, This Is An Area Under Police Investigation - Keep Out.

Brendan stood by the front door and looked around at the street and other houses, blanking out Chris's house he reflected on the innocent normality presented by the quiet street and neat little house, and as he did so a thought came to his mind of how sinister ordinariness can be. Three days had passed since the beating outside the house and Brendan had not been able to contact Chris or Rosie. He had rung people that knew them, such as friends and people where Chris worked, but they also could not contact them, and after knocking on some of the neighbour's doors for the second time, with the intentions of asking if they knew anything, Brendan decided to leave. As he walked away he looked over his shoulder at the house, although he did not see the pin sized cameras and microphones that were part of a meticulous twenty four hour surveillance of the house, and sitting in a room was an officer of the security service, monitoring all activities that happened outside the house. She touched a screen to show a close up of Brendan, and then after cross-referencing with another page on the computer a photograph of Brendan appeared on the screen with his name and full details of who he was, where he lived, where he worked; in short, everything about him, and at that moment Chris was waking up in a ward of a regular hospital. His mouth was thick and his head groggy because of the heavy sedative he had been given when he was transferred from the room he was in before when questioned by the policeman.

His questions of where he had been, meaning the room he was in before, went unanswered by hospital staff who were evasive and brusque. Nobody could give him any information on the whereabouts of Rosie and Nina; his frustration turned to deep despair as he waited to speak to a 'specialist' who he was told would be seeing him during the course of the day. The three other patients in the same cubicle as Chris averted their eyes when he looked at them, although he had established what hospital he was in, which was about ten miles from his house.

The 'specialist' arrived in the early evening, and he also avoided all the questions Chris asked referring to his family, where his personal possessions and clothes were, where he had been and who the police officer was that had spoken to him. He only wanted answers to the questions he asked Chris, which were in regard to how he felt, and after shining a torch into his eyes he told Chris that he would be discharged in the morning and he had no information about how the arrangements were to be made or by whom.

Chris waited, lying in the bed, although he could get up but was told only to use the toilet and to return immediately back to bed. He was weak and there was great pain in his legs and body, his ribs were strapped up, and on seeing his face in the mirror when in the toilet he took a short gasp, the bruising and cuts, along with being unshaven, presented the face of a man who had been in the wars and looking a lot older than his age.

He could not settle as evening moved slowly into night, but just before the main lights were turned off in the ward a person who said she was part of the administrative staff told Chris he would be leaving in the morning and that arrangements had been made for him. She did not answer his questions about Rosie and Nina, or Brendan, but only repeated what she had said - that arrangements had been made and things would be explained to him. Chris shouted at her in desperation, wanting to know if Rosie and Nina were still alive and were they hiding it from him. The woman looked at him, and Chris felt he saw compassion in her face, even though it was forced to reside beneath the pragmatic air she had to present for her work, and he was sure he saw the corners of her eyes give slightly at the sight of his plight before assuming her work-like demeanour as she repeated what she said before. It was a massive breakthrough for Chris. He just looked at her, and she gave a repressed smile and touched the sheet on his body, and then gently squeezed his arm as she turned away. It was as if there was life out there, like a man on a desert island Chris had found something, even though only a glimmer of life it gave him hope.

Chris had been given a sedative, not as strong as the medication he had been given before, and because of that the night hours were long as time dragged slowly by. Thoughts crowded in on him and were ready to burst in his mind, and it was then that Chris had an idea; to escape. He got out of bed and walked to the toilet, noting how there were less staff than during the day, and as he passed the desk with two nurses sitting behind it he nodded and pointed in the direction of the toilet, one of them nodded and told him to go straight back to his bed after he had been there. Whilst in the toilet he went over the possibilities of escape, and the more he did so the more he realised it would be hopeless and that it was just a reckless thought borne out of frustration. He passed the nurses on the way back to his bed without acknowledging them, his shoulders having dropped considerably from the short time when he had passed them earlier.

258

The morning routine started early in the hospital ward, 'Six thirty,' the nurse told Chris when he asked her. 'No place for layabouts,' she said with a smile as she looked at the three bedridden men around Chris in their cubicle. Another nurse dropped some shaving things on the table next to his bed and said he was able to shave himself, but she just shook her head and kept walking when Chris asked her what time he would be leaving. Not long after breakfast a doctor came to see Chris and asked how he was feeling. He checked his chart as he spoke to Chris and then told him he should be leaving shortly, but not to ask him any questions about his discharge and that he would find out soon enough what was happening to him.

So, Chris waited, feeling cut off from everything, his family, his life and even from the other patients he shared the cubicle with. It was about an hour later that two men came into the cubicle area and stopped on seeing Chris. One of the men was carrying a holdall and he placed it on the floor by the side of Chris's bed. Their manner was indifferent as Chris was told to get dressed and to use the clothes in the holdall as his own clothes were ruined. Chris got out of bed, but found it difficult to lift the holdall because of the pain in his ribs, so he took what clothes he needed to the toilet and got dressed in there. He did not bother asking the two men any questions about Rosie or even where he was going or what was happening, he just walked by the side of them as they left the ward, with one of the men carrying the holdall. They took the lift and Chris noticed it passed the ground floor and continued to the basement, and he also noticed one of the men watching him, as if for his reaction. The lift doors opened, and there were two men standing there, dressed pretty much the same as the two men in the lift with Chris, in dark suits and long black coats. All the men acknowledged each other with nothing being said and then one of them began to speak, 'Sorry to put you through this Mr Kirby, but we require you to do something before leaving the hospital, and as you're here you might as well get it over and done with and do it now.'

Chris was puzzled as he followed the two men out of the lift, and joined by the other men they all walked down a corridor. Chris asked what it was they wanted him to do, but all he was told that he would find out soon enough, and as Chris asked about Rosie, without getting an answer, he saw a sign on the wall indicating they were walking towards the morgue. He stopped walking, rooted to the spot, blood pounded in his head and his mouth dried so much he could not speak, but he wanted to ask who it was they were taking him to see. Again he was told to wait, only this time one of the men prompted him to keep walking by placing his hand on Chris's arm and firmly guiding him in the direction the others were walking. 'Tell me,' Chris shouted as they stopped at an unmarked door and one of the men entered.

'This way Mr Kirby, this way please,' said the man who was holding his arm, and Chris walked through the doorway into the morgue, his mind rushing as he looked around, and then he stopped looking when he saw a body lying on a slab beneath a sheet. Although not wanting to, he dutifully walked up to the body as another one of the men took his other arm and guided him.

'We believe you can help identify the body, Mr Kirby,' and as Chris screamed, 'No, not Rosie,' his mind raced over possibilities of it being Nina or even Steven. A woman who worked in the morgue appeared from behind a screen and walked to the head of the body, which was visible under the sheet.

'Just to help us with our inquires Mr Kirby,' one of the men said as the women carefully lifted the sheet and pulled it down.

It was Brendan, although it took a few seconds for it to sink in, and Chris did not make a sound and he did not ask any questions. He was not really shocked, he just looked at his face and slowly and quietly said, 'Oh God, Brendan,' and as he went to reach out his hand to touch Brendan's arm he was stopped by one of the men as another one said, 'Don't touch the body Mr Kirby – you do know him then?'

Chris nodded without looking up from Brendan's face.

'Do you?' the man said in a hard voice, and Chris muttered thickly, 'Yes, yes I do.'

'Is this Brendan Vaughan, Mr Kirby,' the man asked, and Chris nodded, very slowly, his eyes locked onto Brendan's face.

'Is it? The man said, and Chris replied as if by remote control, 'Yes, it is, this is Brendan, Brendan Vaughan.'

The man said where Brendan lived and asked Chris if that was correct, and Chris nodded, distant, in his thoughts as he looked at Brendan's face.

'Okay,' the same man said, 'thank you for helping us with our inquires Mr Kirby, we won't hold you up any longer,' and as the women replaced the sheet over Brendan's face the men turned, one them holding Chris's arm and guiding him from the body.

Chris stopped, resisting the pressure on his arm to walk away, 'What - what happened,' he muttered as he turned and looked down at the body.

'Hit and run, I'm afraid, Mr Kirby - did he drink a lot? Have a problem with the drink? There are witnesses who say he was veering all over the pavement and just walked in front of a car - there was nothing the driver could do.'

'And who was the driver?' Chris asked, his voice now definite as he looked into the face of the man who had said it.

The man looked at Chris for a couple of seconds before saying, 'I just said, Mr Kirby, it was a case of hit and run, we don't know, and it was dark, and what with things happening so quickly, and bystanders being shocked, nobody took the number plate,' and he stared at Chris, challenging him to defy what he had said. But Chris was beaten, he looked down at Brendan, the shock made it impossible to form any constructed thoughts, and as he looked at his best friend he began to cry.

Forty-Four

Chris was led out of the hospital and into a car, then he was driven to a building at the back of an old town hall. While in the car Chris gave up asking questions about Rosie and Nina, he was told everything would be explained to him when he met the people who were 'helping and supporting' him. The town hall was in a different part of the city from where Chris lived, in an area he had been to only a few times in his life. His mind raced with hopes that he might very soon be with Rosie and Nina as he walked from the car, into the building and down a corridor leading to the room where they were taking him. Rosie and Nina were not in the room, but there were three men dressed the same as the men who had taken Chris from the hospital; one of whom placed the holdall on the floor, and after all three made eye contact with the men in the room they turned and left.

One of the men stood up and closed the door, and as he did so gestured for Chris to sit in a chair. 'Mr Kirby,' he said in an officious, but intending to be encouraging, voice, 'you are a lucky man.'

Chris looked at him as he sat down, and then he looked around the room and thought of what his life had become as he said in a quiet and fatigued voice, 'What's happening to me, please, and can anybody tell me where my wife and child are? If this isn't a living nightmare, then it must be hell.'

All three men in the room looked at Chris with serious contemplation, but not a word was said, and it remained like that until the man who had spoken before began to speak.

Chris was told he was to be taken to flat, which apparently was going to be where he was to live, and in less than twenty minutes Chris was being driven in a car with the two men who were in the room, but had not spoken, to an area not far from the old town hall that was run down and on the perimeter of a housing project. Chris saw himself as a carcass of a man, or like a lamb he had seen through the slats on trucks being driven to an abattoir. Staring through the side window in a state of prostration, Chris remained impassive as the car slowed and circled its way through the back streets and came to a stop near to an old shopping precinct, and as it did so the man in the front passenger seat pointed up at flats above the small shops and said to Chris, 'There's your place, up there.'

Chris looked from the man to the flats and back at the man, and then straight ahead as he tried to understand what he was talking about. The man repeated what he had said and nodded with an empty smile to affirm what he said was true. Chris looked up at the flats and around the surrounding area, no words were going to leave his lips, it was as if he was observing his predicament from a different orbit. The men got out of the car and stood either side of the rear doors for a few seconds before the one on Chris's side opened the door and said under his breath, 'Home sweet home.'

Chris did not move, he could not, he had lost the ability to and also he could not speak; he had frozen in a bubble where there was no sound or feeling.

'Come on,' the man said as he took hold of Chris's arm, 'on our way now, we have other things to do today.'

Chris complied by climbing out of the car, and then looked around himself like a man rescued from a mine after being trapped for days only to find he had emerged in a place he did not recognise.

'That's it, Mr Kirby, that's it, now you're getting there,' the man said as he led Chris by his arm towards the back of the shops while the other man carried the holdall.

They walked around the back of the shops and up metal steps to a narrow balcony that served four of the flats, and as they made their way on the balcony around to the front of the flats Chris took note of everything he saw, from the discarded rubbish to the empty cans and bottles that once contained cheap alcohol and a life-sized photograph of a baby, which had been taped onto cardboard that was now sodden, dirty and torn; Chris remained silent as he noticed there were not any chickens, but then they were not in a housing project.

The man carrying the holdall opened the door to the flat and entered, walking into the cramped kitchen that had recently been cleaned and decorated in a basic fashion, as had the rest of the flat, which led Chris of think of Paul the artist's flat and the way it had been prepared for the next person to live in; and the thought of it caused his thoughts to blaze to an extent the heat burned his stomach. Chris let out a yell that was long and painful, and as he did so the men hurried him into the kitchen and quickly shut the door. They told Chris to calm down and that someone would be meeting him in a couple of minutes to explain what was happening, but Chris could not hear what they were saying, he just stumbled into the cheap kitchen furniture holding the sides of his head and moaning. The men led Chris into the small living room and sat him down on a settee that been cleaned, but was old and had been put in the room with the other bits of furniture that bore no relationship to each other; they had been placed like props on a set. Chris sat on the settee with his head in his hands looking down at the carpet as one of the men took a mirror that was hanging on the wall and held it in front of Chris.

'Look in the mirror, Mr Kirby, go on, have a look at yourself,' he said in a voice that sounded like it might be used when placing an order for boxes of cleaning products in a warehouse. Chris looked up at the mirror, and felt that everything suddenly stopped and became suspended in a vacuum.

What he saw was not him; it was the reflection of a man in insufferable pain who could have recently survived a car accident by the look of the bruising and cuts on his swollen face and head. A patch of hair had been shaven in order for stitches to be sown above his ear, and although he had seen his refection in the hospital, it was at that moment it hit home.

'Done well for yourself, haven't you, Mr Kirby?' the man holding the mirror said. 'It's a good job you live in a country where people are looked after and supported when things go wrong for them - or they allow their lives to be ruined.'

Chris did not try to say anything, he looked around the room, at the holdall and the two men, and then around the room again; Chris stopped looking on hearing a knock on the door.

A man entered the room and looked down at Chris for a few seconds before speaking in a contrived mood of optimism. He introduced himself and told Chris he had been assigned by the health and welfare authority to support him with his transition from hospital to taking his place in society. He said his name was Bob Morgan and he handed Chris four identical cards having his name and number on them. Chris looked from one of the cards to Bob Morgan; there was something about him that reminded Chris of Steven's health worker, Simon, and even more so when Chris asked about his possessions, such as his wallet and phone. Bob Morgan smiled and told Chris he had raised a matter that was not his responsibility and he was concerned only with Chris making, 'steps to a constructive future.' He said, 'The past is the past - as they say Chris,' and it was then that Chris tried to stand up and attempted to shout at him, but he was too weak; Chris wanted to know where Rosie and Nina were.

One of the men placed his hand on Chris's shoulder, keeping him seated as Bob Morgan studied Chris before speaking, 'Getting worked up and shouting at people isn't going to help your situation, now is it Chris - just think about it.'

And again Chris tried to shout, 'Think about it? Think about it? What the hell are you talking about? I'm asking you where my wife is for Christ's sake, it's a perfectly normal thing to want to know...'

Bob Morgan did not answer, but just looked at Chris in a way that said he would start speaking when Chris calmed down, and then taking a deep breath he began to speak. He told Chris that his life was in danger and

Rosie and Nina were being kept in a safe place for their own safety and it was imperative for security reasons that Chris did not know their whereabouts. Bob Morgan just shook his head slowly when Chris asked who was threatening his family's life and told him he could not divulge what little he knew, but it was people who were agents working against the interest of the state, and it also had something to do with his brother Steven.

Chris stood up on hearing Steven's name, which caused the two other men to react by stepping towards Chris, but that is where it ended, with Chris staring at Bob Morgan for quite a few seconds before quietly saying Steven's name. Bob Morgan's eyes intensified as he looked at Chris, watching his response to what he had just said, and it did not go unnoticed by Chris, which made him think Bob Morgan was working for the police and would be feeding information back on his behaviour; reminding him again of Simon and his relationship with Steven.

Chris decided to say very little about Steven, other than ask how his brother was implicated, but, as he expected, the man calling himself Bob Morgan repeated that he knew very little about Chris's situation, and added that he knew nothing about Steven. A voice in Chris's head told him clearly to say nothing else, because everything he did say was being scrutinised by the man who had been assigned to monitor his thinking, intentions and activity.

Chris sat down and looked at the three men in the small room; and then it became too much and he broke down, knowing his life had changed into the nightmare he had feared it would do. He continued to cry as he went over how he would never see Rosie or Nina again, and as he did so one of the men took things like underpants, socks and shaving stuff out of the holdall and put them on the table while Bob Morgan and the other man watched Chris; all three men remained silent and impassive.

Forty-Five

Chris remained on the settee long after the three men had left the flat. Bob Morgan had left Chris medication for his injuries, phone numbers and addresses for the local authorities to deal with matters related to utilities, and the places and times for Chris to attend in regard to check ups for his injuries and to sign on for what welfare provision he might be entitled to.

He sat looking around the small room, its alienness not sinking in as his eyes merely browsed over the uncoordinated, cheap and basic furnishing, some bits were new while others were old, and quite pathetically the person who had assembled the items in the flat had placed something on a shelf that was intended to make it homely and as if having some personal meaning. It was an old-fashioned milk jug with a print of a sailor and a blue bird on its side, a very inexpensive piece that would have probably been bought in a novelty gift shop at the seaside, and it was while looking at the little jug Chris began to calm down and think clearly about his situation. He made a resolution, and swore himself to stick to it, which was to remain, whatever situation occurred, positive in finding Rosie and Nina and putting his life back together. It was to be a single-minded purpose, and one that was to draw on all of his mental and physical resources in order to fulfil, and in order to be able to achieve his intentions he swore to eat as well as he could, exercise and keep his mind alert and focused. It was a battle, and one he was going to win. Chris leant back, breathing deeply, the challenge had been set and he was ready to take it on.

After some time, Chris stood up and walked into the kitchen, aware of the pain in his chest and side; gently fingering the bruising and cuts on his face and head he was reminded of how injured he was. His hands were badly bruised, one of them felt as if it was broken, in fact his whole body was bruised and as he thought about it Chris counted himself lucky he was not killed or suffered brain damage. His injuries would heal and through it all he was going to stand tall and put his life back together; and then he dropped to the floor letting out a scream as the image of Brendan flashed in front of his eyes. He asked himself how it had slipped his mind, but then accepted it had not, but what with what was happening it was another shock, and one that had not sunk in.

Chris went through a list in his mind; his brother was dead, his wife and child had gone out of his life, his best friend was dead, it seemed his house had gone and God knows what was going to happen with work or what was going to happen to him next. It had only been minutes before he had set himself a task to be committed in finding his family, remaining resolute and positive come what may, but for that moment Chris just curled up in a ball and cried like a baby.

It was a full hour before Chris got up from the floor, telling himself he would stick to his plan of getting his family back together. He walked over to the sink and ran the cold water, and as it was running he opened the door to a cupboard that was on the wall and saw there were a few glasses and cups amongst other crockery. Chris took a glass and filled it with from the tap, and as he sipped the chlorine tasting water he looked through the window out across the square at a view that was not inspiring or uplifting in any way. The concreted area had at one time had some trees and foliage around its parameter and would have been busier, with people coming and going because there used to be shops at the front of the flats, but they closed down years ago and had since been blocked up and painted over. It was a neighbourhood that had become run down, although it had never been an affluent area by any means and quite close to a small housing project. Chris turned and looked around the little kitchen, thinking how the whole flat would have cameras and microphones secreted in different places, and his mind nearly drifted down the path of thinking about the spartan conditions of poverty and state surveillance, and how it is constructed to protect the power and affluence of those in control and having privileges; but he stopped himself going down that track, he had to stay positive and focus on what he wanted to achieve.

The flat had been stocked with basic provisions and there were towels and clothes in a wardrobe for Chris to wear; although his size, they were not all new. In the bedroom there was a single bed and a small table next to it with an old radio alarm clock on top of the table that had been plugged in, but the time had not been set so it flicked out lit digits to a bland and lifeless room. A television was in the corner of the living room and on a small foldaway table was the remote control, and Chris stopped looking as the silence of the flat was broken by the sounds of someone knocking on the door and ringing the doorbell.

Chris was scared. He looked down at the carpet, trying to calm his breathing but the knocking and ringing sounded again, so, steeling himself, he walked towards the door in the kitchen. Chris stopped on seeing there was no spyhole in the door so he looked through the window, but the angle was too acute to see who it was. He opened the door and saw two policemen; one of them was the senior officer from before. He acknowledged Chris with a quick nod as he handed him a sealed plastic bag, 'Mr Kirby,' he said in his abrupt tone, 'here's your personal belongings, you have the vigilance of two of our police officers to thank for getting them back to you' and he went on to tell Chris that at ten thirty the following morning he would be collected from the flat and taken to his house to collect more of his possessions.

'Hope you're settling in, Mr Kirby,' he said as he turned and walked away, followed by the other police officer who looked into Chris's face before turning, but Chris was looking through the contents of the bag he had been given and saw his phone was not in it. He shouted out, telling them his phone was not in the bag, but they kept walking, and he heard the senior officer say, 'Tomorrow, you'll be getting your things tomorrow, Mr Kirby.'

Chris watched them walk down the balcony and around the corner, and he noticed how it was already getting dark, even though it was not yet two in the afternoon. A sudden noise caused Chris to look across the square; a dog was barking as he or she chased and jumped up at an empty plastic bag that tantalised the dog as it twirled in the wind just out of reach.

Forty-Six

The day continued with no change in mood. Chris heated a tin of soup and made a cup of tea in the evening, but besides doing that he sat on the settee not wanting to turn the television on, and every now and then shouted out in frustration as he thought about not having his phone. He looked through his wallet and was pleased to see that nothing was missing, and as the cash had not been taken he assumed the assault had nothing to do with robbery. The keys for his house, car and work were in the bag the senior police officer had given him, and as he looked at them Chris thought about work and what they would have been told about him, but then his mind returned to Rosie and Nina, and he forced himself to keep focused on what he had told himself to do.

Sleep came in patches, at times Chris toyed with the radio, going through different stations, listening to the tone of the voices rather than the content until finally settling on a station playing classical music, most of it having been composed well over a hundred years before, and Chris thought of what life for the ordinary person was like back then. When ten thirty came the following morning Chris was ready and waiting, pacing around the small kitchen, but still not wanting to turn the television on.

It was not long after the arranged time that a knock sounded on the door, and on opening it Chris saw Bob Morgan standing with two men who looked similar to the men who had brought him to the flat the previous day. The first question Chris asked him was about his phone, but he shook his head slightly and told Chris he would be going to his house soon and it would probably be there.

Bob Morgan was quite industrious in his manner as he went through practical information with Chris, such as where to turn the water on and off, radiator keys and fuses. As Bob Morgan did this Chris asked about Rosie and Nina, but was told he would explain the situation after Chris had 'settled' in the flat.

The two men with Bob Morgan stayed in the kitchen while Chris and Bob Morgan went into the living room and sat next to each other on the settee. It was as if Bob Morgan was testing how far he could go without Chris lashing out. He told Chris that a criminal gang had targeted his family because of Steven's involvement in 'certain activities' where he had information that was very important to them. He said that Steven was a clever man, and, 'in layman's terms he had been got at by a gang who saw Steven as an important asset in getting what they wanted.' He then told Chris that Steven had been used by the gang, which they did by blackmailing him with evidence they had of his involvement with activities

269

harmful to the state's security, and also if he did not comply with their demands they would bring harm to Chris and his family as Steven did not have a wife and children of his own.

When Chris finally spoke he asked why there was a need for his family to be broken up and why had he not been in contact with Rosie; but the explanation he was given was totally implausible. 'It minimises risk if you are apart' Bob Morgan said, and he told Chris at present it was best for them not to even know of the other's whereabouts for their own safety just in case the gang got one of them. And when Chris asked why they could not speak on the phone, he was told it was a state security inquiry and that is the way they do things.

'Trust me,' Bob Morgan said with a simple smile on his face, 'your lives are in real danger, and it's lucky for you the security service got to you first - that beating you took, Chris, is nothing compared to what these people are capable of,' and he continued to look at Chris, nodding to confirm what he had said. He went on, telling Chris they would be leaving in a minute to collect some of his possessions from his house, and that Rosie and Nina had already been there and collected their things under the protection of 'special' police officers. On hearing their names the breath stopped in Chris's chest and he looked into the eyes of the man sitting next to him, but they were giving nothing away, they were not cold and hard, they just seemed to be residing behind a barrier that restricted all entry. Chris did not believe a word he had said, and as if reading his thoughts Bob Morgan said it was an extremely important matter that the state's security system had termed as 'classified.'

Chris looked down at the floor; he suddenly felt very tired, but it was in a strange way. A debilitating feeling came over him in waves and the aches and pain in his body throbbed as if being amplified and he heard himself speaking, and on doing so stopped and looked up at Bob Morgan who was staring at him and nodding. Drugs. That is what came to his mind as Chris looked at Bob Morgan, the feelings he had was to do with the drugs he was taking, and he wondered what kind of drugs they were.

'Is there anything you want to tell me, Chris?' Bob Morgan asked, in a friendlier and less formal manner, and it confused Chris, because he felt himself drawn towards him, not in an affectionate way, but as if he was a close friend and he wanted to relax and just talk about anything.

'What is it Chris? What's on your mind - come on, maybe I can help you - I'll try, I'm not that bad you know.'

Chris forced himself to resist from talking, and he realised he was staring into Bob Morgan's face, but he did not say anything and after a while Bob Morgan stood up, smiled and told Chris he was always there for him to talk to if he wanted to get something off his chest. He then changed the mood by telling Chris to get his coat as they were going to his house.

Chris drank a glass of water, which went a small way to clearing his head, and followed the three men out of the door, and he answered in the affirmative when Bob Morgan asked Chris if he had remembered to bring the keys to the flat with him.

It was raining, which gave a limited and blurred view of the areas they were driving through. Chris and Bob Morgan sat in the back of the car with hardly a word being spoken as the car moved slowly through traffic-clogged streets, but every now and then there was a short burst of speed as they drove down open roads. Bob Morgan tilted his head to one side and pulled an expression of finding it difficult to answer Chris when he asked what day Rosie and Nina had been to the house. He finally did answer, telling Chris he was not sure, and it was not within the 'scope' of his 'remit,' and that he would tell him when he had information concerning Rosie and Nina.

Chris could not believe what he saw as the car pulled up outside his house. His stomach tightened as he looked at the words 'paedo scum' daubed on the front of the house and the police tape stuck over metal sheets that had been screwed over the front door and windows. He heard the words, 'What the hell,' passing through his lips and then became aware of the three men in the car looking at him, watching his response to what he had just seen.

'I'll get them back, I'll find Rosie and my baby, and we'll be together, again,' Chris said as he looked in turn at the men in the car, but it did not bring any change of expression on the faces of the men who continued to look at Chris; and all the while Bob Morgan was monitoring how Chris was reacting to his predicament.

As they walked up the path to the front door Chris stared at the other derogatory things that had been sprayed on the wall, and he checked the neighbours' house to see if there was a face at the window. He stopped walking and looked around at the other houses and the street itself, but nothing, there was not any activity or signs of anyone. Chris thought of asking if he could knock on his neighbour's door, after all they had been friends and had done favours for each other, but stopped himself, he knew things had changed to such a degree any hope of trying to maintain a link to the past was hopeless; except, of course, for reuniting himself with his family.

Bob Morgan inserted a key into a lock in what looked liked a plain steel sheet, but was in fact a steel door, and opened it, and then changing keys

271

opened the regular door. 'Where did you get the key to the door?' Chris blurted out, and without turning to face him Bob Morgan said they had made a copy of all keys, and added 'Purely for safety and security reasons.'

Chris followed him into the house with the two men walking behind, all four remaining silent as Bob Morgan turned the lights on, which was necessary because of the windows being covered over, and it was performed in a way that led Chris to feel all loss of ownership of his home and past. It was as it ever was, just the same, except for a feeling of it having been deserted. Bob Morgan checked his wristwatch as he told Chris they did not have a great deal of time and for him to collect things that were important, and then added it was part of the conditions that Chris was not allowed to visit there again until he was given permission to do so, as it was dangerous because the criminals that caused this situation might be watching the house.

Chris did not answer. He did not even nod, but just looked around the living room.

Photographs. There were not any family photographs on the walls, in the cabinet or on the shelves; Chris had intended to take a photograph of Rosie and Nina with him. When Chris mentioned this to Bob Morgan he just shook his head in a gesture of not knowing anything about it and said that maybe Rosie took them all when she had returned to the house. Chris looked from Bob Morgan to the plug on the wall where the charger for his phone was always plugged in; it was not there, and a sickening feeling filled him.

'The charger, for the phone, it's not there,' he said, his voice weakening throughout his sentence as he added, 'I suppose I won't get my phone; that's the way it is.'

Chris thought of how they had decided to keep his phone, and suddenly remembered the other phone he used to contact Simon and people in the 'underground' movement. He kept the other phone in the spare room where he did his work, and as he was thinking this Bob Morgan shrugged and said Rosie could have taken the phone, possibly by accident thinking it was hers. Chris did not answer him, he knew what the situation was and he tried to calm his mind, wondering if they had taken the other phone as well, but whatever had happened he reminded himself that he had a plan and he was going to stick to it.

Chris was followed by Bob Morgan and one of the men as he went into every room, stopping in Nina's bedroom he stared at the bed for a long time and only moved when Bob Morgan said they should be getting on. They went into the spare room and Bob Morgan watched Chris closely as he took some folders, a box with bits and pieces in it and his computer, and he nodded when Chris asked if he could take some of his clothes before saying that Chris did not want to take much with him. Chris remained silent as he handed the man some of his possessions and carried the rest of his things down the stairs. He had tried not to show he was looking for the other phone when gathering his things in the spare room. It was not there and the fact it was missing did not surprise him at all, and without looking back he walked through the front door into the rain.

The car turned around and slowly drove away, and again Chris did not look back at his house or even bother to look at the houses of his neighbours, and he did not see the elderly lady who attempted to come to the aid of Chris when he was beaten outside his house. She watched the car drive away, standing beneath an umbrella and holding the lead to her little dog who was wrapped in her winter coat.

Forty-Seven

It was not until he had got back to the flat that Chris thought about his car. He asked Bob Morgan where it was and was told it had been impounded, and only investigators working on the case were allowed to touch the car because of possible evidence in an ongoing investigation. Chris nodded with a blank expression, as he did not believe what he was told and he did not want to pursue a futile discussion about it.

The three men remained in the flat for no longer than thirty minutes, with Bob Morgan reiterating what he had already told Chris about the different agencies and departments to contact, and that he should make a note of the time and date he had to keep for a hospital appointment in a few days and the police station, which was in ten days time.

Chris did not bother mentioning that not having a phone would make it difficult to contact any of the people he had to call, and of course for him to be contacted by them, or anyone else for that matter, and he felt Bob Morgan was waiting for him to do so in order to crush him a little bit more. He would buy a cheap one, but until then he would have to use a public phone; he noticed there was one in the square outside the flat.

'And remember, Chris, 'Bob Morgan said in a serious tone as he turned in the doorway before leaving the flat, 'if you fail to attend for your appointment at the police station without telling them why - they will be out looking for you, and you could be arrested.'

'Why's that? I haven't done anything wrong have I?' Chris said without thinking, and wishing he had not said it.

Bob Morgan stopped, and looked at Chris in a manner he had not shown before; it was intransigent and formal. He said, 'Let's just say we'll play ball in accordance with the rules of the game - eh?'

He then turned and left the flat, but as he did so Chris heard him say, 'Be careful Chris - be careful.'

And that was it; Chris was alone in the flat. He closed the door to keep the cold out, as well as a few sweet wrappers that had got caught up in the wind, and for a passing second he felt some kind of connection with the sodden wrappers.

Chris took out the things he had collected from his house, the shock of what was actually happening still coming over him in waves. Besides his clothes there was the computer, which he plugged in and put on the table. He looked at the folders, two of them were to do with his work, and the box, which he had put things in like rubber bands, a piece of string, a writing pad, a couple of pens, a few old books and other bits and bobs, and also a newspaper he had kept when he went to see Roger Edgebury in the country. He looked at the paper, his mind zooming back to the hot day with the sun beating through the window of the bus; he could not think about those times any more, so he shoved the paper under the cushion on the sofa. One of the folders contained material to do with the dissident and underground groups he had made contact with. He looked at a pamphlet written by Kim Blakely with the title, Amuse And Control. Chris thought about the people he had met in the groups, and of course Karena. His mind wandered around possibilities of where she was, and even who she was and if he would see her or any of them again, especially as he had not saved their phone numbers anywhere else besides his phone.

Chris could not remember Rosie's or Nina's number, 'Why would I?' he asked himself out loud. It was just a matter of looking up their names and pressing a button, and then he thought about how important and personal information is accessed from a source without hardly knowing how he or she is doing it. It suddenly occurred to him that he did not have a number for Rosie's parents, her sister or her friends, he could ring Rosie's work by getting the number from enquiries, but did not want to do that in case it caused further problems.

Chris dropped that train of thinking and thought about what it meant not to have a phone. The codes one has on his or her phone interacts with their computers, therefore he would be limited to what information is available, and then he realised the difficulty he is going to have trying to travel around. The codes on one's phone required to travel across Zones changed on a regular basis and were used with a card, making fraud impossible for the ordinary person, so from now on he was limited to just the zone covering the area of the city he was in.

An overwhelming feeling of defeat was constricting tighter and tighter, but Chris had to try and shrug it off and maintain his attention on what he wanted to achieve. It was only one fifteen, he told himself he would go out, buy a phone and something to eat, and then he remembered to take the painkillers he had been given. Before leaving the flat he quickly ate a slice of toast and margarine that tasted of what he imagined engine oil to taste like. Walking down the steps at the back of the shops was painful, and it seemed to fit with the weather, the rubbish littering the area and a dark mood encompassing the whole area and everything within it; and he was very conscious how Chris Kirby was now part of that setting he had once just been an observer of.

The short stroll around the square outside his flat took no more than two minutes. Chris knew all of the shops had closed down, but he just wanted to check before asking someone where the nearest bus stop or railway station was so he could get to an area where there are shops. The person he asked was a man who at first Chris thought to be middle aged, but as he spoke to him he realised the man was only in his early thirties. He regarded Chris with suspicion, and after a pause asked Chris what kind of shops he was looking for and if he wanted a large shopping centre or the local, 'G store.'

'Well, I would prefer shops,' Chris said, 'but if you tell me both please, I'll make my mind up.'

It was Chris's demeanour, accent and use of words that increased the suspicion the man had about Chris. He appeared to be uneasy as he told Chris the nearest railway station was a long way off, but gave him directions to the bus stop he needed to get to an area where there were shops or for a Gigantic Store. Chris thanked the man and as he walked in the direction he was given for the bus stop he told himself he had to ward off thinking about the reality of his situation and forge ahead with his plan until he achieved what he wanted.

There was just one person waiting for a bus, a woman in her fifties, but looking a couple of decades older. Chris was careful not to stare at her as he noted her appearance and that the bag she was carrying held a few possessions, which looked like a uniform of some kind and some confectionary that was a very cheap brand. He surmised she was a cleaner or an auxiliary nurse, something of that nature, a good woman, hard working and poor; just the way it is intended to be, Chris thought. The bus arrived, and after stepping back to allow the woman to enter, Chris climbed aboard, showed the driver his travel card and held out some coins, but the driver stopped Chris by holding his hand up as he looked closely at the card.

'That's not enough by itself cocka,' he said, 'gotta have it verified with your phone.'

Chris told the driver he thought the card would allow him to travel in that area, but the man shook his head, 'Sorry cock, it won't,' he said, and when Chris asked how it was the woman did not have any problem without showing her phone, the driver explained that her card was different, and he leant towards Chris, eyeing him surreptitiously as he spoke through the corner of his mouth, 'What, you had a few problems come on top recently, me old cocker?'

Chris looked at the man, not thinking clearly, his mind rushing in too many directions to consolidate a clear thought, and he was taking such a long time before speaking the driver cleared his throat and said, 'In your own time, cocker - I've gotta get this bus going,' but Chris continued to just look at him, and the bus began to pull away with the sound of the door closing behind him. The driver nodded at the coin tray in front of Chris and said, 'put a dollar fifty in there.' Chris looked at him, not understanding what was happening.

'Where you going?' the driver asked Chris, who told him, but remained confused.

'That's all right, just put it in there,' the driver said as he nodded down at the tray, 'I'll give you a shout when we're there,' and he nodded at Chris in a gesture for him to sit down.

Chris sat down and looked from the driver to out of the window. The bus was leaving the depressed area and making its way down wider roads and avenues with trees either side on the pavements, as if dutifully and in a graceful fashion blocking the view through the windows into the flats and houses they were outside of. The journey was not long and as the bus was nearing where Chris was going to get off he had begun to understand the situation with travelling on public transport. He was unaware of not having the required permit to travel, anywhere! So it seemed he was to pay the driver an amount, and he wondered if all the drivers participated in what Chris was beginning to think was just one part of a massive black, or alternative, market that existed, although one did not come into contact with it if you had a good job and the other advantages. One dollar and fifty cents was certainly way over the normal, or legal, tariff, so Chris thought that maybe he would have to barter with drivers until he got the travel permit problem sorted out.

The driver shouted something out, what it was Chris did not know, but it was aimed in his direction so he thought it must have been the signal for his stop. Chris wanted to speak to the driver before getting off, so as the bus was slowing to a stop he walked over to him and asked about the situation with the permit, but the driver was giving nothing away and barely looked at Chris as he asked him how long he had been in his present situation. Chris told him, and it could well have been his honestly and desperation that made the driver think it was safe to speak to him. 'Don't pay any more than you paid just now - whatever the distance,' he said, and nodded without looking at Chris when he asked if it was common practice for this to take place.

When Chris got off the bus he did not move, he stood on the pavement looking at the people passing him and going into and out of the shops, some in a hurry, others at leisure. 'They are alive,' were the words that came from his mouth as he absorbed the life and colour around him. Women and daughters laughed as they held cups of coffee, young men spoke into phones, sometimes with serious purpose or laughing at what was being said to them. It had only been days since this world had been snatched from him, but for Chris it felt a lifetime.

He saw a bank, and if he had had his phone he could have transferred money onto his card at home on the computer, but without it he had to go into the bank to deal with it. As Chris waited to be served he became aware of people looking at him, and how they averted their eyes when he looked back at them. It made him feel uncomfortable, but then it all became apparent when he looked at his reflection in the glass above the counter; of course people would stare at him, he looked like an extra in a horror film. The cuts, and bruising on his face and head, the stubble and stitching and the cheap clothes they had given him made Chris appear as a walking wounded refugee, taken from an alien war zone and dropped in a place of affluence. It was little wonder the man in the precinct was suspicious of him when Chris had asked for directions and the bus driver could so easily identify him as someone who had fallen just like the others from qualified status the driver had seen over the years.

He might as well be holding a banner over his head saying his life was destroyed and declaring he was now a desperate and broken man. His feelings of self-consciousness were unbearable, and more than once he had to tell himself to see it through and stay in the bank to sort his money out. When getting to the counter Chris gave the young woman cashier his card and asked for an amount of cash while noticing how her eyes widened in shock as she looked at him. She took his card without saying anything and stood up, as if relieved the security glass was between them. Chris waited, looking around himself, but not at head height, just sweeping the floor with a beaten gaze and every now and then taking a quick glance up at the people in the bank. And he continued to wait, the other cashier had dealt with at least five customers by the time the young cashier returned with a middle aged woman who was looking at Chris as if he had tried to burgle her home.

She said, 'Mr Kirby, unfortunately your account has been frozen, and therefore you are unable to make any deposits or withdrawals.'

'Frozen,' Chris said as he looked into her impassive face, and she nodded, slightly, saying nothing, as if testing how long it would take before he said something else.

'Why?' Chris asked, his eyes showing clearly how he was suffering yet another wave of torment.

'It says because of suspicious interference,' the woman said, holding a fixed gaze before adding, 'it's to do with security reasons, it could be a number of things - it's best for you to contact the main office.' She watched him, as did the young woman next to her, as Chris looked at her and then at the joints in the frame around the glass partition to up at the tiles in the ceiling and then down at the carpet to finally looking at the woman again, whose expression had remained exactly the same. He stuttered as he asked how he could contact the main office and if there was a phone he could use. The women's face did not move a single muscle as she told Chris there was not a phone for him to use and that he could write to the head office or go in person to make an appointment.

'I'll give you the address,' she said as she took a form by her side and slid it through the opening under the glass. Chris watched her like a cat or dog watches his or her owner take shopping from bags in the hope for getting a treat of some kind. Chris read the address on the form; it was over two hundred kilometres away. There was no way he could get there so he would have to write, but that would take a long time, and who knows, maybe they would deny any knowledge of having received a letter from him. It was terrible, and as he was thinking about his latest problem his attention was broken by the middle aged woman behind the glass screen who was asking him to move away from the counter because people were waiting to be served. Chris looked around and saw a small queue of people standing behind him, and immediately behind him was a woman with a girl of about eleven years of age who was looking at Chris with eyes having great expression, showing a deep curiosity about the man standing at the counter, while the woman with her did not meet Chris's look, but stared at the counter and pulled the girl closer to her side.

Chris shambled, rather than walked, away from the counter thinking of the face of the woman who had just spoken to him, his reflection in the glass, finding out his account had been frozen and the little girl's eyes as she looked at him; he could not have spoken if someone asked him a question, too many things were rushing through his mind. 'The end,' these two words kept repeating in his mind, and he then realised he was saying them aloud as he stood in the middle of the bank with people looking at him.

The wind threw up dust, grit and small pieces of litter, as if demonstrating what lies just beneath the veneer of prissy order and affluence. Chris left the bank, walking in the direction to somewhere he did not know, only that he would find out where it was when he got there. He stopped suddenly and stood in a doorway, taking his wallet out of his pocket he counted the money he had, calculating how much a cheap phone would cost, and then remembering he did not bring Bob Morgan's number out with him; he wanted to let him know the situation. There was enough money in the wallet to buy a phone, but if he did it would leave him short to get by, and he did not know when his financial affairs would be put in order. Chris put the wallet in his pocket and looked up at the goings on in the street from his position in the doorway and saw there was a shop that sold phones not far from where he was standing.

Chris entered the shop, and as he did so was aware of the two young men behind the counter eyeing him with suspicion. There was only one other person in there, and she was browsing, looking over the array of phones on one of the walls.

Chris went to the counter and asked one of the young men about a cheap phone. It was probably his accent and manner that put the young man at ease and he came from behind the counter to show Chris what they had, but after Chris explained he had to pay cash, and told him the amount he had it was clear that the cost was too much, and also there was something else, the shop assistant was hesitant in saying what he wanted to say, so Chris prompted him by diplomatically asking if there was anything he else he should know. The young man told Chris that people could not buy phones in shops for cash, the transaction had to made with a card or phone, and then he added as he looked closely at Chris, 'Although, as you know there are other ways to get one.'

The response Chris gave to what the young man said to him was to just stare rather dumbly in his direction. The assistant looked around before telling Chris in a quiet voice how one can buy a phone quite easily in the projects, and that any of the shops will sell a reconditioned one for cash; and then he raised his eyebrows in a gesture that said it was food for thought considering his present predicament.

Chris left the shop, having asked the young man where the nearest project was, and asking himself if what he was doing was going to dig him deeper into the rotten trench he was now in.

To save money Chris walked to the project, which was apparently a small one, but all the same he wanted to be out of there before it got really dark. It took him twenty five minutes, and he had to slow his pace because he felt so weak. The projects were all the same in that there was an atmosphere of depression and aggression lying heavily over the area. The ring road circling the project was busy, it was a popular area and it felt there was not enough room in that part of the city to accommodate the economically deprived. Chris thought about how the area the project stood on would soon be claimed by the authorities to build residencies for middle class property owners, and even for the rich. He crossed the ring road, walked past lines of low rise housing and within a minute was near the centre of the project where there was a row of shops with a bar at the end of them surrounded by small houses that had been crammed into a limited space along with a few blocks of flats.

280

As Chris walked towards the shops he thought back to a time a few years earlier when he went into a project that was definitely a no-go area for someone like him. It was a project that is in practice segregated for 'foreign nationals' and maintained at a level of being extremely run down. He had no business to go there and, although knowing it was a dangerous thing to do, he was urged by curiosity and he also knew the likelihood of being helped by the security services would have been less than minimal if something had happened to him. The project resembled something he imagined to be in a far off land. English was hardly spoken and the smells and sights were unfamiliar. He saw half a sheep lying in the gutter and a handcart laden with broken computer parts. The culture was totally unlike the world Chris had grown up in, and it would be obvious he did not come from there, which meant he could be a spy, but he hoped the people around him would know the authorities would not be that blatant because of him being so conspicuous. The military and civil police made violent intrusions to arrest people, but it was never to break up fights, restore order or monitor rape, abuse and murder. It was to capture those who, allegedly, were committing crimes against the state and consequently threatening the country's security.

Chris was scared, extremely scared and although he regretted entering the project he felt excited by it. There are spies operating in the projects that work for the state. These people are B B'S, Blended Blood, themselves, and being foreign nationals it is easier for them to mix and participate in daily life. It would be impossible for a regular or orthodox agent to operate in such an alien enclave. Chris had heard how the foreign national spies were paid very little money and were given meagre benefits for the service they perform. He had also heard they are not paid at all but press-ganged into being a spy with threats of blackmail involving their families if they did not pry for information, and are then often arrested and charged with being terrorists themselves.

As Chris stood on the pavement looking at the shop he was going to enter, a shop selling a variety of everyday things, he became aware of not being afraid or self-conscious; he had become anaesthetised by the things that had happened to him.

The shop was similar to those he had been in before, but what was different from the last time he went into a shop in a project was the response of the person working there. He was then watched closely, but now it was obvious that he had become a person like many others who had fallen from grace, or at least from the world he once inhabited as a qualified person. It was not a Rubbish Room, but a shop that opened long hours selling an assortment of practical products as well as various lottery tickets, cheap toys, basic groceries, cigarettes and confectionary, but not alcohol. Standing behind the counter was a young man, and on the wall above his head was an old digital clock; it read Friday: 14:55. Chris looked at the clock, wondering where it was when it was first put up on a wall, and he thought about what life was like back then, but here it was, in the here and now, in a shop on a housing project; just like him, a relic from a past age trapped in awful conditions. There was one other person in the shop, a woman in her thirties, looking at cheap birthday cards, touching them carefully as though the cards were precious objects and incredibly expensive to buy.

The young man behind the counter did not move the tiniest of muscles as Chris walked towards him, leant on the counter and asked if he sold phones. He looked at Chris through the lenses of his glasses for as long as he felt necessary before folding his arms and breathing heavily as he asked Chris what kind of phone he was looking for.

They talked about phones and how much Chris could buy one for, but then Chris had second thoughts about the idea as the young man explained how buying a 'black' phone meant one had to use several 'chips' and frequently change the number to, 'avoid detection.'

It seemed so complicated to Chris, and he knew it was because he was weak and tired, but the whole convoluted process put him off, and so he told the young man he would go away and give it some thought.

'How long since it happened?'

Chris stared at the young man, shocked by what he had asked him, and in such a matter of fact manner.

'Since what happened?' Chris said to him, following closely any movements the young man's eyes might make. The young man looked at Chris for a few seconds before giving a slight shrug of his shoulders and turning away, as if it was not his problem and it was up to Chris to explain himself. Chris watched the young man's slim fingers as he opened a box of plastic whistles. They were children's toys, and on the front of the box was a coloured drawing of a whistle having a cheeky face with the name, Wolf Whistle printed above it. The young man handled the whistles like they were meaningless pieces of waste matter he had pulled from a blocked up drain, his face showing stoical reserve all the while as he performed a task that was part of the whole of which his existence was made up of.

Chris looked at the selection of cigarettes and saw they sold packets of five, not of his normal brand, but they were not the cheapest ones. Thinking how he had to carefully budget his money he bought five cigarettes and a bar of chocolate; the young man served him as if he they had never spoken to each other before.

Once outside the shop Chris did not look around his surroundings, but walked as quickly as he could to get out of the project, and as luck would have it on the road circling the project he could catch a bus that took him close to where his flat was. He held one dollar fifty cents in his hand, like a child who had been given the correct money to pay for something, and although knowing the distance was further than his previous journey Chris remembered the driver telling him that a dollar fifty is the amount to pay. When the bus came Chris looked the driver straight in his eyes and told him where he wanted to go, and then looking around before speaking as he wanted to keep their transaction to themselves he said, 'no permit,' and placed the money in the tray.

The driver looked at Chris, casting a long look over his face, and then looking ahead gave the briefest nod of his head to acknowledge his acceptance, and with great relief Chris thanked the driver and made his way to the upstairs of the bus.

There were only a few empty seats and the one Chris chose was behind two girls wearing their school uniforms. He looked out of the window at a world he felt distant from and increasingly fearful of. Chris just hoped he could get back to flat without breaking down; that is how bad he was feeling. The voices of the girls averted his attention from the dark trouble weighing heavily upon him. He listened to the tone of their voices, their way of speaking and how easily they broke into laughter, and then he began to listen to what they were actually saying. 'Ugh, I look away when they start screaming,' one of them said as she smiled at the girl next to her. 'I know it's got to be done, and they're not worth bothering about, but, sometimes, they make such a fuss - my dad says I shouldn't be so stupid and I should just enjoy it instead.'

The other girl looked at her and said, 'Of course, that's what the offenders want you to think, like they're normal people, that's what my mum says, and all they're doing is trying to trick you, so you've got to be careful, because they're bad people, otherwise they wouldn't be on the show.'

'I know,' the first girl said, 'my dad said I'm sensitive, and that will only get me nothing but trouble.'

They looked at each other and giggled, seemingly at a private joke.

'Don't tell Steve you're sensitive then,' the second girl said, and they both laughed, but Chris had switched off from listening to the girls and their conversation.

She had said 'Steve' and his mind retreated back to thoughts of his brother, and then to the implications of what the girls were talking about, of getting into 'trouble' with a boy she knew. Chris thought about Steven when he was the same age as the girls, of how he never had relationships at that age, or when older. He was an outsider, a bright person, but one that did not fit in because he appeared different, and strange, although there was no harm in him, he was a good man, as he was a good boy.

Chris tried to stop thinking about Steven and looked at the girls in front of him. He guessed they were about fourteen, and as it hd been Nina's birthday a few months before she would soon be the same age as them; and the words came into his mind, 'that's if she's still alive.' The spontaneous effort he used to throw the thought as far away from his mind as possible caused Chris to physically shudder and violently jerk his head to one side, and so much so he checked to see if anybody had noticed; one of the girls had. She looked at her friend pulling a face as she gestured at Chris, and her friend turned in her seat to look at him. They both looked straight ahead, suppressing laughter, and Chris stood up, wanting to get away from the situation. He went to the downstairs of the bus, standing for the rest of the journey, holding onto a pole for support; he felt weak and pain throbbed through his ribs.

Forty-Eight

Chris got off the bus, walked home and, after making some soup and having bread rolls that tasted like one would imagine wallpaper paste to taste, went to bed. He was exhausted as he lay down and listened to a piece of classical music, and although his mind was tortured with worry he immediately fell asleep.

The following day was Saturday, a day he had previously always enjoyed, especially when Nina was younger, because they would go out as a family to seek out activities and interests together. He had planned to go to the college where he and Steven worked to see if he could collect his things; there was nothing of great importance, but they were his possessions. After taking a shower for just the lower part of his body, because of the strapping around his ribs, Chris made a concoction of powdered egg and dehydrated soya protein that was meant to taste like beef sausages, and looking at the side of the packet the bread rolls were in he saw they could be eaten until a date over three months in the future.

He set out at ten-thirty, wondering if he would be able to get into the college, as he no longer worked there. In regards to how far he was allowed to travel due to the limitations Chris found he could go to the college, his house and quite a large area of the city and suburbs; even though he was travelling illegally without a permit, to travel outside the zone he would be allowed to travel in when he got the permit would evoke severe consequences and was not worth risking. It was for this reason Chris decided against going to Rosie's parents and her sister's, because they lived outside the zone he could travel within, and he gave up on the idea of visiting Nina's friend's house because of the trouble it would undoubtedly cause; he told himself just to focus on staying strong and work towards being reunited with his wife and child.

He caught a bus that took him part of the way to where the college was and then had to catch another one, and although catching a train would be quicker Chris knew he was confined to bus travel because one had to use a machine in order to buy a ticket for the train and one's ID had to be used, and that would show he did not have a permit. It was as before, both drivers on the different buses he got on barely acknowledged Chris as they gestured to put the money in the tray. Chris thought how common it must be for people to just give the driver money without having a permit and why the authorities had not clamped down on the situation. It would be easy enough to have someone get on the bus and do what he had been doing in order to catch the drivers out. It led him to think of just how threadbare the system is in certain ways, and that the poor and disenfranchised live in what can be seen to be a parallel society, existing within and on the margins of the orthodox structure.

Chris walked through the main gate of the college and into the car park that led to the main entrance, wondering if his ID would allow him entry let alone to move throughout the college now they had removed things from it. He placed his ID on the plate next to the doorway, and to his surprise he heard the buzzing sound that was the signal to push the door open. Catching sight of his reflection in the glass of the door caused his shoulders to drop as he was reminded what he looked like, which did not instil confidence in speaking to the people that worked there; although it had been only recently since he walked down the corridors it might well as have been a lifetime. Students passed him, fortunately none that he taught, and just as he was approaching the staff room where he was based, a man came walking towards him who he recognised as a tutor in the department of practical and building construction skills. He raised his eyes at Chris, while mindful to look down at the cup of something he was holding, and Chris nodded to the man as he prepared himself to enter the staff room.

There were two people in the room, Chris used to speak to one of them, although not being close they would talk about the college and pass pleasantries. The man looked at Chris as if seeing someone he thought had died, but Chris remained purposeful as he said hello to him and asked if his course supervisor was around; Chris had to speak to this man to get the key for the locker where he had his belongings.

'Should be back here in about fifteen minutes,' the man said, and he nodded at Chris, in what seemed to be a belated response to Chris saying hello to him. Chris went over to the drinks machine and said he would get himself a drink while he waited, but the man did not speak, he just nodded and looked down at a journal he was reading.

As Chris sat down and started to sip the coffee-flavoured drink the other man stood up, remarked to himself that he better get on with things and left the room. It was quiet in the staff room with the two men saying nothing as Chris looked around at nothing in particular and the man read his journal, but eventually other tutors came into the room, some giving Chris a brief nod and finally the supervisor turned up, who stopped momentarily on seeing Chris.

Chris stood up and motioned for the man to go to the corner of the room for privacy. The man's eyes studied Chris carefully as Chris told him he wanted to collect his things, and barely gave a shrug of his shoulders when Chris said in an ironic tone that he supposed he had finished working at the college. The man took a key from his pocket and handed it to Chris as if what he was doing was forbidden, and leaning close to Chris he asked to see him in his room after he collected his things because he had something he wanted to give him. Chris took a small bag from his locker and left the staff room without bothering to try and make eye contact with anyone. He walked down the corridor and knocked on the supervisor's door. On hearing 'come in,' Chris entered the room, and as he did so the man gestured for Chris to close the door.

'Got something here that was given to me by Steven's supervisor, Chris,' he said and his eyes searched Chris's face. The man was uncomfortable as he explained how Steven's supervisor had given him the biscuit tin that was on the table in front of him. He told Chris how a man had been to the college who said he was from the health and social department and that he was dealing with Steven's affairs, and it had been agreed with the senior management at the college for him to collect Steven's things.

He went on to say, 'Steven's supervisor had given the man a few books and the computer memory sticks Steven was using that had course material on them, but had not seen the biscuit tin until some time afterwards, so he thought he would give it to me and I could give it to you when we meet.'

He then looked around nervously as he said, 'In all honesty, the tin should be handed in and for that chap from the authorities to come and collect it, but you are his - was, his brother, Chris,' and his eyes skated everywhere in the room other than Chris.

Chris looked at the man, thinking how what had happened to Steven was not even going to be mentioned, and how terrible it is for everyone to be this scared. The man standing in front of him was a good person, and it was obvious that he wanted to talk to Chris, ask him what happened, talk to him about his brother and why it is Chris suddenly does not work at the college, and how did he come to look so awful; but he could not, because that is the way it is.

Chris placed the key of his locker on the desk and said, 'Thanks,' and although he thought his voice sounded crumbly and weak he felt the two of them, together, as hesitant as they were, had a strength, a defiance and hope that had not been broken even against the overwhelming odds of the system's force and power to control and beat people down.

Chris asked him if he knew the name of the man who came to collect Steven's things, thinking it might be Simon, but he did not know his name and had not seen him. Chris picked the biscuit tin up, feeling its weight, and, surprised by how light it was, gave the tin a gentle shake, but there was no noise such as a rattle indicating loose objects of some kind.

The two men did not say anything else, although their eyes conveyed a shared understanding of the situation, and thanking him Chris turned, opened the door and left the room, hearing the man's hushed words as he walked though the doorway, 'good luck Chris, with everything.'

Forty-Nine

Chris could barely wait to leave the college before opening the tin and finding out what was inside it. Standing outside the gates of the college he placed his fingers under the lip of the lid and prised it off. There were two white envelopes, both unsealed, and in the rushed amount of time he spent looking inside them he saw there was hand written notes on a few pieces of paper and an old fashioned memory stick for a computer in one of them, which was good because the computer Chris had could accommodate it. This excited Chris, tremendously, and he put the memory stick into his pocket feeling it was a connection that brought him close to his brother. As Chris walked down the road from the college he was not only examining the tin, but also cherishing it. It was a link to Steven, and the only one he had, besides the memory stick and the two envelopes, and as it became too much for his shattered emotions he began to cry, and he did not care if people saw him doing so, because he would have said proudly, 'this tin, it belonged to my dear bother, and I loved him.'

The tin had given Chris hope, at last there was something, and even through the powerful emotions he was feeling, Chris suppressed a smile as he looked at the tin and wondered where Steven got it from, because buying a 'family' tin of biscuits was certainly not a thing he would have done; and as Chris smiled again at the thought of Steven and the tin he then suddenly stopped dead in his tracks. Rosie had given Steven a tin of biscuits as a Christmas present; was it the same tin he was holding in his hands? Chris could not think clearly, his immediate thought was to ask Rosie, but that door slammed in his face and the tin suddenly became a symbol of how isolated he was and how much his life had changed for the worse.

There was not anyone he could talk to, he could sense that people he knew would shy away from him because of fear, and Brendan, his best friend, he was dead, and he had to force from his mind that this nightmare was now his reality. Chris got on a bus he knew would take him to an area where there were shops, with intentions of having a cup of coffee, finding a quiet corner and reading what was in the envelopes. It was the same as it seemingly always was, one dollar fifty cents in the tray and the driver gave a short nod to acknowledge the transaction, which Chris performed without giving any thought.

As Chris got off the bus he thanked the driver, who said, 'Anytime buddy, be careful.'

The driver's words caused Chris to look at him, and he saw the driver nod whilst not looking at him, but it gave Chris a feeling of support, and that maybe, however bad our situation, we are not alone. It had a positive effect on Chris, it gave him strength and he reflected over how even against the odds there still exists kindness and concern amongst people.

It was a trendy and expensive little coffee house with a small seating area selling pastries and coffee beans, whole or ground in chic little bags for people to take home. Although wanting a pastry, Chris decided against it because they were so expensive. He bought a standard coffee and took it to a quiet space next to the wall, and, almost trembling, opened the tin with an eagerness to explore the contents of the treasure within. Taking one of the envelopes he placed it on the table and looked at it, preparing himself to read what his brother had written on the pieces of paper, but then he looked about the small café, suddenly in a panic as he realised he had let his guard down while absorbed in thoughts of Steven. He pulled out the separate sheets and as he spread them on the table to read his breathing seized; he could hear his brother's voice with every word and it choked him. There were four bits of paper bearing the tight scrawl, which was Steven's handwriting and at times difficult to read. Everything he had written was relating to people Chris did not know or internal conversations in which Steven had put pen to paper to clarify his thoughts, but all of it was, seemingly, personal musings and not to be sent to anyone else to read. Chris read through them three times, and then just looked at the pieces of paper, wondering why Steven had carried them around with him, because what he had written did not seem to be important and were just personal reflections that could be left at home.

Chris picked up the other envelope and took out the pieces of paper, and again there were just notes about the same people he did not know or even heard of. A lot of what was written did not make sense, with things such as, 'backtrack lizard, eyes in place but can't see yet – I have explained in G137, that is our salvation, but nexus are travelling down the wrong road - I try and help, but they aren't ready, or able to listen - who am I to criticise?'

Chris had to admit it was disappointing, and kept wondering why Steven would feel the need to keep his innocuous personal ramblings in a tin and carry them around with him. He placed his hand on his trouser pocket, feeling the outline of the computer memory stick and consoled himself with the thought there might be something of more interest on that. He would have liked another cup of coffee, but the restraint of money came to his mind, so putting the envelopes back in the tin he stood up to leave, and catching sight of himself in the mirror on the wall he thought how he did not look so battered and his wounds must be healing, or then maybe he was just getting used to the way he looked.

He weaved his way out of the café, a place filled with a life he was removed from, but was once part of, and once outside looking for a bus stop he checked the time; it was one thirty. While waiting for the bus Chris remembered that Brendan's sister, Mary, lived in an area not far from where he was, and although conscious it was a difficult time for Brendan's family, he decided to visit her. Chris had met her only twice, and it had been a long while back for just a very brief few words. He knew Brendan did not get on with her that well, but all the same, Chris wanted to talk to her about Brendan, and then Chris was struck with the thought of how Mary would not want to speak to him, maybe she would see Brendan's death as being a result of his association with him, and his mind raced and stumbled over different thoughts; but Chris wanted to see her, whatever the outcome.

It was the same routine on the bus, and Chris had to guess which stop would be nearer to Mary's house; it had been a long time since he went there with Brendan and as he had driven, his memory had a different perspective to his surroundings. Whilst walking down the road where Mary lived Chris thought about Mary and what he knew of her situation, which was not much. She had brought her children up by herself, having married a man who drank more than he cared for his family and she now lived alone as her children had grown up and left home. All her children were struggling and living on the cusp of poverty or below it.

Chris prepared himself before knocking on the door, patting his hair and straightening his jacket in an attempt to present himself in a tidy manner as he pressed the bell and rapped his knuckles on the flaking paintwork; he looked at his fingers and saw that some fragments of the aged paint on the door had stuck to his skin.

The door opened, and on seeing Chris, Mary closed it again, leaving it open just enough for her look through a gap between the door and its frame. Her eyes watched Chris as he explained how he wanted to see her and that he was devastated and shocked about Brendan. Chris felt she was not going to invite him inside and her eyes flitted over his appearance. He knew she was wondering what had happened to him, but their meeting was brought to an abrupt end as Mary interrupted him, tears forming in her eyes and her voice constricted with choking up. She told him to, 'stay away,' and her voice trailed off while saying, 'you've brought enough trouble,' as she closed the door.

Chris wanted to speak to Mary, but he was not going to try again, and as he walked away from her house he told himself he would not contact any family member, friend or associate of Brendan until he had resolved his situation.

After leaving Mary's house Chris went for a ride on a bus, going nowhere, just whiling away time in a haze before making his way back to the flat, buying a bottle of wine and a newspaper as he did so.

Fifty

The first thing Chris did when he got back to the flat was put the kettle on, and all the while his mind was on the memory stick in his pocket and what could be on it; knowing Steven he imagined it to be incomprehensible stuff to do with mathematics or physics. He pressed the switch to heat the kettle, planning to have a cup of hot chocolate, which really was not chocolate at all but a substitute flavoured drink, although one he quite liked. Tea and coffee was not in abundance and so its price was forced up to an amount only the relatively well off could afford on a daily basis. There is substitute tea and coffee, but it is so blatantly artificially tasting Chris felt it not even worth bothering with. While Chris was putting the simulated chocolate powder in a mug he realised the kettle was not getting hot, so he switched the kitchen light on to check the electricity; that also did not work, which meant the power had gone off, and when that happens it could be cut for a few hours. Chris had never experienced them before, but the flat was in a neglected area and power cuts are an accepted part of life, and the situation is even worse in the projects.

He looked in the drawers and found some candles, but delayed lighting them for a while as he poured a glass of water and walked into the gloomy dark of the living room; before dropping onto the sofa he turned the television on, knowing it is powered by a different source, and what appeared on the screen caused Chris to swear out loud. It was a talent show called WOW! Its format is of having a panel of experts judging the merits of musical groups and singers appearing on the show, and it is their decision that selects the next famous 'artist' to appear as part of a showcase with other performers; Alan Manville is the leading judge on WOW! The winners are all contracted to the same management and they will tour the country, make recordings, appear on television shows, feature in magazines and every other popular form of media. The companies the 'artists' sign to are subsidiaries to the company that makes WOW, which in turn is a subsidiary of People's Pleasure Corporation; Alan Manville is the main person holding and controlling the contracts of seemingly all popular celebrities.

The existence of musical groups, bands or solo artists using their talent as a vehicle to take a critical analysis of society very rarely happens, and if found out about the musicians and writers can find themselves in court on trumped up charges, usually to do with something like inciting social unrest. There is not the encouragement to think in that way or the facilities to rehearse that kind of material, and also, the limitations on travel makes it impossible for an independent group of people to tour. The culture of attracting young people and using music to counter societal laws and practices has gone. Music no longer asks questions or demonstrates, it is now unquestioning and merely mechanical entertainment.

The show ended, but Chris's hypnotic gaze remained on the credits rolling down the television screen. It was the sound of the kettle hissing, signifying the power had returned that brought him out of his trance-like state. Chris aimed the remote control at the television and pressed buttons, going through the channels in an effort to find something he might find interesting, but it did not take long for him to give up, turn it off and stare at the lifeless screen.

Chris went into the kitchen, took a few slices of the bread, smeared on them the margarine that looked and tasted like solidified engine oil and then a gooey substance labelled as Jam, which tasted of an incredibly sweet syrup gunge injected with some kind of chemical that is supposed to have a flavour resembling a fruit, but in fact actually tasted like something frighteningly alien.

Taking the chocolate flavoured drink and the food into the living room he placed them on the table next to his computer and took the memory stick from his pocket. Chris settled himself, excited to see what was on the stick - he was impatient with the time the computer was taking, and when finally something appeared on the screen he was disappointed to see just a series of scratchy lines on a blank background without sound. Chris stared more intensely at the screen, his heart dropping as he thought Steven must have cleared what had been on the stick, and just as his disappointment was setting in, a picture assembled itself into shape, and it was joined with sound.

The titles of a television programme rolled up the screen and gave way to a series of seemingly random camera shots around streets in a major city, although it was not in this country. Chris guessed it was Italy, and amidst the bustle the figure of the chef who presented the programme was singled out, the picture spun and when it settled he was walking along a busy street among people shopping and going about their way in this country. Chris noted how there were a greater number of people with different coloured skin and cultural presentations than there are now, which highlighted how mono-cultural society had become.

The chef had an act of making out he was a maverick type of character as he went around the kitchen banging pots and pans and using language that was intended to shock, yet it was all conducted within the parameters of acceptability because it did not threaten. After all, it was just a cookery programme and irreverent remarks made about items of food or kitchen staff holding lowly positions were hardly going to raise objections from the state.

The show was at one time one of the most popular programmes on television, which made Chris think how people under a certain age in today's society would find that difficult to understand, even though mass popular cultural icons and entertainment was simple and banal today, so maybe it was more to do with there not being the selection of food nowadays or the freedom of travel, amongst other things, for a programme and character such as the chef to exist. It led Chris to think how it was surprising a programme of this kind was so popular back in a time when there were many choices and options on offer, and for the nation to be transfixed on something like a cookery programme is bewildering. Chris thought of how in a way nothing had changed as the state is still using prosaic everyday activities as trite entertainment with all its superficiality and fake personalities that are presented and promoted to an extent where they become so meaningful to many people as the mechanisms of social control changes to fit the situation in different eras.

The chef spoke of 'fun' in every situation and of how cooking brings the family together. The central message of the show promoted the ideal of a functional family participating in 'creating' a meal, all having their role to play in the kitchen and shopping for the ingredients. He went on about how 'wholesome foods' make 'wholesome families.' The word 'natural' was constantly used as he spoke about the ingredients and explained the healing properties of the exotic foods he was using and the beneficial effects they had. The programme broke for the adverts and the same chef was now promoting the virtues of shopping at a particular chain of stores and of how parents with young children can 'trust' that company for providing 'reliable' and 'honest' food that is 'pure,' and it showed him, with supposedly his family, laughing in a serene country setting on a sunny day rolling down a grassy embankment.

The adverts were different, yet even after thirty seconds they seemed to be the same in a relative sense, but Chris found it fascinating and interesting to watch them, noting the different accents, fashion and different products no longer available. It really was startling to note how there is now, for the general population, far less diversity in terms of the range of items and products, and a television show even as simple as this one with the chef gave evidence to this. The shops back then had commodities now only bought by a minority and the ingredients used in the meals made by the chef were generally unattainable. Yet the adverts were the same in being designed to mould minds into the desired condition to be influenced, and although set in a seemingly hail of consumerism it is not so much the product that is of importance, but a way of life, of values and ideas to be consensually adhered to, meaning a way of living, which in essence is a way of thinking.

As well as fashion, language, the racial make up of the people and choice of products the matter of self and freedom was apparent, or a sense of freedom. An advert aimed at young people and travel showed groups of young people in foreign countries taking part in backpacking and different outdoor activities involving thrill seeking experiences. A trailer for another television programme looking at 'binarism and gender identity' followed the advert. Chris thought about how the subjective feelings of one's own identity is no longer even discussed or understood by the vast majority of people and scoffed at by authoritative contemporary thinking. It has been omitted from all means of education and public information, and as an area of debate was lumped together with other matter that is ridiculed, reviled, hated and blamed as a theory and practice associated with the demon enemy that is 'liberalism.'

The show returned and a young woman who was described as a comedian joined the chef. The main thrust of what she said was to make jibes about fat men and of how things were now 'cool' because 'archaic values' had been swept away. She said society had people like the chef to thank for the 'cool' changes that had happened and he had 'revolutionised' cooking and 'what it means.' She spoke of how women were 'free to express themselves' because 'roles and expectations' had changed, except for in some pockets of culture inhabited by 'fat lumpen men' who 'ate rubbish' and were 'disgusting.' She went on to describe how these men continued to maintain 'negative values' and use 'inappropriate language.'

Chris thought about how language had changed. Terms like 'inappropriate' was part of a language that had been discarded and demeaned as 'liberal,' and therefore loaded with connotations that prophesise an ideological dogma serving the interests of a system now gone. Chris felt the chef and the comedian could be seen as little more than agents used to propagate ideology serving the interests of liberal policy and facile consumerism, just as glib celebrities were doing in today's society. As Chris watched the end titles run down the screen his final thoughts were how fruit like mangos are no longer flown around the world for general consumption, and there is no longer such a thing as 'inappropriate', because things are either wrong or right.

Chris stopped the film because he wanted to think about what he had just seen. Although he was not a young child when the transformation in society happened his memories of life before the 'big change' were confused and felt very distant, but he had always been engrossed in finding out about what it was like in those days. He had researched what material he could find and asked older people for their accounts, but found it very frustrating because, however hard he concentrated, he could not conjure up a vivid image or create any meaningful feeling of what life was like back then. The reason for this being so, Chris thought, was undoubtedly because of the misinformation that is relentlessly disseminated by the state through the various all-encompassing means it has at its disposal, and therefore true history is destroyed. Chris thought back to when he was a young boy and his inquisitive nature of wanting to know why things are the way they are, and how his mother would tell him, and Steven, not to bother with preoccupations about the way of things and the injustices in society, but to get on with life and take what the society they live in has to offer. She told them if they worked hard and kept their heads down they could have a good standard of living and enjoy a quality of life not shared by the majority of people in the world, or even in the country where they live.

Chris pulled the stick from the computer, saving its contents for another time - he did want to gulp his treat in one go. He opened the bottle of wine, and discovering there were not any glasses in the flat he used a mug, but before sitting back down Chris took a film clip from the box he had brought over from his house and plugged it into his computer. As well as many films there was one he had downloaded from a person he had met who attended the meetings he went to that was popular within the 'underground' culture. It presented a satirical depiction of a state department having responsibility for art and literature; the film was called The Laughter Machine. It was poorly made, and one had to be a supporter of its intentions to have patience with it. While watching the film Chris thought of many of the people he had met who were involved in the underground movement. He thought of their aims and the way they were, and he felt his brother would not have anything in common with them. Chris could not imagine Steven sitting in a room drinking wine and discussing the contradictions and faults of the society we live in; it was just not Steven at all. Chris tired with the film so he turned it off and sat for a few moments sipping the cheap wine from the mug, thinking of everything and not one thing in particular. He broke from his thoughts and took from the box some literature he had been given by people involved in the 'underground' movement.

Chris opened a folder and pulled out a journal with the initials PUM printed on it. PUM stands for the People's Universal Movement, which is the largest organisation that is part of a network of underground groups having a critical observation of society. They produce a well-circulated periodic journal, relatively that is for a covert counter organisation. The journal is printed on what Chris thought to be cheap quality paper that had a pulp feel and smell to it, and it had often crossed his mind that maybe the journal, and others like it, were produced by the state and consciously made to look amateurish and home printed when contrasted with the glossy magazines in mainstream culture. He opened the journal without looking at the photographs on the cover, which were of graffiti in a city on the other side of the world with people marching and holding up banners to a backdrop of an artificially created scene of buildings burning all around them. He stopped flicking through the journal on seeing a photograph of Alan Manville in the centre of the page; written over Manville's face was an article entitled, The Functional Dysfunctional.

Before reading the article he looked at the photograph of Manville and thought how well they had presented his image as the normal sheen was taken away. It was stripped down, basic and grainy, his staring eyes emphasising an austere and perverted rectitude. The subtitle of the article read, Extinguished By And For Entertainment.

Flicking through the pages Chris stopped on seeing the title, The Truth Will Kill You. He looked down and read what was written: *The seeker of truth will be ostracised, condemned and attacked. The ordinary people fear the seeker. Their hostile response is a result of harbouring feelings of self-loathing, which they feel because of their compliance to the state of things, and so they grudgingly go through their lives.*

DON'T THINK.

The delving, questioning mind is challenging for the state. There is the provision for means of expression through groups and subcultural cliques that are deemed acceptable and so sanctified by the state…

And so it went on. Chris thought back to the group meetings he had been to, going over the tone of the voices and their discussions about matters such as how we live in a police state and how the interests of an elite are protected, and of how international financiers cooperate in a mass manipulation and monopoly of power, and international armies are employed in different countries where there are rigged and fake political outcomes, and how statements on television are constructed by those working in the interest of people having complete ownership of the media, and how we live in a situation where there is designed chaos to justify a heavy military presence in all areas of society.

Chris looked down at the journal, flicking through the pages, and again stopped on seeing an article, which was about large prisons that have consistently been built over the years and always in out of the way places where access is limited. Although the prisons have different functions, some are not prisons at all, but training centres; others are domestic detention centres used to hold dissidents of various types as well as the basic unruly troublemakers. The article concluded with a piece about Kim Blakely, written in sycophantic tones it described the notorious figure as an almost mythological cultish guru giving hope to the dissident types that work in groups and communicate to each other through methods not easily detected by the state, but against the odds these 'free thinkers' work at spreading a dissenting voice with evangelical zeal.

Chris put the journal down, wearied by its contents. He considered how people have a need for heroes in their lives, and he sat for a long while, finishing the bottle of wine as he thought about different things, but for never one moment did Rosie and Nina leave his mind. He noticed the remote control, it broke his solemn torpor and picking it up he aimed the inanimate device at the television, pressed a button and watched life come into being on the screen. He pressed other buttons, not interested in the images that showed themselves, all the while without sound, and then stopped; Mistress T's face appeared on the screen.

'Fuck,' he said the word to himself remembering it was Saturday evening and The Offender's Nemesis was on. Keeping the sound off, Chris looked at the face of the woman called Mistress T. It seemed surreal and slapstick in the obviousness of a woman playing the part of the 'mistress', who was an actress, or failed actress, and it was all made evident with the absence of sound with the hysterical laughter to build up the character and atmosphere. Her performance and the presentation was so poorly acted and fake it was grotesque, and yet designed to be so in that it was simple, and maybe based on the caricatural style exhibited in the very early days of silent cinema, which caused Chris to think about how sophisticated capabilities in technology have been passed over for the stagy presentation that is uncomplicated, basic and easily palatable for an uneducated audience.

The feigned and unconvincing friendliness and sincerity of the presenters on the show contributed to a cartoon-like quality and un-reality of the whole thing, and Chris began to think even the audience were also fake and that maybe a large percentage of them were police or security officers. And then he turned it off, watching the dying images disappear as if they were diseases having lost their power. He stared at the wall by the side of the television, noticing the imperfections in its surface that had been coated in paint, but showing the divots and scars left by hooks and nails and adhesive that had once been hammered and stuck into and onto it, the wall's history, having had photographs hung onto it or maybe maps and the faces of people that had once lived in the flat, the faces of relatives, photographs recording family celebrations, babies, cats or a pet dog. Chris felt the wall symbolised his situation, a blank, but damaged canvas that was once furnished with meaning and purpose for the people in his life, his parents, his brother and sister, his wife and child, but now ruined; he crumpled forward with his head bowed towards the floor, and he began to cry.

Fifty-One

The next day started with the type of weather that one knows will not improve. The heavy clouds were set too deep and daylight, at its best, would have a dirty yellow tinge and a mood as if it had been begrudgingly pulled from darkness. Chris did not have any intentions of leaving the flat, telling himself his first priority was to get well, he decided to rest. He sat at his computer, writing down his thoughts and the plans he aimed to fulfil. During the course of the afternoon he began to look around the flat; being small there was not that much to explore, but his heart quickened pace when finding a phone in a cupboard in the kitchen, albeit an old-fashioned one. Finding the socket in the living room he plugged it in, and to his surprise found that it worked. It felt to Chris like he had unearthed a lifeline, and he kept checking it to see if the phone actually did work. He wondered why the man who was called Bob Morgan had not told him about it, but then maybe he did not know the phone was in the cupboard, or maybe they were watching his every movement with spy cameras and seeing how long it took for him to find it, and Chris shouted out loudly, 'I've found it - I've found the phone, left in the cupboard for me to stumble across - well done - well done - you're all doing a good job for your country.'

Chris settled down, and cursed himself for not knowing Rosie's number, let alone Nina's. He sat looking at the phone thinking who he could ring; besides his home and work number he did not know any more, and had not written any down. It hit him how few people he had around him that he actually knew, and that thought totally consumed him. He was convinced there would be a security officer listening in to everything he said on the phone and every number dialled would be checked out.

Without consciously doing so Chris dialled his home number; there was not a dialling tone, just a constant hissing sound that seemed to symbolise the disappearance of his life into the ether.

Chris phoned where he worked the following morning, and on hearing the voice that answered he jumped up from the chair he was sitting in. It was a man he knew well and got on well with, but on hearing it was Chris on the end of the line his manner changed from its normal friendliness to being distant, with an obvious feel of not wanting to be involved in whatever it was that had created the situation. He ignored the questions Chris asked and passed him over to the boss; and there it ended, because after half a minute of silence the line went dead. Chris tried again, and the same man answered the phone, and when hearing it was Chris he put the phone down; but Chris was desperate and he attempted to make contact another three times before giving up. He had been discarded, all the years he had known the people he was ringing, all the things they had spoken about and shared was now gone, as if friendships and professional association had never existed.

Chris phoned a number he had been given, to do with welfare provision, and an appointment was made for the following Thursday, but gaining information on getting a travel permit was met with vague answers and a number that led him back to the one he had previously rung. He tried to contact Bob Morgan, but with no luck, and then he asked about Simon, Steven's health worker, but again he got nowhere.

The following day Chris went to the hospital as was arranged. His strapping was removed and he was given more tablets, some were the same as before, others were different, and when Chris asked what they were he was told they would help him relax and for him to take them as prescribed and they made an appointment to see him in two weeks time. Later that day, and the day that followed, Chris tried to contact Bob Morgan, but again without success, and it was the same outcome with trying to sort out the travel permit and any other matter he wanted information about. On Thursday he went to the office that dealt with welfare benefits, where his situation was again brought home to him by the company of the people he shared the waiting rooms with and the manner of the staff that dealt with him. He was given coupons for food and candles and the addresses of a branch of statuary agencies that provided 'emergency aid,' but when Chris asked about getting some money he was told his claim for financial provision had not yet been processed and that he would be notified when it has been. It was plain Chris had to budget his money and so spending nothing that day and the Friday he walked to the nearest shops that took the coupons.

On Saturday Chris left the flat at midday, he had been itching to look at the film on Steven's stick, but having such little stimulation he kept putting it off, and he also felt very upset at the thought of what he might see. A cold wind greeted him like being hit with a stick as he opened the door of the flat, and thoughts he was having of not being able to contact Bob Morgan were replaced with the need to buy a pair of gloves. He was drifting without conscious direction as he walked to the main road and wrestled with the indecision whether to get on a bus or not. His resolve did not last and so offering the driver cash without regard Chris took a seat in the upstairs of the bus and looked out of the window at a world and its people as if there was far more than a pane of glass separating him from what he was looking at.

He had decided to go round to Bill Copley's flat even though he knew it would be futile; but Chris felt he had to do something. It was just the one bus that was needed to take him close to where Bill Copley lived, and as Chris saw the grey concrete buildings making up the project his heart sank as he asked himself had it been such a short amount time since he last went there, a time when he was still with his family.

The familiar path leading across the green in the project took on a homely feel, something Chris would have never felt possible, but it was only because it represented a link to his past. He looked at the shops, wondering if the old couple were still there, and now he too was also like them, living in a nightmare, and how quickly this thing had fallen upon him, as it does to most people in their position. He quelled a momentary thought of going into the shop to see if they were there and asking them, 'Do you remember me? I wasn't like this when you last saw me; I was a different person.'

While walking up the steps to Bill Copley's flat Chris realised the environment of the project posed no fear as it once had, because what could its inhabitants do to him that was any worse than had already happened? The smell of chicken waste matter seared the hairs in his nostrils as it did before, but not to the same effect. Chris was aware his senses had been dulled, not only by the drugs they given him at the hospital, but since what had happened to him his mental state had been so traumatically affected. He knocked on the door to Bill Copley's flat, but there was no answer. Chris stood there for over fifteen minutes, waiting, counting time, not able to see inside the room by the door because the curtains had not been drawn and a tough piece of fabric had been wedged on the inside of the letter box and so making viewing through the rectangular space impossible. There were not any sounds coming from inside the flat, and the scene had a feel of dereliction, as if nobody had ever really lived there anyway, and it was nothing more than a theatrical stage set having been constructed by the state to lure and trap wayward citizens.

Chris left the balcony, not bothering to look across the project at the austere surroundings - it no longer felt foreign as he was now personally attached and belonging to it, and besides that, he was more alienated than most of the people that live there.

He walked towards a bus stop with a mechanically driven desire of wanting to see Karena, ambling in an uneven step as he walked, leaving the project with its sounds and smells, and the shouting of its inmates in an atmosphere that crushed the life from any being that had a will to change for a positive end.

It was a journey that took one bus and a long walk, and as he stood on the pavement next to the main road outside Karena's flat he asked himself why he had gone there, but his mind could not form a clear notion or idea as all his thoughts were vague, yet a nagging feeling behind them kept telling him something was wrong.

Chris rang the bell and knocked on the door, knowing there would not be an answer, because he now inhabited a world of isolation. Sure enough there was not an answer, and after knocking and ringing a few more times Chris turned from the door with a lumbering walk that said he is walking from a place he had once been to where he had spoken to a person he did not know, and that is all it ever was. His mind became a void, although his emotions were slashed and he was close to tears. Chris did not stand at a bus stop, he just walked, at times stumbling and bumping into walls and the front of shops, not aware of the looks people gave him or a mother pulling her child from his path.

The afternoon passed and the evening installed itself with the weather growing colder, and so Chris got on a bus and spent over an hour on it, keeping warm, sitting by the heater, drifting in and out of consciousness he regarded people around him with detached abstraction.

Chris travelled towards his flat, although in no hurry to return there he did not know what else to do. He was hungry and as he walked down a high street close to the flat he thought about going into somewhere for something to eat, but knowing he could not spend his money he decided to have something when he got back to where he now lived. As Chris walked towards the virtually defunct shopping precinct where the flat was he passed a bar, and just as he was passing it the doors opened and out tumbled two men and a barrage of noise, a noise made up of the sounds created in a busy bar on a Saturday evening; a sound, that for Chris, was inviting as it symbolised life.

The warmth inside the bar found every tired part of Chris's being and in doing so exacerbated his weariness. His hands and face prickled with the new sensation of heat and his head thickened and became heavy. The smell of cigarette smoke filled his nostrils and bit into his sinuses, and Chris knew he really wanted to have a drink. The counter was crowded and further along at the other end a group of men cheered and shouted at a television showing a football match. The bar was rougher than Chris would have expected, but then, on second thoughts he realised it was very close to where he was staying, which was in a run down area. Chris got served and ordered two large glasses of beer; they had an offer of when buying a large beer another large beer could be bought for half price. He turned from the counter, seeking a quiet corner and if possible a place to sit. The quiet corner was possible, but not somewhere to sit, so Chris leant back against the wall and, closing his eyes he sipped the beer flavoured drink, recounting some of the thoughts that zoomed in and through his head. He no longer thought he stood out from the crowd in that kind of bar in that kind of area; he was now a familiar figure, maybe not an unqualified labourer having a beer in the local bar, but one of the fallen types that are not uncommon to see.

The football was inciting loud behaviour, but besides that the bar seemed to be full of people having a drink before going elsewhere or maybe on their way home from work. There were a few regulars, or so they looked as being such, sitting or standing alone, contemplating whatever thought it was that turned their minds inward. Chris was aware of how weak he had become, and not eating did not help. The alcohol immediately affected him, giving him a slight headache and causing a buzzing sensation in his hands and chest, but he wanted to drink more and break out of the prison of the damned, which was the place where he now existed. He finished the beers and walked towards the toilet, not noticing the people he bumped into or those around him. The walls in the toilet were scrawled with graffiti having the basic content and humour of that written by schoolboys of a low educational level. Chris reminded himself the doodles and rhymes were actually drawn and written by adult men, men who would beat you to death without needing or wanting to know the reason why they were doing so.

He decided on buying more of the beer, an elixir to aid escape from one's state of mind, it was obvious, it is part of the human condition, this is what Chris told himself as he stood at the counter waiting to be served alongside other souls that were reaching for their escape from whatever it was they were trying to break away from. And then he snapped; Chris raised his voice, telling the girl behind the counter he was next in line to be attended to and not the man she was serving. The girl flicked on an expression of disregard, but the man she was serving glared at Chris and shouted at him. 'What's your problem, matey?'

Chris retreated from the confrontation and shrugged his shoulders, looking elsewhere, away down the counter, making it obvious he did not want to pursue the matter any further; but the man was not going to let go of this opportunity to vent aggression at another person.

'Who the fuck are you? You'll be going back to the hovel where you live in an ambulance.'

The man stared at Chris, and as he did so the young woman smirked, ever so slightly, as she looked from the man to Chris.

'Get out of here - you pest, standing there like a useless article - about as much use as a broken light bulb.'

The man paid for his drinks, and looking over at Chris as he handed the money to the young woman he said, 'Dig the useless cunts into the ground, that's what they should do - making the rest of us pay for them to walk around.'

The young woman nodded without looking at the man or Chris as she turned, concentrating on counting his money before putting it in the till. The man gathered his drinks and nodded at Chris in a way that said he had been warned and the young woman made a point of not serving Chris as she gave him a look of disdain and served someone else. Chris thought of how the man recognised his situation, and that he had turned into the vulnerable victim just like the man he saw getting baited and bullied in the pub that evening. A man appeared behind the counter and served Chris, telling him if he wanted another two beers he better order them as there was only ten minutes to go before the time is up on buying cheap beer. Chris told him he did not want any more and just the two would be fine.

'Well, just telling you sunshine, vodka, whisky, rum, it's all cheaper now, I don't want you missing out,' the man said, and all the while as he was speaking he did not look at Chris for the briefest of moments, but looked down at the beer he was pouring and at the other people waiting to be served.

Chris returned to his place in the corner, again leaning with his back against the wall drinking the beer flavoured liquid, and then he became aware of someone standing close by to him; it was a man of about forty years of age. He nodded at Chris and said in the neutral tone adopted in pubs and bars, 'Had a hard day?'

Chris nodded back, intending to smile, but the action of actually smiling would not form on his mouth or face.

'I saw that,' the man said, and what he had said alerted Chris that the man was still there, standing next to him.

The man continued, 'I saw that, the fella at the bar - what an idiot, getting aggressive with people like that.'

Chris nodded, not wanting to engage in conversation, but the man had attracted his attention and Chris looked at him, at what type of person he looked like and what he was wearing. The man appeared to be what is often described as a 'regular' person, a man popping in the bar for a drink who would soon be on his way home to a family and all the concerns that brings.

'Got to be careful,' the man went on, 'this isn't a bad place, but there is an element - it's because of where it is of course,' and he nodded in the direction of the housing project. 'Any bar close to a project attracts undesirables - it's the way they are, and it's not worth giving it any more thought than that - that's just the way they are.'

Chris looked at him, realising he was nodding in agreement. He did not have the energy to get involved with any discussions about social behaviour and the societal effects of one's environment; he could not think about it, all his attention was on his plight, and he was aware of this as he acquiesced with the man's opinion.

After looking around the bar, the man's gaze returned to Chris and he said that he had not seen him in there before that evening. Chris gave hardly any more than one syllable grunts, as an explanation it was the first time he had been in there.

'Live locally, then?' The man asked, and Chris nodded, telling him where the flat was, and the man asked how long he had been there. Chris told him, his answers coming without thought, just responding to what he had been asked, and when the man told Chris he would buy him a drink, Chris accepted, as it was not so much an offer but a statement.

Chris was feeling the effects of the alcohol to a great degree, and he was aware of muttering to himself as the man spoke in his firm and direct manner, like a person of substance with a clear conscience, which was the antithesis to how Chris felt about himself, which was weak, uncertain and in need of help. The man eyed Chris closely, and increasingly so as he spoke with greater confidence in asking more personal questions, such as if Chris was married, his background, parents, where he grew up, where he worked and if he had children; and Chris told him, answering what the man had asked, at times the back of his head rolling against the wall, lolling from side to side with his words becoming slurred, and, feeling as if he knew the man from somewhere else, he felt quite at ease talking so frankly to him.

Consciousness of the moment slipped and when he became aware of what he was saying it confused Chris, but he continued to speak, telling the man how his father could not take the strain of what happened after the 'big change' what with the regulations, the way things were tightened up and not being able to travel. His work demanded the need to travel abroad, regularly, and a lot of his clients were foreign and a lot of his sales were in other countries. The international trade dried up, people were forced out of business, and he was one of them. He owned a small company, which he had built up himself and was proud about giving people employment. Chris spoke of how his father said it meant a lot to him and when the company dissolved he worried about his employees and would talk about what they were going to do as Christmas was looming and jobs were scarce, and everything was made worse with the 'austerity measures' they brought in, and which are still in. Chris became aware of what he was saying and so he stopped speaking, and after a couple of seconds the man said, 'Just the two of you was it, you and Steven?'

What the man had asked him confused Chris, but he was confused all the time. He must have told him about his family, and Chris started speaking, telling him about his sister, Helen, and the man became very interested in her and was persistent in wanting to know if he was in contact with her, when was the last time he spoke to her and where she lived. Chris lost track of what he was saying, but realised he was talking about Steven and when he was young - with the special education teachers, how the school did not address his needs, and that he got picked on and ridiculed by some of the boys, and how Chris wanted to punch the bullies for picking on Steven. Chris was staring at the floor, shaking his head as he told the man about his mother dying, of her lying in bed looking up at Chris and asking him to get on with his own life, but to also keep an eye on Steven.

Chris told the man how she tried to touch his arm and said, 'I know you will.' And then Chris began to cry.

The man put his hand on his shoulder, and speaking quietly he told Chris to 'let it out,' and not to worry and to just, 'go with the feeling - it will make you feel a lot better.'

He persisted with his questions, this time about Rosie, and as he said her name Chris realised he must have told him about her, probably about everything, and Chris heard himself tell the man how he met her when she was studying to be a midwife, and how she told Chris she hoped she could make a difference for women who struggled in labour, and she believed bringing children into this world should be a joyous experience and one to celebrate, rather than for it to seen as a burden.

Chris stopped talking, all of a sudden, and he tried to remember what he had told the man about Rosie and Nina. His head started to clear as he became conscious of what he was doing and the man spoke quickly, as if realising Chris had become aware of what he was saying to a stranger, and he changed the subject back to Helen, but the atmosphere had changed, the moment had gone and Chris just looked at the man.

Chris was thinking the man was most likely not what he was making himself out to be, and was not just a random man in a pub having a drink and passing the time with a man who is upset. The questions were too directed and formed, as if pursuing a goal and placing already known bits of information together; and Chris had the information that would complete the jigsaw. Chris panicked, putting down his glass he pulled a cigarette from his packet, and not able to speak coherently he told the man he was going and that he did not feel well. As he turned away something came into his head; it was what the man had said earlier about the aggressive man at the bar. 'Undesirables' is what the man said, which is language used by the media when talking about state security.

Chris carried on walking through the crowd and out of the door where a cold wind seemed to be waiting for him.

Fifty-Two

Chris stayed in the flat on Sunday, the remorse and worry of the man in the bar and what he had said plaguing him. He asked himself why he told the man all those personal details about his life. He wondered if it was because of loneliness and being desperate with the need to talk to someone, or was it because of the medication he was taking and maybe he was being drugged with some kind of chemical used by the state's security to break down mental defences.

Late on Monday afternoon Chris went to the police station as he was instructed to do, which was not far from the flat. After checking in at the desk he was taken to a room where he was told to wait until the officer who was going to speak to him arrived. He sat in a chair looking around the bland room, which was furnished with a table and three hard backed chairs for about five minutes, and finally the door opened; it was the senior police officer he had spoken to before. He asked Chris some questions about fulfilling his 'obligations,' such as attending the hospital and seeing about his benefits. Chris told him he had done what was asked of him, and the police officer watched him closely in a manner that made it obvious he was concerned with other matters relating to Chris.

Nothing was said for a long while as the two men looked at each other in silence. The police officer's eyes were unflinching and hard, boring into Chris until finally he broke.

Chris collapsed over table and began to cry, and through sobs he asked the police officer what had happened to his wife and child and why was he in the situation he had found himself.

'You drink too much, Mr Kirby,' the police officer said, 'you're wandering around in a drunken haze talking rubbish to people - meeting undesirables in pubs and bars can be dangerous, Mr Kirby - you have to be careful, after all, you've been though a lot and you aren't in good physical shape - no wonder your wife and child had to be taken into care, after the trouble you've brought upon them.'

Chris asked what he meant, but the officer shook his head and said he was not going to say anything other than it had been decided by a court ruling to separate him from his family and he was just following the orders of his superiors.

He went on, 'You've been loitering outside your old house, Mr Kirby, going to the college where you worked and making a nuisance of your self - they rang us and said you were there, wanting your belongings, and getting to the point of being aggressive.'

'What the hell are you talking about?' Chris said, but the officer's gaze was that of steel and he was not going to falter from his task as he snapped, 'What did they give you?'

Chris told him he went there to collect his personal belongings, and then stopped before telling him about Steve's biscuit tin, but the officer suspected there was something else and his stare became more intense. Chris recognised the officer's searching look and changed the subject, asking him why he should not collect his things and why he should be separated from his family without having any contact, and why was this happening to him. Chris was thinking the officer wanted something, they were looking for something and he was being monitored, the man in the bar on Saturday evening was probably a member of the security services, and not having a travel permit was part of it as it meant he had to use buses, and that limited the distance he could travel, making it easier to follow his movements.

The police officer's eyes had remained trained on Chris, and after a while he said, 'There are people out there, Mr Kirby, who are a threat to your life - we are trying to protect you from them.'

Chris looked into the man's eyes, they were still and flat, and very quietly Chris asked him what had happened to Steven's body; but the eyes remained as they had been, giving nothing away and not showing the slightest hint of emotion, and just as Chris was beginning to lose control and raise his voice as he repeated what he had said, the officer stood up and told Chris their time was up.

'You are a very difficult man to deal with, Mr Kirby, speak to the officer at the desk to make an appointment for next week – let's just hope you become helpful, shall we?'

He turned and left the room, his face grim at an unresolved matter he had been assigned to deal with. Chris watched him leave, knowing there was something, what it was he did not have a clue, but there was something that was going to come to the surface, and it was most probably going to come to light soon, or so he hoped, no matter what it was.

Fifty-Three

Chris went home after making an appointment at the police station for the following week. The evening passed with Chris sitting in the small living room, the television off with the only light coming from the kitchen; he was waiting for a power cut, only because it was just something to think about that distracted him from his thoughts. This continued for a couple of hours and then Chris decided to read something. He got up, turned the light on and pulled the newspaper out from under the cushion on the sofa; the paper he bought when he went to see Roger Edgebury the previous summer. Chris wondered what the area around Roger Edgebury's home looked like in the winter, and he thought about how the man was so conceited and his daughter so precocious, for a while before concentrating on the newspaper. Looking at the paper took him back to that day with the smells, heat and peacefulness. He thought about the little station, of how quaint it was, but then he remembered his anxiety while waiting on the platform for the last train back. He read the paper, enjoying the stories of local interests and concerns; it all seemed so small and even petty in its provinciality. There were gripes over the depth and height of hedges along the sides of the road and whether traffic lights should be erected on a temporary basis on a road junction during certain times of the day. The upcoming events amused Chris, although he did not mean be arrogant, it was just that he could imagine the local community elite, the inner clique organising the village festival and the names of three women were given who had arranged the flowers at the church.

There was a story on one of the inside pages about a man who had been stopped for questioning by the police and was found not to be in possession of the relevant permit allowing him to be in the area. The man was doing some building work on the side of a public house and said he was sure he had a permit, but he was arrested and waiting to stand trial with the prospect of looking at a very severe sentence. The manager of the pub claimed everything was in order, but the authorities did not accept his claim and took his licence away so that he would never be able to manage a public house again, and he got five years' hard labour. Chris read a column, which apparently was a regular piece written by a woman on behalf of a local association she presides over. She spoke about church affairs and the good work she and her association does. Some of the adverts made him smile; there was one about a 'local handyman' offering his services, and another was a chimney sweep whose family had an 'established business' in the area for over a hundred years. It all had a simple feel about it, but then there was something else that suddenly made Chris feel sad.

Thinking of the day he went to see Roger Edgebury had reminded Chris of his childhood in many ways. There was the countryside, the quietness and slow pace of life, the heat that settled heavy in long afternoons, to be away from everything and that feeling of being just a visitor. It was an occasion, an experience, and knowing one has to return to where one comes from, leaving it all behind and never to belong there, for if one did it would change everything. They were special times for Chris and ones he cherished.

He remembered his uncle and aunty who he used to visit when he was a young child. They lived in the country and the paper reminded him of their lives. They had a son and a daughter, both a fair bit older than Chris; they were his cousins. This was obvious, but it became increasingly significant the more Chris dwelled on the fact that he had close relatives, cousins, but did not have any contact with members of his family. Chris thought about what they might be doing, what they looked like and where they might live.

It hurt Chris to think this separateness he felt should be so and he asked himself why, and everything about them felt so distant, as if they had never existed and that it was all so meaningless. He wondered if his sister felt the same way, and for a few seconds he had to think what her name was. Helen that was her name. That is her name he told himself. And his cousins, he asked himself if they might feel the same as him. It then came to his mind that maybe he was the only one in his family who felt that way.

A feeling of upset gripped Chris as the realisation of being alone flooded through him.

He stood up quickly in an effort to shake off his mood, and seeing an old world atlas he had brought over from his house he picked it up and sat back down, looking at the different continents and countries, the regions and towns; it came from another world, or that is how it felt to Chris. The atlas was a present from his mother when he was about twelve years of age, and he looked at his handwriting as he had written his name on the inside of the cover. He looked through the atlas for quite a while, thinking how interesting and diverse the world must have been compared to what was now presented; and then, taking the computer stick from his pocket he looked at it. Chris could not resist looking at what was on it, so he plugged it into the computer and watched the screen with excitement and curiosity. Steven had not titled any separate files or sections to identify what was on the stick; there was just a line of dots, each one representing different sequences. He went through what he had already seen and clicked on the next dot, and what he saw made him gasp and cry out loud; it was film his father had taken when he was a boy; Steven must have put it on a computer and saved it onto the stick.

There he was, Chris, a seven-year-old boy in the back garden of his house with his birthday cake on a table and his mother clapping and singing a song; although there was no sound on the film. His mother was laughing and patting his sister on her shoulder, telling her to join in, but all she did was pull an exaggerated smile and self-consciously raise her glass that contained fizzy pop. His sister looked wooden and embarrassed. It was not her scene because she was a twenty-year-old woman, and this was her little brother's birthday party. Every now and then there was a glimpse of her boyfriend, Chris tried to remember his name, but he knew he was not the one his sister married. She had left home by the time this birthday celebration was filmed, having gone to college to study art and photography. She travelled abroad, quite extensively, and although he could remember his parents being not too pleased with what she was doing, Chris could not really remember the details. He believed that Helen had gone travelling with a young man of about her own age who was interested in music and played guitar. Well, that was what Chris's parents told him. He never met the young man who sounded interesting and played a guitar. Helen very rarely came home, Chris believed a lot of it was to do with Steven, but there was always a tension between her and his parents.

Chris looked at his sister. At her face, the way she smiled and the way she was standing. She did not want to be there at all, there was a distance about her and her surroundings, even though it was her family, although at the time Chris thought she was as excited as him about it being his birthday, and that was why she had made such an effort to travel the distance home with her boyfriend. It was common for there to be family rows, not on that particular day, but at other times. Chris remembered his father saying she only came home to get some money off him. She always seemed to be short of money and it caused disagreements to occur between Chris's parents. His mother used to stick up for his sister when his father said Helen should behave differently, and then he would blame Chris's mother for being too soft. Chris realised the naivety he had as a child in thinking everything was okay just because people smiled at him and said 'Happy Birthday,' and as Chris looked at his face when he was a child, he felt the innocence, and it struck him that he had not really changed.

The images on the screen flickered and disappeared, but were replaced with more family film, this one taken when on holiday. Chris was wearing swimming trunks, standing on a beach with the sea in the background and pulling faces as he held up a sandwich and pointed at it, and again Chris looked closely at his face; it was a face that held an open expectation.

Chris remembered the beach was abroad, on an island that had something to do with Spain, a place that nowadays is never heard about. It was hot and sunny every day.

Chris picked up the atlas and searched for the island, and finding it, he placed his finger upon it and was surprised to see how close the island was to Africa. He remembered his parents speaking to people about holidays abroad, and of the different places people went to. That had all now gone. He returned to the film, but there was not much more of the holiday stuff left. The screen went to white, and it was as if his childhood had been bleached from the memory of the world. Chris clicked on the next dot, but it was just squiggles and lines and after looking at them for a while he decided to leave the remainder of the stick for another time.

Chris sat with his head in his hands thinking of everything at once, his past, his present situation and what might be coming next, struggling to keep to his pledge of staying positive in his objective to be reunited with his family; it was as if he was battling against time itself, a pursuit that nobody can ever conquer, and he wondered why Steven did not tell him about saving the holiday films his father took.

315

Fifty-Four

The following day passed by as a period of time having a dream-like quality in that thoughts were distant and Chris had to keep reminding himself how long he had been at the flat. On Wednesday he left the flat just before midday; he had to get out after spending over an hour holding the telephone in his hand without calling anybody, but just going over things in his mind.

Chris got on a bus, and without knowing where he was going he gave the driver one dollar fifty cents and stayed on the bus for the duration of its route. Getting off at the terminus, he wandered down a high street that had a variety of shops, which were housed in substantial buildings built about a hundred and fifty years ago. Chris felt he was in a state of limbo as he walked amongst people, stopping every now and then to stare into a shop window. He entered an arcade that had several shops and a Viewing Centre at the end of it. Viewing Centres are referred to as VC's and are buildings that show government information films. They are located all over the country in every town and city, but this one struck Chris as out of place with its surroundings. Sometimes they are used for seminars and students go to them to attend meetings and see films that reiterate the state's line on history, culture, commerce and political events at home and aboard. There is always some occasion to celebrate and commemorate that the authorities has achieved, and of course crime is a subject high on the list of matters to be discussed.

The letters A.O.C. stood large and distinct on a hoarding above the frontage of the Viewing Centre. There were planned celebrations to mark what had been called the new Age Of Consciousness and the Viewing Centre was showing films about law and order and the industry of 'professionals' that proliferated from crime as it grew into a vast business. Chris knew the films would be discrediting and ridiculing 'liberals' and other 'professionals' from the past. Their practice and language would be analysed with contempt and how criminals audaciously flouted the law, acted in selfish interests and sneered at their victims in a system run by so-called 'professionals.'

Chris decided to go in, he was tired out and it was somewhere to rest for a while. The entrance fee is kept low to encourage people to enter, and it is usual to see those down on their luck dozing in the theatre, as it is a place giving shelter for a few hours on a cold day. While Chris paid the young woman the fifty cents entrance fee he momentarily lost consciousness of who he was, what he was doing and where he was, and again he felt like he was in a dream; it was as if he was watching himself in a film. He felt numb as he walked down the aisle inside the almost empty theatre and sat in a seat in one of the empty rows; Chris noted there were just three other people in the theatre, all of whom were middle aged men, and two of them were asleep.

The narrator's voice boomed over what looked like hastily filmed evidence of an act of arson that took place years before the 'big change'. It showed a burned out flat that was the result of a drug related crime. The narrator spoke of how widespread the practice of burning people in their homes had become and also how incidences of kidnapping had risen dramatically. A comfortable looking home in a wealthy area appeared on the screen as the narrator told of how a young girl who lived in the house with her parents was kidnapped by people working on behalf of a notorious drug baron. The film continued with other stories of kidnapping and of how the system that was in place at the time was powerless to do anything about it.

Another film showed footage of a group of young men walking down a road in a housing estate. The gang were swaggering along with beer cans in hand, one of them kicked the side of a car and they all laughed, and as they were laughing one of them climbed onto the roof of the car and jumped up and down. They walked off, laughing and belching and throwing their beer cans into people's gardens. The narrator of the film told of how a week before a young girl was raped in that same road in front of her father. A gang of youths had held the man down and made him watch as other gang members raped his daughter. They then cut her with a knife and set her on fire before beating the man to death. His head was stamped on with such force that every bone in his face and head was broken. A community leader spoke of 'societal conditioning' and how there are, 'Challenges that have to be met, but the responsibility lies with the authorities in being brave enough to commence action that will have a positive effect and will be meaningful for youths like the ones involved in the murders of the father and daughter.'

A lawyer acting on behalf of a youth, who had been accused of murdering an elderly woman, appeared on the screen. He spoke of how his 'client' was, 'Not acting on initiative or incentives of his own making, but was responding, as many youths do, to a cultural president that has become prevalent and acceptable within the cultural framework making up norms and a world view held by youths in particular situations in society.'

The narrator explained how the liberal management of crime had brought about a state of affairs where an act of crime was perceived and dealt with as a 'victimless situation.' Policies shaped a standard where it would be an infringement of a person's human rights if a person committed a crime against another person and was labelled a 'wrong-doer,' because that label had negative connotations. There were no 'wrongdoers', but only an 'act' that had taken place, and it was the 'situations' in which those 'acts' took place that were to be 'evaluated.' The two parties involved in the 'act' are 'equal participants', meaning that if both of them were not there in the same place at the same time the 'act' would not have taken place. A young man might well rob an old person to relieve the effects of relative poverty he is suffering because maybe he is 'environmentally deprived'. His dilemma will be resolved, which was something that had to be understood in a 'progressive' society. What was central in this thinking was the preference of the individual. It was that preference that had to be upheld and not discriminated against, and it does not matter what an individual might choose to do, whether it is a sexual preference or an involvement in what could negatively be described as acts of crime.

The narrator spoke about how 'academic verbosity' had pervaded the area of law and order to a point where the fact that a person had been harmed was lost under a multitude of various people, bodies and agencies contributing a theory that justified their involvement. There was talk of 'dynamic responses' borne from positive results brought about by a cross-fertilisation of methods and theories coming from psychologists, sociologists and anthropologists who had positive working practices with partners in the medical and political spheres. All these people created an extensive industry that was vague and inconclusive in providing any findings or answers as the theories and therapies contradicted one another.

The narrator emphasised that it is little wonder resentment grew against this 'liberal hierarchy' that earned large incomes and enjoyed generous state pensions. The regular person became increasingly conscious of the ineffectual function of 'professionals' who wanted to help criminals and limit the freedom of innocent people. It was obvious to them that the system that had been put in place to deal with law and order had lost its way.

The next film was about the history of crime and punishment. It examined society in the late seventeenth century and of how punishments were expected to fit the crime and bear some relation to the act that had taken place. For example, fraudulent financial crimes had penalties of fines, thefts meant having personal assets seized and murderers faced the death penalty. It was seen as correct and fair; but a new era was establishing itself. Where before crimes were seen to be against the King, they were now seen to be against society, and society wanted to be recompensed for the crimes committed against it. Criminals were put on view, as in the case of working on the developing public roads and people went to watch them, even taking their children to make an occasion of it. The consequences were public humiliation, which also acted as a warning to those who thought about committing a crime. Prison was just one penalty, and not favoured because it was too expensive and seen by many as a place for thugs to loaf and idle while others had to work. Prisons were also seen as places that served as learning centres for offenders to make a career as a criminal.

Yet, after time detention and incarceration became the dominant form of punishment, but aspects of education and ethics were incorporated. The prisoner was to be educated and taught the error of his or her ways and to become a reformed member of society. The industry of law and order was growing in an evolving liberal society with its scientific reasoning with an emphasis on judgement, measurement and curing in an elitist climate that took the act of physical punishment out of the public's view. Prisons became standardised and the prisoner became a subject of evaluation by a multitude of professionals who attended to spiritual, mental and physical needs, while the public were deprived of witnessing a punishment against a criminal who had transgressed against them.

The narration of the film told of an evolving 'progressive, altruistic class' that had another objective, which was to take control over what they had named as 'society'. It was 'their' society. The prison was a place of detailed observation with every facet overseen by the 'professionals'. Offenders were trained to be normal in a process of being positively socialised under the constant gaze of 'professionals' who knew best. And as the criminal carved a career out of the evolving system, so did the 'professionals' as a spectrum of behaviours, personality types and the classification of different crimes demanded an increasing number of the new social engineers to attend to them.

It was the development of an administrative class who pushed aside the crown and God as they feasted on each new subject matter they constructed. This new liberal elite wallowed in 'progressive' hypothesis, but imposed stringent laws that bound the innocent working person whose life was changing from agrarian to industrial work.

And as time went on there were those that wondered if these 'professionals' with their banks of 'knowledge' were really interested in solving crimes, or were they more concerned with wanting to prosper financially, gain a qualified status and enjoy the power that goes with it.

319

The film concluded by stating that prisons had created more criminals as 'professionals' normalised crime, decriminalised the criminal and failed the innocent working person.

Immediately after the titles of the film faded another film took its place, which was really a continuation from the previous one, but brought up to the time in history just before the 'big change'.

The narrator spoke of the terminology that was created under the system years ago when things were different. He brought criminologists to task because of their use of language, with terms such as 'mugging.' The narrator explained how the word assumed the victim was stupid for allowing him or herself to be robbed and could even possibly be blamed for allowing the crime against him or herself to happen. The narrator told of how psychologists working within the remit of criminology placed the onus on the victim, which the narrator pointed out was a contradiction when there was 'victimless' crime and just a 'social act.' Factors such as architectural environments, which could be living areas with alleyways and dark stairwells where a person could waylay someone, took precedence in the importance of understanding the causes of crime. There was also the idea that an old pensioner had responsibility for how she or he behaved in terms of presenting positive body language rather than passivity that might draw the attention of a young man, or indeed a group of young women who are short of money. Presenting weakness is to attract acceptable and understandable behaviour within the appropriate situation, which might be the taking of money or possessions from the old pensioner, because within the value system of certain young people's culture there is nothing wrong in acquiring money from certain people, just as an animal singles out its prey.

The use of semantics was a popular scheme adopted by the 'professionals' to evade responsibility while taking money from the taxpayer to fuel their industry. Their scientific analysis of the situation became worthless as it was seen to be disingenuous, and as time went by the whole industry was discredited.

The obsession with self-analytical thought that dominated debates on deviance with a mission to satisfy the preference of the individual came in for criticism. It was blamed for creating a culture of selfishness where the vulnerable were a powerless victim of the actions of the selfish who were given carte blanche to pursue their interests and desires. Drug taking and sexual experimentation was sanctified in a society where the fashion for life-coaching, self-stimulation and wanting to satisfy personal whims was supported by a 'liberal elite' who were unwittingly signing their own death sentence because of the negative effects it had on society.

The film spelt out clearly that this way of thinking was a major factor in breaking society apart with sexual deviancy, drug related crime and slovenliness, and nothing was done about it because the legal parameters of acceptance accommodated this behaviour. The age of what was called 'psychodynamic reasoning' had failed the people. The narrator spoke passionately about how things had moved completely away from the public witnessing an offender punished, to seeing criminals as part of what was perceived the norm in an age where the authorities preached a mantra for 'fairness', but it was not felt to apply for the average working person. The narrator told of how the public wanted revenge. They wanted to see the perpetrators of crime dragged back into public view and made to suffer. The slippery 'professionals' with all their deceit and conceit had let them down. They wanted the criminals back where they belonged, as people, not a product that is detached and utilised for the benefit of a 'professional' class, but right in front of them, vulnerable and ready to suffer. The people wanted to feel they had some control over what affected them.

Chris's mind was drifting. His thoughts blurred and at times seemed unreal. He woke with a start, and not sure if he was watching a different film because the narrator's voice sounded the same. The man spoke in a dull monotone. It was endless as he went on about statistics, variables, research methodologies, the psychology of crime, emotions of victims, and the victims in this case being the people who committed the crime. The film looked at the contradictions that existed under the liberal management of law and order, and the mountains of data, and the conflicts arising from what was called 'trusted social partners,' and Chris realised he had lost consciousness for a short while because the film he was looking at was different from before, and although it was not the same narrator his voice was similar in tone and content as he went on about scientific analysis, suitable victims, motivated offenders, progressive medial models, genetical reasons, psychometric evidence based approaches and criminogenic triggers.

Chris felt delirious. The narrator's monotonous voice said the same thing over and over, seemingly without end, talking about statistics and theoretical hypothesis in an unrelenting drone.

Another film followed that looked at the privatisation of crime, but Chris became confused because it seemed familiar, and he realised it was the film that was on when he had entered the Viewing Centre. It was about the amount of 'yobbish' behaviour that existed previously in society, and claimed it was even encouraged by social policies and the media, as society accepted that disrespectful behaviour and aggressive attitudes had become the norm. Chris dozed off one more time and then decided to leave the Viewing Centre.

As he was walking out he looked to see if the same young woman was in the kiosk as when he arrived. She was still there, reading a magazine about game shows and their presenters. It was a popular magazine with simple puzzles to solve and lots of competitions to enter. Chris watched her as he passed, noticing her small snub nose, her soft mouth and her eyes, seemingly lifeless as they scanned the page of the magazine. There was something about her that Chris liked, which is why he looked to see if she was still there, and for a bursting second he wanted to say something to her, but stopped himself as he knew what he wanted to say would sound deranged and shock the young woman. He wanted say, 'They killed my brother and have taken my family away from me - and there is nothing I can do about it.'

He kept walking, his mouth clamped so tightly closed his jaw hurt, and as he left the Viewing Centre he started to cry; he felt he was losing his mind.

Chris stood in an alley, away from people and out of sight. Staying in the alley until he calmed down, he went and bought a cup of coffee. After having a rest he walked around the streets for a long time, trying not to catch his reflection in the windows as he passed by. He went into a shop that looked as though it might be interesting as there was an unusual collection of miscellanea in the window, such as old hats and photographs. It was not an antique shop and it was not just junk; it was a curiosity shop with items that would be of interest to collectors. There were old railway magazines going back way before the 'big change' that took Chris's interest, and he hungrily looked at the photographs, not of the trains, but of the people on platforms, what they were dressed in and what they looked like. There were helmets and tunics in the shop, worn by soldiers many years ago, one or two were foreign, but Chris was interested in the photographs, some in a family album, taken sixty years ago. There was a magazine called, 'Beat Groups', and Chris read of how the groups were a bad influence with their long hair and, 'slovenly couldn't care less attitude.' There were old vinyl records, some in cardboard sleeves with the photograph of the groups or artists on the cover. Some of the covers were very artistic and surreal, and some had the scrawl of a person's name on them, and one had an amusing personal message written all along the edge of the cover. They were all very expensive, in fact everything in the shop was very expense, and Chris thought surprisingly so.

In one rack, as if hidden in the corner by the wall, was a collection of sex magazines that had been put in plastic sleeves for protection; they were incredibly expensive and as Chris flicked through them, quite mindlessly, a man who worked in the shop stood at his side and placed a small pile of magazines next to him and nodded at Chris in a sordid manner that said there was also more stuff he might be interested in. Chris looked from the man to the magazines that dealt with perverted and deviant forms of sexual gratification, and he looked through the pages, gazing at the images in a semi-conscious state, his eyes passing over photographs of men having sex with animals and sado-masochism in its different forms with the various fetishes as well as men having sex with men; since the 'big change' homosexual relationships had been made illegal, it is a criminal offence, although it is prevalent between consenting adults, and the state knew it was.

Chris suddenly became aware of what he was doing and looked from a photograph in the magazine to the man, who was watching him closely with a faint leering smile; the photograph was of a young girl tied to a table with blood all over her nearly naked body and a man snarling next to her with his penis in his hand and a knife in the other. Chris dropped the magazine and walked from the shop, not believing he had stood there looking at the magazines, and he knew the authorities would be monitoring the shop very carefully as well as the people who went in there, and without doubt the man working in the shop would be a police officer of some kind.

Chris made his way home, and when close to the flat he went into a shop to buy a bottle of the cheapest vodka.

Fifty-Five

When he got back to the flat Chris decided not to have the television on, preferring to listen to the radio, but listening to the radio demanded a certain amount of concentration and he felt the need for the simple distraction provided by the television. He flicked through channels, programmes with noise and flashing colours merged with solemn narration and the images of destruction caused by war, and then stopped searching as he saw Alan Manville trying to placate a baying audience; it was Wednesday evening and it was the midweek edition of The Offender's Nemesis.

A hooded man was standing between two security guards as Alan Manville explained how the country's security has been to great lengths and used great bravery in bringing the man beneath the hood to justice. Manville read out the man's crimes, which ranged from petty subversive activities to trafficking illegal immigrants into the country, some of which are infamous terrorists in the countries they come from.

Manville sneered, 'They are the most violent scum, having no regard for normal life or its values - they only wish to cause carnage and destruction, wanting to murder innocent people because it satisfies their sick, warped minds to do so. Well, we have the ringleader,' and he pointed at the hooded man. 'He has led our security service a merry dance, but now it is his turn to take to the stage.'

Manville nodded at the security guards and said, 'Take the hood off and reveal this cowardly gutter filth...'

Chris pressed a button taking him to another channel, one about Greyhound racing and how a champion dog is trained, but after a short while Chris returned to The Offender's Nemesis; he just could not resist returning to it.

Lights flashed across the stage as the audience cheered in a state of wild stimulation and the camera targeted supposedly random people caught up in the excitement of it all. There were close-ups of different people in states of hysterical laughter or crazed anger with humorous comments written in childish style and colours over their faces. The camera shot pulled back, showing the audience in its continuing state of noisy frenzy, and then the shot drew back further so it was seen from Alan Manville's point of view as he stood on the stage watching them, smiling, nodding, his eyes searching through the audience and as the lights caught his face he said, 'Have we got a treat for you tonight.'

A close up shot on the side of his face was momentarily illuminated by a flash of light and for a second it revealed a fine scar running beneath his chin and along the underneath of his jaw to his neck. With his smile set in place he continued to speak, 'You very lucky people - but be careful what you wish for.'

Manville turned to another camera and said, 'Here's a couple of cocks - remember them? They chose to fight each other for their freedom, and we thought, how do we do this? Have them dress as gladiators from ancient Rome, or as modern storm troopers, maybe?

But no - these are pieces of waste matter who do not understand what bravery means, they acted like chickens, so let them dress like chickens - well like cocks, fighting cocks, and let them fight to the death...'

The remainder of what he said was drowned out by the screaming roar from the studio audience, and a few seconds later two men appeared on the screen standing in a makeshift arena that was a slapstick re-creation of the Coliseum. The men were wearing cockerel heads and large mock feathered tails with spikes on leather wrist straps and large spurs on their ankles, and Chris noticed they also had something looking like a sharp pointed dagger attached to the front of the headdresses they were wearing. A young woman walked into the arena, which caused great applause and cheering from the audience, as she was probably a well known media celebrity, and smiled inanely as she waved at the camera, but then she held her face in her hands in faked shock, although ostensibly unable to stop from laughing as a siren sounded and the two men attacked each other. They were slashing, grabbing, punching and kicking in a desperate fight and music pounded as the men grappled and fell to the floor, each one trying to jab the spiked daggers into the other man's face; a caption appeared on the screen written in childish writing, 'Cock a doodle do - I want to kill you.'

Chris changed the channel - having seen enough. He looked at the screen, not conscious of what was being shown on it.

'Be careful what you wish for,' Manville had said, and Chris pondered over his words, and the expression on his face when he said it, as if it was a veiled warning to inmates of an institution that employs extreme repressive measures to control behaviour. The words and the way in which they were said by Manville stayed with Chris, and he wondered if Manville was on the side of the ordinary person, and if so, did he feel he was also just a piece of the machine that had a role to play and was as powerless as anyone else to do anything about it. Chris snapped out of his thoughts, the alcohol was causing his mind to waver and wander into delirium. He turned the television off and stared at the dead screen for a long time. Knowing he would have difficulty sleeping, Chris picked up the bottle of vodka, looked at it for a short while and without bothering to pour it into the glass he just placed the bottle in his mouth and tipped it up, swallowing in gulps the remains of the clear, but potent liquid.

The vodka lessened his fear of going to bed, a place where he was alone and which became a torture pit as his thoughts grew to be unbearable. Although sleep came quickly for Chris on that night, his tired mind and body craving the escape in the dark tunnels leading to unconsciousness, but the world of blackness was also a place of fear and horror filled with images that terrified and disturbed his restless mind, until he finally surfaced from that place with an image in his mind of men dressed in cockerel outfits. He immediately stared at the clock to see he had only slept for just over an hour; there really was no escape.

Chris had dreamt about the small women he had seen outside the school, her voice and what she said, 'smash him' was vivid as she looked at the young men with hatred creasing her face. 'Smash him' she had said, and Chris thought about her use of words and the expression on her face. He had also dreamt of the girls who were on the television with their school project about medieval tortures. His dreams were clear, but exaggerated, and Alan Manville was smiling at the girls, playing his role of the high priest of vulgarity, spite and ignorance, and the fine scar running under his chin was something Chris had not noticed before. It was as if it was a false face, a mask, which Manville could pull off to reveal, what? Chris gave a judder as he saw a reptilian face, a monster creature revealed under the face of a human man.

The rest of what his mind had flitted over was a confused fusion of rage and dread, with images from the magazine he had looked at in the shop, and the face of the man who worked there, and the films in the Viewing Centre, and the young woman who worked there, the looks on the faces of people he had seen during the day, but then his head jerked to the side in an attempt to shake off an image of a man, a 'criminal', who was completely sealed in a plastic sheet that made him like a tube, or a worm. He had dreamt there was a bar full of people, and the man was kicked and beaten by a jeering crowd, and someone took a running jump and landed on the man's head, and this made some others shout out not to do that as they did not want to finish him off quickly because they wanted more fun. The crowd carried a bench into the bar, which they called the 'crushing board' and they placed it on top of the man. A group of men and women got on top of it, there were lots of them, too many to fit on the board so they sat on each other's laps. 'Squish - squish - squish' they chanted as they bounced up and down, and finding their rhythm, they bounced together. The man's bound head hid his identity, although

326

he would now be dead as his lifeless body shuddered under the weight coming down upon it.

Chris took in a sharp intake of breath to dispel the images and voices; looking at the clock he saw he had fallen asleep for twenty minutes.

Fifty-Six

Chris felt terrible the following morning, not only because of the alcohol, he had hardly slept and when he did fall asleep distressing dreams and images besieged his mind. He was tired out, his nerves were frayed and his feelings of alienation were becoming increasingly amplified.

The day was spent in what he felt to be a state of suspension, without feeling part of anything Chris was waiting for an end to his wretched existence. He took a short walk in the afternoon, just as it was getting dark, around the precinct outside his flat and then a little further down the high street. His mind repeated a clouded search over possibilities and thoughts about people he had met, people like Karena, and he wondered if she was a spy working for the state. He remembered the way she would sometimes look at him, and although he did not take much notice at the time it did register, and now he was thinking how she might have been observing him and feeding back the information to a superior in the security service; and all the while, as he thought about different things, his mind kept returning to the woman in the hospital who touched his arm in a sympathetic manner. Chris went over and over the way she looked at him, her eyes, her smile, the compassion, the way she squeezed his arm and how it lifted his spirits. He could not stop thinking about her, and it grew to an extent in his mind that he wanted to go to the hospital and see if he could find her, to find the one person in the world he felt would be kind and just for a second to feel safe and reassured there was love in the world.

Before returning to the flat Chris went into a shop to buy some milk and while waiting to pay he saw a magazine on the counter that drew his attention. It had an 'exclusive' story on the cover about Alan Manville and Mistress T and how, according to an 'insider,' they could be secret lovers. Chris picked the magazine up and saw the story was spread over eight pages with photographs of the two celebrities interspersed with information, 'supplied by a trusted confident' whose identity must be kept secret because news of the affair, 'will rock the nation to its foundations.'

When back at the flat Chris sat for over two hours in a chair in the living room, staring at the wall with his mind turning over and over like an old reel of film having come to its end but continuing to go round.

Later in the evening Chris wanted to do something, although he felt terrible, his mind was beginning to clear. He plugged the stick into the computer and clicked on the dot that took him back to the holiday film when he was a young boy. Chris watched it all, and going back over parts of it before closing it down and clicking on another dot. It was just more squiggles and lines, but then there was some writing in a caption that was crudely cut into the chaos of lines and shapes. 'And all the words will make a sound - that can stop the world from turning round.'

Chris read the line a few times before closing the file down and opening the last one. He clicked on the dot and watched more squiggles and shapes fill the screen, but then there was a picture, it was film of a room in a house and sitting on the sofa and chairs were Brendan, Rosie, Steven and another woman he did not know.

Chris could hardly breathe. His mind seized up as a gushing noise filled his head. He cried out, touching the screen with his fingers he repeated Rosie and Steven's name, and he sobbed when looking at Brendan, the image of his corpse vivid in his mind when he saw him in the mortuary. Chris collapsed, falling onto the floor he held his head in his hands and cried; wailing loudly he stayed on the floor for over half an hour.

Chris tried to calm himself as he stood up with an objective of watching the film, which again did not have sound. He looked at the four of them chatting and at times laughing in the living room of the house. The film lasted for about two minutes, and then the shapes and squiggles appeared on the screen; and that was all there was on the computer stick.

Chris played it again and again, his breath laboured, crying out intermittently as he looked at his brother, wife and best friend. He studied their faces, and for a second a feeling came over him where he thought he did not really know the people on the screen; but he snapped out of it. He began to wonder what they were doing in the room, why they were there and where it was. It looked as though it had been filmed recently, probably not long before Steven was killed. Chris became annoyed because he felt left out from what they were doing, he had not been told about their meeting and he asked himself if they were involved in something he did not know anything about. His anger increased and he cursed them for looking so detached and smug and comfortable, and he was the outsider, not knowing anything about it. He looked at the woman with them; Chris did not know her at all. She was older than the others, but then there was something about her, about the way she stood and held her glass.

Chris suddenly shouted out; the furniture, he recognised the room and he knew the house they were in. It was the house Rosie went to for the women's group meetings, Chris dropped her off there a few times and on one occasion had gone inside to wait for her. He studied the room, memories of the evening when he was there waiting for Rosie filled his mind. The woman in the film was not there, he had not seen her in the house when he was there; but there was something about her, something familiar.

Chris went to bed late, but hardly slept because his mind was full of what he had seen. He planned to go to the house in the film the following day, and the excitement at the thought of doing so burned through his stomach and chest.

Fifty-Seven

It was the middle of the morning by the time Chris left the flat, it took two buses to take him close to where the house was and then a short walk; he made the journey as if being propelled there by remote control. Chris did not walk straight up to the door, but stood on the pavement looking at the front of the house, thinking back to when he had dropped Rosie off there and what he had seen on the film the previous night. He did not feel as if he had to summon courage to knock on the door, he was eager to do so and hoped there would be someone that was going to open it.

Chris knocked on the door and waited, and just as he was going to knock again the door opened. A pleasant looking woman with an academic air about her, who was probably in her early sixties, looked at Chris and asked him what it was he wanted. He realised he had stood there looking at her without saying anything, and it struck him he had not thought of what he was going to say. He did not recognise her and was sure he had not seen her before when he had been to the house.

'I'm sorry to bother you,' he said, 'but my wife, Rosie, used to come here - well - has, been coming here for quite a while to attend meetings…'

The woman interjected, smiling warmly as she told Chris she was aware of Rosie coming to the house and the meetings, and she opened the door wider as she asked him to enter.

Chris felt so relieved, he shook his head, smiling at the woman as he entered and while wiping his feet on the doormat he told her when it was he had last dropped Rosie off there. He followed the woman into the kitchen, but Chris wanted to see the living room, which was across the hallway and he craned his neck to see in there, but the door was shut. The woman asked Chris why he had come to the house as she lifted a mug with both hands and drew it to her lips, but just as Chris was going to speak, although he was not sure what he was going to say, she asked him if he would like a drink. Chris accepted, gratefully, as it gave more time to think of how to word what he wanted to say.

'I hope there is nothing wrong,' she said with her back to him as she filled the kettle.

Chris looked at the woman, the room, the quietness of the house and its studious feel. It had substance, and a feeling he craved for. He began to speak, but was immediately upset and he bumbled and rushed as he told her a lot of what had happened to him and his family, telling someone he had never met far too much.

She placed the mug of coffee on a table in front of Chris and nodded as he spoke, her small eyes appearing to change shape as she focused on him.

The woman spoke in a calm and deliberate manner as she asked him why he had come to the house; Chris had not told her about the film at this point, but then he did. She nodded as he told her everything, about Brendan, his brother, what had happened to him and going to the college and getting the biscuit tin with the envelopes and the computer stick and what was on it. Her only response was a soft creasing in her skin around her mouth and eyes as she presented an expression of sympathy, and then putting down her mug she apologised to Chris for having to leave the room, but she had to 'attend to something' and would return in a minute. She told Chris to sit down on one of the chairs by the kitchen table and make himself comfortable, which he did, looking at the door the woman had closed on her way from the room. Chris looked down at the cloth on the table, it caused pangs of painful emotions in his stomach as it looked so homely and reminded him of sights and feelings from his past.

The woman returned, her smile was quiet and restful as she went on to tell Chris he was welcome to stay in the house while she 'popped down to the shop' to buy a few things she was short of. She told Chris to relax and that she was making lunch when she returned and would like him to have a meal with her as she felt he needed to eat something. He said that it was very good of her, and added she must be a very trusting person to leave him in her house, but she just smiled and told Chris she was a good judge of character and she just wanted to help him.

Chris heard the front door shut and he was aware of how quiet it was in the house. He thought about the noise around the flat where he was staying and how privacy is not respected in poorer areas; Chris sat listening to what he felt was the sound of emptiness. His thoughts then changed to the woman leaving someone she did not know in her house. It began to bother him, and his mind raced from one moment of fear to feeling he was getting somewhere in finding Rosie. He stood up, resisting the temptation to go into the living room and look at the place he had seen on the film, where his brother, Rosie and Brendan were, the most significant people in his life, and it was just a few footsteps away; but he did not. Chris walked around the large kitchen before sitting back down at the table. He looked down at the tablecloth and, trying to focus his attention on positive thoughts, he kept telling himself he was making steps to finding Rosie and Nina.

The sound of the front door closing took Chris from his thoughts and he looked up at the kitchen door as it opened, a man entered the room; it was Garman. He stood in front of Chris without saying a word. Garman stared at Chris like the hunter he was, having got his prey he would not be satisfied until he had destroyed it.

Chris looked up at the solidly built man, and saw there was another man standing in the doorway, both men were dressed in long black coats and dark suits, just the same as the men who had taken him from the hospital to the flat.

'Where is the lady?' The voice that asked the question was weak, so weak it could barely say the words. It came from somewhere inside Chris as he looked at the man standing in front of him, just like a sick child might ask a doctor or policeman where his or her mother is.

'Where is the lady?' Garman said, his eyes hardening as he stared at Chris and relished the prospect of questioning him.

'Oh God, no - help me - please help me,' Chris cried out as he held his face in his hands and dropped forward.

'Get up,' Garman's voice was harsh, and what with the look in his eyes and the way he took a small step forward it looked as if he was going to strike Chris.

'Up, Mr Kirby, and let's do it like a man - get up, and walk out of this house with us – stand up now!'

Garman shouted his order, but Chris did not move, because he could not move; fear, weakness and fatigue had rendered him motionless.

Chris found himself standing and moving through the doorway with Garman and the other man holding him up and pushing him forward. When outside the house they stopped on the pavement where there was another man dressed in a long black overcoat standing next to a car; on getting a signal from Garman he walked around the car and got behind the wheel.

The car was large and expensive, and despite the shock and dazed state Chris was in, he noticed the weather had taken a turn for the worse. Garman eased Chris into the car and prompted him to move across the seat. Chris was surprised how quickly Garman got in the car and sat next to him, pressing him against the other man so he was sandwiched between the two men. Garman's body was solid, he was cleanly shaven and there was a strong smell of shaving lotion, which smelt as if it could be the stale smell of alcohol; and Chris froze. The solid body suddenly became familiar and it was the same smell he smelt on the bus when the man sat next to him on the day he went round to Paul's flat; it was the same person. Chris slowly ventured a look at the large man sitting next to him, looking into the side of his face. Garman turned his head, and looking directly at Chris he said, 'Who do you think I am?'

Chris looked down and slowly shook his head; he was too beaten and exhausted to respond.

The car ticked into life, and as it hovered away from the kerb Chris felt he had immediately entered another world and the street with all the people in it and those that lived around there were left behind in a universe he would never see again.

Chris looked from Garman to out of the windscreen, looking straight ahead as he slumped in his seat, gazing out at what seemed to be nothing more than a television showing meaningless images with no sound.

His eyes dropped down and fixed on the inside of the door, but Garman's voice sliced through him like a knife.

'Don't try the handle - all the doors are locked, and anyway, where would you go?

And besides that, you look like you've reached the end of the road - do you know how terrible you look?'

Chris slowly shook his head, unable to speak or even blink, and hardly able to breathe.

He heard words being spoken that sounded distant, dry and feeble, but they were not coming from anyone else in the car, so he deduced it must have been him saying them.

'Where are we going?' he asked.

Garman looked at him, and with no change in his expression said, 'Where are we going?'

Chris knew he was staring at the man, who just levelled his steely gaze at him.

'Where are we going? Garman repeated after a short while and he watched Chris scream out, collapse forward and cry hysterically with his face in his hands.

In between crying Chris shouted out and pleaded, 'No - please - no, please - this can't be happening.'

'Oh, this is happening all right,' Garman said as he looked down at the back of Chris's head with disgust.

Fifty-Eight

Nothing was said as the car made its way through lanes of traffic, across a bridge and into less populated districts that Chris was not familiar with. The car carried on travelling out of town, and all the while Chris looked at road signs to see where he was and to calculate where he was going. Chris could not speak, he sat in shock, his mind falling in upon itself over and over again as the car continued to glide along streets, quiet roads and through little towns and villages.

They drove into a small town called Fieldstead End. Chris had heard of it but had never been there. It had a busy atmosphere in its centre where there were shops, and Chris saw a sign that said a market was held in the town one day every week. The place had retained a feel of its past, when it would have been a significant market town serving the area. It was now a prosperous town with shops selling quality products. The people were smart and going about their personal business and Chris thought of how it contrasted so differently with the way people look in the housing projects.

The car stopped at what seemed to be the only set of traffic lights in the little town. Chris looked at the faces of the people and the term 'parochially minded' came to him as he thought about the local paper he bought when visiting Roger Edgebury. He could imagine the people he saw outside the car fitting in with the stories that were in the paper; and he felt it to be sinister, because marbled through the presentation of a staid middle class, or qualified class, life was fearful with feeling the need to compete and retain the status they aspire to. Chris saw them as exhibiting the pretence of comfort while to remain safe, adopting strategies such as being selectively ignorant to certain matters concerning the working of, and methods employed by, the state. He looked at the men passing by, men who probably held down professional jobs and in their leisure time tinkered in the garden, sat on committees of local associations, and maybe went into the old fashioned pubs off the high street to meet friends and talk of local events and the national news that is presented to them. The women were dressed to conventional expectations, with the more mature women dressing conservatively and smart. Chris watched them standing on the pavements with an air of haughtiness about them as they spoke to one another; overtly it was an ordered and polite society.

And then all thoughts suddenly fell away. Fear totally consumed Chris as he remembered The Offender's Nemesis is made nearby to Fieldstead End.

The car set off from the lights and continued on its smooth passage, isolated and impenetrable, travelling down a road stretching into fields and vast open spaces, but there were woods in the distance, and it was towards the woods that the car turned and quickened its pace.

The Offender's Nemesis is filmed in one of a group of buildings owned by the state that are accessed by a road that winds through the woods, which eventually opens to a clearing where a series of heavily armed barriers block the road leading to the buildings.

The audiences are bussed in from various points, but usually each show has an audience that comes from the same area. Chris looked at the faces of the armed guards as they stood around a barrier. Some of them looked into the car, most did not bother, they just surveyed the area, looking into the woods and fingering the triggers on their guns.

'How long have you been watching me?' Chris asked Garman, and, as before when he had spoken, what he had said sounded disconnected from him.

'You don't ask the questions - we do,' Garman said; and his attitude and tone of voice had changed to being very hard.

Some of the buildings were white concrete and some were brick, but they all seemed to be silent and soulless. The light began to dissipate as the car drove under a large canopy, and it disappeared more quickly as the car drove slowly down a ramp, and as the light completely faded in the car a thought crossed Chris's mind - that he might never see daylight again.

Fifty-Nine

As soon as he entered the building Chris was taken to a room. It had a bed, shelves on the wall for books, which were empty, and a connecting room where there was a toilet and shower. The three men had led him from the car, into the building and down corridors with nothing being said. Chris had looked at the people who worked there, men and woman, administrator workers, carrying files down corridors, sitting behind their desks, taking no notice of him as he walked past them flanked by the three men who looked nothing like they did. The offices and corridors were plain and had a military feel to them.

Garman and the other men left Chris in the room without saying anything, and since then nearly twenty-four hours had passed. Chris had not seen anyone that following morning; the last time he spoke to somebody was in the early evening the day before, when a man brought in a tray that had a small bland meal on it and a cup of artificial tea, which he had drank only half of. The man did not respond when Chris thanked him, he just turned and left the room as if Chris was not there. Chris knew the door was not locked, there were bars across the windows that were made of thick glass, but the door was just closed shut. What might happen if he opened the door and walked out was a thought Chris did not allow to form in his mind.

Chris still had all his personal belongings on him. He took out a packet of cigarettes from his jacket pocket, the ones made of synthetic tobacco, and smelt them. He then took out the other cigarettes and looked at the packet. These cigarettes meant something else. They belonged elsewhere; they represented freedom.

Chris put the cigarettes in his jacket pocket, not wanting to light one because he knew it would not be allowed. He sat on the side of the bed looking at the tray he had placed on the floor for a while before standing, picking it up and putting it on the bed next to him. Thoughts rushed through his mind at such a speed they were unable to be completed. A constant fear ticked inside him, but there was nothing else. Chris struggled to remember clearly when he had arrived the previous afternoon. He thought about the drive in the luxurious car, the residents of Fieldstead going about their day, the expression on the guard's faces at the barriers, and then driving towards the woods and into the building where he was now; and then his thoughts suddenly stopped as the door opened. Chris looked up and saw Garman standing in the doorway, but to Chris he was just the main man who had walked into the kitchen of that house less than twenty fours ago; he did not know his name. Chris thought about how the man had been home, rested the night, showered and shaved, put on fresh clothes and was now back at 'work.'

'Time we spoke,' Garman said as he entered the room carrying a chair. He placed the chair in the middle of the room, sat down and looked at Chris, who looked from Garman to the tray next to him on the bed; he was thirsty and the last thing he had to drink was some of the artificial tea the day before. Garman took a notebook from his pocket, sniffed and regarded Chris in an offhand manner as he spoke.

'Okay, Chris Kirby, you are going to tell me things we want to know.'

Chris looked at Garman and spoke quietly. 'Are there cameras watching me in here?'

Garman repeated Chris's question, 'Are there cameras watching me in here?'

'We ask the questions, not you.'

Garman adjusted his seating position and looked closely at Chris as he said, 'You're going to get to know me.'

Chris wondered why it was just the one man interrogating him. He imagined there would be a few of them, but then maybe that was going to happen later.

They looked at each other. Everything Chris felt about the system he lived in was encapsulated within the man's eyes. Nothing was said, they just looked at each other, until finally Garman began to speak. 'You're in a bit of a mess, aren't you?'

Chris looked down at the floor, noticing for the first time how worn the carpet was; it was that hard he did not realise it was a carpet.

'This is getting us nowhere,' Garman said, and his eyes glared, but all his words did was prompt Chris from looking at the floor to down at his lap.

Garman went on, but Chris did not look at him. 'And you drink too much - meeting undesirables in bars and pubs, telling people your life story.'

Chris realised how he must have been monitored the whole time and his mind spun as he tried to think of all the times they were watching him, on buses, at his house, the Viewing Theatre, that little shop; everywhere.

Chris spoke, slowly and quietly, his eyes staying on the carpet just in front of him.

'Is everything I drink drugged - to make me talk - I know it is, the tablets from the hospital and what I've drank here, with some kind of chemical that induces a person to tell the truth.'

Garman watched Chris as he said, 'Have a drink of your tea before it gets cold,' and then he smiled; it was a cruel smile.

Chris spoke, again down at the carpet. 'A chemical that releases deeply guarded information in the brain - a truth drug.'

'Truth,' Garman said, and he geared himself up for, what was for him, some enjoyment. 'All this supposition of freedom, discipline - reason, religion - punishment, power - morals - controlling elites, liberals to tyranny - deception, perception - the transference of governing ideologies - manipulation of law, shifting practices to maintain order - propaganda.

'Where is your place is in this chaotic experience called life?' He raised his voice as he said, 'What the hell do you think is happening?'

Garman's words stayed in the room as if they had been constructed as a set of metal shelves.

'You and your type have a great deal to say - always asking questions, but when asked a simple question you clam up - just like naughty children, because that is all you are.' The man spoke with what seemed to be growing anger. He stood up and Chris flinched, pulling back a little as Garman took a step towards him.

'What is it? Are you scared I'm going to punch you? Hurt you? Is that it? Is that why you flinched like a little girl? Eh?'

He looked at Chris as if considering his deficiencies and then sneered as he spoke. 'Rhetoric, and self-imposed worth by failed people - that's what you are, and nothing more than a pain - your effect is only that of a pest, like an irritating fly buzzing in the corner of the room - an annoyance that needs to be squashed so that everyone can get back on with what they are doing in peace now the inconsequential little shit-eater is gone.'

The two men looked at each other.

Garman spoke, staring into Chris's eyes. 'Was she seeing him?

Chris just looked at him.

'Did you ever have any thoughts that they were seeing each other?'

Chris frowned, confused as to what he was talking about.

'Did you know she was seeing him? Did you hide it somewhere in your mind - deny it was happening - Chris, Kirby? Father of a thirteen year old girl, Nina.'

Chris leant forward, staring at him, and Garman continued in the same manner.

'Was she? What do you know?'

'Who? Who?' Chris said at first and then shouted, 'Who? Who are you talking about?'

'Who am I talking about?' Garman said, his eyes lifeless yet staring through him. He sat on the bed, very close to Chris.

'Don't mind me sitting here do you?'

339

Chris shook his head.

'Sure?' Garman said, and Chris shook his head again.

He took something from his pocket and showed it to Chris. It was a card. It was the scratch card with Paul's face. Garman watched Chris as he looked at it.

'Know him?' he asked.

Chris nodded.

'Where do you know him from?'

As Chris told him, Garman nodded as an adult listens to a child who is telling a fantastic tale. Chris said his real name is Paul.

'No it's not,' Garman said, and he pointed at the card. 'Look, it's got his name here - Nick, there it is - his name is Nick.'

He stared at Chris for a long time before putting the card back in his pocket.

'Who do you know that has been on TON with a different name from what you knew them as? Tell me, tell me Chris - you see, because I think you've made the whole thing up - you should have been stopped earlier, much earlier, when you were very young - you should have been brought to your senses, but now all sense has gone - you live in gaga land - lost in the clouds.'

Chris turned slowly to face Garman; his own face was that of a mask showing utter despair. 'My brother - my brother was on that show,' his voice thick as it came from a place so deep it can only be known when experiencing the most distressing emotional pain. 'They used a different name, and not his - Steven.'

Garman looked at Chris before speaking; his look was one of deep consideration.

'I sat next to you, Chris, on the bus when you went round to where this man you call Paul lived - a colleague of mine nearly bumped into you at the bottom of the stairs.'

Chris stared at Garman, startled at what he had said, and then remembering the heavy set man sitting next to him on the bus and how yesterday he recognised the smell of the shaving lotion in the car.

Garman leant close to Chris, his manner bullying, amusing himself as he sang the words in tune with no change of expression in his hard eyes.

'Getting to know you, getting to know you - getting to know all about you.'

Garman watched Chris for a while and then said, 'I've got a photograph here of one of the dissident agents who has been working against the interests of the state - in fact working to bring it down.'

He took the photograph from his pocket and showed it to Chris; it was Rosie.

Garman stared at Chris, watching his response, which did not show itself outwardly, because he was imploding and it was as if every memory and thought was being sucked into a vortex.

Garman's eyes nearly closed, although his staring look maintained it's probing severity as he said, 'What's going to happen now?'

Chris was instantly scared and covered in a cold sweat.

'Now!' Garman shouted in a loud growling order and the door burst open. An armed guard rushed into the room and pointed a machine gun into Chris's face.

'Was he? Was he? Was he fucking seeing her?' Garman shouted.

Chris looked from Garman to the security guard; it was impossible to see his face because it was covered with a visor. Chris was so nervous he was unable to speak.

Garman gestured for the security guard to leave, and as he closed the door Garman looked at Chris and said, 'You will tell me - if you know something we want to know, you will tell me.'

Chris realised his mouth was open, but it felt so dry he could not close it.

'Do you know who I'm taking about? Garman said, but Chris could only shake his head.

'Steven,' Garman went on, 'your brother - was she seeing him? Did you know, but denied it? Because it was too painful? Was it Chris? Was it, Chris Kirby - the innocent man, who is caught up in the middle of things, and he knows nothing about anything.'

After a long pause Garman continued. 'Was your wife - your dutiful, faithful, loving wife and mother of your dearest child, having an affair with your brother? The socially incompetent genius physicist, who you have felt a lifelong responsibility to look after - and have always been worried about his welfare.

'Well, was she?'

Nothing was said as Garman watched Chris look down at the floor, down at his lap, trying to understand what he had asked him. Garman was waiting for Chris to respond; the skilled interrogator who enjoyed his work. He studied Chris as an engineer watches a machine go though its different processes and movements, detached, observant and patient. After a long while he spoke, his voice quiet as he continued to scrutinise the side of Chris's face.

'She was you know - seeing Steven, and had been for years - found him fascinating, with his intellect - she loved his mind.'

341

Chris began to shake his head, at first slowly, but then gaining speed until he was vigorously flailing it from side to side and shouting out that it could not be true; and all the while Garman watched him, as if checking off points and ticking boxes, measuring Chris's outburst and reaction.

Garman started to speak, the quiet tone now gone as the hard edge returned.

'Chris, oh Chris, oh Chris - why are you so naïve? Eh? Your brother - the person you were always anxious about? Well, in reality it was the other way round - he felt a responsibility to protect you, Chris - to give you an example, like the time you went to the shop to meet X. We told him, to let him know that his caring brother was poking around and making a fool out of himself - so when you met Steven in the café afterwards he couldn't tell you who told him, because he's working for us - I told him - he was trying to protect you - he told you to keep out of it and concentrate on your family - but you didn't, because you're a fool, and fools don't listen to people when they are trying to give them good advice - I was there in that store, when you met Steven in the café area - I was watching, like I have been watching you all the while since I have been on your case.'

Garman sneered as he said, 'X - you pathetic cunt, there is no X - what the hell were you thinking about? Why couldn't you just get on with your little life and let the grown ups fight among themselves?'

Garman watched Chris for a long while before continuing; his manner pitiless and unrelenting, but Chris did not say anything, he just looked down at his lap, sitting, waiting, not able to think and unable to speak.

'And there was your *friend* Karena,' Garman said, 'who you got on with and who told you she had been seeing Kim Blakely - I take it, or I hope, you know he's a creation of the security services - there is no such person - he doesn't exist.'

Chris was aware that he was nodding, and that he was staring helplessly at Garman.

Garman stood up, his manner now more brisk, 'Oh, and by the way - just if you were thinking - if you can think that is - Karena and Roy are government security officers - as is Bill Copley - what did you expect? But, Karena, I think she likes you Chris, and maybe you liked her - so much for Mr loyal family man.'

Chris thought back to the times he was with Karena, the time he went to her flat, the way she smiled at him, and told him about how she was seeing Kim Blakely, about the workings of the underground groups and the way she said how she had told him too much and he must not tell anyone about what she had said, because it was just their secret; and there was that time in the kitchen, when she stroked the side of his face and said something about how she wished she could help him, and she told him about Simon, the supposed health worker, and the state agent, Garman, who looks what he is, a powerful man with grim features and a feared reputation that has given him notoriety.

'He's an assassin,' she said, and that he tortures people, an ex-military man, a soldier for the state who does what he's asked to do with no questions of moral consideration or ethics.

Chris remembered how he thought of what Paul had told him when Karena was telling him this; Paul had told him about a 'state official - a hulking bloke.'

Chris looked into Garman's face, and he began to speak, very slowly, 'Garman - you, you are Garman.'

Garman studied Chris before speaking. 'She told you about me I suppose - Karena,' and he grinned, 'She would, toying with you, it wouldn't do any harm, she knew that,' and he smirked, 'Yes, my name is Garman - we won't shake hands, and I'm not pleased to meet you - but let me tell you about your wife - Rosie. She began her involvement with dissident activity when she was seventeen and had built up international connections, although the vast majority of them are creations set up by the authorities to lure people like her and her type - by the way, her involvement was only in an intellectual capacity and not part of an organisation engaged in bombing or posing a physical threat to those or that they see as their enemy - but all the same, she was involved.

'She hid it from you Chris, she lived a double life - and from not long after she met you she was attracted to your brother, Steven, and he reciprocated, finding her attractive, and so it continued, the two of them, having an affair - and guess what? Your best friend Brendan knew all about it, and had done for years. Brendan was involved with the same people as Rosie - but, Steven didn't share their views - and he made them swear not to get you involved or even let you know about their involvement.'

Garman stood up straight, looking down at Chris, his eyes narrowed and he licked his lips before speaking in a dispassionate manner, telling Chris his house had been searched by the secret police and that, over a year before, bugs were planted which recorded all conversations between the family, and phone calls.

Chris looked up at Garman and mouthed the name 'Nina,' but Garman ignored what Chris was trying to say and walked towards the door; turning just as he reached it he said, 'more later,' and he was gone.

Sixty

Chris stared at the carpet, trying to think; but clear thinking and reason was impossible. He just could not accept that Rosie was having an affair with Steven, or that she was involved in dissident activity at any level. He forced himself to remember things Rosie had said, but his mind was heavy and memories were indistinct. He tried to think of things that might have suggested or given something away about her activities, or supposed activities. Chris thought back to times when Brendan was 'out of town,' or doing something at the same time Rosie was at her 'women's group meetings'.

He wondered what else he was going to find out? Garman had said, 'more later' as he left the room. Chris could only see Rosie smiling at him, and there was Nina, a strong image of the three of them, but then Nina's expression changed, the smile drained from her face and she began to scream, screaming in fear and torment as she was trying to reach Chris, trying to be beside him on the bed, in the room, and her distress increased as she threw herself at Chris, and Chris leapt from the bed, screaming, it was him who was screaming, and he realised he had been for some time.

Chris lay on the bed, his mind racing, and a thought popped into his mind, it was something Simon had said when they were in the café. He had asked him about Rosie and her relationship with Steven; because he knew what was happening maybe he was fishing for any suspicions Chris had about Rosie and Steven.

The door opened and a man entered carrying a tray with drinks and food; but when Chris looked again the man had gone.

Light faded from the room; time was leaking away without measurement, but it must have been the middle of the night, a time when sounds are different and pronounced. Motor vehicles convey their mechanical voice more distinctly and animals cry out as they always do, but in the still darkness the pitch and meaning of their cries and calls are felt with clarity.

Chris felt too scared to sleep, but he did, and when he woke he found himself lying on the floor. Daylight had established itself and Chris listened to the sounds of the early morning workers, sounds that would set the foundation for the coming day. Chris was waiting, and he asked himself what was it he was waiting for; and then he relaxed a little as he remembered it was Garman he was waiting for.

But Garman did not come. Nobody came into the room and the nothingness went on, all day, and darkness began to cause shadows to appear in the room.

'There is no mirror.' Chris said the words aloud, lying on the floor, in the dark, listening to the same sounds as the previous night. Chris was not thinking in a way that drew conclusions or made references. It was just a mind unreeling, like a spool of film rolling across the floor exposing more images the further it rolled. Chris waited for daylight, no longer waiting for Garman - he was waiting to be dragged from the room by his tethered wrists and ankles, like an animal in a slaughterhouse; that is what he was waiting for.

Sixty-One

'Get up – up – get up!' The voice was hard and it was pulling Chris from a place that felt like a deep swamp; Garman was standing in the doorway looking down at Chris, who was lying on the floor. It was now daylight, and it felt to Chris as though it had been for a while. Garman told Chris to sit on the bed as he closed the door. It took Chris a while to get onto the bed, and as he did so Garman looked at him, watching every movement and struggle Chris had to make to perform the task.

Garman took two phones from a bag he was holding and showed them to Chris. 'Recognise these?' he said. Chris nodded, looking at his phones.

Garman went on. 'Of course - you knew everything as simple as a phone is monitored, but,' he held up one of the phones, 'you used this one to contact the people you met connected with so called dissident activities.'

He looked at Chris. 'We went through what's on them,' putting the phones in the bag dismissively he added, 'nothing there of importance or significance whatsoever.'

Garman watched Chris as his half closed eyes looked down at his lap and then to the floor.

'But this is significant,' Garman said. Chris looked up and saw Garman holding the computer stick.

'I will tell you, Chris Kirby, this,' and he shook the stick at Chris, 'is what we have been looking for, along with the pieces of paper in the envelopes - and you kindly led us to it by telling the woman at the house about the biscuit tin - and she told me, because she is a colleague.'

Garman paused, not rushing his words - his timing was measured and skilful as he delivered his words and watched his prey for a response.

'Yes, we were very worried - thanks for helping us Chris, and looking after it, your country is extremely grateful to you, which I'm sure will please you greatly.

'Who knows what would happen if it landed in the wrong hands -- it could have been devastating for the security of our country - yes Chris, the bits of paper and the computer stick - clever man, Steven, encrypted information presented through convoluted symbols that look like just meaningless lines and shapes - but then messages and suggestions are embedded everywhere in society - as you must know Chris, because you're a switched on kind of guy.'

The room was silent for a short while before Garman continued to speak.

'We brought your friend Brendan in for questioning - it was thought that maybe Steven had given him something to keep or pass on - we drew a blank, and then couldn't ask him again because he had the accident - accidents - they do happen.'

And then there was silence until Garman began to speak.

'Oh what a merry dance this has been.' He started to sing to the tune of the song, 'I could have danced all night, I could have danced all night, and still have begged for more.'

He watched Chris.

'Do you like musicals, Chris?

'I do - your sister, Helen, liked music.'

'That's right, your sister - remember her?'

Chris looked up at him.

'That's right, your sister - remember her?'

Chris just stared at him; what was not already numb in his mind had now become so.

'A different kind of music of course, not entertainment, but using music as a medium to convey messages of dissent and criticism of the country that had provided a good home and life for her and people like her to live in.'

Garman had mentioned his sister, and said her name, 'Helen,' and all Chris could do was to look down at the carpet as Garman carried on talking.

'It's like that fucking idiot you visited, Edgebury, the smug little part-time country dweller - we got him in a few years ago Chris, just for a few questions and to scare him - he's harmless, and when asked about any people he knows or knows about in the so called underground movement he sings more than any of the birds that gather around his eco-friendly small holding. The conceited little hypocrite - the man's a disgrace, nothing but a fraud - he's profited very well out of the system, exploited it for his own ends, and then puts out the pretence of being a caring person - when he's nothing more than a selfish little creep that has written banal music and jumped out of his station.

'He told us about you - he's told us about everybody he has ever met. The man would do anything to save his own skin - that's all he and his type care about - that's why it's easy to keep them in line - he would put his mother in the frame if it meant he got something out of it.

'You had a nice little chat down at his mini-estate didn't you? Watching films and talking, discussing theoretical propositions - all very dangerous, drinking a cup of piss that is passed off as some kind of organic broth for the progressive thinkers, and then retire for a meal of home-resourced food that has not been contaminated by the real world. My, what a couple of foot soldiers for the revolution you two are.

'It goes without saying he is about as dangerous to the authorities as a sick child - we toy with him, Karena amuses herself with the thought of him - the man lies, telling people he's a close friend to the non-existent Kim Blakely, because it adds to his swollen ego.'

Nothing was said for a while before Garman continued.

'Oh yes, we've looked at the notes you made about the meetings you went to, and the people that go to them, and those magazines, or journals they read and get stuff they've written published in. Yes, meetings where the 'enlightened ones' gather, and call everyone else 'ordinary' and 'unthinking' - yes, criticising people they have never even spoken to for not being 'conscious' - when in reality the 'ordinary' people are the ones that are difficult to control, not the 'enlightened' intellectuals. It's easy to deal with them - the state knows what they want - it's to have their egos massaged - they're just a collection of inadequate fools - gloating at having the rubbish they've written printed and read out in what they imagine to be a secret location - they are children.'

He smirked as he said, 'Functional dysfunctional' - what a lot of rubbish is that for a grown man to write down? And look at the quality of the paper these journals are made out of - it has been designed to use this paper and in a style to fool the stupid bastards - and it works! They imagine it has been run off a press by committed associates in a covert place - it isn't! The state's printing department produces it. It's easy - and it's pathetic - it would only fool the most self-obsessed who are blind to anything other than that which feeds their need to inflate their own self-importance - these people are failures, feeling they can't cut it in the real world they invent a haven where they feel safe and set out on a journey of self-deception, until finally they are so deluded they are mentally disabled.

'And that stupid film you watched - The Laughter Machine - you actually thought it was good, didn't you? An intellectual insight beyond the capability of the minds of common people - The Laughter Machine - it's just another tool, contrived and produced by the state.

'I have a record of you saying the, "controlling eye of the state is omnipresent." So why didn't you listen to what you were telling others?

'The arm of the state extends to all areas of society - you are quite correct - even to harmless pursuits such as model trains, or boat enthusiasts. All activities are monitored and agents working for the state watch the participants.

'What do you think you're going to put in place of what exists? Eh? What plan that will enlighten the masses and bring a new dawn of consciousness? A place where every citizen will have opportunities to maximise their potential as a valued individual - and it could happen, but only in an imaginary world run by people like Chris Kirby, where iniquity and inequality is legally banished, and it will all be presided over by people like you, saviours of freedom for the masses.

Chris finally spoke, the breath escaping from his mouth in a great gasp as he did so.

'I knew, I knew, that all, or most the so called non-conformists were just playing at it and this dissident stuff attracted stupid people, and that the state would know what was going on, but considered them to be harmless - I knew...'

'But,' Garman's voice silenced Chris, 'you didn't, or do not, know about your father - do you Chris? The engineering work he did - the contracts he got were for the government, contributing to electronic components used in arms, and your sister, Helen, she didn't like it, she didn't like it at all.'

Chris was not aware that he was slowly shaking his head as waves throbbed through his mind with the power of an ocean tide. He wanted to say he did not believe what was happening, but his mouth could not form the words; hearing his sister's name and what Garman had said about his father overloaded his already fragile emotions.

A knock on the door sounded, but Chris did not look up as Garman told the person to come into the room. A man entered pushing a small stand on wheels that had a television screen on top of it. The man plugged it into a socket on the wall and then handed Garman a remote control before leaving the room. The whole process was performed in silence with Chris looking down at the carpet and Garman looking at the back of his head.

Garman continued to look at Chris for a while longer before shouting, 'Look at me, or I'll have one of your eyes burned out with a blowtorch.'

Chris's head snapped up as he fought for breath.

'And then you won't be able to watch the films on the television over there,' Garman said as he nodded at the screen in the corner of the room, its face blank, imperviously so, yet waiting to be filled by whatever images and sounds that are transmitted into it by a power greater than itself.

'Look at the screen,' Garman said as he pointed the remote control at it. Flickering broke across the screen, which was eventually filled with light and squiggles and lines began to dance over the blank background.

'Recognise it?' Garman said, and Chris nodded. It was the film on the computer stick he had watched, the lines and shapes he thought were meaningless, but were in fact coded information.

Garman froze the screen and started to speak, 'We wanted that information - we felt Steven had secreted it away - and all the while it was lying in a biscuit tin at the college.'

Garman's eyes searched a piece of space on the wall that he was going to blame for the incompetence of a system with all their sophisticated methods and powers to observe and spy, and the banks of people working in what is called 'intelligence', and yet the smallest and ostensibly insignificant things can trip it up to show the vulnerability of the state's security, as in this case with vital information left in a biscuit tin that had not been handed in, and that alone could jeopardise the security of the country.

Garman looked from the wall to down at Chris, his manner less aggressive and his tone of voice softer.

'Steven is an expert in the field of laser technology - sophisticated weapons used by the state, and Steven was a principal figure in the scientific team.'

Chris looked up at Garman; even though his mind was numb he picked up on the use of the present tense, 'is' when referring to Steven. He watched Garman as he continued to speak, unaware Garman had noticed that Chris's attention had intensified when he said, 'is.'

'He was, slightly, blackmailed into doing the work, as are many others - some will do anything for money, some have values - ethics. He had to keep up a show of being out of work, the unemployable boffin - it's just a cover, living in a crummy flat, doing that part-time college job you got him, processing the next batch of imbeciles to muddle through their days on earth - his presentation of dissatisfaction and being at odds with society - but it wasn't true - just as you imagined your brother as a vulnerable person who might get brought in by the state security, because you saw him as being different - but it wasn't so, and all the while he was working for the state.

'That's how it's done - sometimes - there are a lot of bad people out there Chris, and the country has to protect itself from them. And also, his condition, the autism, or whatever it's defined as, it makes them play by the rules - that's why they're useful, the state needs minds like Steven's because once they lock into something they can't pull themselves from it - caught in the loop, over and over again. He didn't have to be cajoled that much, it was just explained to him that he was to do this work - wind him up, and off he goes - like clockwork - although he had to be watched, especially as he was having a relationship with your wife, a woman with anti-establishment views and involved in dissident activity.

'But it was harmless enough, we kept an eye on things, and Steven said everything to do with his work stayed with him and the people he works for; i.e. the science and technology department of the state's security.

'He was under no threat Chris - you were under no threat, but you started nosing around and making a fool of yourself, with ideas of getting Steven out of the country and to a place of safety. You were worried about him, and he was worried about you - trying to protect you.

'But, you persevered with your meddling, and unsettled the water, and in doing so released all the murky matter that puts two and two together and makes five. We need to maintain a firm grasp on dissenting activity, and although there are many state plants and spies, there does also exist those who are out to harm the country's welfare - and it was those people who became alerted to Steven - inadvertently you placed him, your family and the security of the country in danger.

'You did a good job at ruining Steven's life. He became concerned when we told him about you, and that we might have to take measures to stop your activities - he flipped, told his superiors to shove their work and that he wasn't going to contribute towards the project he was working on again - finished, and that was it, his focused mind had re-focused elsewhere, which was to do nothing and withdraw, and it was impossible to move him on it. He had information - he was maverick, like a lot of his sort are, you just have to let them have their quirky way - he kept vitally important information on his person, but always maintained it was in a format that wouldn't make sense to anyone else who came upon it.

'We wanted that information, Chris - but he threw a tantrum and wouldn't tell us where it was, saying he would one day, but he wanted time to think - but too much time passed, and those that can pose a real threat were moving in, and still he remained obstinate and wouldn't tell us.

'So - we...

'Staged his death,' Chris said.

Garman nearly smiled, 'Very good - very good, Chris, now that is impressive - through all that your brain and soul has been subject to, and you fathomed that out and cut in sharp as a razor.'

'The whole of fucking society is a film set - and you work in the wardrobe and props department - you cunt, turning cartwheels for the producers,' Chris said, and because he did not look up he did not see Garman slowly nodding his head as if in agreement with him before speaking.

'Yes, he's still alive, Chris - do you want to know the details of his staged death?'

Chris did not move, just stared down at the floor, concentrating on what was left of the fibres of the carpet, seeing each strand as a living thing; as like a person.

Garman continued. 'He had to be seen to have been killed, and so out of the scene - technology is very advanced, and what people see is not necessarily what they think it is. The man, the image of the face on the screen after the beating was so disfigured, even if closely scrutinised it would be impossible to compare with the face shown on the screen earlier - we do not kill one of our agents for no reason - oh, and by the way there aren't any repeats of certain editions of The Offender's Nemesis, and because of the way it's encrypted there can't be any pirate recordings - a one off blast to the eyes and senses.

'In some situations funerals are staged, but they are just a presentation to satisfy suspicions and enquiring minds.'

Nothing was said. Chris remained hunched on the bed staring down at the floor with Garman watching him; the silence continued for a while until Garman spoke, and what he said caused Chris to look up.

'Steven told your wife, your friend - your sister, he didn't want you involved in any anti-establishment activity.'

Chris watched Garman point the remote control at the television and press a button that brought the squiggles and lines on the screen back to life. Chris could not bring himself to say his sister's name, his mouth dropped open as he looked at the screen as images fast forwarded until there was the film of them all in the room in the house. Chris shook his head, at exactly what, he did not know, but it was something.

'My sister? Helen?' Chris said as he looked at Garman, 'What do you mean?'

'Look at the film, Chris, look at the film, and tell me who you see.'

Chris looked at Steven, Brendan and Rosie, and the woman he did not know, the older woman.'

'Who's the woman with them, Chris?' Garman's voice sounded distant.

Chris did not answer Garman as he looked at her, the woman he did not know; it then clicked into place, the woman he did not recognise. When seeing the film for the first time he felt there was something about her, the way she stood, there was just something about her.

Garman watched Chris, looking through his eyes and into his mind, watching him think.

'Didn't recognise her did you Chris? But then again it was a long time ago that you last saw her - but you can see it's her now, can't you?'

Chris instinctively nodded his head as he looked at the woman, the woman who was his sister.

Garman spoke, his tone of voice returning to as it was before, because it had softened for a short while. 'Yes, it's Helen – Steven was always trying to persuade the three of them to stop with their futile mission to bring down the system.'

Chris looked at his sister, at her face, at the shape of her features, her lips, her mouth, having forgotten what her voice sounded like he tried to remember.

Garman continued. 'Helen didn't want you to be involved - she's fully immersed in so called dissident activities, the hippy drippy days of idealism didn't leave her, too naïve to understand who really made that *protest* music - and when she learned it was produced by the same corporation that made arms and pharmaceuticals she decided her calling was to challenge that system, which she saw as ruining the world.

'When she was young she became what was known as at the time, a radical feminist, a Marxist, but with a desire to live in a private property, and of course one in an expensive area away from *ordinary* people. After the *big change* her discontent with the running of society deepened, and she has strived for a thing called liberty, and a return to a time where individual preference is to be realised - even by ordinary people, who she has never shared anything with.'

'Where is she?' Chris asked in a quiet and low voice.

'She's okay Chris, she's being looked after - we had to have her in for questioning, but as we've got what we wanted, a decision will be made as what to do with her.'

Over fifteen seconds passed before Chris spoke, asking Garman if Brendan had really died, or if it had been staged. Garman told Chris that Brendan was dead and a car hit him, and it was an accident that happens, 'every day to everyday people.'

Chris asked if Brendan and Rosie knew Steven was still alive and had they been seeing him all along. He was told they had not been and their shock was real, as they believed Steven was killed.

Garman went on, 'We snatched Steven and kept him in a safe place, he hasn't had contact with anyone - but, of course, now we have what we were looking for, well, it's safe for him to return into society - his holding back on where the information was put the fox amongst the chickens, and so he will be returning to a different farmyard scene - what with some people no longer alive, the eruptive effect of his relationship with your wife now known to you - you becoming aware of your family, your father's work and about your sister.'

Garman paused before continuing, 'But you know what Chris? I think Steven will pick up with his work again, working on his project - it means

353

too much too him, he needs to have that mind of his stimulated - and just settle down - now that everything is in the open.'

The room fell silent

'Settle down with Rosie?' Chris said, in a voice so thin it was not even brittle. Nothing was said for a long while, and then Garman started to sing, 'Love and marriage, love and marriage, goes together like a horse and carriage, this I tell you brother… da da da da – fill in the rest of the words yourself Chris.'

'And Nina?' Chris asked.

'Ah,' Garman said, 'now she doesn't like it one little bit at all - daddy's not well, but she doesn't want to ditch him, and she wants to see him - she only has a patchy sketch of the picture that's been going on around her - but all the same Chris,' he sang in tune to the song, 'I've written a letter to daddy - saying, I love you.'

He stopped singing and said, 'Although, she knows you're not in 'heaven above.'

Chris stared down at the carpet, trying to grasp what was being said to him, but emotions had thrown every thought out of kilter.

Garman watched Chris for a while before speaking. 'Your head is spinning, and you are asking yourself how can all this be true?'

After continuing to look at Chris for a while longer, Garman turned away and left the room.

Chris tried to lie down on the bed, but could not as thoughts of his brother, sister and father poured through his mind, a mind that was thick, hazy and constantly rushing with indistinct thoughts and images. It was too much, he tried to concentrate on what he had been told, but it was impossible to comprehend, filter and rationalise the things Garman had said, and then there was Nina; Chris felt his heart was physically breaking when he thought of her, but his mind could not form any lucid thoughts.

Chris sat on the edge of the bed looking down at the carpet, and rather than thinking about what had just been revealed, information that was so incredible, he concentrated on the everyday sounds going on around him. Ordinary sounds such as the engines of cars starting, doors shutting, people walking down the corridor, and here he was, in a room, right next to people going about their daily work. They go home in the evening, attend children's recitals, take dogs for a walk, have sex, have rows about money, and then go back to work the next day, and all the while the man who has been brought in for questioning is in the room along the corridor as they go about their day. He continued to sit on the side of the bed not aware that over an hour had passed, his eyes fixed down on the carpet, his mind assessing inconsequential pieces of matter until his attention was broken by the door to the room opening.

A man entered carrying a tray with a glass of water and a sandwich on it. He placed the tray on the floor, picked up the other tray and left the room without anything being said.

Chris looked from the closed door to down at the tray; it could have been five miles away at the foot of a large valley, and then emitting a deep groan he rolled onto his back.

He tried to stop breathing, hoping it would take him peacefully into death. It was ridiculous, he knew it was, but he lay still, with his mouth open, seeing himself as a decaying corpse with insects crawling around his gums and teeth, nothing more than something, a piece of a vegetable lying on the ground, rotting, in a state of decomposition and infested with maggots and flies. Images and hallucinations, Chris knew he was drugged, he knew it was in the food and drink. He looked over at the television, at the legs of the stand it was placed on. The legs narrowed down to small wheels, but he saw the legs turning into shinning daggers with their points pressing on the centre of human eyes, and Chris wondered why the eyes did not burst with the pressure bearing down onto such a small sharp point, but then they did burst, and out of the puss that broke from the eyes were human babies in the embryonic stage of development, and their faces were visible and clear, they had already formed as adults, and they were screaming in torment, and Chris also screamed, at the unbearable images torturing his mind, because they were dragging his concentration from wanting to think about Nina, Rosie and Steve, but Nina, there was hope, Nina, his daughter, his love, but he could not think about her, he could not form clear thoughts, and it went on and on, and then a voice was speaking; it was speaking to him.

He closed his eyes, not wanting to hear the voice because he wanted to think about Nina, but all thoughts of his daughter dissipated as the voice became clearer. Chris realised the voice was coming from the television; it was Garman's voice. He turned and looked at the television, but the screen was blank, as if not turned on, although Garman's voice was coming from it; Chris began to listen to the words he was saying.

'And there they were, the little darlings, emerging from what they like to call the "technological revolution." "Revolution," they like that term, it makes them think they have some control in the changes that occur during their lives, and yes, and it is now as it was then, self-important theorists, sitting in their boudoirs and academic garrets, loving their intellectual exclusivity, toying with a construct they called 'reason' - imagining they had come upon a new way of thinking by applying the scientific method to understanding human behaviour in a changing "modern" world, and their poor deluded minds proposed a belief in what they called the "individual" - a conscious, "aware" individual who interacts in the order of things called a society - "society," a construct that became such a valuable product for the men of ideas to tinker with and suggest ways to "progress" this society and the individual. And then the trend took root to banish "ignorance," seen quite contradictory as an "evil," - and by doing so show to all that "freedom" was no longer a privilege enjoyed by an elite few because through the use of reason we can see that all men are born equal and there is nothing "natural" about inequality, and some contradicting themselves again by saying all people are "created" equal, and it is the "situation" they are born into which had been constructed by man, and so it can be changed, as everything changes and evolves so can a person - even criminals - criminals can change, they could be "reformed" to their supposed natural state of being good, because they supposed to be equal is to be good, and it is this "good" that the social reformers can mould the criminal into - a born again good person - Chris.'

Chris stopped breathing on hearing his name, and he looked at the blank screen as Garman's voice continued to come from it.

'But they didn't reckon for the power that continued to reside in other forms of thought - like religion, a way of thinking considered by the new intellectual elite as "immature" - its "reason" may not be scientific, but it satisfies people, giving them answers to matters they are concerned with - it's confusing, and people can become very confused as to what is true, of what is worthy, and when given strong guidance, if the circumstances are conducive, they respond and "believe" in that guidance - because it answers questions they want and feel they need to be answered - ignorance is a good thing, Chris.

'The progressive thinkers had failed, and the people wanted revenge, distracted from what really motivates the society they live in they will lash out - but Chris, you know all this.'

Chris was not hearing Garman's words, he was seeing them, as shapes, as squiggles on a film, dancing around a blank screen, they were things without meaning, and the rasping tone of Garman's voice was pushing Chris, herding him, as a man with a prod or steel pole goads and shoves an animal against the bars of a pen; Chris closed his eyes in an effort to try and find an escape from the lines and darting shapes.

After having fallen into a fevered sleep, Chris opened his eyes and looked about the room, as if re-acquainting himself with a place he had visited many years before. It was as he remembered it, with the television, strangely attentive, yet silent in the corner of the room.

Sixty-Two

When Chris opened his eyes again he was lying on the floor, and he continued to lie where he was, not wanting and unable to move. He remained conscious, looking at the carpet until the door opened and his eyes averted slowly in its direction. Garman stood in the doorway looking down at Chris before closing the door and entering the room.

'You haven't eaten your sandwich - or drunk your water,' he said.

The thought of answering was too much of an effort, and Chris did not fully understand what he was saying, but he did try to speak, although the sound that came from his mouth did not sound anything like his voice.

Garman looked down at Chris before speaking, examining him, as if he was a specimen under a microscope.

'You know nothing do you Chris? We are fully satisfied you really do not know anything that has been going on - nothing at all - your father, your wife, brother, sister, and bestest and closest friend Brendan - what they had been up to - and there you are, Chris Kirby, living your life, imagining you are an *informed* thinker, one step ahead of the game in keeping one's nose clean and hoping for better days to come - living the deluded life of smug complacency that is a package deal offered by the authorities - it is cheap and easy - and it is all done for you - just sign up and go with the ride.

'Drink!' Garman raised his voice, and Chris jumped. 'Drink the water - now!' Garman commanded.

Chris found it difficult to crawl over to the tray.

'Drink it,' Garman ordered, and he watched Chris drag himself across the floor, lift the glass to his lips and sip the water.

'Drink it all,' Garman said, and adopting a quiet and soothing tone he said, 'Go on Chris, it's soft, delicious, cool, cold water.'

Chris held the glass between his hands and continued to drink until it was empty. He looked down at the carpet, fragments of images and half-finished sentences were rushing through his mind, and he looked up at Garman who was watching him in a way as if he knew everything that was going on in the processes of Chris's brain.

'Rosie,' Chris said in an abstracted way, and then 'Nina?'

Garman nodded and Chris repeated her name, now seeing himself as a baby, on the floor, looking up at an adult, gurgling and repeating a name.

Garman stared at Chris as he spoke slowly and clearly, but Chris could not understand or decipher the words being said to him, and not conscious of what he was doing, Chris began to nod his head, staring up at Garman and continuing to nod his head and stare dumbly.

Garman knelt down and leant in close to Chris, speaking in a quiet tone, and Chris nodded, his mouth trying to form words, but his breathing was so short and his mouth was parched.

'What are you trying to say Chris?' Garman said, 'Are you trying to tell me something?'

Chris felt his tongue had swollen to such a size it took up the whole of his mouth. He nodded, but now his eyes were beginning to plead with Garman, who spoke quietly into his ear.

'What are we going to do with you? What is the penalty?

'You can hear me Chris, but you can't respond.'

Garman placed a scratch card on the carpet in front of Chris's face. It was from with the show The Offender's Nemesis, and it had Chris's face on it.

Chris expected fear to explode inside him, but it did not, he just looked at the card and began to flick at it with his hand, as a cat might when tired.

Garman spoke. 'What if you went on the show, paraded as an intellectual agitator? God, they hate people like you and your type, venting heartfelt feelings of justice and criticising the system, yet taking from what the system offers - self-seeking people on a sanctimonious mission to expose malpractices in society and propagate equity for all - while feeling anything but equal to the common person as they share nothing of his or her values.

'How do you think it will go down?'

He grinned maliciously, 'I don't think they will like it - especially if it is added that you wanted to smuggle in terrorists to blow their children apart in shopping centres.'

Garman stood up, and before turning to leave the room he looked down at Chris with what would be difficult to describe as a smile as he said under his breath, 'but, then you are just an innocent, Chris Kirby - and your daughter wants to see you.'

Chris did not look up at him, he was staring down at the carpet, and Garman watched dribble running from the corner of Chris's mouth with interest as it trickled down his chin and dropped onto the carpet.

Sixty-Three

The television was on, but the room was empty; Chris was no longer there.

The Offender's Nemesis was on the television and the sounds of the show filled the dark room, which was lit by blinking flashes coming from the screen. A chorus, comprising of inane lyrics set to a simple melody and beat, was sung by four young women dressed as cheerleaders who looked to be competing with one another to see who could stretch the biggest smile; and then suddenly all light and sounds stopped as the stage became dark and silent for a few seconds with only the odd cheer and call from the audience being heard.

A single light lit the centre of the stage showing a hooded figure wearing a baggy boiler suit flanked by two security guards dressed in their militaristic combat uniforms. A drum roll sounded, and then quietened to maintain a steady roll and another light lit the stage next to the three figures; Alan Manville was standing alongside them, nodding as he looked at the hooded figure. He pointed from the person in the boiler suit to the audience and waited for their cheering to subside before speaking.

'Oh yes, and here it is, good and honest people, as promised, because we never break our promises - here is a disgrace of a human being, an undesirable who is just a piece of waste matter - nothing more than scum, and it is lucky for us all that we have an ever-vigilant and dedicated security service that works tirelessly to flush out these rats - and yes, good people, we will honour your wishes and eliminate it by the use of a giant rat trap.'

The audience exploded into cheering and chanting and the camera swooped amongst them showing some holding up large cardboard animal traps.

Manville smiled before adopting his judicious pose, and pointing into the camera he said, 'Reveal this diseased human rodent now!'

The audience erupted in frenzied hysteria as the two security guards pulled the hood over the person's head to an accompaniment of music, and a line of young women dressed in rat costumes shook their whiskers in the air as they danced across the stage.

ABOUT THE AUTHOR

I was born in West London and became interested in writing at an early age. I began writing plays after success as the drummer in the punk group The Lurkers. I left school at fourteen and did a variety of jobs, mainly working on building sites, but I have also worked in a crematorium and amusement arcades. After drumming in the group – we went on Top of the Pops and other television shows, made albums and toured Europe and the USA – I went to university. I have worked as a Support worker for many years in the community with people with learning disabilities and mental health difficulties.

I lived for a while in West Belfast, where I worked as a project worker in a victim's group; I worked with people living with trauma caused because of the conflict in Ireland. An early work, Thank Your Lucky Stars, was performed at the Edinburgh Fringe, running for three weeks to excellent reviews and I had a short play produced at The Bush Theatre in London that went down very well. I have had four books published, two are novels, and have written a small scene for Steven Berkoff, which was in a recently released film.

Lightning Source UK Ltd.
Milton Keynes UK
UKOW02f1032310716

279546UK00001B/48/P